HIS NAME IS Z'LANDAR

Book Two of the Riverborn Saga

Kevin D. Fraser

Biscuits & Gravy Publishing
Cave Creek, Arizona, USA

Table of Contents

HIS NAME IS Z'LANDAR

Book Two of the Riverborn Saga

An Original Novel by Kevin D. Fraser

Book One: The Heart of the Loch

Book Two: His Name is Z'Landar

Book Three: ???

HIS NAME IS Z'LANDAR

An original novel by

Kevin D. Fraser

His Name is Z'Landar

Published by Biscuits & Gravy Publishing Cave Creek, Arizona USA

First Edition, 2025

Author's Page: kevinfraser.me

A **Kelpie** is a haunting water spirit from Celtic folklore, often said to inhabit the deep, black lochs and rivers of Scotland. In most tales, it appears as a magnificent horse with a dripping mane, its coat sleek and glistening as though sculpted from the surface of the water itself. The creature is both alluring and treacherous — it can shift shape to resemble a handsome human, but its true nature always betrays it through some telltale feature: a sheen of dampness, reeds tangled in its hair, or a glimmer of otherworldly eyes. Travelers drawn to its beauty or tempted to ride it soon discover the horror beneath the surface, for the Kelpie's hide becomes adhesive, binding its victims fast before it plunges into the depths to drown and devour them.

Yet the Kelpie is more than a simple monster; it embodies the wild, merciless power of the natural world. It is the spirit of deep waters — cold, untamed, and impossible to master. To the ancient Celts, it served as both warning and symbol: a reminder that beauty and peril often flow together, and that beneath every mirror-still surface lies a force older and darker than humankind can ever truly understand.

A **Selkie** is a creature of transformation — neither wholly human nor seal, but something in between, bound to the tides and the moon's quiet pull. In the chill waters of the North Atlantic, she swims with the grace of the sea's own heartbeat, her sleek form gliding through currents like liquid night. Yet when she sheds her seal skin upon the shore, she becomes a woman of haunting beauty, her eyes dark and reflective as the depths she came from. Legends say that if her skin is taken, she is trapped upon land, bound to the will of whoever possesses it — a captive soul aching for the sea.

The Selkie is a living embodiment of longing: the eternal call between two worlds. She is love and loss intertwined — the wild heart yearning for freedom, the gentle soul mourning what cannot be reclaimed. To those who glimpse her upon the rocks, half-hidden by mist and moonlight, she is both a promise and a warning: that the things we try to hold too tightly are often meant to slip back into the waves.

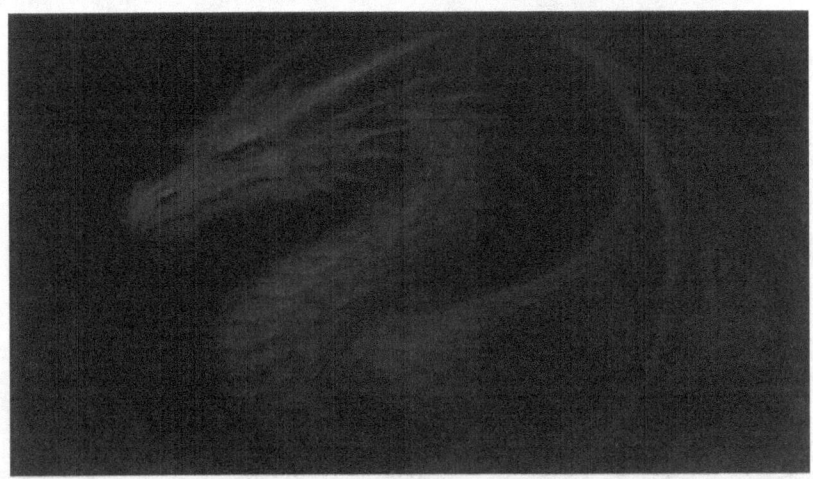

Caoránach, sometimes called *the serpent of Lough Derg* or *the mother of all demons*, is a being born of ancient wrath and shadow — a Celtic dragon whose essence is tied to the primal chaos of the earth itself. In the oldest tales, she slumbered beneath still waters or within the hollows of forgotten hills, her breath the mist that rolls across bog and moor. When roused, her eyes burned like molten stone and her scales shimmered with the sheen of black iron. She was said to devour cattle, poison rivers, and bring ruin to any who dared trespass upon her lair. Even saints and heroes spoke her name with caution, for Caoránach was not merely a beast, but a force of nature, relentless and unbound.

Yet there is tragedy woven through her legend. Caoránach embodies the world's ancient ferocity — the fierce, untamed spirit that existed before man's dominion. To defeat her is to impose order upon wildness, to silence the raw voice of creation itself. In this way, the dragon's tale becomes more than myth: it is a reminder that even darkness has its place in the balance of the world, and that every conquest over chaos leaves the world a little quieter, a little less alive.

Balor of the Evil Eye was the dread king of the Fomorians — a towering figure of ruin and ancient might, whose single eye could fell armies and scorch the earth itself. Born under a prophecy that he would be slain by his own grandson, Balor became consumed by fear and cruelty, sealing his daughter away to defy fate. His eye, heavy with venomous power, was so destructive that it required the strength of several warriors to lift its lid; when opened, it unleashed a beam of death that blighted all it touched. Tales speak of him striding from the mist-shrouded sea, crowned in iron, his gaze a curse upon the living.

But Balor is more than a monster — he is the embodiment of tyranny and foreknowledge, the terror of those who try to outwit destiny. In him lives the ancient dread of the old gods: vast, wrathful, and unyielding. His downfall at the hands of Lugh, his grandson, marks the turning of an age — the triumph of youth and light over the dark weight of ancestral fear. Yet even in defeat, Balor's legend lingers like smoke after battle, a reminder that no power, however great, can blind the eye of fate forever.

The **Fomorians** were the shadowed ancestors of chaos — ancient beings who ruled before the gods of light came to shape the world. Rising from sea and mist, they were creatures of storm and deep water, their forms both human and monstrous: one-eyed giants, tusked warriors, or beings whose limbs seemed carved from the sea's own darkness. They were said to dwell beyond the western horizon, in a realm where sun and moon seldom touched, emerging only to wage war upon the land-dwellers and claim tribute from the mortal tribes. Their rule was harsh and cold, reflecting the untamed world before order and harvest, before the rhythm of the seasons was set.

Yet the Fomorians were not purely evil — they were the embodiment of **raw nature**, the primal forces that creation itself was built upon. To the ancient Celts, they were as necessary as they were terrible. In their battles with the Tuatha Dé Danann, the shining tribe of gods, the old chaos met the dawn of civilization. The Fomorians' defeat did not erase them; it buried them deep within the bones of the earth and the black waters of the sea — waiting, perhaps, for the world to forget the balance they once kept.

The **Aos Sí** — often called *the People of the Mounds* — are the
luminous remnants of an older world, the hidden folk who slipped
beneath the earth when the age of men began. To mortal eyes they
are both beautiful and terrible: tall, radiant beings cloaked in shadow
and light, their movements like wind through grass, their voices soft
as twilight rain. They dwell in the hollow hills, within ancient
barrows and mist-covered raths, where time drifts differently and
mortal footsteps are not welcome. The Aos Sí guard these thresholds
fiercely, for they are the keepers of what was once divine —
fragments of the Tuatha Dé Danann, faded gods who chose
enchantment over extinction.

To encounter one is to stand between worlds. They are beings of
grace and peril, capable of generosity or vengeance without warning,
for their nature obeys older laws than human hearts can grasp. Gifts
from them may bless a lifetime or curse a bloodline; a glance may
enthrall, a dance may steal away years. The Aos Sí remind mortals
that beauty and danger are twin faces of the unseen realm — that
beneath every green hill and quiet glen, the ancient light of forgotten
divinity still stirs in the dark.

The **Púca** is a mischievous and unpredictable spirit of Celtic lore — a shape-shifter born of twilight and trickery. Most often, it appears as a dark horse with eyes like lanterns and a mane that ripples like smoke, though it can just as easily take the guise of a goat, dog, or even a charming human with something subtly amiss — a glint too wild, a shadow that lingers too long. The Púca delights in leading wanderers astray, luring them down moonlit paths or across bogs that vanish come dawn. Yet unlike darker fae, its intent is rarely purely malevolent; the Púca embodies chaos itself — neither good nor evil, but ever restless, a reflection of nature's untamed spirit.

Those who meet the Púca speak of fear and fascination intertwined. It may whisper secrets, grant a sudden burst of insight, or leave behind gifts no mortal can easily keep. Farmers once left offerings at Samhain to win its favor, hoping the spirit would bless rather than spoil their crops. In every form, the Púca stands as a reminder that the veil between order and wildness is thin — and that laughter, danger, and wonder often share the same dark breath of the night.

A **Water Sprite** is a fleeting shimmer between worlds — a spirit of rippling currents and moonlit pools, born from the stillness of water and the whisper of wind upon its surface. Unlike the graceful Selkie or the terrible Kelpie, the sprite is more elusive, more dream than flesh. It appears where reflection and motion mingle — a glimmer beneath reeds, a face in a ripple, a song half-heard through mist. Sometimes it takes form, slender and fluid, with limbs like flowing water and eyes that hold the gleam of hidden depths. Its voice is said to soothe, to lull the weary into calm, yet always with the danger of being drawn too deep beneath the mirrored surface.

The Water Sprite is the gentler spirit of the dark lochs and woodland streams — a guardian, a temptress, a fragment of nature's soul. It embodies the dual nature of water itself: serene and nurturing, yet cold and merciless when stirred. In Celtic lore, sprites remind mortals of the fragile balance between peace and peril, beauty and oblivion. They are the sigh of the river at dusk, the ripple that breaks the moon's reflection — silent witnesses to the eternal pulse between the mortal and the elemental.

14

A **Merrow** is the sea's melancholy child — a being both wondrous and mournful, caught between two realms that can never truly meet. In Celtic legend, the Merrow appears as a beautiful sea-maiden with hair the color of kelp and eyes that shimmer like green glass beneath the waves. Her voice carries the sorrow of the ocean's depth, a song that can enchant sailors or draw them into a dream from which they never wake. Clad in a magical cap or cloak that allows her to slip between sea and land, the Merrow sometimes comes ashore, but if her cap is taken, she becomes bound to the mortal world, unable to return to her ocean home.

The Merrow is the embodiment of longing — a creature torn between freedom and affection, duty and desire. Unlike the Selkie, whose stories often end in tragedy, the Merrow carries a deeper wisdom: she knows that love, like the sea, cannot be possessed without consequence. Her presence is said to calm storms or stir them, to weep pearls or whisper prophecy. To glimpse her at dusk upon the rocks is to see the ocean itself made flesh — ancient, beautiful, and forever mourning the distance between the surface and the deep.

15

The **Banshee** is the lamenting voice of fate — a spectral woman who walks the threshold between life and death, her cry echoing through mist and midnight to foretell a passing. In Irish tradition, she appears at the edge of moonlight, her form veiled in tattered grey or pale white, her hair long and streaming as though caught in an unseen storm. Her wail, part grief and part fury, carries a sorrow older than any mortal heart — not a curse, but a mourning for what is inevitable. To hear it is to feel the air tighten and the world fall still, for the Banshee's song is not meant for the ears of the living, but for the soul soon to depart.

Yet she is not a creature of malice. The Banshee is a spirit of compassion as much as dread — a guardian of passage, bound to ancient families, mourning their losses with a love that has outlived flesh. Her presence reminds humankind that death is not an ending but a return to the unseen. In her voice trembles the memory of every tear ever shed, every farewell whispered beneath the moon — the eternal echo of grief made divine.

The **Sluagh**, the *Host of the Unforgiven Dead*, are the restless shades that ride the twilight winds of Celtic legend — spirits who were denied peace and wander forever between worlds. They are not buried, nor blessed, nor remembered; instead, they drift as a murmuring storm of wings and whispers, gathering in flocks across the darkened sky. In old tales, they sweep through the night like tattered crows, skeletal and hollow-eyed, their movements marked by sudden chills and the flutter of unseen feathers. To see their shadow is to feel the air thicken, for the Sluagh come to claim the souls of the dying, carrying them away before the light can reach them.

Unlike the fair or noble spirits of the Aos Sí, the Sluagh are the remnants of humanity's darkest hearts — those who defied both gods and death. They fear sunlight, dwelling in the cracks of forgotten ruins, in the spaces where prayers no longer echo. Some say they were once men and women who betrayed their kin, cursed to drift until the end of days; others claim they are simply the embodiment of guilt itself, a living wind of regret. Wherever they pass, silence follows — and when their wings blot the stars, it is best to turn your eyes to the ground and whisper a prayer to be left unseen.

Prolog

The lochs remember.

Even when wind scours their faces to glass and silence, even when mountains grind themselves to bone, water keeps the memory. It runs through peat and stone and the slow lungs of the earth, whispering to whoever still listens. I have listened longer than most—longer than the names of kings, longer than the faith of bells that dared to ring against the sea.

My name is Maelis. The villagers call me tide-witch or widow, depending on how hungry their fear is that day. I let them. A name is only as strong as the memory behind it, and theirs run shallow. I was born before the Selkies hid their sealskins and before the Kelpies learned the taste of iron. I have walked these shores since the moon wore a closer face and the stars burned bluer than grief.

At first light I walk the inlet with a basket on my arm. The tide leaves its offerings at my feet: coral scoured to chalk, a green bottle turned soft as sea-apple, a spindle of bone no bigger than a child's thumb. I keep them in a chest of driftwood and whale-rib because everything the sea gives is part of a story, and stories do not like to be misplaced.

Sometimes a child follows me. They come from the village with pockets full of curiosity and crumbs. They sneak along the dune grass to watch the witch touch the water. They never wait for the answers. The moment I speak, they run, for it is one thing to watch the sea and another to hear it speak back.

This morning the sea feels heavy. Not angry—anger foams and breaks. This is weight. The air tastes of copper. Kelp knots itself against the stones. The gulls circle inland without troubling to cry. I ken that silence; it is the same that comes before the first rock lets go of a cliff.

I kneel in the surf and lay my palm to the surface. Cold climbs my arm like breath drawn in surprise. Beneath the skin of the loch a pulse beats, slow and immense. It is not the tide—the tide obeys the moon. This comes from the earth's marrow.

"Is it you again?" I whisper. "You have slept long enough."

No voice answers, but ripples braid themselves into a pattern: four beats, a pause; four beats, a pause. I ken that cadence. It once belonged to the Oilliphéist, the mother of dragons, whose sleep was a covenant older than churches and the nets of men. I thought her dreaming finished. Perhaps I wanted it so.

The water smooths, then sketches a word upon itself as if a finger drew through light.

Z'Landar.

The name strikes me like a blade of ice. When I speak it, the gulls hush and the otters slide from sight. The loch has not given me that name since the last war.

He was a child the first time I saw him—half Selkie, half Kelpie, born in a night when the stars leaned close as lanterns. The loch lit itself to greet him; seals rose in circles and the river's mouth sang. He grew tall, proud, and kind—a rare balance. He made peace where none thought possible, binding sea and shore to a single vow. They called him the Bridge of Waters. I called him hope.

I thought his story ended there. But peace is not an ending; it is a breath.

Now his name returns through water thick with memory, and I ken what it means: something beneath the waves has turned over in its sleep.

A north wind comes wet and cold. I draw my shawl tight and start toward my cottage. The village wakes behind me: smoke lifting from two chimneys, a dog scolding the tide as if it would listen. Ruarc, a young fisherman with hands already older than his face, hails me from the dock.

"Storm coming, Maelis!" he calls. "Sea's got teeth today."

19

"Storm's been coming a long while," I say.

He laughs because he thinks I am joking, then looks past me to the water and stops laughing. He has the good sense to cross himself. He does not have the luck to be heard when he prays.

At the bend of the path I look back. The loch has gone still as thought. Even the reflection of the clouds has withdrawn, as if the water refuses to mimic the sky. That is how the deep prepares for change—by remembering itself.

My cottage sits above the inlet in the lee of a black rock shaped like a sleeping seal. The roof is thatch; the door is driftwood worked smooth by years of hands and weather. Inside, the hearth is cold. I feed it kelp and shavings, and the flame comes up blue, then steady. Shelves line the walls: jars of shells, jars of tears, and one jar of air sealed the night the old king drowned. On the table lies my book bound in kelp and hide— The Chronicles of the Depths. The ink fades as centuries do, but the words still hum when my fingers find them.

Tonight they hum louder.

I open the book and the pages turn as if remembering where to go. They stop at the leaf I swore never to read again. The script is thin as a spider's patience:

When the four hearts of Caoránach beat as one, the sea shall reclaim what the land has stolen.

The house gives a small, tired shudder. The flame gutters and flares green. From far away—perhaps the other side of the world, perhaps beneath my feet—I hear it: thoom … thoom … thoom … I tell myself it is only the storm. The lie goes down like a stone.

"Not again," I say. "You promised."

The sea never keeps its promises. It keeps its balance.

I pour water into a shallow silver bowl and stare down. My face withdraws. Another rises—the face of a young man at the edge of a lake at dawn, cloak dark with rain. The light behind him is the color of iron.

He does not see me. I see him: eyes like storm glass, mouth set against a question he has asked too many mornings without answer. Z'Landar.

"Do you feel it too?" I ask the water. "The heartbeat beneath the calm?"

The surface ripples. Behind him, deeper than sight, something moves— long, coiled, luminous. Four pale orbs stir like moons under snow. Each beats once; the lake shivers. Each beats again; the world tightens around its breath. A shape coils them all, vast as a continent turned in on itself. The mother opens one eye, and for a moment the room grows warmer as if the earth exhaled through my walls.

Her voice arrives without sound. Did you think peace could chain fire? Did you think water forgets?

The bowl cracks down the middle. Water runs across the table and soaks the book's tether. Outside, thunder unspools along the hills and returns as if the mountains were drums. Rain begins in earnest—heavy, metallic, smelling of new blood and old iron.

I relight the lamp and steady my hands with work. I take the quill made from a cormorant feather and the ink I mix from ash and brine. The first line blurs before it dries:

Thus begins the second drowning of the world.

The window rattles. The tide climbs the rocks two steps higher than it should at this hour and under this moon. I ken better than to bar the door—wood is not stronger than the sea's intention—but I set the iron poker beside my chair to comfort the part of me that still believes in objects.

Between gusts, the old language comes up from the loch. I hear the names of the lost and the questions of those not yet born. They speak of the boy with two tides in his veins. They speak of the woman whose eyes carry starlight. They call them the Balance and the Breaker, though none can tell me which is which. Prophecies prefer riddles to maps.

The storm peaks and breaks, as all tempests must. In the hush after, I walk outside. Rain blinds me for a breath, then thins to veils. I can feel the water rising around my ankles, cold and conversational. Lightning unzips the sky and the surface flashes white. For a heartbeat I see shapes moving—vast and slow and sure—far below.

I am old and I am not afraid. I have outlived husbands and harvests, kings and winter fevers. I have nothing left to barter except memory, and memory is what the sea collects. I step from the stones into the shallows, and the loch meets me like an old friend whose news is too grave for the doorstep.

"Very well," I say. "If the story must begin again, let it begin."

The water takes my weight and bears me a pace. It is not drowning. It is a carrying, a small rehearsal of the larger carrying that waits for all of us. When I step back, my dress clings heavy as silt, and the house breathes behind me like something waking from a bad dream.

In the gray morning a child waits on the path—Fia, with a missing tooth and a rabbit's courage. She holds a basket of limpets and a question.

"Are you a witch?" she asks.

"Only when I have to be," I say.

"Da says the sea's wrong today."

"Your Da is right. Keep inland for a while."

She looks past me at the loch. It looks ordinary again. Children are better than men at believing what they cannot see. She nods and runs, and I love her for it, though love is the first thing the sea will ask me for when it comes to take its due.

By noon the wind slants from the west, warmer than it should be. Fishers bring in nets half-burned though they swear no fire touched them. Kelp washes ashore in ropes like black hair. A bell rings from the chapel—a thin sound meant to tame fear by rhythm. The sea does not care for small rhythms. It follows the larger ones.

I take the long path along the cliff to the headland where the old stones stand. No one goes there now; even the goats refuse it. The circle is broken—two uprights fallen, one lintel tilted like a jaw. When the first wars ended, we laid our oaths here, sea and river alike. I bring a flask of rainwater, a ribbon from my wedding, and a shard of glass I picked from the tide the year the old king drowned. Offerings must remember their stories.

The sky lowers as I set them out. The first drop of rain strikes the stone and steams. I lay my hand upon the lintel and speak the names of those who taught me. Some are Selkie, some Kelpie, one a midwife who never learned letters but remembered every cry. When I finish, the wind has stopped. Even the heather listens.

"I call no storm," I say. "I ask only for a path."

The answer is not a word but a feeling—a slackening, like a knot deciding to be easier. Far down the coast a line of lighter water appears where no light should be. It runs west, as steady as a promise. I ken the look of a road when the sea draws one.

I go home to pack. An old woman should not cross two counties in weather, but prophecy is less patient with age than with doubt. I wrap bread and cheese in cloth, tuck the book into oilskin, and hang my mother's knife at my belt. When I lift the latch, the door refuses me for a breath, swelling on damp and reluctance. Then it opens, as doors do when we have to go.

On the threshold I pause, because leaving and arriving are sisters and deserve respect. The room holds its breath. I look at the shelves with their jars and the chair that knows my shape and the hearth that remembers all my winters. Places have memories too. I tell the house I will come back if the story lets me, and that if I do not, I release it from remembering me kindly. Houses, like seas, prefer balance to sentiment.

The path to the village is a ribbon of dark mud and bright puddles. Two men argue by the boats about whether saints or seamanship better keep a man alive. A woman sorts fish with the speed of a prayer. Ruarc stands on the dock with a coil of rope and an expression like a torn net.

"You look set to travel," he says.

"I am," I answer.

23

"Where to?"

"Where the road lies—west."

He nods, as if this were an answer that merited nodding, and then blurts, "Maelis—if I have offended the sea—"

"You have not offended the sea," I say gently. "Offense is a human word. The sea concerns itself with hunger and measure. It is very good at both."

He swallows. "And if I drown?"

"Then you will learn a language without air," I say, and touch his cheek. "But not today. Keep to the shallows. Listen when the tide refuses you."

He kisses my hand in the old way. I do not tell him that the old way is what the sea recognizes first when it comes to count. He will learn as all of us do—by water.

A cart takes me as far as the fork where road becomes track. The driver refuses coin but accepts a blessing he pretends not to believe. From there I walk. The world smells of rain and peat smoke and something hidden loosening its jaw. Twice I hear thunder where there are no clouds. Once I see fire where no man could carry fire. The west pulls at me the way a tide pulls at a swimmer who has forgotten for a moment that water has a will of its own.

Near dusk I reach the high bluff above the long beach men call the Strand of Gray Hares. I set down my bundle and let my breath catch up to my bones. The ocean spreads before me, dull pewter under a lid of cloud. Far out, a seam opens—not in the sky, but in the sea itself. Light wells up from underneath, pale as breath on glass.

I ken a door when I see one. I have guarded enough to recognize the shape even when it pretends to be a mistake.

"Not yet," I say to the opening. "Not for me."

It narrows obediently. Even doors respect a voice that has spoken them often.

I sleep in a cleft in the rock with my cloak for a roof. Dreams come at once and do not feel like mine. I walk under a lake beneath a mountain, and the water is ringing with a sound like bells closing over. I see a woman with hair like foam and eyes filled with far light; she reaches for a child who is not yet born. I see a giant lifting an iron lid from his eye and the world catching fire in silence. I see four eggs pulsing and the mother curled around them, and I understand that love and hunger are not enemies to dragons. They are the same thought said two ways.

Toward morning the dream opens into waking without a seam. I lie in the gray light and listen to the waves talk among themselves. They are not gossiping anymore; they are planning. It is a different sound. Tides arrange themselves when the world decides to change.

I sit up and the first gull of the day cuts a white arc across the cliff wind. My knees ache; my heart does not. I have a cane carved from driftwood and names, and it knows my step. I raise it and draw a circle in the sand at my feet, not to bind anything, only to show myself where I stand. There is use in that.

"Listen," I tell myself, and I do.

At first there is wind. Then there is the unique hush the sea keeps for the instant before a wave decides whether to climb higher or fall back. In that hush I hear it: a name crossing water against the wind, a name that makes the hairs on my arms lift as if they remember being younger.

Z'Landar.

The sound does not come from my mouth. It comes from the sea, and from the veins under the sand, and from the memory of a loch that has decided peace is a kind of neglect. I answer without speaking, because some conversations are better kept out of air.

Yes, I say to the tide. I hear you.

The name comes again, and with it the image of a man standing at a different shore under a different sky, looking west the way I am.

25

Between us lies the old road the sea draws when it wants two points to behave like neighbors. I have walked that road before. I am old, but I am still the keeper, and keepers go when called.

I shoulder my bundle. The first rain of the day begins, gentle as apology. The path down to the strand is slick and steep, but my feet know every stubborn stone. At the bottom, the sea lifts a little as if to say, There you are. I am here, I answer, and step into the water until the cold decides I am paying attention.

"Listen," I say again, but this time to the world. "Listen to your own heart."

The wave that answers is not large. It comes up to my knees, folds around my calves, and falls away. When it does, it leaves a line in the sand that was not there before. It points west, as straight as perhaps. The door I refused last night opens the width of a breath.

I smile because I have always liked stubborn stories. They respect a spine.

Behind me the cliff keeps its counsel. Before me the road lies shining. The sea has made its choice. I make mine to match it.

Thus begins the second drowning of the world, I think, and it is not a sentence of despair. It is only a measure. Not all drownings end in death. Some end in remembering what breath is for.

I step forward and the tide takes my weight, and the lochs remember, and somewhere a young man of two waters lifts his head because the sea has spoken his name in a voice he recognizes as his own.

His name is Z'Landar.

Not "the boy," as we called him in those desperate years when prophecy walked among us wearing a half-grown face. Not "child of two worlds," though that truth runs deeper than most know. Not "King," though two thrones now sit empty, waiting for him to claim what blood and sacrifice have earned.

Z'Landar, son of Brannach the Thundering, King of the Kelpie realm.

Z'Landar, son of Nerina of the Silver Eyes, daughter to Queen Mhairi who rules the Western Selkies still.

The name tastes of old magic on my tongue. Of destiny fulfilled and destiny yet to unfold.

Ten years have passed since the Battle of Loch Ness, when the Great Wurm rose from depths that should have remained sealed, when Duncan MacAuley fell to corruption and rose again as something worse. Ten years since Z'Landar—barely more than a boy then—called the First Waters to his hand and drove the ancient darkness back into the abyss from which it had crawled.

We thought it was an ending.

Fools, all of us. Peace is not an ending. It is merely a pause between breaths.

The Highlands flourish now in ways no bard's song had ever promised. The rivers run silver again, free of the poison that once choked them. Fish leap in numbers not seen since my grandmother's grandmother swam these waters. The lochs reflect stars undimmed by shadow. Human and water-folk trade openly at certain shores where once only violence met the brave or foolish who crossed those boundaries.

Children laugh where warriors bled.

It should be enough.

But I am old, and I have learned that peace—like water—never stays still. It pools in the low places, seeps into cracks, and sometimes... sometimes it hides what festers beneath.

Chapter One: The Weight of Peace

The Kelpie realm struggles without a king.

After Brannach fell—giving his life that his son might be born into a world with hope—the Council of Elders took command. Wise folk, most of them. Old in years and older still in memory. They know the river paths, the ancient treaties, the proper forms for every ceremony from birth-blessing to war-making.

But wisdom is not leadership.

I watch them now as they gather in the River Hall carved beneath Loch Slochd, that great dark water where Brannach once held court. Seven elders, representing the seven major rivers of the Highlands. They sit at the lightning-struck oak table their ancestors hewn before men built stone castles, and they argue.

By the stars, how they argue.

"The northern tributaries report incursions from the mountain Kelpies," declares Tormod of the Rapids, his voice a grinding of stones. "They claim fishing rights that belong to our kin."

"Let them," mutters Eilidh of the Deep Pools, her silver-streaked hair floating in the water-heavy air. "We have plenty. Why shed blood over where a salmon swims?"

"Because blood defines boundaries!" Tormod's fist crashes against ancient wood. "Because if we yield the north, next they will want the south, and then—"

"And then what?" Eilidh's laugh is bitter as brine. "You would have us return to the old ways? When Kelpie drowned Kelpie over pride and territory? We are not so many that we can afford such waste."

28

The arguments circle and eddy like whirlpools, going nowhere, accomplishing nothing. Three moons have passed since this particular dispute began. Three moons, and still no resolution.

They need a king.

They know it. Every soul in the River Hall knows it. But to speak it aloud—to call for Z'Landar to claim his birthright—that requires courage these elders lack. For acknowledging Z'Landar means acknowledging what he is: not pure Kelpie, but something other. Something that makes the old laws tremble.

The Selkie realm fares little better.

Queen Mhairi still rules from the Silver Depths, that gleaming court built into sea-caves beneath the western isles where sunset paints the waves crimson and gold. She is three hundred years old—young for a queen of her lineage—and by all rights should reign for centuries more.

But the years since the wars have worn on her in ways time alone cannot explain.

I see it when I visit the court on Z'Landar's behalf, carrying messages between the divided realms. The queen sits on her throne of pearl and coral, beautiful as the dawn, regal as the tide itself. Yet something in her eyes has dimmed. Some light that once burned bright now flickers like a candle in a storm.

She speaks to her council with the same authority, issues her decrees with the same confidence. But I hear the weariness beneath the words. I see how her hand trembles—just slightly, just enough—when she reaches for the ancient staff that marks her office.

"My grandson," she said to me once, during a private audience when the formality dropped like a discarded cloak. "Tell me true, Maelis. Does he think of us?"

"Every day, Majesty."

"Yet he does not come."

29

"He believes..." I chose my words carefully, knowing they walked the knife's edge between truth and injury. "He believes the peace is fragile. That to claim the throne might shatter what was so hard-won."

"Peace built on division is no peace at all." Her voice carried the weight of tides, the patience of the deep waters. "It is merely postponement."

She was not wrong.

Among the younger Selkies, restlessness grows. They remember the alliance, the battles fought alongside Kelpie and Highlander. They have tasted unity, and the old hatreds sit bitter on their tongues. They whisper that Z'Landar should rule both realms, that only through him can the promises made in blood be kept.

But the old families resist. Three centuries of mistrust cannot be washed away by a single decade of peace, no matter how blessed. They remember too well the wars before Z'Landar's time, when Kelpie raiding parties slaughtered Selkie children for sport, when Selkie magic turned rivers toxic and sent whole Kelpie villages to painful death.

Memory is longer than hope.

And so both realms drift, leaderless in all but name, waiting for something—or someone—to force the choice they lack the will to make themselves.

Z'Landar dwells in the in-between places.

Not human, though he walks on land when needed and speaks the tongue of the Highlands with easy grace. Not fully Selkie, though the seal-form comes to him as naturally as breathing and the sea calls to him in the voice of his mother, whom he never knew. Not purely Kelpie, though his father's blood runs fierce in his veins and the rivers recognize him as their own.

He is water itself—river and sea, fresh and salt, wild and gentle.

He has grown into his power these past ten years. The uncertain youth who stood against the Great Wurm now stands two meters tall, his frame carrying the breadth and strength of his father's line. His hair remains dark as midnight waters, perpetually damp as if he has just emerged from the depths. His eyes shift like the moods of Loch Ness itself—sometimes the tempest-gray of storm clouds gathering, sometimes the deep blue-green of his mother's distant gaze.

He moves through the Highlands like a legend half-remembered, appearing at this loch or that river when he is needed, disappearing again before gratitude can become expectation. The human clans honor him, and some few—those who married Selkie wives or whose ancestors swore old oaths—offer him hospitality without question.

But he does not stay.

He cannot, perhaps. To remain means to rule, and Z'Landar has spent ten years running from that truth.

I find him often enough, when the water-folk need his voice or his hand. He never hides from responsibility when it finds him. But neither does he seek the crown that waits, gathering dust in the Kelpie vaults and salt in the Selkie treasury.

"Why?" I asked him once, three summers past, when we stood together on the shores of Loch Morar, watching the sunset paint fire across water.

"I am not my father," he said simply.

"No one asks you to be."

"They do, though." He turned to face me, and I saw the weight he carried—heavier than any crown. "Every time they look at me, they see him. His strength, his certainty. The king who would have united the realms if darkness had not taken him."

"You could unite them."

"Perhaps." The word hung between us like mist. "But Brannach was only Kelpie. Nerina was only Selkie. I am both and neither. What right have I to rule what I cannot fully be?"

31

"The right of sacrifice," I told him, my voice sharp as broken shells. "The right your parents bought with their lives. The right earned by every warrior who bled beside you when the darkness rose."

He smiled then—sad, distant, like moonlight on black water. "Rights can be inherited, Maelis. But wisdom must be earned. And I am not yet wise enough to take what I cannot hope to hold."

We spoke no more of it that day.

But the question lingers, patient as tides, inevitable as dawn.

The younger generation does not understand his hesitation.

Fionnuala, his aunt but always considered his half-sister—youngest born to Queen Mhairi, younger even than Z'Landar himself, and raised as his sibling. Sired by a Selkie lord who thought to ease the queen's grief— swims up from the Western Isles every few moons seeking her brother. She has their silver eyes and stubborn heart.

"He is being foolish," she tells me, not bothering to hide her frustration. "The realms need him. Why does he hide?"

"He does not hide. He prepares."

"For what? It has been ten years! How much longer must we wait?"

I have no answer that satisfies her. I barely have an answer that satisfies myself.

Caelan—who fought beside Z'Landar in the wars and now leads patrols in the northern rivers—echoes her sentiment with fewer words but equal conviction. Alasdair Fraser, grown old now but still sharp as his clan's blade, sends messages from Beauly asking when the young king will come claim what is his.

Even the water sprites whisper questions as they dance across the lochs at twilight: *When? When will he rise? When will the promise be fulfilled?*

32

The pressure builds like water behind a weakening dam.

And Z'Landar feels it. I see the strain in the set of his shoulders, hear it in the silences that fall when kingship is mentioned. He knows what is asked of him. Knows what is needed.

But knowing and accepting are different tides entirely.

I dreamed last night, and my dreams are rarely kind.

In the vision, I stood on the shores of Loch Ness beneath a sky empty of stars. The water before me boiled and churned though no wind stirred. From the depths rose smoke—not the clean smoke of hearth-fires, but something darker, fouler. It carried the reek of burning scales and ancient malice.

Across the water came wings.

Great wings that blotted out the absent stars, wings that beat the air into submission and sent waves crashing against stone. Eyes like forge-fires pierced the darkness, and a voice—old beyond reckoning, cruel beyond measure—spoke a single word:

Soon.

I woke gasping, my sealskin cloak tangled around me, my heart hammering like a trapped bird against my ribs.

The young ones ask me to tell tales of Z'Landar's valor. They want to hear how he stood against the Great Wurm, how he called the First Waters to break the ancient curse, how he forged unity from hatred's ashes.

What they do not ask—what they cannot know to ask—is whether the war truly ended that day beside Loch Ness.

Or whether it merely slept, gathering strength, waiting for the moment when hope had grown comfortable and the hero had forgotten how to reach for his crown.

I am old. I have seen peace shatter more times than I care to count. And I know—with the certainty that comes from living through ages when others barely survive decades—that something stirs in the waters once more.

Something that will not wait for Z'Landar to decide when he is ready.

Something that will force his hand whether he wills it or not.

The younglings gather in the shallows, waiting for my stories. I smile and begin the familiar tale, watching their eyes grow wide with wonder. But even as I speak of past glories, my thoughts drift to the dream, to the smoke and wings and that single terrible word.

Soon.

The weight of peace, I have learned, is heavier than the weight of war.

For war at least is honest about what it demands.

Somewhere in the depths of Loch Ness, Z'Landar swims the cold dark waters, alone with thoughts no one else can share. The pendant at his throat—the Heart of the Loch, that ancient relic of his birth—pulses with steady light, illuminating nothing but the path before him.

He does not know yet what comes.

But he will.

The tides of fate, once turned, never cease their flowing.

And soon—very soon—the weight of peace will give way to something far heavier.

The weight of destiny itself.

His name is Z'Landar, and his story is far from finished.

Chapter Two: The Depths Know

The waters of Loch Avon held a clarity found nowhere else in the Highlands. Cradled high in the Cairngorms, the loch lay like a jewel of liquid sky, so pure that a seal could see the stones at forty fathoms as if they rested but an arm's length away. The humans called it the "blue loch" and told tales of drowned climbers whose bodies never surfaced, of depths that led to other worlds, of strange lights seen dancing beneath the ice in winter.

The water-folk knew better than to believe human tales.

But they rarely swam here regardless.

Too high. Too cold. Too far from the comfortable territories where their kinds held sway. Loch Avon belonged to the mountains and the sky, to the eagles that nested on its cliffs and the red deer that came to drink at dawn. The few Kelpies who ventured this far found the waters too thin, lacking the weight and substance of the lowland rivers. The Selkies avoided it entirely, uncomfortable so distant from the sea's embrace.

Which made it perfect for solitude.

Z'Landar surfaced in the center of the loch, breaking through the mirror-smooth water with barely a ripple. He floated on his back, human-formed, staring up at clouds that drifted past like ships on an inverted ocean. His dark hair spread around his head like ink in water. The sun, already westering toward evening, painted the surrounding peaks in shades of amber and bronze.

Alone.

Blessedly, peacefully alone.

He had swum for three days to reach this place, taking the seal-shape through the rivers and smaller lochs that connected like veins through the Highlands' body. Stopping only briefly to hunt, to rest in hidden pools where the current whispered rather than roared. Avoiding the places where his name carried weight, where eyes would turn and expectations would press against him like physical things.

The pressure had grown unbearable these past weeks. Not from anything spoken aloud—his people were too careful, too aware of his flight from the throne, to demand openly. But he felt it nonetheless. In the way conversations halted when he appeared. In the glances exchanged between Kelpie elders. In Fionnuala's increasingly pointed questions.

In Maelis's ancient, knowing eyes.

They wanted their king.

The weight of their wanting threatened to drown him more surely than any depth.

He closed his eyes, letting the water hold him, feeling the cold seep into his bones. This high, this far from the warmer lowlands, the temperature bit with teeth sharp enough to numb. He welcomed it. Pain—even the mild discomfort of cold—was honest. It demanded nothing but endurance.

A shadow passed across his closed eyelids.

Not cloud. Too swift, too purposeful.

Z'Landar's eyes snapped open. He twisted in the water, diving beneath the surface in a single fluid motion, the seal-form flowing over him like a second skin. His vision sharpened, adapted, showing him the underwater world in crystalline detail.

There.

A figure descended through the blue, moving with grace that made his own considerable skill seem clumsy by comparison. Not seal. Not quite human either, though the form held that shape. Something between. Something other.

She wore her humanity like a garment chosen deliberately rather than a shape born into. Her hair—neither blonde nor brown but something that caught light strangely, shifting between colors like sunlight through amber—streamed behind her as she swam. Her body curved in ways that spoke of both strength and an elegance that went beyond mere physical beauty.

But it was her eyes that arrested him.

Even underwater, even at this distance, he saw them clearly. Large. Luminous. The color of no ocean he had ever known—deeper than blue, brighter than gray, holding depths that had nothing to do with water.

She had come for him. That truth settled into his bones with the certainty of tides.

No chance encounter, this. Not in Loch Avon, where the water-folk rarely ventured. She had sought this place. Sought him.

The question was why.

Z'Landar held his position, neither fleeing nor advancing. Watching. Waiting. The predator in him—the Kelpie inheritance that sang in his blood—assessed threat and opportunity with cold calculation. She was alone. Unarmed, at least visibly. Her movements showed no aggression, no fear.

Confidence, then. Either foolishness or certainty.

He suspected the latter.

She stopped perhaps ten yards distant, hanging suspended in the blue with a stillness that spoke of perfect control. For a long moment, they simply regarded each other—two creatures of water, circling like thoughts unspoken.

Then she smiled.

And the world tilted.

Andralia

I had wondered what he would be like.

The stories paint him as a dozen different men—hero, warrior, reluctant savior, bridge between worlds. Maelis speaks of him with the reverence usually reserved for prophecy made flesh. The young ones whisper his name like a prayer. Even my parents, who have seen empires rise and fall across a hundred worlds, speak of Z'Landar with something approaching awe.

But stories are shadows cast by the truth, and shadows tell only shapes, not substance.

I see him now, and the stories suddenly seem... inadequate.

In seal-form, he is magnificent. Larger than any true seal, his coat the deep charcoal of storm-waters, marked with subtle patterns that catch the light like oil on dark glass. Power radiates from him—not the crude strength of muscle alone, but something deeper, more fundamental. As if the water itself recognizes him and moves differently in his presence.

But it's his eyes that hold me.

Even through the seal's form, they remain unchanged. Storm-gray shot through with that impossible blue-green, holding intelligence that goes beyond animal cunning, beyond even human sapience. Old eyes in a young face. Eyes that have seen too much and carry it without complaint.

Eyes that see me.

Really see me, in ways that make my pulse quicken despite two decades of training to remain unmoved.

I knew he was beautiful. The legends mention it—son of Brannach the Thundering, whose human form could stop a heart, and Nerina of the Silver Eyes, who was counted fairest among the Selkie queens. But knowing and seeing are different things.

And knowing and *feeling* are oceans apart.

Focus, Andralia. You came here for a reason.

I let the smile touch my lips—the one my mother says makes me look too human, too warm. The one I rarely show because it reveals more than I intend. But with him, I find I want to reveal. Want him to see.

Dangerous, that desire. But inevitable.

I have always known this moment would come. My parents prepared me for it, as much as anyone can be prepared for the inevitable collision of fate and choice. They told me what he was. What he would become. What role I might play in that becoming.

They did not tell me he would make my breath catch. That thirty seconds in his presence would undo twenty years of careful cultivation of detachment.

The stories, it seems, left out the most important part.

He shifts—a ripple of transformation so smooth it seems more like water changing shape than flesh—and human-form flows over him like a tide. Suddenly he stands before me in the deep blue, suspended as I am, bare-skinned and unashamed. Two meters of contained power, dark hair floating in the water-current, eyes holding mine with an intensity that should frighten me.

It doesn't.

"You're far from home," he says, and his voice carries clearly through the water—a trick that takes considerable skill, shaping sound through liquid medium. His accent holds traces of both river and sea, Highland and otherworld. "Whatever home is, for one like you."

Observant. My form betrays me to eyes trained to see the differences. I am not Selkie. Not Kelpie. Not quite human. Something other.

"As are you," I reply, matching his trick of underwater speech. "Unless solitude counts as a homeland now."

A flicker crosses his face—surprise, perhaps, that I dare match him so directly. Most approach Z'Landar with either reverence or fear. I offer neither.

"Solitude chose me," he says. "I didn't seek it."

"Liar."

The word hangs between us, sharp as broken glass. His eyes widen fractionally—shock that I would challenge him so bluntly, so soon.

But I see the truth beneath his surprise. Recognition. Relief, even. How long since someone spoke to him without the weight of his legend pressing down on every word?

Too long, I suspect. Far too long.

"You swam three days to reach the most remote loch in the Highlands," I continue, my voice soft but unyielding. "Avoiding every settlement, every clan holding, every place where your name carries meaning. That's not solitude choosing you, Z'Landar. That's you choosing to run."

Anger sparks in those storm-colored eyes. Good. Anger is honest.

"And who are you," he says, his voice dropping to something dangerous, "to judge how I spend my time?"

"Someone who knows what it costs to carry weight that isn't yours to carry." I tilt my head, studying him with the same intensity he offers me. "Someone who understands that running from thrones doesn't make them disappear. It only makes them heavier when you finally turn around."

He stares at me for a long moment, and I can almost see his thoughts moving behind his eyes. Trying to place me. Identify my kind, my purpose. The Kelpie in him assesses threat. The Selkie in him seeks connection. The human part—the part that makes him more than either alone—simply tries to understand.

"You came here deliberately," he says finally. Statement, not question.

"Yes."

"To lecture me about thrones?"

"To meet you."

"Why?"

The question holds layers. Why seek him? Why here? Why now? Why speak to him as if his legendary status matters less than air?

I could answer with truth—that I have watched him from afar for years, that my parents tasked me with finding him when the time was right, that destiny has plans neither of us fully understand.

But truth can wait. For now, curiosity will suffice.

"Because I wanted to see if the stories were real," I say, letting my smile widen just slightly. "If Z'Landar, son of sacrifice and prophecy, was truly as remarkable as they claim."

"And?"

"The stories," I say carefully, "did not prepare me."

His expression shifts—confusion, wariness, and something else. Something that looks almost like hope, quickly hidden but not quickly enough.

"For what?"

"For you."

I swim forward before he can respond, closing the distance between us to an arm's length. He tenses but doesn't retreat. Pride, perhaps. Or curiosity matching my own.

This close, I see details the distance obscured. The faint scar along his shoulder blade—legacy of some battle I know only through secondhand accounts. The way his pulse beats at his throat, slightly elevated, betraying interest he tries to hide. The shifting colors in his eyes, like storm and sea constantly at war.

"I'm Andralia," I tell him, offering the name freely where others might guard it. "Born of Loch Etchachan, daughter of the deep waters."

"Etchachan." His brow furrows. "The highest loch. But you said deep waters."

"Deeper than you know. Deeper than most imagine."

I extend my hand—a human gesture, formal and strange here in the blue depths where such things should have no meaning. But I want to touch him. Need to, with an urgency that goes beyond curiosity or mission.

He stares at my offered hand for several heartbeats. Weighing. Deciding.

Then he reaches out.

The moment our fingers touch, the world explodes into light.

Not physical light—nothing so simple. This light comes from within, from between, from the spaces where reality thins and other truths bleed through. I feel it surge through me like lightning, like the moment a star is born, like the first breath after drowning.

And in that light, I see.

Not Scotland. Not Earth. Not anything bound by the small truths of this single world.

I see infinity stretched across impossible distance. Galaxies wheeling like dancers in the dark. Worlds beyond counting, each one holding life in forms beautiful and terrible and everything between. Civilizations rising and falling like waves on cosmic shores. And threading through it all— connecting star to star, world to world, heart to heart—currents of something that might be called fate or destiny or simply the recognition that some things are meant to be.

I see my parents' world, where I have walked beneath three suns.

I see places I have never been but somehow recognize.

I see him, standing at the center of it all, light pouring from him like water from a broken dam.

And I see myself, reflected in that light, amplified by it, completing some circuit that was always meant to close.

The vision lasts perhaps three heartbeats. Perhaps three lifetimes.

When it fades, we're still standing in Loch Avon, hands clasped, staring at each other with identical expressions of shock.

"What—" His voice cracks. He tries again. "What was that?"

I should tell him. Should explain about his heritage, about what he truly is, about why I'm here and what my parents know and what role we're meant to play in whatever comes next.

But looking into his eyes—seeing the wonder and fear and confusion written there so plainly—I find I can't. Not yet. He's not ready for those truths.

And perhaps I'm not ready to give them.

"A greeting," I say instead, which is both true and utterly insufficient. "Between those who recognize each other."

"I don't know you."

"No." I squeeze his hand once before releasing it, already feeling the loss of that connection like a physical ache. "But you will."

I swim backward, putting distance between us before the urge to close it again becomes impossible to resist. His eyes track my movement, still holding that mixture of confusion and something hungrier, more dangerous.

"Wait," he says. "You can't just—we need to talk about—"

"Later," I promise. "Soon. But not today."

"Why not today?"

Because if I stay, I'll tell him everything. Because that vision shook me more than I expected, more than my careful training prepared me for. Because I came here to assess him, to begin the slow work of revelation, and instead I find myself undone by a single touch.

Because I'm afraid of what it means that the stories were wrong.

He's not just remarkable. He's necessary.

And I think I might be falling in love with him.

"Because," I say, already turning to swim away, "some truths need time to settle. And we both need to understand what just happened before we speak of it."

"Andralia—"

My name in his voice sends shivers down my spine. But I don't turn back. If I do, I'll never leave.

"Three days," I call over my shoulder. "Meet me at the River Garry where it joins Loch Ness. Dawn, three days from now. I'll explain what I can."

"And if I don't come?"

I smile, though he can't see it. "You will."

Then I'm swimming, taking the seal-form that's almost natural to me, letting the shape carry me swift and sure through the crystal waters toward the outlet that will lead me home. My heart hammers against my ribs. My hands still tingle where our skin touched.

Behind me, I feel his gaze following until I'm lost to distance and depth.

Three days.

It seems both forever and not nearly enough time to prepare myself for what comes next.

For what he'll ask. For what I'll have to reveal.

For the moment when he learns that the legends only scratched the surface of his truth.

Z'Landar floated in the center of Loch Avon long after Andralia vanished from sight. The sun continued its descent, painting the peaks in shades of fire and shadow. The water grew colder as evening approached. His body registered the temperature drop, the need to seek shelter, to eat, to attend to the practical demands of flesh.

He ignored them all.

His hand—the one that had touched hers—still trembled slightly. He stared at it as if it belonged to someone else. As if simple flesh and bone could somehow contain what he had seen, what he had felt.

Stars. He had seen stars. Not as they appeared from Earth's surface, tiny lights scattered across the black, but as they truly were. Vast. Burning. Alive in ways that defied understanding.

And he had felt... connection. Recognition. A sense of rightness so profound it made every other certainty in his life seem fragile as morning mist.

"Who are you?" he whispered to the empty water.

But he already knew the answer would not come easily. Would not come at all, perhaps, until he met her again at the appointed time and place.

Three days.

He had three days to decide if he was brave enough—or foolish enough—to show up.

Three days to wonder if the woman who had just shattered his careful solitude was answer or complication.

Three days to ignore the truth settling into his bones like stone:

He would be there at dawn. Wild horses couldn't keep him away.

And somehow, he suspected, everything was about to change.

Chapter Three: When Darkness Calls

Dawn came to the River Garry with mist thick as wool, turning the world to shades of pearl and silver. The river itself flowed swift and cold where it joined the greater waters of Loch Ness, its voice a constant whisper against stone and gravel. The junction point—where current met stillness, where river became lake—had held significance since before the clans remembered to count years.

A threshold between worlds. A meeting place for those who needed neutral ground.

Z'Landar arrived an hour before the appointed time, unable to sleep, unable to stay away. He stood at the river's edge in human form, barefoot on the cold stones, watching the eastern sky gradually surrender its darkness. His hair hung loose past his shoulders, still damp from the journey through underwater channels. The Heart of the Loch rested against his chest, its familiar weight somehow feeling heavier these past three days.

Three days of restless swimming. Three days of trying to make sense of what he had seen when their hands touched. Three days of telling himself he should not come, that prudence demanded distance, that mystery was another word for danger.

Three days of knowing he would come anyway.

The water sprites had followed him for the last mile, their tiny lights flickering with curiosity as they whispered among themselves. They knew something unusual stirred—Z'Landar did not typically arrange meetings with strangers at dawn. But they kept their distance, sensing perhaps that this was not their business.

He paced the shoreline, nervous energy finding no outlet. What would she tell him? What could possibly explain the vision—galaxies and stars and connections that stretched across distances that defied comprehension? And why did the memory of her smile, that knowing curve of lips that held secrets she would not share, make his chest tighten in ways that had nothing to do with fear?

"You came early."

Her voice carried across the water before he saw her. Z'Landar spun toward the sound, his pulse quickening despite himself.

Andralia rose from the river like morning mist given form, water streaming from her hair and shoulders as she took the shallows in long, unhurried strides. She wore simple clothing—a tunic and leggings woven from some material that shed water like sealskin—but moved with a grace that made simplicity seem deliberate choice rather than lack.

And her eyes. Those impossible eyes that held depths no water could match.

"I couldn't sleep," he admitted, surprised by his own honesty.

"Neither could I." She stepped onto the shore, close enough now that he could see droplets clinging to her lashes, could catch the scent of deep water and something else—something that reminded him of star-bright nights and distances too vast to name. "Three days felt like three years."

"And three minutes," he added quietly.

Her smile bloomed like sunrise. "Yes. That too."

For a moment they simply stood, the river rushing past, the mist curling between them like curious hands. Z'Landar found himself cataloging details—the way she tilted her head when studying him, the slight curve of her collar bone, the silver trace of what might have been an old scar along her forearm.

"You have questions," she said, breaking the silence.

"A thousand of them."

"I can answer some." Her expression grew serious. "Not all. Some truths aren't mine to give."

"Then start with what you can." He gestured to a flat rock near the water's edge. "Please."

Andralia

He's different in daylight, or what passes for daylight through this Highland mist. More vulnerable, perhaps. Or maybe just more honest. The careful control I sensed at Loch Avon has frayed at the edges, revealing the young man beneath the legend.

I like him better this way.

We settle onto the rock, close but not touching—both of us wary of repeating what happened before. Not out of fear, exactly. More like the caution one shows approaching fire. Recognition that something powerful waits, ready to ignite with the smallest spark.

"Loch Etchachan," he begins, choosing his opening carefully. "You said you were born there. But it's barely deep enough for spawning salmon, let alone..." He trails off, uncertain how to phrase what I am.

"Let alone creatures like me?" I finish for him, allowing amusement to color my voice. "Loch Etchachan is deeper than maps show. Deeper than most believe possible. The waters there connect to... other places. Through channels no human geographer has ever charted."

"Underground rivers?"

"Among other things." I watch his face, seeing the intelligence working behind those storm-colored eyes. He's piecing it together, or trying to. "The Highlands are riddled with passages, Z'Landar. Some carved by water over millennia. Others shaped by forces older and stranger."

"And your parents live there. In these hidden depths."

It's not a question, but I answer anyway. "Yes."

"What are they?"

50

The question I've been dreading and anticipating in equal measure. How much truth can he handle? How much should I reveal before the world forces our hands?

"They're old," I say carefully, choosing each word like stones for a cairn. "Older than the clans. Older than the division between Kelpie and Selkie. They came to these waters before humans learned to carve stone or name the stars."

His eyes narrow. "You're speaking in riddles."

"I'm speaking in truths you're not ready to hear."

"Try me."

The challenge in his voice makes something in my chest tighten. He's brave, this one. Braver than he knows. But courage alone won't prepare him for what I need to say.

"Your parents," I begin, shifting the conversation deliberately, "were remarkable. Not just for loving across the divide, but for what that union created. You're not simply half-Kelpie and half-Selkie, Z'Landar. You're something that hasn't existed since the First Waters were young."

He goes very still. "Explain."

"The division between river and sea—it wasn't always so. Once, all water-folk were one people. The separation came later, forced by circumstances I don't fully understand. But the potential for reunion always existed, waiting for the right... catalyst."

"You're saying I'm that catalyst? That's not new information. The prophecies—"

"The prophecies don't know half of what you are." I lean forward, needing him to understand even if I can't tell him everything. "You were born in the Heart of the Loch, yes? Where your parents gave themselves to the waters?"

"Everyone knows that story."

"They know the story. They don't know the truth." I pause, gathering courage. "The Heart of the Loch isn't just a place of power, Z'Landar. It's a threshold. A meeting point between Earth and—"

A disturbance in the water cuts me off. Not the normal flow of the river, but something larger, more deliberate. Z'Landar is on his feet instantly, every line of his body gone taut with readiness.

"Something comes," he says, his voice dropping to that dangerous register I heard at Loch Avon.

I feel it too. Multiple somethings, moving through the deeper channels where river meets loch. Large forms, powerful, radiating intention that presses against my senses like a hand against glass.

"Not hostile," I murmur, reading the currents. "But not friendly either. They're..." I search for the right word. "Desperate."

The water churns. Breaks.

And from the depths rise five figures that make Z'Landar's hand move instinctively toward where a weapon would hang if he carried one.

They were giants, or close enough to make no difference. Three meters tall at minimum, their bodies massive with corded muscle that spoke of deep-water pressure and ancient strength. Their skin held the gray-green pallor of those who dwelt in the darkest trenches, and their eyes—cruel and calculating—fixed on Z'Landar with an intensity that bordered on violence.

Fomorians.

Z'Landar had heard stories of them—pre-Celtic beings of chaos and storm, raiders from the western waters of Ireland who came in the night and left devastation in their wake. The clans whispered their names to frighten children. The Kelpies avoided their hunting grounds.

And now five of them stood dripping on the shore where he'd hoped to have peaceful conversation with a woman whose mysteries already threatened to undo him.

"Z'Landar, son of Brannach," the largest said, his voice like boulders grinding in deep water. "We come bearing warning. And we come seeking yours."

"Mine?" Z'Landar kept his tone neutral, his body relaxed despite every instinct screaming readiness. Showing fear to Fomorians was invitation to violence. "I give warnings, not seek them. What brings you so far from Ireland's waters?"

"Necessity." The speaker stepped forward, and Z'Landar noticed for the first time the fresh scars across his arms and chest. Battle wounds, recently healed. "And fear."

That admission—from a Fomorian—sent cold spreading through Z'Landar's gut.

"Speak plainly."

"A dragon stirs in Ireland," another said, this one female with eyes like storm-tossed seas. "Caoránach, the Mother of Serpents. She carries eggs."

The world seemed to still. Even the river's voice dimmed.

"Dragons," Z'Landar said carefully, "haven't walked these lands in recorded history."

"Then perhaps," the first Fomorian replied, "your history has gaps."

Beside Z'Landar, Andralia rose to her feet, her expression gone cold and focused in ways that made her seem suddenly older, harder. "How many eggs?"

The Fomorians' eyes shifted to her, assessments being made and recalculated in the space of heartbeats. They recognized power when they saw it, even if they couldn't name its source.

"Four," the female said. "Four eggs when legend says there should be one. She hides them in separate places—two in Ireland, two in Scotland."

"Scotland?" Z'Landar's voice sharpened. "When? Where?"

"Already done. Three nights past, she swam beneath dark of moon, bearing precious cargo in her jaws. We tracked her as far as Torr Head before losing her trail in the deeper channels." The largest Fomorian's expression twisted with something between respect and fear. "She is fierce beyond measure, protecting what she carries. We lost one of our number simply attempting to follow."

Z'Landar's mind raced, processing implications. Dragons. Eggs. Scotland. "What does she want? Why bring them here?"

"Safety," Andralia said softly, her gaze distant as if seeing something the rest of them could not. "Scotland has known peace these ten years. No wars, no great upheavals. Ireland..." She glanced at the Fomorians. "Ireland still churns with old conflicts."

The female nodded reluctantly. "The Tuatha Dé Danann stir again. Powers wake that have slept since before our time. The dragon seeks calmer waters for her brood."

"And if they hatch?" Z'Landar asked, though he already knew the answer.

"Then four dragons will rule these lands," the largest Fomorian said flatly. "They will burn and they will feed and they will grow. And no power in Scotland or Ireland will be strong enough to stand against them."

The silence that followed held weight enough to crack stone.

Z'Landar looked at Andralia, seeing his own understanding reflected in her impossible eyes. This was why she'd come. Why their meeting had been necessary. Somehow—through whatever means her mysterious parents possessed—she'd known. Or suspected.

"You came to warn me," he said to the Fomorians. "Why? Your kind owes allegiance to no one."

54

"Because," the female said, and something almost like respect entered her voice, "we remember what you did ten years ago. We watched from our depths as you stood against the Great Wurm. We saw you unite water and land against darkness that would have devoured us all." She paused. "You are... worthy. If anyone can stand against what comes, it is you."

The weight of her words settled on Z'Landar's shoulders like a physical thing. The throne he'd run from. The crown he'd refused. The responsibility he'd spent ten years avoiding.

All of it calling to him now, inevitable as morning.

He turned to Andralia, found her watching him with an expression he couldn't quite read. Pride, perhaps. Or sadness. Or both.

"You knew," he said quietly. "Not the details, maybe. But you knew something was coming."

"I knew the peace couldn't last," she replied, equally soft. "And I knew you would be needed."

"Needed." The word tasted bitter. "For what? I'm not king of anything. I have no army, no authority beyond what people choose to give me."

"Then perhaps," she said, and reached out to touch his arm—just briefly, just enough to send that current of connection crackling between them, "it's time to stop running from what you are."

Before Z'Landar could respond, the largest Fomorian spoke again. "There is more. A Merrow named Muirgheal tried to bring this warning days ago. She and her Muckie companion came to Scottish waters, seeking to alert your people. None would listen."

"A Merrow?" Z'Landar frowned. "They rarely leave Irish waters."

"She left because she saw the danger. Saw Caoránach swimming east with eggs in her grasp." The Fomorian's expression darkened. "She was turned away at every shore, dismissed as a teller of tales. Your people did not want to believe that dragons were real."

Shame burned in Z'Landar's chest. His people. Leaderless, scattered, without authority to make them listen even when truth came bearing warning.

"I'll find her," he said. "This Muirgheal. I'll hear her story properly."

"Do more than hear it," the female Fomorian said. "Believe it. Act on it. Because the dragon will not wait for you to decide you're ready." She turned to the others. "We have delivered our warning. The rest is his to carry."

They moved toward the water, those massive forms slipping beneath the surface with barely a ripple despite their size. Within moments, only disturbed water remained to prove they'd ever been.

Z'Landar stood staring at the spot where they'd vanished, his thoughts churning like the river at flood. Dragons. Eggs. Four of them, hidden somewhere in the Highlands.

And somehow, he was supposed to find them. Stop them. Save both Scotland and Ireland from a threat that shouldn't exist.

"Z'Landar." Andralia's voice pulled him back. "Look at me."

He did, finding her standing close now, close enough that he could see the flecks of silver in her impossible eyes.

"The Fomorians are right," she said. "If anyone can face this, it's you. But not alone." She took a breath. "I'll help you. Whatever comes, you don't have to carry it by yourself."

"You barely know me."

"I know enough." Her smile was sad, certain. "And I know what you are, even if you don't. Not yet."

"Then tell me." Frustration bled into his voice. "Stop speaking in half-truths and mysteries. If you know what I am, if you know something that can help—"

"I will," she promised. "Soon. But first..." She glanced toward Loch Ness, where the Fomorians had vanished. "First we need to find proof of what they claim. You'll need evidence to convince the clans, the councils. They won't mobilize on the word of Fomorians alone."

She was right. Of course she was right. The Kelpie elders would demand verification. Queen Mhairi would require certainty before committing Selkie forces. The Highland clans—by the stars, convincing them would be nearly impossible without proof.

"Ireland," he said, pieces falling into place. "I need to see this dragon myself. Witness the eggs, if possible."

"And I'm coming with you."

"Andralia—"

"Don't." She held up a hand, forestalling his protest. "You said it yourself—you have no army, no authority. But you have me. And I have abilities that will prove useful, whether you understand them yet or not."

He wanted to argue. Wanted to tell her this was too dangerous, that he couldn't risk someone he barely knew. But the truth was simpler and more complicated: he didn't want to face this alone. And something in him—something deeper than reason—recognized that she was meant to stand beside him in whatever came next.

"Three days ago," he said softly, "you were a stranger who appeared in Loch Avon uninvited."

"And now?"

"Now I can't imagine doing this without you." The admission cost him something, but felt right. "Which terrifies me more than dragons."

Her laugh was soft, genuine. "Good. Fear keeps you sharp." She sobered. "When do we leave?"

Z'Landar looked toward the east, where Ireland lay beyond the horizon. The journey would take days, even swimming at full speed. And every hour they delayed was another hour the dragon had to prepare, to protect, to ensure her eggs remained hidden until hatching.

"As soon as I send word to Maelis and the clan chiefs," he said. "They need to know what's coming. Even if they don't believe it yet."

"I'll help you compose the messages." Andralia moved toward the water. "But Z'Landar? When we find proof—when you return with evidence of this threat—you'll need to do more than share information."

"What do you mean?"

She turned back, and in her eyes he saw certainty that went beyond her years. "You'll need to claim the throne. Both thrones. The water-folk will need a king to follow into this storm. And whether you're ready or not, that burden falls to you."

The weight of prophecy. The weight of legacy. The weight of every hope and fear and desperate need that had been building for ten years.

Z'Landar felt it settling onto his shoulders like armor he'd never asked to wear.

But looking at Andralia—at this mysterious woman who had appeared in his life mere days ago yet already felt essential as breathing—he found unexpected strength.

"Then I'll be ready," he said. "Somehow."

"You will be," she agreed. "Because you won't face it alone."

As they began preparing messages to send by water sprite and river current, as the sun climbed higher and burned away the mist, Z'Landar felt the last of his carefully constructed solitude crumbling away.

The peace had ended. The weight he'd carried for ten years would only grow heavier.

But perhaps—just perhaps—he wouldn't have to carry it alone anymore.

And that single thought, fragile as new ice but real nonetheless, gave him hope that maybe, just maybe, he could be what they needed him to be.

What the world needed him to be.

King.

The word still tasted strange. But he was beginning to believe he might learn to wear it.

If he survived what came next.

Chapter Four: The Calling Tide

The water sprites scattered like dandelion seeds on the wind, each carrying fragments of Z'Landar's message burned into their ephemeral forms. They would reach every loch and river within a day's travel, whispering warnings to any who had ears to hear: *Dragon. Eggs. Ireland. Proof needed.*

Simple words for a complex threat. But simplicity carried further than elaborate explanation, and speed mattered more than poetry.

Z'Landar watched them go from the shore of Loch Ness, their tiny lights flickering against the morning sky like stars that had forgotten to fade with dawn. Beside him, Andralia worked her own magic—speaking in low, melodious tones to the river currents themselves, sending messages downstream toward the Selkie territories. Her methods were subtler than his, requiring no intermediary spirits, just will and water responding to will.

He envied that ease. That certainty of being understood.

"The Kelpie Council will debate for three days before deciding whether to take your warning seriously," Andralia said, breaking her concentration. "The Selkies will be more receptive, but Queen Mhairi will demand corroboration."

"Which is why we go to Ireland." Z'Landar ran a hand through his damp hair, feeling the weight of decisions made in haste. "Proof first. Crown after."

"If there's time for 'after.'" She moved closer, her shoulder almost but not quite touching his. "Dragon eggs don't wait for convenient moments."

"No." He glanced at her, this woman who had appeared in his life three days ago yet already felt woven into it like a current he couldn't escape. "Do you regret coming?"

"No." Her answer came without hesitation. "Do you regret accepting my company?"

"I don't know you well enough to regret anything yet."

Her laugh was soft, slightly sad. "Fair enough. Though I suspect you know me better than you think."

Before Z'Landar could ask what she meant, a disturbance in the loch's surface caught his attention. Not the sprites returning—their touch was lighter, more ephemeral. This was something with substance. With age and purpose.

Maelis broke the surface twenty yards from shore, her seal form cutting through the water with the ease of one who had swum these depths for centuries. She shifted to human shape as she reached the shallows, her silver-streaked hair hanging in dripping ropes past her shoulders, her amber eyes finding Z'Landar with laser focus.

"Dragons," she said without preamble, water streaming from her clothing. "Of all the threats I expected to face in my lifetime, dragons were not among them."

"You received my message."

"Your sprite nearly gave me heart failure, appearing at dawn shrieking about fire and eggs." Maelis waded onto shore, her gaze shifting to Andralia with an assessment that held layers of meaning. "And you are the mysterious one from Loch Etchachan."

"Andralia," she offered, inclining her head with respect that seemed automatic. "You're Maelis. Z'Landar speaks of you often."

"Does he?" Maelis's expression remained neutral, but Z'Landar caught the sharpness beneath. "How curious, given he's only known you a handful of days."

The air between the two women suddenly felt charged, like the moment before lightning strikes. Z'Landar stepped forward, positioning himself subtly between them.

61

"Maelis, I need your help," he said, pulling her attention back to him. "The Fomorians were clear—four eggs, two already in Scotland. But without proof, the councils won't mobilize. I have to go to Ireland, see this dragon myself."

"Foolishness," Maelis snapped, though her eyes held worry rather than anger. "You're one person, Z'Landar. What happens if this Caoránach decides you're a threat? Dragons don't negotiate."

"Which is why I'm going with him," Andralia said quietly.

Maelis's gaze sharpened on her. "And who are you, exactly? You appear from nowhere, just as ancient threats emerge. You speak of things no one your age should know. You..." She paused, studying Andralia with intensity that made Z'Landar uncomfortable. "You carry magic that tastes wrong. Not bad, not corrupted. Just... other."

"Maelis—" Z'Landar began.

"No." Andralia raised a hand, stopping him. She met Maelis's gaze squarely. "She's right to question. In her position, I would too." She took a breath. "I'm not what I appear to be. My parents are older than most beings walking this earth. I carry knowledge passed down through bloodlines that predate the division of the water-folk. And yes, my magic is 'other' because I come from places you haven't seen."

"Places," Maelis repeated. "Not families. Not territories. Places."

"Yes."

The single word hung between them, heavy with implication. Z'Landar looked between the two women, feeling pieces of a puzzle he couldn't quite see shifting into new configurations.

"Maelis," he said carefully, "what do you know that you haven't told me?"

The old Selkie's expression shifted—something between resignation and relief crossing her weathered features. She gestured toward a cluster of rocks further up the shore, away from the water's edge and any curious ears.

"Come. If we're to speak of this, we do it properly."

They followed her to the makeshift shelter, settling onto sun-warmed stone. Maelis took her time arranging herself, as if gathering courage or choosing words with unusual care. When she finally spoke, her voice carried the weight of years held silent.

"Ten years ago," she began, "when you defeated the Great Wurm and drove back the ancient darkness, I dreamed. In that dream, I saw your parents—Brannach and Nerina—standing at the Heart of the Loch. But they weren't alone. Behind them, barely visible through a veil like morning mist, stood others. Figures that hurt to look at directly, as if light bent wrong around them."

Z'Landar's pulse quickened. "You never mentioned this."

"Because I didn't understand it." Maelis's gaze found Andralia. "Until three days ago, when the sprites brought whispers of a strange woman seeking Z'Landar in Loch Avon. A woman from the highest loch. A woman who carried that same wrong-bent light."

Andralia's expression remained calm, but Z'Landar saw her hands tighten slightly. "You've seen star-travelers before."

"Once. Centuries ago, when I was young and foolish enough to swim the deepest trenches where even Kelpies fear to go." Maelis's voice dropped. "I found a door. Not made of wood or stone, but light and intention. I had the sense not to open it, but I watched it for three days. On the third day, someone—something—passed through. They didn't see me. Or perhaps they did and judged me harmless."

"What were they?" Z'Landar asked, though part of him already guessed.

"Not of Earth," Maelis said simply. "Not in the way we understand origin. They wore forms that could have been human, but the way they moved, the way light caught them..." She shook her head. "I swam away. Never spoke of it. Tried to forget."

"But you didn't forget," Andralia said softly.

"No. And when I saw them again in my dream, standing behind Z'Landar's parents at the Heart—" Maelis turned to him, her amber eyes luminous with certainty. "I knew then that your birth was more than prophecy. That you were meant for something beyond these waters."

Z'Landar felt the ground shifting beneath him, metaphorically if not literally. Everything he thought he understood about himself suddenly seemed inadequate, like trying to hold an ocean in a cup.

"My parents never mentioned—"

"They couldn't," Andralia interrupted gently. "There are rules. Ancient rules about interference, about revealing too much too soon." She hesitated, then continued. "But circumstances have changed. The threat is real and immediate. Some truths can't wait for perfect timing."

"Then tell me." Z'Landar's voice came out harder than intended. "No more half-answers, no more mysteries. If there's something about my birth, my nature, that will help me face what's coming—tell me now."

Andralia and Maelis exchanged glances, some wordless communication passing between them. Finally, Andralia nodded as if accepting a burden.

"The Heart of the Loch where you were born—it's not just a place of power. It's a threshold. A meeting point between Earth and other worlds. Your parents didn't just sacrifice themselves to create it. They were chosen by forces older than Scotland, older than humanity. Chosen to create a bridge."

"Between what?"

"Between Earth and everywhere else." She met his eyes, her own holding that vast depth he'd glimpsed at their first meeting. "You're not just Kelpie and Selkie, Z'Landar. You're Earth and stars. Bound to this world but connected to infinite others. That's why the vision happened when we touched. That's why I can help amplify your power. We're..." She searched for words. "Compatible. In ways that go beyond blood or magic."

The implications crashed over Z'Landar like a wave. He thought of the vision—galaxies wheeling, distances impossible to comprehend, the sense of connection stretching across void. He thought of his strange abilities that went beyond what either Kelpie or Selkie could explain. The way water responded to him not just as element but as conscious thing.

"I'm..." He couldn't finish the thought.

"You're exactly what you need to be," Maelis said firmly. "Whatever your origin, whatever strange forces shaped your birth—you are still Brannach's son. Still Nerina's child. Still the one who stood against darkness when it would have consumed us all."

"But now," Andralia added quietly, "you know why the dragon threat matters beyond Scotland. Beyond Earth, even. You're being watched, Z'Landar. By powers that hope you'll prove worthy of what you could become."

"And if I'm not worthy?"

"Then we all suffer for it." She reached out, took his hand despite Maelis's sharp intake of breath. The connection flared between them— not as overwhelming as before, but present, undeniable. "But I don't think unworthiness is your problem. Fear is."

She was right. Of course she was right. He was terrified—not of dragons or eggs or ancient monsters, but of becoming what everyone needed him to be. Of accepting that his life was never meant to be his own.

"The throne," he said quietly.

"Eventually. But first—" Maelis rose, decisive. "First you survive Ireland. You gather your proof. You return alive." Her voice gentled slightly. "Then we worry about crowns and destinies and whatever cosmic forces have opinions about your future."

Z'Landar appreciated her practicality. Whatever revelations had been shared, whatever truths had shifted the foundation of his understanding, immediate concerns remained unchanged. Dragon. Eggs. Threat.

"I need supplies," he said, forcing himself to focus on what could be controlled. "Provisions for the journey. And I should speak with Fionnuala before I leave—she'll be furious if I vanish to Ireland without word."

"I'll handle your half-sister," Maelis said, though her tone suggested this would not be an easy task. "You focus on preparing. How long do you estimate the journey?"

"Three days there, perhaps four." Z'Landar calculated distances, currents. "If we swim hard and avoid unnecessary encounters. A day or two in Ireland gathering proof. Three days back."

"Ten days minimum, then." Maelis's expression tightened. "Much can happen in ten days. The eggs could begin quickening. The dragon could strike. The councils could fall to infighting without your presence to unite them."

"Which is why we must move swiftly." Andralia stood, ready. "No delays. No side ventures. We find evidence and return."

Maelis studied them both—these two young people about to venture into waters that had claimed better swimmers. Then she did something unexpected. She bowed. Not deeply, but enough to show respect given rather than demanded.

"I underestimated you," she said to Andralia. "Forgive an old fool's suspicion."

"There's nothing to forgive." Andralia returned the bow with equal grace. "Suspicion keeps him alive. I'm grateful for it."

Something passed between them—understanding, perhaps. Or simply the recognition of two who loved the same person and would fight to keep him safe.

"Go then," Maelis said. "I'll hold the chaos at bay as long as I can. But Z'Landar—" She gripped his arm, her fingers strong despite her age. "Come back. Whatever you find there, whatever proof you gather—come back alive. We need you."

"I will," he promised, though the future felt suddenly murky as storm-water. "Take care of them while I'm gone. The councils, the clans. Keep them from each other's throats."

"I've been doing that for three centuries. I can manage ten more days." She released him, stepped back. "The sprites will carry word if anything urgent develops. Otherwise—move fast, trust your instincts, and remember that you're stronger than you believe."

With final nods exchanged, Maelis returned to the water, her seal-form cutting south toward the Selkie territories where her particular brand of wisdom would be needed most.

Z'Landar watched her go, feeling the weight of revelation still settling on his shoulders. Star-travelers. Thresholds between worlds. A destiny that stretched beyond Scotland, beyond Earth itself.

"Overwhelming, isn't it?" Andralia said softly beside him.

"Yes."

"Does it change anything? Knowing what you are?"

He considered the question carefully. Did it change things? He was still himself—still the boy who had stumbled from the Heart of the Loch, still the young man who had fought beside Highlanders and water-folk, still the one who carried his parents' legacy in blood and bone.

But perhaps he understood now why that legacy weighed so heavy. Why the throne mattered beyond politics or prophecy. Why he couldn't simply be Z'Landar, son of sacrifice, and nothing more.

"It changes everything," he admitted. "And nothing. I still don't want the crown. I still fear becoming what they need. But..." He turned to face her fully. "I understand now why running was never really an option."

"Because fate doesn't take no for an answer?"

"Because some debts transcend personal choice." He managed a wry smile. "Even cosmic ones."

Andralia's expression softened. "For what it's worth—I didn't come here just because my parents asked. I came because I wanted to meet you. The legend, yes. But also the person behind it." She paused. "I'm glad I did. Even knowing what comes next."

"We barely know each other."

"We know enough." She mirrored his earlier words back at him, and the echo made him smile despite everything. "Ready for Ireland?"

Z'Landar looked west, toward waters he'd never swum, toward dangers he could barely imagine. Ten years ago, he'd faced the Great Wurm armed with little more than desperate hope and borrowed courage. Now he would face dragons with slightly more experience and significantly more questions about his own nature.

"No," he said honestly. "But let's go anyway."

They took the seal-forms together, slipping beneath Loch Ness's dark surface side by side. The water closed over them like a benediction, cool and certain, carrying them toward the channels that would lead to open sea.

Behind them, Scotland prepared for war.

Ahead, Ireland waited with fire and secrets.

And somewhere in the depths between worlds, cosmic eyes watched to see if Earth's bridge would hold when pressure came to bear.

Z'Landar swam toward his destiny, not alone but accompanied.

And for now, that would have to be enough.

Chapter Five: The Western Waters

The North Channel stretched before them like a road paved in twilight—gray waters churning with currents that had worn paths between Scotland and Ireland since before memory kept accounts. Z'Landar took the seal-form as naturally as breathing, his body remembering the shape of his mother's people even as his father's strength surged through muscle and bone. Beside him, Andralia shifted into something that was seal but also other—sleeker, faster, touched by depths no ordinary Selkie had ever known.

They swam.

The first day passed in a blur of motion and cold water, the channel currents carrying them southwest toward Irish shores. They surfaced only briefly—to catch breath, to orient by sun and stars, to feel the wind on their faces before diving again into the blue-dark world where sound traveled strange and light bent in ways that defied surface logic.

Z'Landar had made this journey before in his mind, planning routes through underwater valleys and around the known territories of creatures best avoided. But having Andralia beside him changed everything. She moved through the water like music given form, and he found himself adjusting his pace not out of necessity but desire—to stay close, to watch the play of light along her seal-skin, to exist in the shared space between them.

They didn't speak much that first day. The channel waters were too loud, too turbulent for easy conversation. But in the brief moments when they surfaced together, floating in the space between waves, their eyes met with understanding that needed no words.

This matters. This journey. This moment.

Night fell, and they sheltered in a sea-cave along the Scottish coast, still hours from Ireland proper. The cave ran deep into limestone cliffs, ending in a chamber where water met air and barnacles clung to stone like ancient script. They took human form, shivering despite skin that knew cold as comfort, and built no fire for fear of attracting attention.

Z'Landar sat with his back against rough stone, feeling the fatigue of a full day's swimming settle into his bones. Across from him, Andralia wrung water from her hair, her movements graceful even in exhaustion.

"You're quiet," she said, breaking the silence that had stretched comfortable between them.

"Thinking."

"About what Maelis told you."

Not a question. She knew. Of course she knew—she always seemed to know what moved beneath his surfaces.

"About what *you* told me," he corrected gently. "Star-travelers. Thresholds between worlds. My parents chosen by forces I can't begin to understand." He leaned his head back against stone. "Ten years I've known my birth was unusual. But this..."

"Changes things," she finished.

"Everything. Nothing." He managed a tired smile. "Both at once, as seems to be my fate."

Andralia shifted closer, careful to maintain space but reducing the distance between them. In the dim light filtering through the cave entrance, her eyes held that impossible depth—not the blue-green of Earth's oceans, but something vaster, darker, shot through with light that came from nowhere and everywhere.

"Does it frighten you?" she asked softly. "Knowing what you are?"

"I don't know what I am. That's what frightens me." Z'Landar's hands curled against his thighs. "I thought I understood myself. Kelpie and Selkie, water and river, the bridge between two peoples. That was complicated enough. But now—" He gestured helplessly. "Now you tell me I'm descended from the stars themselves, that my birth involved cosmic forces, that entire worlds are watching to see what I'll become."

"Not watching to judge," Andralia said. "Watching to hope."

"Hope for what?"

She was quiet for a long moment, and Z'Landar watched emotions play across her face—the same struggle he'd seen before, that war between what she knew and what she was permitted to share.

"My parents' people," she began carefully, "have rules about interference. Strict rules about letting worlds develop naturally. But those rules also create... limitations. They can observe, they can hide, they can exist quietly among the humans and other Earth-born creatures. But they can't lead. Can't unite. Can't be what you are."

"And what's that?"

"Free of their restrictions." Her smile was sad, knowing. "You're Earth-born, Z'Landar. Whatever star-heritage runs in your blood, you were born here. The rules that bind my parents don't apply to you. You can act. You can lead. You can become something neither fully of Earth nor fully of the stars, but greater than either alone."

The weight of that truth settled on his shoulders like water—heavy, all-encompassing, impossible to escape.

"I never asked for that burden."

"No one asks for their destiny. But some of us are strong enough to carry it anyway." She reached out, her fingers stopping just short of touching his hand. "You proved that ten years ago when you stood against the Great Wurm. You're proving it now, swimming toward danger to protect people who can't protect themselves."

"I'm not swimming alone this time."

"No," she agreed, and her fingers closed the final distance, settling over his with warmth that drove back the cave's chill. "You're not."

Andralia

I feel it the moment our skin touches—that surge of connection that should be familiar by now but still catches me unprepared. The vision doesn't come this time, no galaxies wheeling or distances spanning. Just him. Just me. Just the certainty settling into my bones that this—*this*—is where I'm meant to be.

I've traveled to worlds so distant there are no Earth words to name them. I've stood beneath triple suns and walked through cities built of light and crystal. I've seen wonders that would break a human mind with their beauty and strangeness.

None of it compares to sitting in a limestone cave with Z'Landar's hand beneath mine, feeling his pulse steady against my palm.

My parents warned me this would happen. That once I met him, once I understood what he was, I would be lost. They used gentler words— "connected," "bonded," "essential to each other"—but the meaning was clear. Some forces transcend choice. Some attractions answer to laws older than consciousness.

I should tell him everything. Should explain that my parents sent me specifically to find him, that I've known for years what he represents, that the dragon threat is only the beginning of challenges he'll face. Should confess that I'm falling for him not despite our destiny but tangled inextricably within it.

But looking at his eyes—storm-gray and exhausted and carrying burdens no one his age should bear—I find I can't add more weight. Not yet. Not when he's still processing revelations that would shatter lesser men.

"Tell me about the stars," he says suddenly, surprising me. "You've been to other worlds. What are they like?"

Relief and trepidation war in my chest. This is safer ground. Sharing wonder rather than burden.

"Different," I begin, then laugh at my own inadequacy. "That's obvious, I suppose. But it's true in ways that are hard to explain. Some worlds have

72

water that thinks, that remembers. Others have no water at all, just gases that flow like rivers and creatures that swim through air."

"And the people?"

"As varied as Earth's life, only more so. Some look almost human— you'd pass them on a Highland road without a second glance. Others are so different that your mind struggles to process them as alive." I pause, remembering. "But all of them understand certain truths. The importance of balance. The danger of darkness left unchecked. The need for bridges between different ways of being."

"Like me," Z'Landar says quietly. "A bridge."

"Like you."

We sit in comfortable silence, his hand still under mine, our breath synchronizing in the way of those who've shared close spaces and closer purposes. Outside, waves crash against cliffs with the patience of water that has worn stone for eons and will wear it for eons more.

"Andralia," he says, and my name in his voice sends warmth through places I didn't know were cold. "When this is over—when we've found the eggs, stopped the dragon, saved Scotland and Ireland from whatever darkness thinks to claim them—will you stay?"

The question catches in my throat like a fish hook. *When this is over.* As if there's any guarantee of survival, any certainty we'll both walk away whole. As if I don't know with the certainty my parents' teaching gave me that great victories demand great prices.

"Yes," I say anyway, because it's true even if the staying might be different than he imagines. "Where else would I go?"

His smile breaks like dawn. "The stars. Your parents' worlds. Anywhere in the infinite cosmos."

"I choose here." I turn my hand, threading my fingers through his. "I choose you."

The words hang between us, weighted with meaning beyond romance, beyond even destiny. A choice made freely despite all the cosmic forces trying to dictate our paths. In that moment, in that cave with water whispering at our backs, we become something neither fate nor star-travelers nor ancient powers can fully claim.

We become us.

Z'Landar leans forward slowly, giving me time to pull back, to laugh it off, to remind him we barely know each other despite the intensity burning between us. I don't pull back. When his lips meet mine, the connection explodes through every nerve—not vision this time but pure sensation, the recognition of two who were always meant to find each other across whatever distances separated them.

The kiss is tentative at first, questioning. Then deeper, certain, as if our bodies understand what our minds still struggle to accept.

When we finally part, both breathless, his forehead rests against mine.

"I've never—" he starts.

"Neither have I," I admit. "Not like this."

"Is it always—?"

"No." I smile against his cheek. "This is us. This is what happens when Earth and stars finally remember they were never meant to be separate."

We don't sleep that night, not truly. We talk in whispers about small things and cosmic truths, about his childhood in the water and mine split between depths and distances. We share stories of loneliness—his running from crowns, mine caught between worlds with no clear home. We trade kisses like currency precious beyond gold, each one settling something restless in both our souls.

And when dawn breaks gray and cold over the Irish Sea, we return to the water as something we weren't before.

Partners. In every sense that matters.

The second day brought them fully into Irish waters. Z'Landar felt the difference immediately—a subtle shift in temperature and taste, in the way currents moved and ancient magics pressed against his senses. These were older waters than Scotland's, carrying memories that predated even the longest Selkie songs.

They surfaced near midday, treading water while Z'Landar oriented himself. The Irish coast rose green and dramatic to the east, cliffs crowned with grass and stone ruins. Somewhere beyond those cliffs, a dragon nested. Somewhere in these waters or hidden in secret places on land, two eggs waited to hatch into monsters.

"There," Andralia said, pointing north along the coastline. "Do you see the discoloration?"

Z'Landar followed her gesture and felt his stomach tighten. A section of cliff face bore marks that couldn't be mistaken for natural weathering. Black scorch marks climbed the stone like flame frozen in time, and the vegetation for a hundred yards in either direction had withered to ash.

Dragon fire. Above and below the waterline.

"Recent," he judged, reading the patterns. "Within the last fortnight."

"A warning." Andralia's voice held grim certainty. "She's marking territory. Telling any who see: *Stay away. This is mine.*"

They swam closer, careful to approach from underwater where the dragon's sight couldn't easily find them. Up close, the destruction was even more apparent. Stone had melted in places, refrozen into glass-smooth surfaces that spoke of heat beyond any natural fire. Fish avoided the area entirely—the water itself tasted wrong, poisoned by whatever ancient magics the dragon carried in her flames.

"How do we fight something that can do *this*?" Z'Landar asked quietly, running his hand along scorched stone.

"Carefully. Together." Andralia's fingers found his beneath the water. "And with knowledge she doesn't expect us to have."

75

Before Z'Landar could ask what she meant, a voice carried across the water—female, melodious, touched with sorrow old as Ireland itself.

"You're the ones from Scotland. The warning-bringers who came too late."

They turned to find a figure floating twenty yards distant, having appeared with the silence of one who knew these waters intimately. Green hair spread around her shoulders like kelp, and when she raised a webbed hand in greeting, Z'Landar recognized what she was.

Merrow. The Merrow who had tried to warn them.

"Muirgheal," Andralia said, and the Merrow's eyes widened slightly at being named.

"You know me?"

"The Fomorians spoke of your courage," Z'Landar said, swimming closer but maintaining respectful distance. "You tried to warn Scotland. We didn't listen. I'm sorry."

Muirgheal's expression softened from wariness to something like relief. "You believe now."

"Hard not to believe evidence like that." Z'Landar gestured to the scorched cliff. "We came seeking proof. Seems we've found it."

"There's worse." The Merrow's voice dropped, glancing around as if the dragon might be listening from the depths. "Come. If you truly seek proof, I'll show you what Caoránach has wrought. But not here. Not in the open where her eyes might see."

She dove before they could respond, her form cutting through the water with practiced ease. Z'Landar and Andralia exchanged glances—part question, part understanding—then followed.

Muirgheal led them along the coast, staying deep where sunlight barely penetrated and the water pressed with the weight of fathoms. They swam for an hour, maybe two, until the Merrow angled upward toward a hidden inlet protected by standing stones that predated human memory.

They surfaced in a natural harbor surrounded by cliffs carved with spirals and symbols Z'Landar recognized from the oldest Kelpie legends. The water here ran shallow and clear, untouched by dragon fire but holding an atmosphere of watchfulness, as if the stones themselves stood guard.

"This place is old," Andralia murmured, studying the carvings with something like reverence.

"Older than dragons." Muirgheal hauled herself onto a flat rock, her seal-like lower body settling into human legs as she moved from water to air. "Older than most things that walk Ireland now. The dragon avoids it—there are protections here even she respects."

Z'Landar pulled himself up beside her, taking human form with relief. The seal-shape was natural to him, but long hours in that form still brought fatigue. "You said there was worse. Worse than scorched cliffs?"

"Aye." Muirgheal's green eyes held depths of sorrow. "Three days past, Caoránach rose from her lair in rage. Something had angered her—perhaps your Fomorian friends' journey to Scotland, perhaps she sensed threats to her eggs. Whatever the cause, she took her fury out on the fishing villages along the western coast."

"How many dead?" Andralia asked quietly.

"Seventeen humans. Burned in their boats or drowned when she overturned their vessels." Muirgheal's hands clenched. "And countless of my people—Merrow who tried to intervene, to protect the humans we've sworn to watch over. She killed them with fire that burns even underwater. I watched friends burn. Watched the water itself catch flame."

Z'Landar felt rage building in his chest—cold, controlled, but absolute. This was why they'd come. This was the proof needed to unite Scotland against the threat. But knowing the price in lives, seeing the grief written on Muirgheal's face—

77

"I'm sorry," he said, the words inadequate but necessary. "We'll stop her. Somehow, we'll find a way."

"Will you?" Muirgheal studied him with intensity that went beyond curiosity. "The Fomorians said you were powerful. That you'd stood against ancient evils before. But Caoránach is older than your Scotland, older than most magics practiced in these lands. What makes you think—?"

She stopped mid-sentence, her eyes widening as they fixed on Z'Landar's chest. Following her gaze, he looked down to find the Heart of the Loch pendant had slipped free of his tunic, catching sunlight with inner luminescence.

"That's—" Muirgheal's voice dropped to a whisper. "Where did you get that?"

"It was my mother's. And her mother's before her. A relic of—"

"The First Waters." Muirgheal's hand trembled as she reached toward the pendant, stopping just short of touching. "I've seen drawings of it in the oldest songs. The Heart of the Loch, they called it. Forged in waters that connected worlds."

Andralia and Z'Landar exchanged glances, and he saw knowledge in her eyes—recognition that Muirgheal understood more than she should.

"You know what it is," Z'Landar said carefully.

"I know the legends." Muirgheal pulled her hand back. "I know that whoever carries the Heart is marked for greatness or tragedy. Often both." Her expression shifted, some calculation being made. "If you truly carry that—if you're the one the old tales speak of—then perhaps there's hope after all."

"Tales?" Z'Landar prompted.

But Muirgheal was already sliding back into the water, taking seal-form before she answered. "Come. If you want proof for your people, I'll give you proof. But prepare yourselves. What Caoránach guards, she guards with fury."

78

They followed her out of the hidden harbor, back into the open waters of the Irish coast. Z'Landar's mind churned with questions—about the pendant, about the legends Muirgheal knew, about what they were swimming toward. Beside him, Andralia swam close, her presence a comfort against the growing dread in his gut.

The sun hung low on the horizon, painting the water blood-red, when Muirgheal led them to a place where the ocean floor dropped away into darkness.

And in that darkness, something massive stirred.

"There," Muirgheal's voice carried through the water, touched with fear she couldn't hide. "She hunts at night. If you want to see Caoránach, if you want proof for your Scotland—stay here. Stay quiet. And pray she doesn't catch your scent."

Z'Landar felt Andralia's hand find his in the deep water, her fingers tight with shared tension.

They waited.

They watched.

And as night swallowed the last of day's light, the dragon rose from the abyss.

Chapter Six: She Who Darkens Waters

The deep waters know their own silences.

There is the silence of winter lochs, frozen beneath ice that muffles even the heartbeat of stones. There is the silence of tide-pools at dawn, holding their breath before the sun remembers to wake them. There is the silence of underground rivers, patient as centuries, wearing mountains grain by grain.

And then there is the silence that comes when predators hunt.

Z'Landar floated in water gone still as held breath, Andralia's hand tight in his own, Muirgheal hovering three body-lengths distant. The Irish Sea had swallowed the last of daylight, leaving them suspended in darkness broken only by the faint phosphorescence of deep-dwelling creatures and the strange luminescence that clung to Andralia's skin like starlight remembered.

Waiting.

Below them, the abyss yawned—not merely deep water, but a trench that plunged beyond measuring, beyond light's ability to penetrate. The humans called it Rockall Trough, that vast underwater canyon carved by forces older than their naming of it. The water-folk knew it by other names, names that tasted of caution and ancient fear.

Here be dragons.

Not metaphor. Not legend carefully embroidered by generations of tale-tellers seeking to frighten younglings into obedience.

Truth, terrible and scaled.

Something moved in the deep.

Not sound, precisely—water this far down carried noise strangely, bending it, distorting it until a whale's song might seem to come from stones and a Selkie's cry from empty water. But Z'Landar felt it nonetheless, that shift in pressure that spoke of massive displacement, of something vast rising through layers of ocean that should have crushed lesser creatures to pulp and memory.

His father's blood sang warning in his veins. His mother's heritage whispered caution through every nerve. The part of him that was neither Kelpie nor Selkie but something other—something touched by stars and cosmic forces he barely understood—went very still, very watchful.

She comes.

The water grew warmer. Impossible, at this depth, in these northern latitudes where cold pressed like iron against skin. But warmth spread upward from below nonetheless, carrying with it a taste that made Z'Landar's throat close: sulfur and char, ancient malice and jealous fury, the reek of things that should have remained buried in ages long forgotten.

Dragon-stench.

Beside him, Andralia's grip tightened until her nails pressed crescents into his palm. He squeezed back, offering what comfort could be given when comfort itself seemed a child's dream, inadequate against what rose toward them.

Light bloomed in the abyss.

Not the clean light of sun through water, nor even the cold glow of deep-sea creatures making their own illumination. This light burned red-gold, pulsing like a heartbeat, climbing through the dark like dawn inverted—rising from hell rather than descending from heaven.

The dragon's eyes opened first.

Two orbs of molten amber, each larger than a man's torso, holding intelligence that went beyond cunning, beyond even the vast and patient wisdom of the eldest Selkies. These were eyes that had watched empires rise and crumble, had seen the very shape of coastlines change as ice advanced and retreated. Eyes that knew the taste of human flesh and found it wanting, that had burned villages for sport and kingdoms for spite.

Eyes that had counted her eggs four times each day for a thousand years, waiting for the moment when new life would break shell and the ancient line would continue.

Z'Landar could not look away. Some terrible magnetism held his gaze locked with those burning orbs, and in their depths he saw his own death written a hundred different ways—crushed between jaws that could snap castle walls, burned by fire that melted stone, drowned in water turned to boiling fury.

Move, his mind screamed. *Flee. Swim. Survive.*

But his body betrayed him, held frozen by the oldest magic of all—the prey's paralysis before the predator's approach.

Andralia's hand released his. Moved to his face, turning it forcibly away from those terrible eyes, breaking the spell with touch that burned brighter than dragon-fire.

"Do not look," she whispered, her voice carrying through water with techniques that spoke of training beyond Earth's teaching. "She hunts with gaze as much as claw. Look away, beloved. Look at me."

Beloved.

The word pierced through terror, found purchase in something deeper than fear. Z'Landar tore his gaze from the dragon to Andralia's face, and in her impossible eyes—eyes that had seen stars beyond counting—he found anchor enough to remember himself. To remember he was not prey. Not helpless. Not without power of his own, however untested against threats like this.

"Better," Andralia breathed. "Hold to me. Watch, but do not engage. We are here to witness, not to fight. Not yet. Not tonight."

The dragon rose past them, so close that Z'Landar could have reached out and touched scales that gleamed like polished obsidian shot through with veins of gold. She was vast beyond his imagining—fifty meters from snout to tail-tip at least, perhaps more. Her body serpentine and powerful, designed for water in ways that made even the most graceful Selkie seem clumsy by comparison. Wings lay folded against her flanks, membrane webbed and translucent, catching the glow from her own eyes and reflecting it in shades of crimson and amber.

Beautiful.

The thought came unbidden, unwelcome. But truth nonetheless. Caoránach the dragon was terrible as storm-surge and deadly as deep-water pressure, but she was also magnificent in ways that made Z'Landar's breath catch. Ancient beyond reckoning, powerful beyond measuring, she was what his people might have become if they had chosen fury over wisdom, flame over flow.

She was everything the water-folk had spent millennia learning *not* to be.

Her head swung as she rose, those massive eyes scanning the darkness for prey or threat. Z'Landar held utterly still, trusting Muirgheal's knowledge of these waters, trusting that the Merrow had chosen this vantage point for reasons beyond mere viewing.

The dragon passed within two body-lengths. Close enough that her wake set them tumbling through the water like leaves in autumn wind. Close enough that Z'Landar felt heat radiating from her scales, impossible warmth in cold depths. Close enough to see scars along her flanks—white lines against dark scales, speaking of battles fought and survived across centuries.

Close enough to see the bulge along her underbelly where something precious rested.

An egg.

The fourth egg, carried within her own body, protected by flesh and scale and the terrible certainty that she would burn worlds before allowing harm to reach it.

Caoránach ascended toward the surface, toward the night sky where stars watched with indifference and the moon painted silver roads across wave-tops. Her tail swept past them—a final dismissal, or perhaps a warning. The water churned in her wake, carrying currents confused and contradictory, speaking of power that bent natural law to draconic will.

She broke the surface a hundred yards distant. Z'Landar watched her rise, water streaming from scales, wings spreading wide as church steeples. She hung suspended for one eternal moment—silhouetted against stars, terrible and glorious, a nightmare given form and purpose.

Then she was gone, arrowing north along the coast, swift as thought, leaving behind only disturbed water and the memory of eyes that burned.

For a long time, none of them moved. Could not move. The dragon's presence had pressed against them like physical weight, and her absence left a vacuum that needed filling before normal motion seemed possible again.

Finally, Muirgheal surfaced, gasping for air despite having spent the entire encounter underwater. Z'Landar and Andralia followed, breaking into night air that tasted sweet as redemption after the sulfur-reek of dragon-passage.

"Now you have seen her," Muirgheal said, her voice shaking. "Now you understand what threatens both our lands."

Z'Landar found his voice after three attempts. "The egg. She carries one within herself."

"Aye." The Merrow's green eyes reflected moonlight. "The fourth egg, kept closest. The others she has hidden—one in Ireland, two in Scotland. But the fourth she will not trust to earth or water or any protection save her own body."

"Then we cannot destroy it," Andralia said quietly. "Not without killing her first."

"And she will not be easily killed." Muirgheal swam closer, urgency replacing fear in her expression. "You've seen her now. Witnessed her size, her power. Do you still believe your Scotland can stand against her?"

84

Z'Landar thought of the Highland clans, brave and fierce but mortal as autumn leaves. He thought of the Kelpie elders, ancient and wise but aged beyond their strength. He thought of Queen Mhairi's Selkies, numerous and skilled but unaccustomed to warfare against threats like this.

He thought of his own untested power, the cosmic heritage he barely understood, the potential that burned within him like a star waiting to ignite but remained frustratingly out of reach.

"We must," he said simply. "What choice remains?"

"Many choices," Muirgheal replied, and her voice carried weight of sorrow earned through watching friends burn. "Flee. Submit. Offer her Scotland freely, beg mercy for your people, hope she grants quick death rather than slow."

"Those are not choices." Z'Landar's voice came out harder than intended. "Those are different forms of surrender."

"Then what is your choice, son of Brannach? What will you do against a creature that has survived since before your clan-names were spoken?"

He looked at Andralia, found her watching him with expression caught between hope and heartbreak, as if she saw futures branching before them and knew—somehow knew with certainty her parents' teaching granted—that not all paths led to victory. Not all endings held joy.

But she nodded. Permission, or perhaps simply acknowledgment that this was his decision to make, his burden to carry.

"I will unite the water-folk," Z'Landar said, the words falling from his lips with weight of prophecy he had spent ten years fleeing. "I will take the thrones my parents died to grant me. I will gather forces from Highland and depth, from river and sea, from every creature that calls Scotland home and values it enough to fight."

"And then?"

"And then we will do what must be done. We will find the eggs she has hidden. We will destroy them, one by one, until only the fourth remains within her." He paused, feeling destiny closing around him like water, inescapable as tides. "And then we will face her. All of us together. And we will stop her."

"You speak brave words." Muirgheal's expression held something between admiration and pity. "But words are wind, and wind does not defeat dragons."

"No," Andralia said softly, speaking for the first time since the dragon passed. "But destiny does. And he carries more destiny than any creature I have known, born of Earth or stars."

The Merrow studied them both—this young king-to-be with his cosmic heritage and untapped power, this mysterious woman who spoke of stars as if she knew them personally. Something shifted in her expression, some calculation being made.

"The Merrow will stand with you," she said finally. "When you return to Scotland, when you unite your people and prepare for war—send word. We cannot come in numbers, our kind being few and scattered. But what aid we can give, we will give. Ireland may lack a leader like you, but we are not without courage. We are not without fury of our own."

"Thank you," Z'Landar said, and meant it deeper than words could carry.

"Do not thank me yet. You have not won. You have only seen the size of what you must overcome." Muirgheal turned toward the Irish coast, where distant lights spoke of human villages unaware how close death had passed. "Rest tonight in the hidden harbor. Tomorrow I will show you more proof—the burned villages, the scorched earth where she has marked territory. Gather your evidence, then return to your Scotland. Move swiftly. The eggs will not wait forever."

She dove before they could respond, leaving them floating in waters still disturbed by draconic passage, beneath stars that watched with whatever emotions stars were capable of feeling.

Z'Landar felt exhaustion pressing against him like the deep itself. Two days of hard swimming, revelations about his nature, the first stirrings of romance with a woman touched by worlds beyond his understanding.

And now this—the dragon herself, vast and terrible and carrying within her flesh the seed of Scotland's destruction.

Too much. It was all too much for one person to carry.

But then Andralia's arms came around him from behind, her body warm against his back, her voice soft in his ear.

"You are not alone in this. Whatever comes, however dark the waters grow—you swim with me beside you. Always."

He turned in her embrace, found her eyes luminous with light that came from no moon, no stars, but from something within her that spoke of home-worlds distant beyond mortal comprehension. He kissed her then, tasting salt and determination and love that transcended cosmic design to become something chosen, something real.

"Always," he echoed against her lips.

They swam back to the hidden harbor, past standing stones that had watched the world turn for ages uncounted, seeking shelter in waters protected by magics older than dragons.

Tomorrow would bring more evidence, more proof of the threat. Tomorrow would begin the long journey back to Scotland, carrying news that would force his people to face what they could no longer deny.

Tomorrow would start the march toward crowns and thrones and the weight of leadership he had fled for ten years.

But tonight—tonight he held Andralia in the shallows of an ancient harbor, and let himself be simply Z'Landar. Not king. Not bridge between worlds. Not cosmic curiosity watched by distant planets.

Just a young man, holding the woman he loved, stealing moments of peace before the storm arrived in earnest.

The dragon hunted in the darkness above them, flying north to wherever she kept her terrible secrets.

And in the depths below, ancient forces stirred, drawn by the convergence of destiny and desire, of power waiting to be claimed and choices that would echo across worlds.

The tale was far from finished.

It had barely begun.

Chapter Seven: The Burned Lands

Dawn came to Ireland wrapped in mist thick as wool, turning the world to shades of pearl and ash. Z'Landar woke in the shallows of the hidden harbor with Andralia's warmth pressed against his side, her breathing soft and even, her hair spread across his chest like dark water caught mid-flow. For one precious moment before full waking claimed him, he allowed himself to exist in that space between sleeping and knowing—where dragons were myth and crowns were other men's burdens and the woman in his arms was simply that, without cosmic complications or destinies written in stars.

Then memory returned, bringing with it the weight of what they had witnessed.

The dragon. Vast and terrible. Carrying death within her and doom beneath her scales.

He did not move, unwilling to wake Andralia, unwilling to surrender these final moments of peace before the day demanded they continue their grim cataloging of destruction. Above them, gulls cried their harsh morning songs. Beyond the harbor's protection, waves crashed against cliffs that had stood since before the clans learned to name themselves.

The standing stones watched, patient as they had been for ages uncounted, their spiral carvings catching the first light in ways that made shadows dance.

"You're awake," Andralia murmured against his chest, not moving, not opening her eyes. "Your heartbeat changed."

"How long have you been awake?"

"Long enough to memorize the sound of you breathing." She shifted slightly, tilting her face toward his. Her eyes opened—those impossible eyes that held depths no ocean could match. "Long enough to wish we could stay here. Just here. Just us."

"We can't."

"I know." She pressed her lips to the hollow of his throat, just once, a benediction or perhaps a farewell to peace they both knew couldn't last. "But I can wish it anyway."

They rose together, taking the water as seal-forms, swimming the short distance to where Muirgheal waited at the harbor's mouth. The Merrow had not slept, Z'Landar guessed—her green eyes held the particular weariness of those who had spent dark hours keeping watch, ensuring no threats approached while others rested.

"The villages lie north," she said without preamble, her voice carrying the flatness of one who had seen too much grief, spoken of it too many times. "A day's journey along the coast, if we make good time. Are you certain you wish to see? The proof you carry already— the dragon herself, witnessed in her terrible glory—surely that suffices?"

"It must be seen," Z'Landar replied, though his heart rebelled at the necessity. "The Highland chiefs will demand accounting. They will ask: How many dead? What destruction wrought? They will need numbers, details, evidence that goes beyond one man's word."

"Even if that man is Z'Landar, who stood against the Great Wurm?"

"*Especially* if that man is Z'Landar." He managed a bitter smile. "They will say I seek the throne, that I manufacture crisis to justify my claim. Better to show them truth so stark it cannot be denied."

Muirgheal studied him for a long moment, some calculation being made behind those ancient eyes. Finally, she nodded. "Then come. Bear witness to what Caoránach has wrought. But steel yourselves—

90

the burned speak more loudly than the living, and their testimony breaks the hardest hearts."

They swam north along the Irish coast, keeping to deeper waters where the sea floor dropped away and currents ran swift with the mixing of ocean and channel. The morning grew brighter as they traveled, mist burning away to reveal a sky of that particular crystalline blue that comes after storms, when the world has been washed clean and light falls pure as prayer.

But the beauty above made bitter contrast with what waited below.

The first body floated a mile from shore, caught in kelp beds that swayed with the tide's rhythm. Human—what remained of him. The sea had already begun its work of reclamation, fish and crab attending to flesh with the efficiency nature grants her cleaners. But enough remained to show the manner of his death.

Burned.

Not by normal fire, which would have been quenched by water, which would have left different marks. This burning had occurred underwater, impossibly, flesh charred black despite the sea's embrace. The man's mouth hung open in a scream that had found no air to give it voice.

Z'Landar felt his stomach clench, bile rising. He had seen death before—ten years past, the Battle of Loch Ness had painted waters red with blood and sacrifice. But those deaths had come in combat, warriors choosing to stand against darkness. This man had been a fisherman, his boat's oars still clutched in hands burned to the bone. He had been hauling nets, feeding his family, living the small and precious life that mortal men are granted.

And the dragon had burned him for the crime of existing in waters she claimed as territory.

"There are sixteen more," Muirgheal said quietly. "Scattered along three miles of coast. Some in boats. Some who tried to swim to shore when their vessels burned. The dragon took them all—men, women, two who had barely seen thirteen summers."

"Children." Andralia's voice came out strangled. "She killed children?"

"Dragons do not distinguish between warrior and innocent. All are equal in their eyes—equally worthless, equally disposable." Muirgheal gestured north. "Come. The villages will show worse."

They left the fisherman to the sea's mercy, swimming past two more bodies before the coast bent eastward and the first village appeared.

Or what remained of it.

The settlement had held perhaps three hundred souls—a respectable size for coastal Ireland, where communities clustered around harbors and fishing grounds that could support them. Stone cottages with thatched roofs, a small kirk for Sunday worship, a market square where traders would have gathered weekly. Simple lives, honest labor, the everyday miracle of humans making home in a world that offered them no particular welcome but no active malice either.

Until the dragon came.

The harbor lay choked with charred debris—boats reduced to blackened ribs, nets melted into lumps of twisted fiber, a pier that had stood for generations now collapsed into waters that still tasted of ash. On shore, the cottages had fared no better. Roofs gone, walls crumbled, everything that could burn reduced to carbon and memory.

And the bodies.

Z'Landar forced himself to count. Forced himself to witness each one, to acknowledge the life that had been, the person who had woken that morning expecting to see sunset. Nine in the harbor itself, caught trying to flee or fight or simply too shocked to move when fire descended from the sky. Twelve more in the village proper, including an entire family—mother, father, three children—huddled together in what had been their home, seeking shelter that offered none.

Twenty-one souls. Twenty-one lives snuffed out because a dragon decided this place offended her.

"The other two villages lie further north," Muirgheal said, her voice gone flat as winter sea. "Smaller than this one. Seventeen dead between them. The survivors have fled inland, abandoning the coast entirely. They say the sea is cursed. They say the old gods have returned to punish hubris."

"Not gods," Z'Landar said, his voice rough as stones grinding. "One dragon. One ancient evil that should have remained in whatever pit spawned her."

"Does it matter to the dead what name we give their killer?"

No. It did not matter. The dead cared nothing for distinctions between dragon and god, between myth and monster. They cared only that they were gone, that their families wept, that the world continued without them as if they had never drawn breath or known love or hoped for futures now impossible.

Z'Landar surfaced in the harbor, taking human form despite the danger, needing to stand on land and feel the weight of what had happened. Andralia rose beside him, her hand finding his automatically, her presence the only thing keeping him from howling his rage at skies that offered no answers.

"We stop her," he said, the words coming out sharp as broken glass. "Whatever the cost. However many must stand against her. We end this."

"Yes," Andralia agreed simply.

They walked the village in silence, bearing witness to each ruin, each body, each small and terrible proof that evil had passed this way. Z'Landar committed it all to memory—the burned kirk where villagers had sought sanctuary and found only death, the blackened bones of livestock that had died in their pens, the children's toys scattered among the ashes like accusations.

This. This was what awaited Scotland if he failed. If the eggs hatched. If four dragons took wing instead of one.

This multiplied by hundreds. By thousands.

Entire clans burned. The Highlands reduced to ash and memory. The water-folk hunted in their own depths, fire finding them even in the places they had always considered safe.

Everything he loved, everyone he had sworn to protect—gone, as these Irish villagers were gone, mourned briefly and forgotten quickly by a world that held no space for grief when survival demanded constant vigilance.

"I need to see the scorched earth," he said abruptly. "Where she marked territory. Muirgheal said there were places she burned not for killing but for claiming."

The Merrow had accompanied them to shore, keeping watch from the water's edge. Now she nodded, understanding in her ancient eyes. "Aye. Three miles inland. But Z'Landar—the land-creatures there may not welcome our kind. The Unseelie Court holds those territories, and they take unkindly to water-folk venturing beyond shore."

"Then I go alone."

"You do not," Andralia said firmly. "Where you walk, I walk. Unseelie Fairies can threaten what they like—they'll find me more dangerous than they expect."

Something in her voice made Muirgheal's eyebrows rise, some edge of power or certainty that spoke of abilities kept carefully hidden. But the Merrow only nodded.

"Then I will wait here. Three hours—if you have not returned by then, I will assume the worst and carry word back to Scotland myself."

"We'll return," Z'Landar promised. "I've not come this far to fall to fairies."

They left the harbor behind, following a path that wound inland through countryside that should have been green and lush with late spring growth. For the first mile, Ireland showed her typical face— rolling hills crowned with heather, stone walls marking boundaries between farms, ancient trees that had sheltered generations of cattle and sheep.

Then the burned lands began.

The transition was abrupt, unnatural. One moment: grass and growth, life abundant. The next: char and devastation, a perfect circle of destruction that spoke of fire falling from above with draconic precision.

The circle stretched perhaps three hundred yards across, its edges sharp as if drawn with a blade. Within that boundary, nothing lived. Nothing remained that could sustain life. The earth itself had been scorched down to bare stone in places, melted to glass in others where heat had exceeded anything natural fire could produce.

And at the center, burned into rock with dragon-fire's permanence, a symbol.

Not words. Not pictures. Just a spiral—ancient, simple, carrying meaning that needed no translation.

Mine. Stay away. This place belongs to the dragon.

Z'Landar walked to the circle's edge, stopped just short of crossing into the burned zone. Power radiated from that boundary, a warning written in heat and ash and the bones of small creatures that had been caught within when fire fell from the sky.

"She's marking nesting sites," Andralia said quietly, studying the symbol with eyes that saw more than surface meaning. "Claiming territories where her eggs might be placed. Or perhaps—" Her eyes widened. "Or perhaps where they already rest. Hidden just beneath the surface, in places prepared specifically for hatching."

The implications settled like stones in Z'Landar's gut. "You think this is one of them? One of the egg sites?"

"It could be. The heat required to create this level of destruction—it would serve dual purpose. Warning off threats, and simultaneously heating the earth beneath for incubation." She knelt at the boundary, not crossing but reaching out to feel the air above burned ground. "Still warm. Days after the burning, and the stone still holds heat."

Before Z'Landar could respond, laughter drifted across the burned lands—high and crystalline and wrong in ways that set his teeth on edge.

"Clever water-children, clever indeed!" The voice came from everywhere and nowhere, surrounding them like mist. "Seeing truths the locals miss, making connections the Merrow never managed. But cleverness buys no passage through our lands. Cleverness saves no one from Unseelie justice."

Figures materialized from the unburned grass, stepping into view with the casual arrogance of those who ruled their territories absolutely. Seven of them—Unseelie Fairies wrapped in glamours that hurt to look at directly, their true forms flickering beneath like flames beneath oil. Beautiful and terrible, ancient and amoral, they watched Z'Landar and Andralia with eyes that held no humanity, no mercy, no recognition that the strangers before them might deserve consideration beyond prey status.

The tallest stepped forward—female, perhaps, or wearing a female shape for this particular moment. Her hair moved like grass in wind that didn't exist, and her smile promised cruelty wrapped in honey.

"Turn back, water-children. This is not your shore, not your land, not your concern. Turn back, or learn why the Seelie Court calls us kin only when forced by treaty and tradition."

Z'Landar felt power gathering in his chest, responding to threat with readiness he barely understood. His father's strength, his mother's grace, the cosmic heritage Maelis and Andralia had named—all of it churning beneath his skin, seeking outlet.

But before he could speak, Andralia stepped forward.

And the world bent.

Not physically—or not only physically. Reality itself seemed to ripple around her like water disturbed by a stone's splash. The air took on weight and texture, and her eyes—those impossible eyes—began to glow with light that came from somewhere beyond Earth's small horizons.

When she spoke, her voice carried harmonics that shouldn't exist, layers of meaning woven through each word like music complex beyond mortal composition.

"We claim guest-right by the old laws, the laws that predate your courts and your petty territorial squabbles. We walk here bearing witness to dragon-fire and seeking knowledge to save our homes. Turn us away, and you break laws older than your queens. Attack us, and you'll learn exactly why my parents' people set rules about interference—rules I am rapidly reconsidering."

The Unseelie Fairies recoiled as one, their glamours flickering, their certainty cracking. The tall one's smile vanished, replaced by something between fear and fury.

"You—what are you? You wear water-folk shape but carry power that tastes of—" She stopped, unable or unwilling to finish the thought.

"Elsewhere," Andralia supplied, her voice gentling slightly but losing none of its edge. "I am from elsewhere. And I stand with Z'Landar, son of Brannach, heir to two thrones, and you will grant us passage or I will remind you that some powers transcend mortal courts entirely."

Silence, broken only by wind through unburned grass.

Then the tall fairy laughed—genuine this time, surprised and almost delighted.

"Well then. It seems Ireland's dragon has drawn more interesting players than we anticipated." She bowed, mockery and respect mixed in equal measure. "Guest-right is granted, by old laws you invoke correctly even if we'd prefer to ignore them. Walk where you will. See what you must. But be warned—the dragon's marking is for your kind as much as ours. She cares nothing for old laws or guest-rights. If she finds you trespassing, she'll burn you as readily as she burned those foolish villagers."

"We'll take that risk," Z'Landar said, finding his voice, trying not to show his shock at what Andralia had just done.

The Unseelie Fairies faded back into grass and shadow, watching but no longer threatening. Andralia's glow dimmed, reality settling back into normal configurations, though Z'Landar thought he saw her sway slightly before catching herself.

"What was that?" he asked quietly. "What did you just do?"

"Later." Her voice carried exhaustion he'd never heard before. "Let's finish here. I'll explain everything when we're safely back in the water. I promise."

They examined the burned circle for another hour, confirming Andralia's suspicions about heat and purpose, finding evidence that suggested—though didn't prove—an egg might lie beneath. Then they retreated, walking back through land that grew greener and more alive with each step away from dragon-claimed territory.

The Unseelie Fairies watched them go but did not interfere.

By the time they reached the harbor where Muirgheal waited, Z'Landar's mind churned with questions about what Andralia had revealed, about powers she clearly possessed but had kept hidden, about what "elsewhere" truly meant when spoken by one whose parents traveled between stars.

But those questions could wait.

First, they had to return to Scotland. Had to show the councils what dragon-fire wrought. Had to convince stubborn elders and ancient queens that the time for hesitation had passed.

The proof had been gathered. The evidence collected.

Now came the harder part: making them believe.

Making them fight.

Making them follow a king they'd spent ten years refusing to crown.

Chapter Eight: The Trickster's Truth

They returned to the hidden harbor as afternoon shadows lengthened across standing stones, bringing with them the weight of what they had witnessed. Muirgheal waited where they had left her, her green eyes reading their faces before words could be spoken.

"You saw," she said. Not question. Statement.

"We saw." Z'Landar's voice came out hollow, scraped clean by grief and rage held too tightly contained. "Thirty-eight dead. Three villages destroyed or abandoned. And inland, marked territories where eggs may already rest."

"Then you have your proof." Muirgheal gestured toward deeper water, toward the channels that would carry them home. "Scotland awaits. As does the reckoning you've spent ten years avoiding."

Z'Landar nodded, too weary for argument. But before he could move toward departure, Andralia touched his arm, her expression troubled.

"Wait. There's one more I think we should seek." She turned to Muirgheal. "Is there a Puca near? One who might trade knowledge for... whatever price Pucas demand these days?"

The Merrow's face shifted through several expressions—surprise, wariness, something that might have been grudging respect. "Aye. There's one haunts the waters between here and Torr Head. Finvarra by name, though he wears a dozen others depending on mood and company. But Z'Landar—" She fixed him with a stare sharp as broken shells. "Pucas are tricksters born. Shapeshifters and riddlers and speakers of truths so twisted they become lies. Why seek such counsel when you carry evidence enough already?"

"Because evidence shows what has happened," Andralia replied before Z'Landar could speak. "But a Puca might know what comes next. Dragon movements, egg locations, plans she has not yet enacted. Information that could save lives."

"Or cost them, if the Puca decides mischief serves him better than honesty." Muirgheal shook her head. "But I see the set of your jaw. You've decided already. Very well—I'll take you to where Finvarra most often appears. But whatever bargain he offers, whatever price he names—consider thrice before accepting. Puca debts have a way of coming due when least convenient."

They swam north along the coast, following Muirgheal through waters that grew rougher as channels narrowed and currents fought between ocean and land. The sun hung low now, painting everything in shades of amber and shadow, turning the sea to molten copper.

Where the waters churned most fiercely, where rocks rose like broken teeth and tide-pools frothed white with trapped foam, Muirgheal stopped.

"Here," she said. "Call him. Speak his name thrice with water in your mouth, and he'll come—if he chooses. If he judges you interesting enough."

Z'Landar exchanged glances with Andralia, saw determination mixed with caution in her impossible eyes. Together they surfaced, treading water in the churning space between stone and sea.

Z'Landar took a breath, let water fill his mouth, tasting salt and ancient minerals and the particular flavor these Irish waters carried. Then he spoke, the name coming out garbled and strange through liquid:

"Finvarra."

Nothing. Waves crashed. Gulls cried. The world continued indifferent.

Again: "Finvarra."

The water rippled, disturbed by something more than current. A presence gathering, curious, amused.

Third time, with all the force of command his father's blood granted him: "Finvarra!"

Laughter bubbled up from the depths—high and wild and wrong, like music played on instruments that had no names in human tongues. The water between the rocks began to *shift*, not in normal ways but as if reality itself had decided solidity was optional, fluidity was negotiable, and the laws governing matter were merely suggestions.

A shape rose from the churning—horse-like at first glance, but wrong in every detail. Too many legs, or perhaps too few. A mane that might have been seaweed or serpents or simply darkness given form. Eyes that glowed yellow-green and held intelligence that danced between brilliant and mad.

Then the shape *changed*, flowing like water poured from vessel to vessel, and suddenly a man stood before them—or wore a man's shape, at least. Tall and thin, with hair black as midnight and skin that seemed to absorb light rather than reflect it. His smile showed too many teeth, all of them sharp.

"Well, well," the Puca said, his voice carrying echoes of that bubble-laughter. "What brings water-born royalty to seek counsel from poor Finvarra? Come to bargain? Come to beg? Come to threaten, perhaps, though that would be unwise given I know seven hundred ways to drown a Kelpie and twice that many to make a Selkie forget which shape is his own."

"We come seeking knowledge," Z'Landar said carefully, remembering Muirgheal's warnings about twisted truths. "About the dragon Caoránach and her eggs."

"Ah! The mother-monster and her precious brood." Finvarra's grin widened impossibly. "Everyone seeks knowledge of eggs these days. The dragon hoards them. The Fomorians whisper about them. Even old Balor takes interest, though his reasons remain as murky as his favored depths." He tilted his head, bird-like and unsettling. "But knowledge costs, young king-who-runs-from-crowns. What do you offer poor Finvarra in trade?"

"What do you want?"

"Ah, the dangerous question! The open-ended offer!" The Puca clapped his hands in delight, and the sound echoed wrong, as if it came from six different directions simultaneously. "I could ask for your voice. Your shadow. The memory of your mother's face. The color of your lover's eyes—" He gestured toward Andralia. "Though I suspect those would prove difficult to take, wouldn't they, star-child?"

Andralia's expression went very still, very cold. "Speak carefully, shapeshifter. Some names carry weight beyond your playing."

"Oh, I speak with utmost care! Care upon care upon care!" But Finvarra's smile had dimmed slightly, his yellow-green eyes studying Andralia with newfound wariness. "No offense meant to those whose roots stretch farther than Ireland's shores. I seek only fair exchange—knowledge for knowledge, perhaps? You tell me something I don't know, and I'll tell you something you don't know. Fair?"

It was a trap. Had to be. Pucas didn't trade fairly—they traded *technically*, finding loopholes in every bargain, twisting words until agreements became prisons.

But they needed whatever information Finvarra held. And Z'Landar suspected he had one piece of knowledge the Puca couldn't possibly possess.

"Agreed," he said, ignoring Andralia's sharp intake of breath. "But you answer first. Then I'll share knowledge you lack."

"Ho! The water-prince has *stones*!" Finvarra's laugh rang wild. "Very well. I'll trust the son of Brannach keeps his word—Kelpie honor being slightly more reliable than morning mist." He leaned forward, and his voice dropped to something that might have been genuine. "Four eggs, as you've heard. Two hidden in Ireland—one beneath Lough Corrib where the Fairy Queen guards it with magics that would give even dragons pause, another in the deep caves of Cruachan where darkness itself has weight and form, this one in the dragon herself. Two in Scotland—one in waters so pure it blinds, another in a place of old death where Kelpies once dwelt."

Z'Landar's mind raced. The Kelpie village—the dragon would claim an abandoned settlement, use its magical residue for protection. And "waters so pure it blinds"—where? What loch held such description?

"The dragon moves at night," Finvarra continued, clearly enjoying having an audience. "Flies her patterns, checking on each egg, ensuring no threats approach. She's obsessive, our Caoránach. Counts them. Speaks to them. Promises them kingdoms once they hatch and grow strong." His grin turned vicious. "And old Balor—ah, he's promised to guard the final hatching. Some bargain struck between dragon and giant, though what she offered him I cannot say. Perhaps simply the joy of destruction when four dragons take wing instead of one."

The information settled like stones in Z'Landar's gut. Four locations. Dragon's nightly patrols. Balor's involvement confirmed.

"Now," Finvarra said, his teeth gleaming. "Your turn, prince-who-would-be-king. Tell me something I don't know."

Z'Landar took a breath, committing to the gamble. "I know what the Heart of the Loch truly is. What power it carries. And I know it was created by beings older than dragons, older than Pucas, older than Ireland herself."

He pulled the pendant free of his tunic, let it catch the dying sunlight. Finvarra's eyes went wide—genuine surprise, perhaps the first honest emotion he'd shown.

"That's—" The Puca stopped himself, clearly torn between curiosity and the bargain's terms. "You truly know its nature?"

"I know it was forged in waters that connect worlds. I know its power isn't what legends claim—the truth runs deeper and stranger." Z'Landar tucked it away again. "And that knowledge you won't get from me, because our bargain is fulfilled."

For a long moment, Finvarra stared at him, emotions flickering too fast to name across his too-sharp face. Then he threw back his head and laughed—genuine this time, delighted.

"Well played! Oh, *very* well played!" He sketched a mocking bow. "You'll make a fine king, Z'Landar son of Brannach, if you survive long enough to claim your crowns. Knowledge for knowledge, fairly traded, and both of us walking away wanting more." His form began to shimmer, reality remembering he wasn't quite real. "A final gift, free of bargain: the dragon fears you. Specifically you. She doesn't know why yet, but her dreams are troubled by a figure of water and starlight who stands against her. Make of that what you will."

Then he was gone, dissolved into foam and shadow, leaving only his laughter echoing between the rocks.

Z'Landar turned to Andralia, found her watching him with an expression caught between pride and concern.

"That was dangerous," she said quietly.

"All of this is dangerous. But we have locations now. Real information, not just suspicions."

"If we can trust a Puca's word."

"Can we?"

Andralia considered, her gaze distant. "In this? Yes. He told truth—twisted and incomplete perhaps, but truth. Pucas lie through omission and misdirection, not through false statements. The locations are real." She paused. "But Z'Landar—what you told him about the Heart—"

"Later," he said, echoing her words from earlier. "When we're home. When we have time to speak of cosmic matters and powers I don't understand. For now—we return. We begin the campaign that should have started ten years ago."

Muirgheal swam close, having watched the exchange from safe distance. "The Puca gave you what you sought?"

"And more." Z'Landar straightened, feeling something settle in his chest—determination, or perhaps simply acceptance that running had ended, that the weight he'd fled now must be shouldered. "We return to Scotland. Tonight, if we can make the crossing before full dark."

"Then swim hard and swim fast," the Merrow advised. "And when you reach your shores—when you begin gathering your forces—remember that Ireland watches. Remember we have dead of our own to avenge. Send word when battle comes, and you'll find allies across the water."

"I will." Z'Landar clasped her hand in the old way, warrior to warrior. "You have my word. And my thanks."

They left Ireland behind as sunset painted the western sky in shades of blood and gold, swimming east through channels that would carry them home. The journey took three days of hard swimming, stopping only briefly to rest in hidden coves and hunt fish in the deep currents. They spoke little, conserving strength, each lost in thoughts of what awaited.

The third day brought them to Scottish waters as dawn broke clean and cold. Z'Landar felt the difference immediately—not just temperature or taste, but something deeper. Recognition. The water itself knowing him, welcoming him home even as it whispered warnings of duties owed and debts come due.

They surfaced in Loch Ness where it all had begun a decade past, where the Great Wurm had risen and been defeated, where his parents' sacrifice had created the Heart of the Loch and given him life. The morning mist curled thick across the water's surface, and through it Z'Landar saw the familiar cliffs, the ancient trees, the shore where Alasdair Fraser had once stood with drawn sword and desperate hope.

Home.

And everything that word entailed.

"It begins now," Andralia said softly beside him. "Once we set foot on that shore, once you send the first message—there's no more running. No more pretending you can be anything other than what you are."

"Aye, I know."

"Are you ready?"

Z'Landar looked at her—this woman who had appeared in his life mere days ago yet felt essential as breathing, who carried powers she wouldn't explain and heritage that stretched to stars, who had chosen to stand beside him despite knowing what it would cost.

"No," he admitted. "But I'll do it anyway."

They swam to shore, took human form on stones still wet with morning dew. Z'Landar raised his face to the sky—to Scotland's sky, gray and vast and holding storms yet to break. Then he turned his attention to the water, to the currents and flows that connected every loch and river in the Highlands.

He had learned this trick years ago, taught by Maelis in the quiet times after the wars. How to send his voice through water itself, carrying messages farther than any sprite could fly, reaching into the depths where the oldest water-folk dwelt.

Z'Landar knelt at the water's edge, placed both hands beneath the surface, and *spoke*—not with voice, but with will and water and the authority he had denied for too long.

I am Z'Landar, son of Brannach the Thundering, son of Nerina of the Silver Eyes. I have returned from Ireland bearing witness to dragon-fire and destruction. The threat is real. The danger comes whether we acknowledge it or not. I call the Kelpie Elders to council. I call Queen Mhairi and her advisors. I call every water-folk who values Scotland's survival. Three days hence, at Loch Slochd where my father once held court. Come. Hear what I have seen. And prepare yourselves—for the time of choosing is upon us.

The message rippled outward, carried by current and connection, spreading through the network of lochs and rivers like roots through earth. Within hours, every water-folk in the Highlands would hear it. Would know he had returned. Would understand that the ten years of waiting had ended.

Beside him, Andralia stood watch, her presence a comfort and a promise. When Z'Landar finally withdrew his hands from the water, she took them in her own.

"They'll resist," she said.

"I know."

"The Kelpie Elders will argue you're too young, too different. The Selkies will claim Queen Mhairi rules yet. The old hatreds will surface. The fear will be stronger than reason."

"I know all of it." He turned to face her fully. "But I also know thirty-eight Irish villagers lie dead because no one stopped the dragon when they might have. I know these eggs wait to hatch into destruction. I know Balor hunts the waters, and ancient evils stir because ten years of peace created space for darkness to gather strength."

"And so?"

"And so I claim what is mine. By right of birth, by right of sacrifice, by right of being the only one who can unite them." His voice hardened with certainty he'd never felt before. "I take the throne—both thrones—whether they grant it willingly or I must fight for every inch of acceptance. Because the alternative is watching Scotland burn the way those Irish villages burned."

Andralia smiled—sad and proud and knowing. "Then let us begin. You have three days to build support before the council. Three days to gather allies, to shore up weakness, to prepare for the battle that comes before you ever face the dragon."

Three days.

It seemed both forever and no time at all.

Z'Landar spent the first day visiting the Highland clans, taking human form to walk among those who had fought beside him a decade past. Alasdair Fraser welcomed him to Beauly with fierce embrace and fiercer pride, immediately pledging Clan Fraser's support. Simon Fraser, ancient and infirm but still sharp of mind, gave his blessing from a chair by the fire, his weathered hands clasping Z'Landar's with surprising strength.

"We knew you'd return," the old man said, his voice like wind through autumn leaves. "Knew the peace couldn't last. But by God and the old ways both, it's good to see you standing tall. Your father would be proud."

Other clans proved more cautious. Clan Sinclair sent word they would attend the council but made no promises. The Border Reivers—Halls and Grahams—remembered the wars but wondered whether dragon-fire in Ireland truly threatened Scottish soil. They would wait. They would watch. They would decide when evidence proved beyond doubt.

The second day brought responses from the water-folk, and Z'Landar read the currents with growing frustration. The Kelpie Elders sent formal acknowledgment that they would attend council, but nothing more—no welcome, no recognition of his authority, no hint whether they would support his claim. Queen Mhairi's response came through Maelis, who swam to Loch Ness with news both hoped-for and feared.

"The Queen will attend," Maelis reported, her amber eyes troubled. "But she brings her full court, including those who oppose any union with Kelpies. She tests you, Z'Landar. Tests whether you have strength to stand before three hundred years of pride and hatred and make them bend."

"I won't make them bend," Z'Landar replied. "I'll make them *see*. There's a difference."

"Is there?" Maelis studied him with that ancient, knowing gaze. "Sometimes seeing requires bending first. Pride blinds more surely than any darkness."

By the third day, word had spread throughout the Highlands— water-folk and human alike buzzing with news that Z'Landar had returned, that he called council, that something stirred which might shatter the decade of peace they'd grown comfortable within. Some welcomed it. Others feared it. Most simply waited to see which way the currents would flow.

On the eve of the council, Z'Landar stood at the shore of Loch Ness with Andralia, watching sunset paint the water in shades of fire. Tomorrow would determine everything. Tomorrow he would stand before the gathered powers of Scotland's water-folk and demand they accept him as king. Tomorrow the campaign would become reality or collapse into failure.

"Nervous?" Andralia asked.

"Terrified."

"Good." She leaned against him, her warmth driving back the evening chill. "Fear keeps you honest. Keeps you sharp. Better to go into tomorrow terrified and prepared than confident and blind."

"Will they accept me?"

"Some will. Some won't. But you don't need all of them—just enough. Just the critical mass that tips the balance from resistance to inevitability." She turned to look at him, her impossible eyes holding starlight and certainty in equal measure. "You'll find the words. When the moment comes, when you stand before them—you'll know what to say. Trust that."

Z'Landar wanted to believe her. Wanted to feel the certainty she seemed to carry like a cloak.

But mostly he felt young and inadequate and acutely aware that tomorrow he would attempt what his parents had died to make possible—the unification of peoples who had spent centuries perfecting their hatred.

No pressure, then.

He allowed himself one moment of doubt, one breath of fear held close and private. Then he released it, letting the wind carry it across waters that had known him since birth, that had shaped him and tested him and now called him to purposes he could no longer deny.

Tomorrow he would be king.

Or he would fail trying.

Either way, the running had ended.

The campaign had begun.

Chapter Nine: The Weight of Thrones

Loch Slochd lay in the shadow of mountains older than memory, its waters dark as obsidian and twice as sharp. The humans avoided it—had done so since before the clans learned to mark their territories with stone and blood. Too deep, they whispered. Too cold. Too full of things that watched from below with eyes that held no love for surface-dwellers.

They were right to fear it.

This was Kelpie water, pure and undiluted. The River Hall lay carved into the loch's depths, a chamber hewn from living stone by magics that predated human arrival in these lands. Here Brannach had held court, dispensing justice and wisdom with a voice like thunder over rapids. Here the Kelpie kings stretching back ten generations had sat upon the throne of lightning-struck oak, commanding respect through strength and the deep certainty that their word held weight enough to move mountains.

Here Z'Landar would stand before those who had known his father, and ask them to accept a son who was only half what Brannach had been—and perhaps more than any of them could understand.

Dawn broke cold over Loch Slochd as Z'Landar and Andralia arrived, having swum through the night from Loch Ness. Already the waters churned with gathered bodies—Kelpies rising from their river territories, Selkies who had braved the journey inland from western seas, water sprites flickering like fallen stars in the depths. Even a few Merrow had come, having crossed from Ireland in the three days since word spread, drawn by curiosity or solidarity or simply the scent of history being made.

Hundreds. Perhaps a thousand. More water-folk gathered in one place than Z'Landar had seen since the Battle of Loch Ness a decade past.

His heart hammered against his ribs. His mouth tasted of copper and fear.

Too many. Too much expectation. I am not ready for this.

But Andralia's hand found his beneath the water, her fingers threading through his own, and her voice carried through the currents with certainty he desperately needed to borrow.

"You are Brannach's son. Nerina's child. Born of sacrifice and prophecy. You do not need to be ready—you only need to be *present.* The words will come."

He squeezed her hand, drawing strength from the connection that had formed so quickly yet felt ancient as these waters. Then he released her, taking the seal-form that came most naturally, swimming down through gathered crowds toward the River Hall's entrance.

They parted for him. Not with reverence—not yet—but with recognition. Whispers followed in his wake, names spoken like incantations: *Brannach's son. The boy who stood against darkness. The bridge between waters. The one who runs from crowns.*

Let them whisper. Let them doubt. He would show them truth sharper than any gossip.

The River Hall opened before him like a throat swallowing, the entrance carved with spirals and runes that pulsed with faint luminescence. Z'Landar took human form as he passed the threshold, feeling ancient magics assess him—*blood of the king, blood of the sea, blood of something other*—and finding him acceptable, if unusual.

114

The chamber beyond stretched vast enough to hold five hundred standing shoulder to shoulder, its ceiling lost in darkness that no light could fully penetrate. The walls bore carvings of every Kelpie king since the first had claimed these waters, their names and deeds preserved in stone and memory. And at the far end, elevated on a natural dais carved by water over millennia, sat the throne.

Empty these ten years. Waiting.

But not for him. Not today. Today he came as supplicant, as messenger, as the one bearing warnings they would rather not hear.

The seven Kelpie Elders had already assembled, seated at the great lightning-struck oak table that occupied the chamber's heart. Z'Landar knew them by reputation if not by face—ancient, powerful, each representing one of the seven major rivers that fed the Highlands' lifeblood.

Tormod of the Rapids sat at the table's head, his face carved by centuries into something resembling weathered granite, his eyes holding the gray of storm-water. Beside him, Eilidh of the Deep Pools, silver-streaked and sharp as broken ice. Then Caelan of the Swift Current, young by Elder standards—barely three centuries— but fierce enough to earn his seat. Morven of the Quiet Waters, Fiona of the Crossing, Niall of the Hidden Channels, and ancient Seoras of the Source, who some claimed had been alive when the first humans crossed into Scotland.

They watched Z'Landar approach with expressions carefully neutral, revealing nothing of welcome or hostility. Guardians of the old ways, Maelis had named them. Not enemies. Simply those who moved slowly, who valued tradition over innovation, who saw change as threat rather than opportunity.

He would have to move them. Somehow.

Behind the Elders, arranged in careful hierarchy, stood Queen Mhairi's court. The Selkie Queen herself sat upon a chair of woven kelp and pearl, her silver hair cascading past her shoulders, her face still holding the beauty that three centuries had failed to diminish. But her eyes—by the stars, her eyes looked weary in ways that went beyond physical exhaustion. She had ruled through wars and peace, through alliance and betrayal, through the loss of her daughter to a Kelpie king's love.

She had buried Nerina. Had mourned a child who chose death over life without her beloved.

Looking at her now, Z'Landar saw his mother's features reflected in his grandmother's face, and grief he thought long-buried stirred fresh and sharp.

Not now. Grief later. Duty first.

Maelis stood at the Queen's right hand, her amber eyes finding Z'Landar's across the crowded chamber, offering silent encouragement. Fionnuala—his half-sister, barely known but fiercely loyal—hovered near the court's edge, her silver eyes bright with anticipation.

And Andralia took position near the entrance, close enough to offer support, far enough to let this be his moment. She had changed to human form, and even among the gathered water-folk her presence drew eyes—something in her bearing, in the way light seemed to bend around her, marking her as *other* in ways they couldn't quite name.

Z'Landar reached the center of the chamber, standing before the oak table where his fate would be debated, judged, decided. He did not bow. Did not genuflect. He stood straight, shoulders back, meeting each Elder's gaze in turn before turning to face Queen Mhairi with respect but not submission.

"You know me!" he said, and his voice carried through water and stone with authority he hadn't known he possessed. Gone is the voice of the boy. Gone is the subtle reluctance of youth thrust in conflict. The rightful king of both undersea empires now speaks. "Son of Brannach the Thundering, who held court in this very hall. Son of Nerina of the Silver Eyes, beloved of the western Selkies. I come bearing witness to threats that care nothing for our divisions, our hesitations, our comfort with peace that has grown soft around the edges."

"We know who you are," Tormod said, his voice like boulders grinding in deep current. "The question is: why are you *here*? You have spent ten years avoiding this hall, refusing the throne that stands empty, ignoring the calls from both Kelpie and Selkie to assume your birthright. Why now? What has changed?"

"Dragons," Z'Landar replied simply. "What has changed is that ancient evils no longer content themselves with sleeping in the dark. They wake. They move. They kill."

Murmurs rippled through the gathered crowd. Some skeptical. Some intrigued. All listening.

"Dragons are legend," Eilidh said, though her tone held less certainty than her words. "Tales to frighten younglings. There have been no dragons in Scotland since before written history."

"No," Z'Landar agreed. "Because they were in Ireland. Sleeping. Waiting. But one has woken—Caoránach, the Mother of Serpents. And she carries eggs. Four of them. Two hidden in Scotland already. One concealed somewhere in Ireland. And the fourth—" He paused, letting the weight settle. "The fourth she carries within her own body, protected by scale and fury and the absolute certainty that she will burn worlds before allowing harm to reach it."

"You have seen this?" Queen Mhairi's voice carried across the chamber, musical but edged with steel. "Or do you bring us rumors and speculation dressed as truth?"

"I have seen her, Majesty." Z'Landar turned to face his grandmother fully. "Three nights past, in the waters off Ireland's coast, I watched her rise from depths that should have crushed lesser creatures. Fifty meters long at minimum, scaled in obsidian and gold, breathing fire that burns above water and below. I felt the heat of her passing. I saw the intelligence in eyes that have watched centuries turn. I witnessed the bulge in her underbelly where the fourth egg rests."

The chamber had gone silent, every eye fixed on him.

"And I walked the ruins of what she wrought," he continued, his voice hardening. "Three Irish villages, burned to ash and memory. Thirty-eight dead—men, women, children. Fishermen hauling nets. Families seeking shelter in their homes. Two younglings who had barely seen thirteen summers, reduced to charred bone and nightmare."

He gestured, and water sprites darted forward, carrying between them images they had preserved—not solid things, but impressions captured in enchanted water, showing glimpses of burned cottages, scorched harbors, bodies floating in kelp beds.

The gathered water-folk recoiled from the images. Some turned away. Others stared with growing horror.

Z'Landar pressed forward, relentless. "The dragon marked territories inland with fire that melted stone to glass. Perfect circles three hundred yards across, claiming land for purposes we can only guess—perhaps egg sites, perhaps simple territorial warning. The heat remains in the earth days after burning, hot enough still to raise blisters on human skin."

More images. The spiral symbol burned into rock. The devastation that spoke of power beyond natural fire.

"I met with survivors," Z'Landar said. "Spoke with those who fled. They told of a nightmare descending from the sky, of fire that should have been impossible, of screams that found no ears to grant them mercy. They told of bodies that burned beneath the waves, impossible but real. They told of a mother who held her three children as flame took them all."

He stopped, letting the silence stretch, letting the horror settle into bones and memory.

"And I spoke with a Puca," he continued, "who told me—in exchange for knowledge he desperately wanted—that four eggs rest scattered between Scotland and Ireland. Two in our lands already, hidden where we would least expect them. One in waters so pure it blinds. Another in a place of old death where Kelpies once dwelt."

Tormod's expression shifted—recognition dawning. "The abandoned village. The one we lost to plague three centuries past."

"She would use that place," Eilidh breathed. "The magical residue. The protection still lingering."

"And the pure waters—" Morven of the Quiet Waters leaned forward. "That could be any of a dozen lochs. How do we narrow the search?"

"We search them all," Z'Landar replied. "Systematically. Carefully. Before the eggs hatch and four dragons claim Scotland as hunting ground."

"One dragon has killed thirty-eight humans," Queen Mhairi said quietly. "Four would kill thousands. Tens of thousands."

"If we're fortunate," Z'Landar agreed grimly. "If we move swiftly, unite our forces, act with purpose instead of debate. But if we wait— if we cling to comfort and peace and the hope that perhaps the threat isn't as dire as claimed—"

"Then we doom ourselves," Fionnuala spoke up from the court's edge, her voice fierce despite her youth. "We doom everyone. Water-folk and human alike."

"The humans," Seoras said, speaking for the first time, his voice like wind through ancient trees. "You would involve them in this? Bring them into our councils, our plans?"

"I would," Z'Landar said, meeting the ancient Elder's gaze without flinching. "Because dragon fire cares nothing for whether flesh is human or Kelpie or Selkie. Because we learned ten years ago that united we can stand against darkness, but divided we fall to it. Because—" He gestured to the throne standing empty. "Because my father and mother died to create possibility of unity, and I will not dishonor their sacrifice by pretending we can survive this threat alone."

"Pretty words," Caelan of the Swift Current said, though his tone held more challenge than dismissal. "But words are not action. You speak of unity, of involvement, of purpose—yet you have spent ten years fleeing the very throne that would grant you authority to command such things. Why should we follow one who runs?"

The question hung in the water like a blade, and Z'Landar felt every eye turn toward him, waiting for his answer.

This. This was the moment. The edge where everything would turn on truth spoken or left unspoken.

"Because I was wrong," Z'Landar said simply. "For ten years, I told myself I was waiting until I was ready. Until I was wise enough, strong enough, certain enough to bear the weight of crowns I never asked to inherit. But wisdom doesn't come from waiting. Strength doesn't grow in safety. Certainty is a luxury we can no longer afford."

He turned slowly, addressing not just the Elders and Queen but every water-folk gathered in the hall, every creature who had come seeking answers or hope or simply to witness history unfold.

"I ran because I was afraid," he said, his voice carrying to the furthest corners. "Afraid of failing you. Afraid of being less than my father, weaker than my mother, inadequate to the legacy they left. Afraid

120

that claiming thrones I inherited through tragedy would dishonor their sacrifice rather than fulfill it."

Silence, absolute.

"But I have seen what fear accomplishes," Z'Landar continued. "I have walked through ashes that were once homes. I have counted bodies that were once lives. I have witnessed what happens when good people wait too long to act, when fear of failure paralyzes until the only choice left is between bad and worse."

He moved toward the throne, not to claim it but to stand before it, placing one hand on ancient oak that had held ten generations of kings.

"Brannach was strong," he said quietly. "Nerina was brave. They loved across the divide that had separated our peoples for centuries. They chose each other when choice meant death. They gave their lives so I might be born in waters touched by cosmic forces, carrying within me the potential to bridge not just Kelpie and Selkie but Earth and stars themselves."

Murmurs rippled through the crowd at this admission, but Z'Landar pressed on.

"I am not my father," he said. "I am not my mother. I am both and neither and something new that frightens me as much as it frightens you. But I am also the one standing here, now, when action is required. I am the one who swam to Ireland, who bore witness, who brought back truth you need to hear whether you wish to or not."

He turned back to face the Elders, the Queen, the assembled masses.

"I do not ask you to crown me today," he said. "I am not ready for that weight, and you are not ready to grant it. But I ask you to *listen*. To hear what I have seen. To acknowledge the threat approaches whether we name it or not. To begin preparing—gathering forces, making plans, setting aside old hatreds for the sake of survival."

"And if we refuse?" Tormod asked, though his tone had softened from challenge to genuine question.

"Then I will go to the Highland clans alone. I will gather what allies I can among humans who remember standing beside water-folk against darkness. I will do everything in my power to stop this threat—" Z'Landar paused. "But I would rather do it with you. With all of you. As my father would have wanted. As my mother would have hoped. As the future demands if we're to have one worth surviving into."

He stopped, having said all he could say, having laid bare the fear and determination in equal measure. The rest was beyond his control— up to creatures older and perhaps wiser than himself to decide whether truth spoken plainly was enough.

Queen Mhairi rose from her chair, moving with grace that belied her centuries, approaching until she stood before Z'Landar. Up close, he saw tears tracking silent paths down her weathered cheeks.

"You have her eyes," she said quietly. "My Nerina's eyes. That impossible blue-green that holds the sea's vastness." Her hand reached up, trembling slightly, touching his face with tenderness that broke something in Z'Landar's chest. "And her courage. Her willingness to speak truth even when silence would be easier."

"Majesty—"

"Grandmother," she corrected gently. "Here, now, I am not Queen to you but the woman who held your mother as an infant, who watched her grow into beauty and strength, who wept when she chose love over life." Her voice caught. "Who has waited ten years for her grandson to stop running and come home."

Z'Landar felt his own tears threatening, his throat tight with emotion he couldn't quite name.

"The Selkies will listen," Queen Mhairi said, her voice gaining strength, carrying through the chamber to her assembled court. "We will hear this evidence. We will consider this threat. And we will begin preparations—gathering intelligence, shoring up defenses, preparing for possibility that dragons are not merely legend but reality with teeth and fire."

She turned to the Kelpie Elders, challenge clear in her gaze. "Will the river-folk do less than the sea-dwellers? Will you let old fears of change prevent you from facing new threats?"

The seven Elders exchanged glances, some silent communication passing between them. Finally, Tormod rose, his massive frame casting shadows in the chamber's dim light.

"The Kelpies will also listen," he rumbled. "Will examine evidence. Will consider proposals." He fixed Z'Landar with a stare that held weight of centuries. "But understand, son of Brannach—listening is not acceptance. Evidence is not proof. You ask us to overturn how we have governed for ten years, to prepare for war when peace has served us well. That is no small thing."

"I know," Z'Landar replied.

"But neither are we fools," Eilidh added, rising to stand beside Tormod. "We remember what came before—the Great Wurm, the ancient darkness, the battles that nearly destroyed us all. We remember who stood against it." Her expression softened fractionally. "We remember the boy who became a bridge when bridges seemed impossible."

"We will convene," Tormod said. "Kelpie and Selkie together, as we have not done since the wars ended. Three days hence. You will present full evidence, answer all questions, make your case complete. And then we will decide—whether to mobilize, whether to prepare, whether to accept that peace has ended and war approaches."

It wasn't acceptance. Wasn't triumph. But it was more than Z'Landar had dared hope when he'd entered the chamber.

"Three days," he agreed.

"And Z'Landar—" Queen Mhairi's voice carried one more time. "In those three days, you will visit me. Properly. As grandson to grandmother, not supplicant to queen. We have much to speak of. Much that should have been said years ago."

"I will, Grandmother." The word felt strange on his tongue but right in ways that settled something restless in his chest.

The council dissolved, water-folk dispersing to discuss what they'd heard, to process evidence presented, to begin the slow work of changing minds that had grown comfortable with stasis. Z'Landar remained standing before the throne, exhaustion crashing over him now that the moment had passed.

Andralia appeared at his side, her hand finding his with practiced ease.

"You did well," she said quietly.

"I didn't claim the throne."

"No. But you planted seeds. And seeds need time to grow before harvest." She leaned against him, her warmth driving back the chamber's chill. "Three days. And then you make your case complete. And then—"

"And then they decide whether I've earned the right to lead them into fire."

"They've already decided," Andralia said, her voice holding certainty that defied logic. "They simply don't know it yet. But you spoke truth, Z'Landar. You showed them not strength without weakness but strength *despite* weakness. That's what they needed to see. That's what makes them believe."

Z'Landar wanted to share her certainty. Wanted to feel the triumph she seemed convinced he'd earned.

But mostly he felt tired, and young, and acutely aware that speaking truth was only the first battle. Claiming thrones would be harder. And facing dragons?

That would be hardest of all.

But for now, for this moment, he had accomplished what he'd come to do.

He had made them listen.

And listening, he hoped, would lead to something more.

Something like unity.

Something like hope.

Something that might—just might—be enough to stand against the fire descending from Ireland's skies.

Chapter Ten: Waters That Remember

The Queen's chambers lay deep within the western arm of Loch Ness, where the waters ran cold enough to numb and dark enough to hide. Not secret, precisely—any Selkie who sought audience could find them—but private in the way that matters most. Protected by currents that moved in patterns only those born to these waters could navigate, by magic subtle as a mother's touch and twice as fierce.

Z'Landar swam alone through the passages Maelis had described, leaving Andralia to rest in the shallows where exhaustion had finally claimed her. Two days since the council, two days of waiting while Elders deliberated and courtiers whispered and the gathered water-folk processed what they had heard. Two days of building tension, of wondering whether seeds planted would take root or wither.

But today—this moment—was not about councils or crowns or the weight of destinies cosmic. Today, Queen Mhairi had summoned him not as supplicant but as kin, and Z'Landar found himself more nervous facing his grandmother in private than he had been standing before hundreds in the River Hall.

The passage opened into a chamber that took his breath despite having swum these waters all his life. Not large—perhaps twenty feet across—but *alive* in ways that defied simple description. The walls were not carved but grown, coral and pearl and living things that had shaped themselves over centuries into patterns that spoke of tides and time and patience beyond mortal reckoning. Light filtered through from above—impossible at this depth, yet present nonetheless—painting everything in shades of silver and blue-green that reminded Z'Landar of his mother's eyes.

Of his own eyes, when he caught his reflection in still water.

Queen Mhairi sat upon a low seat of woven kelp and polished shell, her silver hair unbound and floating around her shoulders like a living thing. She had set aside the formal trappings of court—no crown, no ceremonial garments, no markers of three hundred years of rule. Just a woman, aged but not elderly, beautiful but not untouchable, watching her grandson approach with expression that held such complex emotion Z'Landar couldn't begin to name all its parts.

"Sit," she said, gesturing to cushions scattered on the chamber floor—actual cushions, salvaged from some long-ago shipwreck and preserved through Selkie craft, an odd touch of human comfort in this wholly aquatic space. "Please. We are not Queen and subject here. Only grandmother and grandson, with too many years between us and too much left unsaid."

Z'Landar settled onto the cushion opposite her, suddenly aware he had no idea how to begin this conversation. What did one say to a grandmother barely known? How did one bridge a decade of distance and grief older than memory?

Mhairi solved the problem by reaching across the space between them, taking his hands in hers with grip surprisingly strong for one who looked so delicate.

"You have questions," she said. "About your mother. About what came before. About who she was beyond the legend that shapes how others speak her name." Her thumbs traced circles across his knuckles—an absent gesture, soothing. "Ask. Whatever you wish to know, I will tell you truly. The time for protecting you from difficult truths has long passed."

"Was she happy?" The question burst from Z'Landar before he could consider whether it was the right one to lead with. "Before—at the end—was she happy? Or did she die full of regret for loving someone she shouldn't have loved?"

Mhairi's expression softened, and something in her eyes went distant—remembering, perhaps, or simply seeing past that only those who live centuries can access.

"She was radiant," she said quietly. "Even knowing what it would cost, even understanding that love between Kelpie and Selkie was forbidden not by law but by hate so old we'd forgotten its origins—she glowed with joy. I have lived three hundred years, raised seven children, watched empires of men rise and crumble. And I have never seen anyone as purely, fiercely happy as Nerina was when she spoke of Brannach."

Relief and sorrow warred in Z'Landar's chest. "Then why—?"

"Why did I not stop her? Why did I not use my authority to forbid the match, to keep her safe even if it meant condemning her to loneliness?" Mhairi's laugh held edges sharp as broken shells. "Oh, I tried. How I tried. I commanded. I pleaded. I threatened. I reminded her of every reason Selkie and Kelpie could never be, of centuries of bloodshed, of the impossibility of their union producing anything but tragedy."

She released his hands, one of hers rising to touch her own chest, above where a heart beat slow and steady.

"But she was my daughter. Stubborn as the tide, brave as the storm, and absolutely convinced that some loves matter more than safety. That some connections transcend history's hatreds." Her eyes found Z'Landar's again. "She told me, the last time we spoke before she went to him, that she would rather burn bright for one perfect year than flicker dimly through centuries of comfortable emptiness."

"And she got neither," Z'Landar said, the words coming out harder than intended. "She got nine months. Nine months of love, then death bringing me into the world."

"Yes." Mhairi didn't flinch from the accusation in his voice. "But what nine months they were. I watched her transform from princess into something greater—not queen, not yet, but the possibility of queens. She saw a future we had all declared impossible, and she *believed* in it with such certainty that even I, ancient and set in my ways, began to wonder if perhaps she saw truly."

The Queen rose, moving to the chamber's far wall where the living coral had shaped itself into something resembling shelves. She withdrew a small object wrapped in kelp-cloth, returning to press it into Z'Landar's hands.

"Open it."

Z'Landar unwrapped the cloth carefully, revealing a shell— unremarkable at first glance, common cockle of the sort that littered every Scottish shore. But when he turned it, catching the strange light that filtered through the chamber, he saw that its inner surface had been carved with minute precision into a map of sorts. Not geographical. Something else. Spirals and lines that connected points in patterns that suggested meaning he couldn't quite grasp.

"Your mother made that," Mhairi said softly. "In the weeks before she went to Brannach, before they conceived you in waters touched by forces neither fully understood. She called it her map of possibility—showing not where things were but where they *could* be. Connections that existed in potential, waiting for someone brave enough to make them real."

Z'Landar traced one spiral with his fingertip, feeling something almost electrical tingle against his skin. "What do the patterns mean?"

"I don't know entirely. She spoke of old magic, of places where Earth touched something beyond itself, of waters that remembered being stardust before they were sea." Mhairi settled back onto her seat, her gaze never leaving the shell. "I thought it was the fancy of new love, the way passion makes everything seem cosmic and significant. But after—after you were born, after I held you for the first and only time before you were taken to the Heart—I wondered if perhaps she had seen truly. If her love had opened eyes to patterns the rest of us were too blind or too frightened to acknowledge."

"You held me?" Z'Landar looked up, surprise clear in his voice. "I didn't know."

"For three heartbeats. Long enough to see your eyes open—that impossible blue-green, her eyes, carrying depths no infant should possess. Long enough to feel the power thrumming through your small body, magic that tasted of river and sea and something I had no name for. Long enough to know that everything we had feared about the union of Kelpie and Selkie was wrong." Her voice caught. "We hadn't created weakness. We'd created something stronger than either race alone."

She reached out again, cupping Z'Landar's face with both hands in a gesture so tender it made his throat tighten.

"You were never meant to be ordinary, child. You were never meant to live a simple life, to choose peace over purpose, to hide from the destiny that burns in your blood. And I—" Her voice broke. "I spent ten years being angry at you for running. For refusing the throne. For seeming to waste what your parents died to create."

"And now?" Z'Landar managed past the lump in his throat.

"Now I understand." She released him, sitting back with the weariness of centuries suddenly visible in every line of her face. "You weren't running from duty. You were waiting until you could bear it without breaking. Until you were strong enough to carry what they gave you without being crushed beneath its weight."

"I'm still not sure I'm strong enough."

"No one ever is." Mhairi smiled—sad and knowing and deeply proud. "That's what makes it courage instead of certainty. That's what makes leaders worth following instead of tyrants worth fearing. You

130

doubt. You question. You acknowledge your fear." She gestured toward the door, toward the loch beyond where Andralia waited. "And you surround yourself with those who shore up your weaknesses and amplify your strengths."

"Andralia," Z'Landar said. "You know what she is."

"I suspect what she is. I know what she represents." Mhairi's expression shifted to something that might have been amusement mixed with caution. "Your mother's map—look at it closely. Look at the central spiral, where all the lines converge."

Z'Landar examined the shell again, focusing on the pattern's heart. There, carved with such delicate precision he'd initially missed it, was a symbol he recognized from elsewhere. The same spiral the dragon had burned into Irish stone. The same shape that marked the standing stones around the harbor where he and Andralia had sheltered.

"The cosmic spiral," Mhairi said. "Mark of powers older than our small disputes. Your mother saw it—understood that you would need connection to something beyond Scotland, beyond Earth even, to fulfill what you were born to accomplish. And now a woman appears who carries that connection in her blood and bones." She leaned forward, her voice dropping to barely above a whisper. "Tell me true, grandson—does she love you? Or does she simply serve some purpose written in stars we cannot see?"

The question struck deep, hitting fears Z'Landar had tried not to examine too closely. Did Andralia love him for himself? Or was he simply destiny made flesh, cosmic inevitability she couldn't refuse?

"Both," he said finally, the admission costing something. "She loves me. I feel it—in every touch, every word, every moment she chooses to stand beside me when she could walk away. But I also think she knew—knows—something about what I am, what I'm meant to

131

become. That her parents sent her to find me for reasons beyond romance."

"And that troubles you."

"Wouldn't it trouble you? To wonder whether love is choice or simply fate playing dress-up?"

Mhairi was quiet for a long moment, her ancient eyes holding depths even three hundred years hadn't fully plumbed. Then she smiled—genuine, warm, almost mischievous.

"Your mother and Brannach were fated. Prophecies spoke of their union before either was born. The old ones whispered that only through their joining could the water-folk hope to survive what was coming. Every force of destiny and cosmic design pushed them together." She paused. "And yet, when I asked Nerina this exact question—whether she loved him or simply surrendered to inevitability—she said the most remarkable thing."

"What?"

"She said: 'Fate gave us opportunity. Love was what we made from it. The stars can push souls together, but they cannot force hearts to open. That choice, Mother, was always ours. And we chose *yes* every morning we woke beside each other, every time we could have walked away but stayed instead.'"

The words settled into Z'Landar like stones finding the bottom of a deep pool—heavy, but somehow right. Not resolving the question but reframing it in ways that made the answer matter less than the asking.

"She was wise," he said quietly.

"She was young. Younger than you are now when she made her choice. But wisdom doesn't require age—only willingness to see clearly despite fear." Mhairi rose, moving to a different section of the

132

chamber's wall where water flowed in patterns that suggested decoration and function both. "I have something else to show you. Something I kept for ten years, waiting for the day you were ready to receive it."

She reached into the flowing water, her hand passing through what appeared to be solid coral but was actually cunningly concealed hollow. When she withdrew, she held a length of braided material that caught the light strangely—neither rope nor cloth but something between, woven from materials Z'Landar couldn't immediately identify.

"Your father's war-braid," Mhairi said, offering it with both hands like the precious relic it was. "Worn when he went into battle, braided from the mane of his horse-form, blessed by every Kelpie elder then living. It survived his sacrifice—was found in the Heart's waters after, still intact despite what should have destroyed it." She laid it in Z'Landar's hands. "It was meant to pass to his heir. To the next Kelpie king. To *you*."

Z'Landar stared at the braid, feeling his vision blur with tears he'd been holding back since entering the chamber. This was his father's. Had touched Brannach's skin, had been worn into battles Z'Landar knew only through stories, had survived the sacrifice that created him.

"I can't—I'm not ready—"

"You are ready," Mhairi said firmly. "You may not feel ready. May not believe you've earned it. But readiness is not feeling, grandson—it's choosing. Choosing to stand despite fear. Choosing to act despite doubt. Choosing to carry forward what was given you, even when the weight threatens to break your back."

She knelt before him—the Queen of the Western Selkies, three hundred years old, bowing to the grandson she'd barely known.

"The Elders will announce their decision tomorrow. The formal presentation, the evidence examined, the questions answered. And at the end—whether they say it explicitly or dance around the words—they will offer you the throne. Both thrones, joined for the first time in known history." Her hands covered his where they clutched the war-braid. "When that moment comes, you must not hesitate. Must not give them space to reconsider or time to let fear override wisdom. You must accept. Claim what is yours. Become what you were born to be."

"And if I fail?" His voice came out small, young. "If I claim the throne and cannot bear its weight? If I lead them into fire and cannot bring them through?"

"Then you will fail gloriously, as your parents failed gloriously, and perhaps in failing you will create possibility for whoever comes after." Mhairi's grip tightened. "But I do not think you will fail. I think you are exactly what these waters need—strong enough to stand, wise enough to doubt, brave enough to carry forward despite carrying doubt."

She released him, rising with grace that belied her centuries, moving toward the chamber's exit. But at the threshold she paused, looking back with expression that held such love it made Z'Landar's chest ache.

"Your mother would be proud," she said quietly. "Not of prophecy fulfilled or destiny accepted. Just of the man you've become despite every reason to break under the weight of what you carry. Remember that, when doubt grows loud. Remember that she chose this—chose you—knowing full well what it would cost. And she counted that cost worthwhile."

Then she was gone, swimming away through passages only she knew completely, leaving Z'Landar alone in the chamber of living light with his father's war-braid clutched tight and his mother's map of possibility burning patterns into his palm.

He sat for a long time, feeling things too large for words or easy understanding. Grief and gratitude, fear and determination, love for parents he'd never known and responsibility toward people who needed him whether he felt ready or not.

When he finally rose, when he wrapped the war-braid carefully and tucked his mother's shell-map safely away, when he swam back through the passages toward the shallows where Andralia waited— Z'Landar felt different. Not transformed, not suddenly certain or ready beyond doubt.

But *decided*.

Tomorrow the Elders would speak. Tomorrow the formal council would conclude. Tomorrow he would face the moment ten years of running had tried to prevent.

And when they offered the throne—when destiny and duty and the weight of two peoples' hopes pressed down—he would accept.

Not because he was ready. Not because he felt worthy. Not because certainty had replaced fear.

But because his mother had seen possibility where others saw only division. Because his father had stood strong even when strength meant sacrifice. Because some burdens cannot be set down, can only be carried forward.

Because he was Z'Landar—son of Brannach, son of Nerina, son of water and stars and something cosmic he barely understood.

And it was time to stop running.

Time to become the bridge his parents had died to build.

Time to be king.

Chapter Eleven: King of All Waterfolk

Dawn came to Loch Slochd with mist that clung to the water's surface like a shroud, turning the world to shades of pearl and shadow. Z'Landar arrived early, the war-braid wrapped around his left forearm where it pressed against skin like a promise, his mother's shell-map tucked safely within the leather pouch at his hip. Andralia swam beside him, rested now, her presence a steady comfort as they descended through gathered crowds toward the River Hall.

More had come than three days prior. Word had spread—not just through the Highlands but beyond, carried by currents and whispers and the particular magic that draws water-folk to moments of historical weight. They lined the passages, they clustered in the depths, they watched with eyes that held hope and fear in measures equal.

The River Hall felt different this morning. Still vast, still ancient, but somehow *expectant*—as if the stones themselves understood that what had been ten years broken would today be made whole, or fail in the attempt and shatter beyond all mending.

The seven Kelpie Elders sat at their oak table, faces grave but not hostile. Queen Mhairi occupied her chair of woven kelp, her court arranged behind her in careful hierarchy. Maelis stood at her customary place, amber eyes finding Z'Landar's across the chamber with expression that might have been encouragement or simply acknowledgment that the moment had arrived.

Z'Landar took his position before the throne—not upon it, not yet— and waited while the chamber filled with those who had earned right to witness. When the last had entered, when silence had settled like snow over deep water, Tormod rose.

"We have deliberated," he said, his voice carrying the weight of stone and river both. "We have examined evidence brought by Z'Landar, son of Brannach. We have questioned. We have debated. We have consulted records older than living memory and wisdom accumulated through centuries of rule."

He paused, his storm-gray eyes sweeping the chamber.

"The threat is real," he continued. "The dragon Caoránach lives. Her eggs rest hidden in our lands and across the water. What was done to Ireland will be done to Scotland unless we act—swiftly, decisively, with unity we have not known since before the oldest among us drew first breath."

Eilidh rose to stand beside him. "The Kelpie Elders acknowledge that our governance these ten years—well-intentioned though it was— has proven inadequate to such crisis. Seven voices speaking in council cannot move with the speed that survival demands. We need singular authority. We need a king."

"But not merely a Kelpie king," Morven added, rising in turn. "Not when the threat spans all waters, all territories, all peoples who swim Scottish depths."

One by one, the remaining Elders stood—Caelan, Fiona, Niall, and finally ancient Seoras, who moved with the deliberate care of one who had seen ages turn.

"We offer the throne of the Kelpies," Seoras said, his voice like wind through trees older than kingdoms. "Freely given, not as burden but as honor. We offer it to Z'Landar, son of Brannach the Thundering, who has proven himself worthy not through strength alone but through wisdom to acknowledge fear, courage to act despite it, and vision to see beyond our small divisions to threats that care nothing for old hatreds."

The chamber erupted in murmurs—some approving, some uncertain, none hostile. Z'Landar felt his heart hammering, felt the

137

war-braid burn against his arm as if Brannach himself watched from whatever place the dead occupy.

But before he could speak, Queen Mhairi rose.

"The Selkies also have debated," she said, her voice cutting through the murmurs like a blade through water. "We have considered what offering a throne means—not surrender of authority but recognition that some moments demand more than tradition can provide. That some individuals carry within them possibility greater than the sum of their parts."

She moved forward, approaching until she stood before Z'Landar with expression that held such complex emotion—pride and grief and hope wound together like the war-braid itself.

"My grandson," she said, and the words carried to every corner despite being spoken softly. "My daughter's son. Born of sacrifice, shaped by prophecy, tempered by years spent learning what it means to carry weight without being crushed beneath it." She turned to address the chamber entire. "The Selkies offer their throne as well. We offer it without reservation, without condition, without the hesitation that old wounds might otherwise demand."

She placed one hand on Z'Landar's shoulder, the gesture both personal and symbolic.

"We offer it because Nerina saw truly—that love across impossible divides creates not weakness but strength. That union of river and sea, of Kelpie and Selkie, of Earth and stars themselves, produces something our peoples separately could never achieve." Her voice strengthened. "We offer it because the alternative is fire descending, death in waters that should be sanctuary, and the end of everything our ancestors built across centuries of struggle."

Silence held for three heartbeats. Five. Then Fionnuala's voice rang out from the Selkie court, young and fierce and absolutely certain:

"Long live the King of All Waterfolk!"

The cry was taken up—first by other young voices, then by those who remembered the Great Wurm and the boy who had stood against it, then by the ancient ones who had lived long enough to see that sometimes the impossible was simply the inevitable waiting for its moment.

"Long live the King!"

"Long live Z'Landar!"

The sound crashed against stone and water like waves against cliffs, building until the chamber itself seemed to shake with the force of it.

Z'Landar looked at the throne. Looked at his grandmother, whose eyes shone with tears she made no effort to hide. Looked at the seven Elders, who watched with expressions ranging from pride to cautious hope. Looked at Andralia, whose smile held certainty that transcended the moment—as if she had always known this would come, had simply been waiting for him to catch up to destiny.

He thought of his father, voice like thunder, standing where Z'Landar now stood. He thought of his mother, brave and stubborn and so certain that love mattered more than safety. He thought of the Irish villagers reduced to ash, of the dragon's terrible beauty, of eggs waiting to hatch into fire and devastation.

He thought of the shell-map pressed against his hip, showing connections that existed in potential. Of the war-braid burning against his arm, survived through sacrifice.

Of the ten years he had spent running, and the moment when running ended.

"I accept," Z'Landar said, and though he spoke quietly the words carried as if the chamber itself had chosen to amplify them. "I claim the throne of the Kelpies, given freely by those whose wisdom guides the rivers. I claim the throne of the Selkies, offered without condition by those whose strength spans the seas."

He turned slowly, addressing not just the Elders and Queen but every creature gathered.

"I claim them not as separate crowns but as single purpose—to unite what has been divided, to protect what is threatened, to stand against darkness whether it comes wearing dragon scales or any other form." His voice grew stronger, carrying the authority his grandmother had told him he possessed, the power that had always lived within him waiting for the moment when doubt gave way to decision.

"I accept the title you offer: King of All Waterfolk. Not Kelpie alone. Not Selkie only. But both and more—the bridge my parents died to build, the unity they believed possible even when possibility seemed purest fantasy."

He placed one hand on the throne's ancient oak, feeling centuries of kingship pulse beneath his palm.

"But know this," he continued, his tone hardening. "I claim these thrones not for glory or power or the weight of crowns that will come when time permits such ceremony. I claim them for war. For the battle that approaches whether we name it or not. For the struggle that will demand everything we have to give and perhaps more than we possess."

The chamber had gone silent again, every eye fixed on him.

"Four dragon eggs wait to hatch. One already moves within the beast who seeks to birth destruction across our lands. We have days—perhaps weeks if fortune favors—before the first breaks shell and Scotland learns what Ireland has already witnessed. Before fire falls from skies and waters run red with those too slow or too stubborn to stand united."

Z'Landar's hand tightened on the throne.

"I will not sit upon this seat and rule in comfort while threats gather. I will not hold court and dispense wisdom while enemies make plans we're too divided to counter. This throne exists for one purpose now: to give us structure enough to fight, authority enough to command, unity enough to survive."

He released the oak, turned to face them fully.

"Grand ceremony will wait. Celebration will come when we've earned it through survival. For now—for today—we acknowledge what has been given and accepted. We recognize that Kelpie and Selkie swim as one people, under one authority, facing one threat that cares nothing for our historic divisions."

"Well spoken," Tormod said, and something in his weathered face had shifted—respect, perhaps, or simply recognition that the young king understood what kingship meant when war approached. "What are your first commands, Your Majesty?"

The title felt strange in Z'Landar's ears, heavy and sharp-edged. But he bore it.

"Summon the Highland clans," he said without hesitation. "Four days hence, at Loch Ness where it all began. Not every clan—we lack time for such gathering—but the chiefs or their first chieftains. Those who fought beside us ten years ago, who remember what united forces can accomplish."

"The humans will come," Queen Mhairi said. It was not question but certainty.

"They must," Z'Landar replied. "Dragon fire burns flesh regardless of whether it walks on two legs or swims in seal-skin. This is not merely waterfolk concern—it threatens every creature who calls Scotland home. We need the clans. Their strength, their steel, their knowledge of the lands where eggs may rest."

He turned to Maelis. "You will carry messages to those who should attend. Clan Fraser first—Alasdair will rally others once he knows the call is genuine. Then the Sinclairs, the Grahams, the Halls. Every clan that holds territory near lochs or rivers where Kelpies dwell."

"It will be done," Maelis said, bowing her head.

"Caelan," Z'Landar addressed the youngest Elder. "You know the rivers better than most. I need searches organized—systematic, careful—of every abandoned Kelpie settlement. The dragon will use places of old magic for her eggs. We need to find them before they hatch."

"I'll organize parties immediately," Caelan replied, already calculating in his mind how many could be spared for such work.

"Fionnuala," Z'Landar found his half-sister in the crowd, saw her straighten at being named. "You'll coordinate communication between search parties. You're young enough to swim fast, known to both Kelpie and Selkie. Messages will flow through you."

Pride blazed in her silver eyes. "I won't fail you."

"I know." He continued issuing commands, feeling the shape of kingship settle around him—not comfortable, not easy, but *right* in ways that went beyond personal readiness. "We need scouts watching the Irish waters, tracking the dragon's movements. We need supplies gathered—healing herbs, weapons that can be used underwater, anything that might prove useful when fire comes. We need—"

"You need rest," Andralia said quietly, appearing at his side with the ease of long practice. "And food. And time to breathe before you burn yourself to ash trying to do everything in the first hour of kingship."

A ripple of something between amusement and approval moved through the gathered waterfolk. Z'Landar felt his lips twitch despite the weight of all he carried.

"My queen speaks wisdom," he said, and watched color bloom in Andralia's cheeks at the title he had not planned to bestow but felt absolutely correct in this moment. "We will reconvene in four hours. The Elders and I will begin detailed planning—strategy, logistics, the thousand small decisions that prepare armies for war. The rest—" He gestured to the assembled masses. "Return to your territories. Prepare your people. Train those who can fight, protect those who cannot. Four days until the Highland Gathering. Seven, perhaps ten before dragon fire tests us in earnest. Move with purpose. Move with unity. And remember—"

He paused, letting the silence build.

"We are no longer Kelpie and Selkie arguing over old wounds and older hatreds. We are waterfolk, bound by common cause and common threat. We are Scotland's children, born of these depths, and we will defend them with everything we possess. That is my first decree as your king. That is the foundation upon which all else will build."

The chamber erupted not in cheers but in the deep-throated calls of Kelpies and the melodious cries of Selkies, blending together in harmony that had not been heard since before memory kept accounts. Z'Landar felt the sound wash over him, felt it settle into bones and blood, felt it transform the fear he carried into something sharper, fiercer.

Purpose.

The gathering dispersed, creatures moving with new urgency, new unity. The Elders remained, as did Queen Mhairi and her closest advisors. Maelis. Fionnuala. Andralia. The core around which everything else would orbit.

"Four days," Tormod said once the chamber had cleared enough for conversation. "Not much time to organize what you're proposing."

"It will have to be enough," Z'Landar replied. "The dragon won't wait for our convenience. Better to gather what forces we can quickly than delay seeking perfection that will never come."

"The clans will have questions," Eilidh pointed out. "About authority, about who commands if water-folk and humans fight together, about—"

"About whether they'll take orders from one they called 'boy' not ten years past," Z'Landar finished. "I know. Let them question. Let them challenge. But in the end, they'll follow. Because the alternative is burning in their halls while debating whose authority matters more."

"You've grown teeth," Seoras observed, and something that might have been approval glinted in his ancient eyes. "That's good. Kings without bite are decorations, not leaders."

They spent the next hours in planning—detailed, practical, the unglamorous work of organizing forces and supplies and strategies. Maps were consulted, ancient ones showing every loch and river and the connections between them. Discussions ranged from how many Kelpies could be spared for egg-searching to what weapons might pierce dragon scales to where scouts should be positioned to track Caoránach's movements.

Z'Landar listened more than he spoke at first, learning from those who had ruled and fought and survived long before his birth. But gradually he found his voice—asking questions, offering suggestions, making decisions when consensus proved impossible. The Elders treated him with respect that would have seemed impossible three days ago, and he worked to earn it with every word, every choice.

When they finally broke—exhausted, hungry, but with the skeleton of a plan beginning to take shape—Andralia pulled him aside to a quiet corner where water flowed in patterns that suggested privacy.

"You did well," she said simply.

"I gave orders. Made demands. Pretended certainty I don't feel."

"That's kingship." She cupped his face in both hands, forcing him to meet her impossible eyes. "You'll spend every day questioning whether you're doing right, making correct choices, leading them toward survival instead of slaughter. That doubt will never leave. But neither will the determination to try anyway. That's what makes you worthy of the crown you'll someday wear."

"Someday," Z'Landar echoed. "When there's time for such ceremony."

"When the war is won," Andralia corrected gently. "When Scotland stands safe and the eggs lie destroyed and the dragon is nothing but cautionary tale for younglings not yet born." She leaned forward, pressing her forehead to his. "When we've earned the right to celebrate, we'll celebrate properly. Until then—we survive. We fight. We protect what's ours."

"We," Z'Landar repeated, letting the word settle. "I'm glad you're here. Glad you chose to stay when you could have—"

"Could have what?" Her smile held edges. "Returned to the stars? Left you to face this alone? Pretended I wasn't meant to stand beside you through whatever comes?" She kissed him softly, briefly. "I told you I choose here. Choose you. That hasn't changed because you've claimed a throne. If anything, it's more true now than before."

Z'Landar held her, drawing strength from her presence, her certainty, her absolutely unwavering conviction that they could survive what approached. Around them, the River Hall continued its work—Elders departing with assignments, courtiers carrying messages, the machinery of newly unified government beginning its ungainly first movements.

Four days until the Highland Gathering.

Four days to prepare the clans, to organize forces, to shore up weaknesses and pray their strengths proved sufficient.

Four days before water-folk and human would stand united once more, facing threats ancient and terrible.

Z'Landar released Andralia reluctantly, knowing work remained, knowing kingship meant sacrificing comfort for duty more often than not.

"Come," he said, taking her hand. "We have a kingdom to defend and very little time to do it. Best we begin as we mean to continue—together, determined, and too stubborn to acknowledge the odds stacked against us."

She laughed—genuine, bright, the sound pushing back darkness that tried to creep into corners even here. "Now *that* sounds like a king worth following."

They swam back toward the planning tables, toward the maps and strategies and thousand decisions waiting to be made. Behind them, the throne stood empty—would stand empty until fire had been faced and victory earned.

But Z'Landar wore the title now, carried the weight, bore the responsibility.

He was King of All Waterfolk.

And the war had only just begun.

Chapter Twelve: The Searching and the Gathering

Part One: Into the Depths

The abandoned settlement lay three days' swim north of Loch Slochd, tucked into a river canyon where water ran cold and dark even at midday. Caelan led his search party through passages that narrowed with each turn, feeling the weight of stone pressing close on all sides. Behind him swam twelve others—six Kelpies who knew these northern territories, six Selkies who had volunteered despite never having ventured so far from open water.

United. As the King commanded. As survival demanded.

"There," Caelan said, pointing to where the canyon opened into a natural chamber carved by millennia of patient flow. "The village proper begins just beyond. Three hundred souls once dwelt here before the plague took them."

"Three hundred years past," murmured Dòmhnall, a grizzled Kelpie whose scars spoke of wars older than most present could remember. "Long enough for the dead to settle. Long enough for their magic to steep the waters."

"Long enough for a dragon to find it useful," Caelan replied grimly.

They swam forward in formation—careful, watchful, weapons drawn though what good steel would do against dragon-fire none could say with certainty. The village emerged from shadow like a ghost made solid: stone dwellings carved into the canyon walls, their windows dark as empty eye sockets. Spirals and runes marked every threshold—protective wards placed by Kelpies who had believed such magic could keep plague at bay.

It hadn't.

The streets—if such they could be called underwater—lay empty. Kelp grew wild through doorways. Fish darted through chambers where families had once gathered. Three centuries of abandonment had turned this place into a tomb, and tombs held their own particular silence.

"Spread out," Caelan commanded quietly. "Teams of two. Search every dwelling, every corner, every space large enough to hide an egg. Look for signs of recent disturbance—anything that suggests the dragon has been here."

They dispersed, Kelpie and Selkie paired, swimming through ruins with care born of respect and fear both. Caelan took Ailsa—a young Selkie whose eyes held depths that spoke of waters far from Scotland—and together they moved toward the village's heart, where the largest dwelling had housed the settlement's leader.

"It feels wrong," Ailsa whispered as they crossed the threshold. "Not just dead. *Wronged*."

Caelan felt it too. A thickness in the water that went beyond silt or decay. A pressure that suggested something watched, something waited, something resented their intrusion into grief left undisturbed for centuries.

The main chamber stretched larger than expected, its ceiling lost in darkness that their luminescent markers couldn't fully penetrate. At the far end, elevated on a natural stone dais, sat what might once have been a throne or simply a leader's chair. And behind it, carved into living rock—

"By the First Waters," Caelan breathed.

A spiral. Massive, intricate, glowing with faint bioluminescence that pulsed like a heartbeat. The same spiral the dragon had burned into Irish stone. The same symbol that marked Nerina's shell-map.

The cosmic mark.

"She's been here," Ailsa said, her voice tight with fear and certainty both. "The dragon. This is her marking, her claiming."

Caelan swam closer, studying the spiral's pattern. The glow came not from the carving itself but from something *behind* it—light bleeding through cracks in stone, suggesting hollow space beyond.

"There's a chamber," he said. "Hidden. The dragon didn't carve this spiral—she found it. Used what was already here for her purposes."

"Which means?" Ailsa moved to his side, one hand on the knife at her belt though both knew such weapons were inadequate against what they might find.

"Which means if we're right about her using this place—if an egg rests somewhere in this village—it will be there. Behind this wall. In whatever sacred or secret space the Kelpies carved when they built this settlement."

They called the others with whistles that carried through water, signals that brought the search party converging on the main chamber. Twelve faces, lit by markers and the spiral's eerie glow, all showing the same mixture of anticipation and dread.

"We need to break through," Caelan said, gesturing to the wall. "Carefully. If there's an egg beyond—if we're fortunate enough to have found one on first attempt—we cannot risk damaging it before destruction can be controlled."

"Or risk alerting the dragon we've discovered her cache," Dòmhnall added. "If she has watchers, if she's set guardians—"

"Then we deal with them." Caelan's voice carried authority he'd grown into these past four days. "The King commanded searches. We will search. And if we find what we seek, we will do what must be done."

They worked in shifts, using tools brought for this purpose—stone wedges, metal prybars salvaged from human shipwrecks, strength accumulated through lifetimes of swimming against currents that would have broken lesser creatures. The wall resisted. Not merely stone's natural stubbornness, but something more—magic laid into rock, wards placed to protect or conceal or both.

But persistence has its own magic, and finally—after three hours that felt like three days—the wall cracked. Groaned. Shifted inward with sound like thunder muffled by water.

The chamber beyond breathed darkness absolute.

Caelan entered first, markers held high, their light pushing back shadow to reveal space that stole breath and replaced it with awe. Not large—perhaps twenty feet across—but so perfectly formed it seemed shaped by intention rather than erosion. The walls bore carvings that predated the settlement above, spirals and patterns that suggested this place had been sacred long before Kelpies claimed it.

And at the chamber's heart, nestled in a depression carved to precise dimensions, protected by residual magic that made the air shimmer despite being underwater—

An egg.

Dragon egg.

Larger than any Kelpie in horse-form, its shell the color of old blood shot through with veins of gold. It pulsed. Not visibly, but they felt it—heartbeat slow and strong, life growing within, something ancient and terrible counting days until it could break free and burn.

"Sweet merciful depths," someone whispered. Caelan didn't turn to see who. Couldn't tear his eyes from the egg, from proof that everything they'd feared was real, immediate, *here*.

"We found it," Ailsa said, her voice shaking. "We actually found it."

"Now we destroy it," Caelan replied, though his hands trembled as he reached for the hammer they'd brought—blessed by Selkie priestesses, forged in fires that burned hotter than any natural flame, designed specifically for this purpose.

He moved forward. Raised the hammer. Felt the weight of what he was about to do settle onto shoulders barely adequate to bear it— ending a life before it began, killing what had not yet earned death, preventing birth because birth meant destruction.

"Wait," Dòmhnall said sharply. "The magic around it. Can you see? The shimmer?"

Caelan paused, looking closer. The egg sat within a sphere of distortion, water bending strangely around it, light catching on nothing visible. Protective magic. Dragon magic. And he would wager his life that breaking that protection would trigger alarm, would send signal screaming across whatever distance separated egg from mother.

"We need the King," he said, lowering the hammer. "And the one he calls Queen. They said she could break dragon spells—proved it in Ireland at the Fairy Queen's cave. We cannot risk alerting Caoránach before we're prepared for her fury."

"Then we guard it," Dòmhnall said. "Set watch. Send runners to Loch Ness. And pray the dragon doesn't come checking before help arrives."

They organized quickly—six to remain, six to carry word. Caelan chose to stay, stationing himself before the chamber entrance with Ailsa and four others whose courage he trusted absolutely. The remaining six departed at speed, racing through passages toward Loch Ness where the King prepared for Highland Gathering.

Where hope and help and perhaps salvation waited.

If they could arrive in time.

If the dragon didn't sense her egg discovered.

If magic and courage proved sufficient against scales and fire.

Many ifs. Too many.

But they had found it. First egg located. First step toward preventing catastrophe.

Caelan settled into watch, hand tight on weapon inadequate but necessary, and waited for the King to come.

Part Two: The Gathering of Clans

Four days had transformed Loch Ness into something unprecedented—a staging ground where water and land prepared for war together. The shores bore campfires by the dozens, clan colors flying from hastily erected standards, the sounds of steel being sharpened and warriors drilling carrying across waters that had not seen such gathering since the Battle of the Great Wurm.

Z'Landar stood on the northern shore in human form, Andralia at his side, watching as the latest arrivals made their way down the slope toward the loch. Clan MacKinnon, their banners showing the stag's head, led by chieftain who had fought beside Alasdair Fraser ten years past.

"Twenty-three clans have answered," Maelis said, swimming close enough for conversation. "More than I dared hope when I first carried your summons."

"And how many refused?" Z'Landar asked, though he already knew the answer. Messengers had reported throughout the past days.

"Seven. Mostly from the far north and western isles. Too distant to mobilize quickly, or too skeptical that dragon-threat warrants abandoning harvest and home."

"They'll learn," Andralia said quietly. "When fire comes, skepticism burns as readily as faith."

Z'Landar squeezed her hand briefly, then turned his attention to the approaching chieftain. Dougal MacKinnon was older now than when they'd last met—hair more silver than black, face weathered by years of Highland sun and wind—but his eyes still held the fierce certainty that had made him formidable in battle.

"Your Majesty," Dougal said, and Z'Landar heard layers in the title—respect, curiosity, perhaps slight amusement that the boy he'd fought beside now claimed kingship over realms most humans barely believed existed. "I received your summons. Clan MacKinnon stands ready."

"How many did you bring?" Z'Landar asked.

"Forty warriors. Not as many as I'd prefer, but harvest season leaves us thin. Those who came are tested fighters—men and women who remember the Wurm, who trust your word even when the threat seems impossible."

"The threat is real," Z'Landar said. "More real than I wish. But your presence honors us. Please—make camp with the others. Tonight we hold council. Every clan chief or their representative. Water-folk and human together. And I will show you exactly what we face."

Dougal nodded, shouted orders to his warriors, and moved toward the camping grounds where other clans had already established their territories. Z'Landar watched them go, counting in his head. Forty from MacKinnon. Seventy from Fraser. Thirty-five from Sinclair. The Border Reivers had sent combined force of fifty. Others contributed what they could—sometimes a dozen warriors, sometimes only five.

Perhaps four hundred humans total. Against a dragon that had killed thirty-eight with casual fury.

"Not enough," he murmured.

"It's what we have," Andralia replied. "And combined with water-folk forces—two hundred Kelpies, three hundred Selkies, sprites and Merrow and others who've pledged support—we number perhaps a thousand. Not overwhelming, but not insignificant."

"Against one dragon. But there are four eggs."

"Three now," came Fionnuala's voice as she surfaced nearby, silver eyes bright with news. "Caelan found one. In the northern settlement, exactly where we thought. Sends word he needs you and Andralia—dragon magic guards it, requires breaking before destruction."

Z'Landar's heart leapt and sank in same instant. Success and complication both. "When did he send word?"

"Runner arrived an hour past. I came seeking you immediately." Fionnuala gestured north. "A full days' swim hard. Less if you take the fastest route and don't stop for rest."

"I should go now," Z'Landar said, already turning toward the water.

"You should lead tonight's council first," Andralia corrected gently. "The clans have gathered because you called them. They deserve to see their king, hear the plan, understand what they've committed to before you vanish into the depths."

She was right. Frustratingly, practically right. Leaving now would undermine the very unity he'd worked to build, would suggest water-folk matters took precedence over human concerns. But waiting meant risking the dragon discovering her egg found, meant—

"I'll go," Andralia said, reading his thoughts as she often did. "Tonight, after council begins. I can swim faster than most, and you said yourself I can break the spell. I'll take guards—Fionnuala,

154

Maelis, perhaps others—and we'll destroy it before the dragon knows to check."

"I should be there," Z'Landar protested. "If something goes wrong—"

"Then you'll be here, leading the clans, preparing forces for what comes next. You're king now, beloved. That means delegating. Trusting others to carry burdens you cannot bear alone." Her smile was gentle but firm. "This is what I can do. Let me do it."

Before Z'Landar could argue further, a disturbance in the water drew attention. Scouts returning, swimming with urgency that suggested news requiring immediate attention.

The lead scout—a young Kelpie named Iain whose speed was legendary—surfaced gasping. "Your Majesty. The dragon. She moves."

Every conversation on the shore stopped. Every eye turned toward the scout.

"Where?" Z'Landar demanded.

"North from Ireland. Flying low over the channel, following coastline toward Scotland. She's been spotted three times in past day by Merrow and human fishermen both." Iain's expression held barely controlled fear. "She's coming here. Whether she knows about the egg or simply patrols her territory, we cannot say. But she comes."

Z'Landar felt the world narrow to sharp focus—plan and counter-plan, risk and necessity, decision and consequence all cascading through his mind in instants.

"How long until she reaches Scotland?"

"If she maintains current speed—perhaps two days. Maybe less."

Two days. Not enough time to destroy the egg, not if Andralia had to swim a full day north before even beginning to assess the egg. Not enough time to fully prepare defenses, to position forces, to—

"We move the council forward," Z'Landar said, decision crystallizing. "Tonight was meant for planning. Instead we act. Every clan chief, every water-folk leader, everyone who commands even a single warrior—gather at sunset. We have hours, not days. The dragon comes whether we're ready or not."

He turned to Fionnuala. "Send our fastest swimmers to Caelan. Tell him to hold position, guard the egg, wait for relief. We'll send a party after council—strong fighters, those who can move swiftly."

To Maelis: "Gather the Elders. Queen Mhairi. Anyone who needs to hear what comes next."

To Andralia: "You're right that I must stay for council. But afterward—we both go. Together. We destroy that egg tonight, and we're back before the dragon crosses into Scottish waters."

"That's—" Andralia calculated quickly. "Nearly impossible. A days' swim each direction, no rest, fighting dragon magic while exhausted—"

"Impossible is what we make possible by refusing to accept the alternative." Z'Landar's voice hardened with authority he'd grown into these past days. "I will not sit safely at Loch Ness while others risk themselves. I will not ask you to face dragon magic alone. We go together, we break the spell together, we destroy that egg together, and we return to lead our people against whatever comes next."

He looked at the gathered scouts, at Fionnuala and Maelis, at the clan chieftains who had begun to gather sensing something significant had shifted.

"The dragon comes," he said, loud enough for all to hear. "Let her come. She'll find us ready. She'll find us united. And she'll find that

Scotland—water and land, ancient magic and human steel—does not bow to fire and scale."

Cheers rose from the shore—clans taking up the cry, water-folk voices joining, the sound building until it echoed off distant mountains.

Z'Landar allowed himself one moment to feel the weight of what he'd just committed to. One breath to acknowledge the fear that still lived beneath the crown's authority.

Then he strode toward where the council would gather, Andralia keeping pace, and prepared to forge an army from clans and water-folk who had barely begun to trust each other.

The dragon came.

They had two days to become ready.

It would have to be enough.

Part Three: Fire Council

Sunset painted the sky in shades of blood and gold as they gathered—an unprecedented assembly of power and will. The clan chiefs sat in rough circle on the shore, their warriors standing behind in silent ranks. In the shallows, Kelpie Elders held position alongside Selkie courtiers, with water sprites providing luminescence that turned the gathering into something otherworldly. Merrow had come from Ireland—including Muirgheal, who had crossed dangerous waters to stand with those who had believed her warnings.

At the circle's heart, Z'Landar stood in human form, visible to land and water both. Beside him, Andralia. Behind him, his grandmother Queen Mhairi, the seven Elders, Maelis with her ancient wisdom, Fionnuala with her fierce determination.

The forces that would stand against dragon fire.

If they could stop tearing at each other long enough to face outward.

"You've called us here on short notice," said Iain MacLeod, chief of his clan, a man whose skepticism showed in every weathered line of his face. "Pulled us from harvest, from preparations for winter. The message spoke of dragons and eggs and threats most of us half-believed were children's tales. Well—we're here. Convince us this wasn't folly."

Direct. Challenging. But not hostile. Z'Landar had known this moment would come.

"I could speak," he said quietly. "Tell you what I've seen, what threatens. But words are wind, and you deserve more than wind. Muirgheal—" He gestured to the Merrow. "Tell them what the dragon did to your people."

The Irish Merrow swam forward, her green hair floating around her shoulders, her expression carrying grief that needed no embellishment.

"Caoránach the Mother killed seventeen of my kinfolk," she said, her voice carrying across the circle. "Burned them with fire that works beneath water as easily as above. She destroyed three villages on Ireland's coast—thirty-eight human dead, homes reduced to ash, families broken. She marks territory with flames hot enough to melt stone to glass. And she does this to protect four eggs that, if hatched, will bring four more dragons to ravage both our lands."

"Why come to Scotland?" demanded Callum Graham, the Border Reiver whose clan had fought Kelpies as often as they'd traded with them. "If her eggs are in Ireland, if she's Ireland's problem—why should we risk Scottish blood?"

"Because two of her eggs are already here," Z'Landar said bluntly. "Hidden in Scottish waters and lands. One we've found—in an abandoned Kelpie settlement one day north. Dragon magic guards it, but we will destroy it tonight. The other remains hidden but exists somewhere in our territory. And the dragon herself flies toward Scotland as we speak, drawn by gods know what purpose—perhaps she senses her egg discovered, perhaps she simply expands her hunting grounds."

He let that settle, watching faces shift from skepticism to calculation to worry.

"You've seen the egg?" Alasdair Fraser spoke up, his voice cutting through murmurs. "Confirmed it's real?"

"Caelan and his search party found it hours ago. They guard it now, waiting for those who can destroy it safely." Z'Landar pulled a marker from his pouch—one Fionnuala had carried from Caelan— and tossed it to Alasdair. "That's marked with the egg's magic. Touch it. Feel what we face."

Alasdair caught it, his expression shifting immediately as power pulsed through the marker. He passed it to the chief beside him, who likewise reacted with visible shock. The marker made its way around the circle, each human and water-folk who touched it feeling the proof of what words could not convey.

Dragon magic. Real. Immediate. *Here.*

"So we have perhaps two days before she arrives," said Dougal MacKinnon, his strategic mind already working through implications. "One egg found but not yet destroyed. One still hidden. The dragon herself incoming. What's your plan, Your Majesty?"

Z'Landar had prepared for this. Four days of planning with the Elders, with Mhairi, with anyone whose wisdom and experience exceeded his own. Now he laid it out, clear and direct.

"Tonight, I lead a party north. We swim hard—no rest, maximum speed. We break the dragon's protective spell. We destroy the egg before she knows it's threatened. We return before she crosses into Scottish waters."

159

"That's nearly three days of swimming compressed into two," Tormod said, concern clear in his voice. "Even Kelpies at full strength would struggle with such pace."

"Which is why I take only the strongest, fastest. Andralia to break the spell. Maelis for her wisdom. Fionnuala for her speed. Perhaps three others—warriors who can fight if we're discovered, who can swim without stopping." Z'Landar's gaze swept the circle. "The rest of you begin preparations here. The dragon will come—either following her destroyed egg's trail or simply because Scotland has caught her attention. We need defenses ready."

"Defenses against a dragon?" Callum's skepticism had returned. "What defense stops something that burns stone and flies faster than arrows?"

"Traps," suggested Iain MacLeod. "Pitfalls concealed, perhaps filled with water or bog to slow her if she lands."

"Projectiles," Alasdair added. "Ballista, if we have time to construct them. Heavy spears that might pierce scale."

"Underwater ambush," said Eilidh. "If we can lure her into the loch, force her to fight in our element rather than hers, we gain advantage."

The ideas flowed—some practical, some desperate, all acknowledged as inadequate but better than nothing. Z'Landar listened, adding thoughts, shaping consensus, feeling the machinery of unified command beginning to function.

"Three priorities," he said finally, pulling threads together. "First— scouts. We need eyes on the dragon at all times. Merrow who can watch the channel, Kelpies who can patrol Scottish waters, humans who can man posts along the coast. She must not surprise us. The moment she crosses into Scotland, we know."

Murmgheal nodded. "My people will watch the Irish side. We'll send word the moment she moves."

"Second—the hidden egg. We must find it. Search parties continue, but now with urgency multiplied. Every loch where water runs 'pure enough to blind,' every place where ancient magic steeps the ground—search them. That egg hatches, we fight two dragons instead of one."

"Third—battle preparation. We assume she comes here, to Loch Ness, where our forces concentrate. We prepare this ground. Traps on shore, positions in the water, strategies for coordinated attack. Human and water-folk fighting as single force, using our combined strengths to overcome her advantages."

Z'Landar moved to the circle's center, standing where all could see.

"I cannot promise victory," he said bluntly. "I cannot guarantee that fire won't fall and blood won't spill. But I can promise this: we will fight. United. With everything we have. And if we fall, we fall having chosen to stand rather than submit to terror. That choice—that unity—is what separates us from the darkness that takes whatever it wishes simply because it can."

The silence that followed held weight.

Then Alasdair Fraser stood, his weathered hand dropping to his sword. "Clan Fraser stands with the King of All Waterfolk. We stood beside the boy ten years ago. We'll stand beside the king today."

One by one, the other chiefs rose. MacKinnon. MacLeod. The Border Reivers. Even skeptical Callum Graham, who grinned fiercely as he pledged his clan's steel.

In the water, the Elders raised voices in ancient Kelpie war-cry. The Selkies answered with harmonics that made the air shimmer. Sprites danced light across the gathering, and Merrow added their melodious calls.

The sound built until earth and water both seemed to shake with it.

Z'Landar felt tears threaten but held them back. This. This was what his parents had died to make possible. This unity forged not from law or heritage but from choice—from humans and water-folk deciding together that some threats required setting aside everything that divided them.

"Then we move," he said. "Council dismissed. Those who swim north with me—prepare for immediate departure. The rest—begin fortifications. We have two days to prepare for fire."

The gathering dissolved into purposeful chaos—warriors moving to assigned tasks, water-folk organizing into their battle groups, chieftains conferring with Elders about logistics and strategy.

Z'Landar found Andralia, pulled her aside to where they could speak privately.

"Are you certain about this?" she asked quietly. "Three days of swimming and magic in two days—you'll destroy yourself even if we succeed."

"Then I'll be destroyed doing what matters." He touched her face gently. "But I don't plan on being destroyed. I plan on breaking dragon magic, crushing that egg, and returning in time to welcome Caoránach to Scotland with steel and spell she never imagined we could bring against her."

Andralia smiled—sad and proud and fierce all together. "Then let's go break some dragon magic."

They gathered their party—Maelis, Fionnuala, and three of the strongest Kelpie warriors who volunteered knowing the cost such speed would demand. Seven total. Lucky number, if one believed in such things.

As sunset gave way to twilight, as stars began appearing in the darkening sky, they slipped into Loch Ness and began swimming north. Fast. Faster than should be possible. Faster than wisdom suggested.

But the egg waited.

The dragon neared.

And time, as always, cared nothing for the desperation of those who needed more of it.

Behind them, at Loch Ness, an army prepared for war.

Ahead, in an abandoned settlement haunted by three centuries of death, an egg pulsed with life that promised devastation.

And somewhere over the Irish Sea, wings beat against wind, carrying fire and fury toward Scotland's shores.

The pieces were moving.

The game had begun.

And soon—very soon—blood would determine whether Scotland stood or burned.

Chapter Thirteen: The Breaking

Part One: The Northern Race

They swam.

Not as creatures of leisure, not as beings who moved through water with the patient grace centuries teach. They swam as prey before predators, as those who race against tides that care nothing for desperation. Seven bodies cutting through Scottish waters with speed that burned in muscle and bone, that turned lungs to fire and minds to singular focus.

North. Faster. Don't stop. Don't slow. North.

The hours blurred into nightmare—passages that should have taken hours compressed into minutes, depths that demanded caution traversed with reckless speed. Maelis led, her ancient knowledge of every current and channel keeping them on the swiftest route. Fionnuala swam rear guard, her youth and speed ensuring none fell behind. Between them: Z'Landar and Andralia, the three Kelpie warriors whose names would be remembered for volunteering when wisdom suggested staying behind.

They spoke little. Breath was precious, saved for swimming rather than words. But Z'Landar felt Andralia's presence beside him like an anchor, felt the determination radiating from her even as exhaustion began carving lines into her face that hadn't been there at journey's start.

Night fell. They swam on, guided by luminescent markers and Maelis's unerring sense of direction. The water grew colder as they traveled north, pressing against skin with teeth that numbed.

Z'Landar's father's war-braid chafed against his forearm, a constant reminder of why they pushed beyond reasonable limits.

For Scotland. For those who cannot swim these waters. For parents who died believing their sacrifice mattered.

Dawn found them in waters that tasted different—older, carrying mineral traces that spoke of stone worn smooth over ages. They had covered ground that should have required almost two days. Had done it in twenty hours of relentless forward motion.

The cost showed in every line of their bodies.

One of the Kelpie warriors—Fearchar, a scarred veteran of battles older than Z'Landar's lifetime—signaled halt at a junction where three passages converged. They surfaced briefly in a pocket of air trapped beneath an overhang, gasping, muscles trembling with exhaustion that went beyond physical.

"The settlement lies two hours ahead," Fearchar said, his voice rough as grinding stone. "We can rest here. Recover strength before—"

"No rest," Z'Landar said, though his own body screamed for it. "The dragon comes. Every minute we delay is a minute closer to her discovering what we do. We press on."

He saw the protest forming in Fearchar's eyes, saw it mirrored in the faces of the others. But he also saw them accept it, diving back beneath the surface, resuming the pace that would break them all before this ended.

Andralia's hand found his as they swam, a brief touch that conveyed volumes. *I'm here. Still strong enough. We finish this together.*

Z'Landar squeezed her fingers once, then released them, needing both arms for the swimming that remained.

Two hours. Two more hours of agony, and then they would face dragon magic that might prove stronger than their combined will.

Two hours until they learned if impossible could truly be made real.

Part Two: The Waiting Guard

The abandoned settlement rose from shadow like a memory given substance—stone dwellings carved into canyon walls, empty windows watching their approach with the particular blindness of the long dead. Caelan met them at the village's edge, his relief visible even through the exhaustion that painted his own features.

"Your Majesty," he said, the title carrying weight of genuine respect. "We didn't think— that is, the speed required—" He stopped, shook his head. "You're here. That's what matters."

"The egg?" Z'Landar asked without preamble.

"Unchanged. Ailsa watches it now, along with Dòmhnall and two others. The remaining pair patrol approaches." Caelan gestured toward the main dwelling. "The magic around it—we've studied it as best we can. It's complex. Layered. Breaking it crudely would send alarm screaming across whatever distance separates egg from mother."

"Then we break it carefully," Andralia said, her voice steady despite the exhaustion Z'Landar could feel radiating from her. "Show me."

They swam through passages Z'Landar recognized from Caelan's descriptions—the empty streets, the kelp-choked doorways, the particular wrongness that clung to places where tragedy had soaked into stone. The main dwelling opened before them, and beyond, the chamber where cosmic spiral glowed with faint bioluminescence.

The wall had been fully cleared, the hidden chamber beyond exposed to view. And there, nestled in its depression, pulsing with slow heartbeat that made the water itself seem to breathe—

The egg.

Larger than Z'Landar had imagined despite descriptions. More real. More *alive* in ways that made destroying it feel like murder despite knowing what it would become if allowed to hatch.

Ailsa rose from where she'd been keeping watch, her young face showing strain of two days spent in this place of death guarding something that promised worse death if left intact.

"Majesty. My lady." She bowed to each in turn. "It hasn't changed. The magic holds steady. But sometimes—" She hesitated. "Sometimes I think I hear it. Not sound exactly. More like... dreaming. As if what grows inside dreams of fire and flight and burning."

"Then we end its dreams," Z'Landar said quietly. He turned to Caelan. "Your party. You've done what was asked. More than asked. Now you return—maximum speed, maximum urgency. Back to Loch Ness. Tell them we've found it, that destruction proceeds. Tell them to prepare for the dragon's coming."

"But Your Majesty—you might need—"

"We need you carrying word more than we need additional guards here." Z'Landar's tone left no room for argument. "The army must know. The preparations must continue. Go. Now. Don't stop until you reach Loch Ness and can report to the Elders that the first egg dies today."

Caelan held his gaze for a moment, then nodded. "As you command." He gestured to his five remaining guards. "You heard the King. We swim for Loch Ness. Carry nothing but the news. Stop for nothing but death itself."

They departed in a rush of displaced water, six bodies arrowing south with the urgency Z'Landar had demanded. Within moments, only seven remained—Z'Landar's party, alone with an egg that pulsed with draconic life and magic that shimmer-guarded it from simple destruction.

"Right then," Andralia said, moving toward the hidden chamber with careful grace. "Let's see what the mother-dragon has wrought."

Part Three: The Breaking of Wards

Andralia circled the egg slowly, studying it from every angle, her impossible eyes narrowed in concentration. Z'Landar watched her work, seeing past the exhaustion to the fierce intelligence that analyzed, calculated, planned. The three Kelpie warriors held position at the chamber's entrance—guards against interruption, witnesses to what would be attempted.

Maelis and Fionnuala flanked Z'Landar, the ancient and the young bracketing their king as Andralia completed her examination.

"It's elegant," she said finally, her voice holding grudging respect. "The dragon didn't just throw power at this. She *crafted* it. Layer upon layer of protection, each one designed to trigger alarm if disturbed. Break one layer, the others shriek warning. Try to penetrate them all at once, they collapse inward and crush the egg before you can prevent it—sending shockwave through every water in Scotland announcing what was done."

"Can you break it?" Z'Landar asked.

Andralia's smile was sharp as broken glass. "I can break anything given enough power and proper leverage. Question is: will breaking it warn the dragon?"

"Will it?"

"Not if I don't actually *break* it." She knelt before the egg—or as close to kneeling as one could manage underwater—placing both hands on the stone to either side of the depression. "Space can be... convinced... to behave differently than it typically prefers. Compressed. Folded. Made to occupy less volume than seems possible."

Z'Landar felt understanding dawn. "You're going to compress the protection. Make it so small it can't function."

"Something like that. The magic will remain intact—technically unbroken. But squeezed so tightly that it becomes irrelevant, like trying to guard something through a window too small to see through." Her expression shifted to something between determination and concern. "But I'll need power. More than I can generate alone. Space doesn't like being told it's negotiable. Requires... significant persuasion."

"How much power?"

"All you can spare. And then some." She met his eyes across the chamber. "This will drain you, Z'Landar. Leave you exhausted in ways that simple swimming cannot. I'll be feeding on your strength, your magic, everything you've inherited from parents who bridged water and stars. It will hurt. And when it's done, we'll both be... diminished... for however long recovery requires."

Z'Landar thought of the dragon flying toward Scotland. Thought of two days—perhaps less—before fire tested whatever defenses they'd managed to prepare. Thought of arriving back at Loch Ness too exhausted to fight, too drained to lead.

"Do it," he said.

Andralia's expression softened—pride and worry and love tangling together. "Come here, then. This requires contact. Requires connection deeper than words or simple touch."

Z'Landar moved to her side, kneeling opposite across the egg that pulsed between them. When Andralia extended her hands, he took them, feeling the now-familiar shock of connection—the sense of circuits closing, of power recognizing power, of two who were meant to amplify each other finally given purpose beyond mere survival.

"Don't let go," Andralia said quietly. "No matter what you feel, what it costs—hold on. The moment you release, the spell collapses, and everything we're trying to prevent happens anyway."

"I won't let go."

"Promise me."

"I promise."

She took a breath—unnecessary underwater but human habits died hard—and closed her eyes. For a moment, nothing happened. The chamber remained unchanged, the egg pulsing with its slow heartbeat, the magic shimmer-guarding it with draconic certainty.

Then Andralia's eyes opened, and they weren't her eyes anymore.

They were doorways. Windows into distances Z'Landar couldn't name, showing depths that had nothing to do with water and everything to do with the spaces between worlds, the gaps where reality thinned and something *other* pressed close.

Her voice, when it came, carried harmonics that shouldn't exist:

"*Space bends. Space folds. Space admits it was never as solid as it claimed.*"

Z'Landar felt the pull—not physically but deeper, felt something within him *flowing* outward through their joined hands. Power he'd barely acknowledged possessing, magic inherited from Kelpie and Selkie and forces older than both, streaming from him into her like water seeking its level.

It didn't hurt. Not exactly. But it *hollowed* him, carved emptiness where strength had been, left him feeling thin and stretched and barely adequate to the task of maintaining consciousness.

Hold on. Don't let go. She needs this. Scotland needs this.

The air—the water—around the egg began to shimmer differently. Not the dragon's protection but something new, something that made Z'Landar's eyes hurt to perceive directly. Reality itself seemed to *squeeze*, as if invisible hands pressed from all sides, making the space around the egg smaller, tighter, compressed into dimensions that defied normal geometry.

The dragon's protective magic resisted. Z'Landar felt it push back, felt layers of carefully crafted wards attempting to maintain their territory, their purpose. But Andralia's power—*their* power, flowing from him into her and through her into the working—proved inexorable as tide.

The shimmer grew smaller. And smaller. Compressing around the egg like a fist closing, like water forced through narrowing channels, like space itself admitting that volume was negotiable when sufficient force demanded renegotiation.

Z'Landar's vision began to gray at the edges. His hands trembled where they gripped Andralia's, his entire body shaking with the effort of maintaining connection while being drained to dregs. Distantly, he heard Maelis's voice—concerned, urging him to stop— but the words made no sense, meant nothing against the imperative of holding on.

Don't let go. Don't let go. Don't—

The protective magic collapsed inward with a sensation like thunder heard through thick walls—present but muffled, powerful but contained. The shimmer compressed to a sphere barely larger than Z'Landar's fist, hovering around the egg's center like a pearl of distorted reality, all its alarm functions and carefully laid warnings squeezed so tightly they could no longer perform their purpose.

Andralia gasped and released his hands.

Z'Landar collapsed, catching himself on stone before he could sprawl completely. His vision swam. His lungs burned despite being underwater where lungs should be irrelevant. His entire body felt wrong—hollow and weak and barely capable of the simple act of remaining upright.

But the egg lay unguarded.

The dragon's protection remained intact—technically unbroken, precisely as Andralia had promised. But compressed beyond functionality, reduced to irrelevance, no more useful than armor shrunk too small to wear.

"Did it... work?" Z'Landar managed through lips that felt numb.

Andralia didn't answer. Couldn't answer. She knelt opposite him, her body shaking with tremors that had nothing to do with cold, her impossible eyes now just eyes again—human and exhausted and carrying the particular blankness of one who had reached too far and paid the price.

Maelis was beside her instantly, supporting her before she could fall. "Easy, child. Easy. The worst is past."

"The egg," Andralia whispered, her voice barely audible. "Destroy it. Before I—before the working—" Her eyes rolled back, and she went limp in Maelis's arms.

Part Four: The Ending of Dreams

Fionnuala caught Z'Landar as he tried to rise, her strength keeping him from following Andralia into unconsciousness through sheer will alone. "The egg, brother. Focus on the egg. We'll tend to her."

Z'Landar forced his vision to clear, forced his body to move despite feeling like he'd been carved hollow. The blessed hammer lay where Caelan had left it—forged for this purpose, waiting for this moment.

He took it in hands that shook, feeling its weight settle with the rightness of destiny delayed too long.

172

The egg pulsed before him, still alive, still dreaming its dreams of fire and flight. Still carrying life that would become destruction if allowed to hatch. And now, finally, it lay unguarded by anything except its own shell and the strength those shells possessed.

Z'Landar raised the hammer.

For one heartbeat, he hesitated. This was life. Innocent life that had made no choices, committed no crimes, done no harm. It simply *was*, following patterns laid down in draconic blood millions of years before Scotland learned to name itself.

Then he thought of thirty-eight Irish villagers reduced to ash. Thought of the mother clutching her three children as fire took them all. Thought of what four dragons would do to Scotland—to the clans gathered at Loch Ness, to the water-folk who had finally found unity, to everything his parents had died to protect.

The hammer fell.

The shell cracked with sound like thunder contained, like reality itself protesting this violation of natural order. Golden ichor—not blood but something other—wept from the fracture, staining the depression's stone with color that would never quite wash away.

The egg's pulse faltered. Stuttered. The heartbeat-sense of life growing within began to weaken.

Z'Landar raised the hammer and struck again.

And again.

And again, until the shell lay in fragments, until the not-quite-formed thing within—serpentine and terrible and mercifully dead before it could fully become what dragons were—lay exposed and ended.

No fire rose from its death. No alarm screamed across the waters. The dragon's magic remained compressed, impotent, bearing no witness to what happened beneath its useless guard.

Silence held in the chamber—broken only by the sound of Z'Landar's ragged breathing, by Andralia's weak stirring in Maelis's arms, by the slow drip of ichor from hammer to stone.

"It's done," Fearchar said quietly from the entrance. "The first egg dies. Scotland is safer by one dragon's measure."

Z'Landar let the hammer fall from nerveless fingers. Let exhaustion he'd been holding at bay finally claim its due. He slumped against the chamber's wall, feeling every hour of swimming, every ounce of power drained into Andralia's working, every moment of the past two days settling onto shoulders barely adequate to their weight.

"How long before she can swim?" he asked, nodding toward Andralia's still form.

"An hour, perhaps," Maelis said, studying her with ancient eyes that missed nothing. "The working took much from her. Space distortion of that magnitude—it's not meant for beings bound to single worlds. She'll recover, but slowly. And the weakness will linger days beyond initial recovery."

An hour. They had an hour before the return journey could begin.

An hour before the race back to Loch Ness, carrying news of first victory and praying it would prove sufficient against what came next.

"We rest here until she can swim," Z'Landar said, his voice carrying authority despite the exhaustion underneath. "The three of you—" he gestured to the Kelpie warriors, "—stand watch. Maelis tends Andralia. Fionnuala, you're with me. We plan the return route— fastest path, minimal stops, every advantage we can gain."

They moved to obey, none arguing against the king's command. Z'Landar forced himself upright despite his body's protests, forced his mind to focus on maps and currents and the mathematics of getting seven exhausted swimmers back to Loch Ness before the dragon arrived to find an army waiting.

Behind him, unguarded now, the shattered egg lay cooling in its stone cradle. The first of four ended. Three remained—two hidden somewhere in Scotland and Ireland, one carried safe within the mother's body.

But for this moment, this small triumph—Scotland was safer by one dragon's measure.

And sometimes, small triumphs were enough to build hope upon.

Part Five: The Return Begins

Andralia woke sixty-three minutes after the spell's completion— Z'Landar had counted every one, watching her breathe, waiting for the eyes to open and prove that the working hadn't broken something fundamental. When her lids finally fluttered, when those impossible eyes found his and held focus, relief flooded through him with force that made his chest tight.

"Did it work?" she asked, her voice hoarse.

"It worked. The egg is destroyed. The dragon's magic never triggered." Z'Landar helped her sit, supporting her weight when she swayed. "How do you feel?"

"Like I tried to fold the universe and discovered it objects to being folded." She managed a weak smile. "But alive. Functional. Ready to swim when needed."

"Can you swim? Truly?"

Andralia tested her limbs, pushing against water with movements that started shaky but gradually steadied. "Yes. Not quickly. Not with any grace. But I can make the distance if we don't press maximum speed."

"We press whatever speed you can manage," Z'Landar said firmly. "I won't risk you by demanding more than you can give."

"The dragon—"

"Hasn't sensed anything. The magic held—compressed but intact. She doesn't know we were here." He touched her face gently. "You did something impossible today. Something that will be sung about when this is over and songs are written. Rest now. We have hours yet before departure makes sense."

They rested in the abandoned settlement, taking turns keeping watch while others recovered what strength could be recovered. Z'Landar found himself drawn back to the chamber where the shattered egg lay, studying the remains of what had been prevented.

The shell fragments held beauty despite their violence—obsidian darkness shot with golden veins, patterns that suggested something beyond random formation. And the creature within, barely formed, its eyes never having opened to see the world it would have burned—

"Don't," Andralia said softly, appearing beside him. "Don't carry guilt for this. You ended a threat. Saved lives that would have been taken when this hatched. The mother may have dreamed of four children— but those children would have been monsters. You did right."

"I know," Z'Landar said. "But knowing and feeling are different tides."

"They are." She leaned against him, still weak but present, her warmth driving back the settlement's chill. "We should go soon. The longer we delay, the less time we have before she arrives in Scotland."

Z'Landar checked the mental calculations he'd been running since Andralia woke. "If we depart now, swim at moderate pace to spare you, stop only when absolutely necessary for rest—we make Loch Ness in perhaps two days. The dragon arrives in two, possibly less."

"So she beats us there."

"By a full day, perhaps more." He let out a breath that held the weight of all he carried. "The army faces her first. Without us. Without their king to lead them."

"They have Alasdair. They have the Elders. They have a thousand warriors who chose to stand together." Andralia straightened despite her exhaustion. "They'll hold until we arrive. And we bring news that makes the holding worthwhile—one egg destroyed, the dragon's protection defeated, proof that we can fight this thing and win."

She was right. Had to be right. Because the alternative—arriving to find Loch Ness burning, the army scattered, the unity so carefully forged shattered by fire and fear—

"We depart now," Z'Landar decided. "Moderate pace as long as you can manage. If you need to stop, we stop. The army can hold one day. They must hold one day. And when we arrive—"

"When we arrive, we finish what we started." Andralia's smile held edges sharp as the destroyed egg's shell. "We show the mother-dragon that Scotland has teeth of its own. And we make her regret every mile she flew north from Ireland."

They gathered the others—Maelis, Fionnuala, the three Kelpie warriors—and departed the settlement as evening fell, swimming south through passages that felt longer now, harder, weighted by exhaustion and knowledge of what raced ahead.

Behind them, the abandoned village returned to its silence. The shattered egg lay cooling in stone that had seen too much death over too many centuries. And the cosmic spiral glowed with faint bioluminescence, marking a place where power older than dragons had been proven insufficient against those determined enough to do what must be done.

Ahead, at Loch Ness, an army prepared for fire.

And somewhere over Scottish waters, wings beat against wind, carrying a mother toward the place where her first child had been ended before its dreams of burning could become real.

The race was on.

The pieces moved.

And soon—very soon—blood would prove which side had prepared better, fought harder, wanted survival more desperately.

Scotland stood ready.

The dragon came.

And between them, seven exhausted swimmers raced against time that cared nothing for their desperation, carrying news that might make the difference between hope and ash.

First egg destroyed. Three remain. The war has begun.

Chapter Fourteen: Fire Descends

She came with the dawn.

Not the gentle dawn that paints Highland waters in shades of rose and amber, that whispers of new beginnings and hope renewed. But dawn nonetheless—the moment when night surrenders its dominion and day claims what darkness thought to hold eternal. In that liminal hour, when the world holds its breath between what was and what might be, the dragon Caoránach crossed from Ireland into Scottish skies.

Those who watched from coastal posts saw her first—a darkness against the lightening east that moved with purpose beyond cloud or storm. Wings that stretched wider than any ship's sails, beating against air with rhythm like thunder's heartbeat. A body serpentine and vast, scales catching first light and throwing it back in shades of obsidian and gold.

Beautiful, in the way that avalanches are beautiful. Terrible, in the manner of forces that care nothing for the smallness of those who stand before them.

The scouts who witnessed her passage sent word racing ahead through waters and across lands: *She comes. The dragon comes. Prepare.*

But preparation, they would learn, was a word that held little meaning when fire descended from heaven itself.

At Loch Ness, the army had grown in the days since Z'Landar departed north. Not merely the thousand who had gathered at the Fire Council, but more—stragglers from distant clans who had needed time to make the journey, water-folk drawn by word of unity forged, those who remembered the Great Wurm and understood that when ancient evils wake, all must stand together lest they fall divided.

Perhaps twelve hundred souls now ringed the loch's shores and filled its depths. Twelve hundred hearts beating with the particular rhythm of those who know death approaches yet choose to meet it with steel drawn and backs unbowed.

Alasdair Fraser commanded the human forces, his weathered face showing the weight of leadership accepted when the rightful king swam north on impossible errand. He had positioned his warriors with care born of decades spent in Highland warfare—archers on the high ground, spearmen in formation along the shore, those who carried shields at the fore to break whatever charge might come.

But how does one position forces against something that flies? Against fire that cares nothing for shields or formation? Against scales that might turn steel as easily as water turns aside a striking hand?

They would learn. Oh, how they would learn.

In the waters, the Kelpie Elders had organized their people with the methodical precision that centuries teach. Tormod commanded the deep positions—warriors who would strike from below should the dragon be foolish enough to enter the loch itself. Eilidh held the shallows with Selkies who could transition between water and shore in heartbeats. Caelan, returned from the northern settlement with news of egg destroyed and king still swimming home, coordinated the mobile forces who would flow wherever need was greatest.

Queen Mhairi watched from a position that balanced safety with visibility—far enough from immediate danger that her death would not shatter Selkie morale, close enough that all could see their former queen had not fled. Around her, the courtiers who had argued against unity now stood silent, their doubts made irrelevant by the reality approaching from the east.

Seasoned warriors moved between water and land, carrying orders, offering wisdom accumulated through generations of survival. Fierce eyes held knowledge that frightened those who looked too closely—the understanding that they prepared to face something beyond their capacity to overcome, that this day would end in blood and grief regardless of courage or determination.

But they prepared nonetheless. Because the alternative was kneeling before terror, and Scots—whether human or water-born—had never learned that particular genuflection.

The dragon reached Loch Ness an hour past dawn, when mist still clung to the water's surface like shroud unwilling to surrender its dead. She circled high at first, a darkness against morning sky, studying what had gathered below with eyes that held intelligence malign and calculating both.

She saw the clans arrayed in their borrowed formations, understood the purpose that had drawn them to this place. Saw the water-folk positioned in depths and shallows, recognized the unity that should not be—that her kind had believed impossible since the First Division when water-peoples learned to hate each other.

She saw, and she understood, and she made her decision in the space between one wingbeat and the next.

These creatures thought to stand against her? Thought their small alliances and smaller courage sufficient to deny her what she would have?

She would teach them the price of opposition.

She would burn their presumption to ash and scatter it across waters that would remember this day when all their names had been forgotten.

She folded her wings and dove.

The first screams began before fire fell—simply the sound of twelve hundred throats releasing terror too vast to contain, a cry that echoed off mountains and made the loch itself seem to shudder. Then came the fire, and screaming found new dimensions.

Dragon-fire burns hotter than forge, brighter than summer sun, with hunger that consumes everything it touches. Stone melts. Water boils. Flesh becomes memory between one breath and the next. The dragon

181

opened her jaws and let fury pour forth in a torrent that painted morning in shades of crimson and gold.

The northern shore erupted into inferno. Warriors who had stood moments before simply ceased—not killed so much as *unmade*, their existence burned away so completely that even ash seemed an insufficient remnant. Trees that had grown for centuries became torches. The very earth caught fire, stone cracking with sounds like the world breaking.

"SHIELDS!" Alasdair's voice cut through chaos, decades of command driving men to action when instinct screamed to flee. "FORMATION! HOLD THE LINE!"

But what line could hold against this? What formation stood before fire that fell like judgment?

The dragon wheeled overhead, vast and terrible, and dove again. This time the eastern shore felt her wrath. More screams. More dead. The scent of burning meat and charred bone and terror made manifest.

In the waters, Tormod gave the order every instinct rebelled against: "ATTACK! STRIKE WHILE SHE'S LOW!"

Kelpies surged forward, taking forms built for speed and power, launching themselves from the loch with force that should have driven them through dragon-scale like spears through leather. They struck her underbelly, her flanks, anywhere they could reach in the brief moment while she remained within range.

And accomplished nothing.

Their strikes that could shatter stone simply slid away from scales that had been forged in fires older than Scotland. Those few who managed to pierce between scales—finding the softer flesh beneath—drew blood that burned as hotly as the fire she breathed, that seared their hands and faces and sent them tumbling back into the water trailing agony.

The dragon's tail swept through their ranks like a scythe through wheat. Bodies—broken and dying—rained back into the loch, staining waters red with sacrifice that would not be remembered because there would be none left to remember.

She rose again, circling, studying her handiwork with eyes that held no mercy, no recognition that those burning below had been living moments before. Just satisfaction. Just the cold certainty of power unchallenged proving itself against those foolish enough to stand where they should have knelt.

"BALLISTA!" someone screamed—perhaps Dougal MacKinnon, perhaps another chief whose name would be lost when this day ended. The siege weapons they had hastily constructed roared to life, heavy bolts screaming through air toward the circling darkness.

One struck true. Pierced the membrane of her left wing. Punched through in a spray of that burning blood, leaving a hole that would heal but that presently caused her flight to falter, to list slightly to one side.

The dragon's roar shook stones from their ancient settings. Shook courage from hearts that thought themselves unshakeable. She wheeled with fury multiplied, dove toward the ballista position with fire already building in her throat.

The weapons crew died without time to scream. The ballista itself melted to slag. The stone they'd positioned it upon cracked and ran like water under heat that should not exist in mortal world.

And still they fought. Because what else remained? Flee into waters where she could follow? Scatter to hills where she could hunt them down one by one? Better to die here, together, having at least attempted to stand.

The Selkies tried their magics—old songs that had turned aside human armies, that had called storms and blessed crops and healed wounds thought mortal. They sang harmony that made the air itself weep with beauty. They offered everything their ancient heritage possessed.

The dragon flew through their spells like they were morning mist. Scattered their magic with her passage. Proved that some forces existed beyond what water-song could touch or turn.

An hour passed. Then two. The dragon circled and dove, dove and burned, with methodical efficiency that spoke of intelligence directing slaughter. She was not maddened—not lost to rage or mindless destruction. She was *teaching*.

Teaching them the cost of gathering against her. Teaching them the futility of resistance. Teaching them that dragons were called dragons not because the word was pretty but because nothing else could name what they were.

The dead numbered in the hundreds now. Perhaps more—hard to count when many had been reduced to ash, when others lay broken in the shallows, when screaming made thinking difficult and smoke obscured everything.

Alasdair fought despite the burns covering his left arm and face, despite watching warriors he'd known since childhood die in fire. He fought because Clan Fraser had never learned surrender, because his king had trusted him to hold until return, because the alternative was kneeling.

Queen Mhairi's voice had gone hoarse from shouting orders, from trying to coordinate forces that grew more scattered with each passing moment. Her beautiful face was smoke-stained, grief-carved. She had watched her people die—Selkies she had ruled for three centuries—and could do nothing but endure and command and pray to whatever forces might listen that survival was still possible.

The dragon landed on the northern shore—the part she had burned first, where nothing lived anymore—and studied them with eyes like burning coals. Studied, and prepared to finish what she had begun. To burn until none remained. To teach a lesson that would never be learned because there would be none left to learn it.

She opened her jaws. Fire built in her throat, visible as a glow that turned the smoke-shrouded morning bright as noon.

And then—

She *stopped*.

Not gradually. Not with the slow uncertainty of one who reconsiders. But instantly, completely, her head snapping around toward the north with violence that spoke of something piercing through her consciousness like a blade.

Those who remained—those who still drew breath and retained capacity to observe—saw her expression shift. Saw intelligence become confusion become *recognition* become something that might have been fear if dragons knew that particular emotion.

Something was wrong. Something had *changed*. Something miles distant but suddenly immediate, suddenly more important than the slaughter half-completed.

Her wards. The magic she had placed around her precious egg, layered with such care, crafted with such precision.

They were broken.

Not triggered. Not screaming alarm across the distance that separated mother from child.

Just... *gone*. Compressed beyond functionality, she realized now in the way one realizes they have been wounded only after noticing the blood. Some magic she could not name had squeezed her protections into irrelevance, had left the egg naked and vulnerable to whatever threatened it.

The dragon launched skyward with a roar that made her previous fury seem gentle by comparison. She arrowed north, wings beating with desperate speed, the gathered forces at Loch Ness forgotten as if they had never existed.

She flew to save what could be saved. To protect what she had thought protected. To kill whatever had dared to threaten the life growing in her first egg's shell.

She flew north toward a settlement already abandoned, where an egg already lay shattered, where only empty chambers and cooling ichor waited to teach her that maternal fury, however vast, arrives too late when it arrives after death.

185

The army watched her depart. Watched the darkness that had been their doom arrowing away toward the northern horizon. Watched until she became a speck, then nothing, then merely memory of terror that had painted morning red.

Then they collapsed.

Not all at once. But in waves—warriors dropping to knees, to seats, to simply lying down where they stood because standing required strength they no longer possessed. Some wept. Some laughed with the particular hysteria of those who have looked into their ending and found it has inexplicably delayed its claim.

Some simply sat silent, staring at nothing, processing what they had witnessed, what they had survived, what they had *lost*.

Alasdair Fraser remained standing through will alone, surveying the devastation with eyes that had seen too much, that would carry these images until death claimed him however many years hence. He counted the dead where counting remained possible, made rough estimates where it did not.

Four hundred. Perhaps five hundred. Dead in the span of three hours. Dead while barely scratching scales that had turned aside their finest efforts. Dead while the dragon barely seemed to notice their resistance.

And yet they lived. Hundreds still drew breath. The army had not been shattered—merely *broken*, which was different, which left hope that mending might be possible.

"Water," he croaked to whoever remained near enough to hear. "Tend the wounded. Count the dead. Find the Elders and the Queen. We need—"

He stopped. Because movement caught his eye—motion in the water where all had gone still, where survivors floated listless, where death had settled in the shallows like a second tide.

Seven shapes. Swimming fast. Swimming with purpose that spoke of those who had not yet witnessed what waited at their destination.

"The King," someone whispered. Others took up the cry. "The King returns!"

Z'Landar broke the surface in the center of Loch Ness, his dark hair plastered to his skull, his face showing exhaustion that went beyond the merely physical. Behind him: Andralia, Maelis, Fionnuala, the three Kelpie warriors who had sworn to follow him north and had kept that oath.

They had swum at a pace that should have killed them. Had pushed through exhaustion and pain and the desperate knowledge that they raced against opponent who flew while they swam.

They had failed. That knowledge settled over Z'Landar like a shroud as he took in the devastation—the burned shores, the bodies floating, the smoke that still rose from a dozen places where fire had caught and refused to surrender what it had claimed.

His eyes found Alasdair. Found Queen Mhairi pulling herself onto what remained of the southern shore. Found hundreds of faces—smoke-stained, grief-carved, carrying wounds that would scar—all turning toward him with expressions that held accusation and hope in measures too tangled to separate.

"Your Majesty," Alasdair said, his voice cracking with smoke and strain. "You're too late. She came. She—" He gestured helplessly at the carnage. "We couldn't stop her. We couldn't even *slow* her. And then she just... left. Flew north like something called her. Just... left."

Z'Landar felt the words settle into his chest like stones. Too late. The dragon had come while he swam south with news of victory that now tasted of ash. Had killed—how many? By the First Waters, *how many had died while he raced homeward?*

"The egg," Andralia said quietly beside him. "The spell wore off. She sensed it threatened." Understanding dawned in her impossible eyes. "She didn't leave because we hurt her. She left because she realized what we'd done."

"Then she flies toward an egg already destroyed," Maelis said. "Toward proof that we can strike her where she thought herself untouchable."

187

"And when she finds it," Fionnuala added, her young voice carrying weight beyond her years, "when she sees what was done—she'll return. And her fury will make this morning seem gentle."

They looked at each other—king and queen, ancient and young, those who had broken dragon magic and those who had held ground against dragon fire. They looked, and they understood that the battle just ended was merely prelude.

The true war had only begun.

And they had three eggs yet to find, yet to destroy, before the mother returned with rage that would make the dawn's burning seem but a candle's flame compared to wildfire.

Z'Landar pulled himself fully from the water, his legs shaking with exhaustion he refused to acknowledge, his voice finding the command that kingship demanded even when he felt like a boy who had failed his first test.

"Tend the wounded. Honor the dead. And prepare—" He looked north, where smoke still rose from shores the dragon had painted in fire. "Prepare for her return. Because she will return. And when she does, we will be ready. We will stand. And we will show her that Scotland—bloodied but unbroken—does not bow to fire."

The army stirred. Not with enthusiasm—that had been burned away with the dead. But with something deeper, more enduring.

With the stubborn certainty that surrender was not written in their nature.

With the knowledge that their king had returned, and while he stood, they would stand also.

The dragon would return.

But so had Z'Landar.

And the fire that had descended would meet water risen to oppose it, no matter the cost, no matter the odds.

Scotland would stand.

Or Scotland would burn.

But it would not kneel.

Never that.

Never.

Chapter Fifteen: The Second Finding

The army had begun the grim work of counting when the water sprite arrived—a flickering thing of light and motion that burst from the loch's depths like a dying star given final, desperate purpose. It spun and darted, its luminescence dimmed by exhaustion that spoke of long travel through waters made dangerous by fire and death, its movements carrying the particular urgency of those who bear news that cannot wait.

Most simply stared, too weary or grief-stricken to process yet another development in a morning already heavy with too much. But Maelis—ancient Maelis who had lived long enough to learn the languages others never knew existed—moved toward the sprite with purpose, her weathered face showing recognition.

"Hush, little one," she said, her voice taking on tones that were not quite words, more like water flowing over particular stones in particular patterns, like wind through reeds that sang meanings rather than melodies. "I hear you. I understand. Rest now. Your message will be delivered."

The sprite pulsed once—gratitude or relief or simply acknowledgment—then faded to barely visible shimmer, conserving what little strength remained after its harrowing journey.

Z'Landar pulled himself fully onto the southern shore, his legs still uncertain beneath him, his body demanding rest his mind refused to grant. Around him, the wounded cried out as healers worked with what supplies remained. The dead lay in rows where they had been gathered, awaiting proper honors when time permitted such things. Smoke still rose from a dozen fires that refused to die, and the air tasted of ash and grief in measures that made breathing itself feel like transgression.

But Maelis's expression—sharp and focused despite the chaos—demanded attention.

"What word does it bring?" Z'Landar asked, moving toward her despite his exhaustion.

"Advance notice," Maelis replied, returning to normal speech patterns. "A Kelpie warrior comes bearing critical information. The sprite raced ahead to prepare us for his arrival—would have come sooner, but the battle..." She gestured helplessly at the devastation. "Fire and fury made the waters impassable for creatures of light. It waited. Watched from a safe distance. And when the dragon departed, it swam with all speed to bring us warning that news approaches."

"What news?" Andralia had joined them, her movements still showing the weakness that lingered from her spell-working, but her eyes alert, focused. "Does it concern the dragon? Her return?"

"The sprite could not say—or perhaps did not know. Only that a warrior comes, swimming with such desperation that the sprite judged the information worth risking burned waters to announce his approach."

Z'Landar's mind raced despite the exhaustion that threatened to drag him into sleep where he stood. A warrior bearing critical news, urgent enough to race through waters still carrying heat from dragon-fire, important enough that the sprite had nearly killed itself bringing advance word—

"The egg," he breathed. "The second egg. He's found it."

Before Maelis could confirm or deny, movement in the loch drew every eye. Not the slow, painful swimming of the wounded returning to shore, nor the cautious approach of scouts ensuring the dragon had truly departed. This was speed incarnate—a Kelpie in full horse-form driving through water with force that sent spray flying, with purpose that spoke of news that could not wait one moment longer than necessary.

The horse reached the shallows and transformed mid-stride, becoming a young warrior Z'Landar recognized from the searches—Beathan, barely past his first century, his scarred face showing equal parts triumph and terror. He stumbled onto shore, chest heaving, water streaming from hair plastered to his skull by speed and spray.

191

"Your Majesty," he gasped, dropping to one knee less from propriety than from legs that could no longer support him. "I bring—the egg—we found—"

"Easy," Z'Landar said, kneeling beside him, one hand on the young warrior's shoulder. "Breathe first. Then speak. Your news will wait the handful of moments it takes to draw proper breath."

Beathan nodded, his chest rising and falling with the desperate rhythm of one who has pushed beyond all reasonable limits. Around them, others had gathered—Alasdair limping over despite his burns, Queen Mhairi pulling herself from the water with Fionnuala's assistance, the Elders who had survived the battle converging with expressions that mixed hope and dread in measures equal.

After perhaps twenty heartbeats that felt like twenty ages, Beathan found voice again.

"Bidean Nam Bian," he said, the mountain's name falling from his lips like a pronouncement of doom. "The egg rests in a high loch beneath the mountain's shadow. Waters so pure they blind when sunlight strikes them. Waters fed by springs that have never known salt, that flow from sources high enough to touch clouds."

"The pure waters," Eilidh breathed from where she had positioned herself among the gathered Elders. "By the First Waters, he's found the second egg."

Z'Landar felt the knowledge settle into his bones with weight that threatened to crush. Bidean Nam Bian—the mountain that marked the heart of Glencoe, that rose higher than most peaks in the southern Highlands, that held lochs and tarns in its embrace like a giant cradling jewels. Six hours' travel from Loch Ness for those who swam hard through connecting rivers and then ran the high country in horse-form. Perhaps eight or ten for those still recovering from battle.

And the dragon—where was the dragon? Flying north toward a settlement where her first egg lay shattered. How long before she discovered the loss? How long before she returned south with fury multiplied?

Hours. Perhaps a day if fortune favored them. No more than that.

They had found the second egg.

And they had no time—*no time at all*—to rest before the race to destroy it must begin.

"Tell me everything," Z'Landar commanded, his voice carrying the authority that kingship demanded even when exhaustion threatened to drag him down. "How did you find it? What guards it? Can you lead us there?"

Beathan nodded, his breathing steadying though his hands still trembled. "We searched every high loch as you commanded—dozens of them scattered through the peaks. Most held nothing. But this one..." He paused, gathering words for what he'd witnessed. "The water itself felt wrong. Too pure. Too cold. Like it had been waiting since before the world learned warmth. And at its heart, in the deepest part where sunlight barely penetrates—"

"The egg," Z'Landar finished.

"Aye. Larger than the first, if the descriptions carried from the north speak true. Pulsing with that same terrible life. And guarded—" Beathan's expression darkened. "Guarded by magic that makes my skin crawl to remember. Not the same as the northern egg's protection. Different. Older, perhaps. Or simply crafted with more care. And, it was the water sprites that finally located it, for the rest of us could not see the egg at all"

"Can you break it?" Alasdair asked, his gaze shifting to Andralia. "The magic. Can you work the same spell that defeated the northern protections?"

Andralia was quiet for a moment, her impossible eyes distant as if seeing things others could not. "Perhaps. If the magic is similar enough. If my strength has recovered sufficiently." She looked at Z'Landar, and he saw doubt there—not in her ability, but in whether her body could survive channeling his power again so soon after the first working. "But we must try. What choice remains?"

Z'Landar's mind worked through calculations that grew more desperate with each passing thought. The army lay broken—not shattered, but incapable of mounting another defense like the morning's. Four hundred dead at minimum. Hundreds more wounded. Morale hanging by threads thin as spider's silk. If the dragon returned before they could destroy the second egg, if she fell upon them with fury fresh and multiplied—

There would be no survivors. None. The slaughter would be absolute, not one heartbeat would remain.

But…

If they destroyed the second egg—if they struck her twice in places she thought untouchable—what would a mother do? What would any creature do when realizing that the enemy could reach her children wherever they hid?

She would flee to protect what remained. Would abandon Scotland entirely to guard the third egg in Ireland where at least she could watch over it directly. Would value the living child over revenge against those who had killed the others.

Unless he was wrong. Unless maternal rage overrode maternal protection. Unless she chose to burn Scotland to ash first and then return to guard what remained.

But he had to believe. Had to trust that dragons—for all their terrible power, for all their alien nature—understood the mathematics of survival. Two eggs lost. One remaining. The living child mattered more than the dead.

"We go," Z'Landar said, decision crystallizing. "Now. Immediately. A small party—those swift enough to make six hours become four, strong enough to fight if fighting becomes necessary. We reach the egg. We destroy it. And we pray that losing two children in as many days teaches the mother to protect the third rather than seeking vengeance for those already gone."

"You've just returned," Tormod protested. "You've swum days without rest. Your body—"

"My body will endure what it must endure," Z'Landar cut him off, his voice sharp enough to draw blood. "The dragon flies north even now. She discovers the first egg's destruction—if she hasn't already. When she turns south again, she comes with fury that will make this morning's burning seem gentle. We cannot stop her. Cannot slow her. Cannot do anything but die if we remain here waiting."

He turned to address all who had gathered—the Elders, the clan chiefs, Queen Mhairi, every soul within hearing who still possessed strength to stand.

"But if we strike again—if we take her second child before she can return to prevent it—we change the calculation. We become not merely annoyance to be burned away, but threat that has proven it can reach what she most values. And threatened children make even dragons reconsider the cost of vengeance."

Silence held for three heartbeats. Five. Then Alasdair—wounded, exhausted, his face still bearing burns that wept clear fluid—straightened as much as his injuries permitted.

"It's mad," he said quietly. "Racing to high country with bodies barely capable of standing. Attempting magic that nearly killed you both mere days ago. Gambling everything on the hope that maternal instinct overcomes maternal rage." He paused. "But it's also the only strategy that gives us chance to survive. Go, Your Majesty. Destroy her second child. And may whatever gods watch over fools and kings grant you the speed you need."

Queen Mhairi moved forward in spite of her injuries, her smoke-stained face showing resolve carved from centuries of rule. "The army will recover what it can. We'll prepare defenses if she returns regardless. We'll tend our wounded and honor our dead. And we'll hold this ground—" her voice strengthened, "—because our King commanded it, and because Scotland does not surrender its heart merely because ancient fire demands it."

"Who goes?" Beathan asked, already knowing the answer would include him. "I can lead you to the exact spot. I know every river and path between here and Bidean Nam Bian."

"You," Z'Landar confirmed. "And myself. Andralia to break the spell. Fionnuala—" his half-sister straightened at being named, "—for her speed and courage both. Maelis, if you can manage another journey when you've barely returned from the last."

"I am three hundred and forty-seven years old," Maelis replied, a smile touching her weathered lips despite the grimness of all that surrounded them. "I did not survive so long by declining to do what must be done merely because it proves inconvenient. I go."

"Five, then." Z'Landar looked at the gathered faces—so many carrying wounds, so many exhausted beyond what flesh should endure. "Five to race the dragon to her second child. Five to gamble Scotland's survival on hope and speed and magic that may fail us."

"Six," came a voice from the water's edge. Caelan pulled himself onto shore, his body showing the morning's battle in cuts and bruises too numerous to count. "You'll need warriors who can fight if the egg proves guarded by more than magic. I've rested and I'm fresh enough. I go."

Z'Landar wanted to argue—wanted to tell Caelan that his wounds required tending, that he'd earned rest after leading search parties and surviving dragon-fire both. But looking at the Elder's face, seeing determination that would not be swayed by commands or concern, he simply nodded.

"Six, then. We leave in ten minutes. Take horse-form or human as your nature allows—the rivers will carry us part of the way, but the high country requires running where swimming cannot reach. Beathan leads. The rest follow at whatever pace we can maintain."

They dispersed to prepare what little preparation ten minutes permitted. Z'Landar moved toward where his father's war-braid lay with his few possessions, intending to secure it properly for the journey ahead. But Andralia's hand on his arm stopped him.

"I cannot take horse-form," she said quietly, and he heard embarrassment in her voice that made his chest tighten. "My nature—the water-forms come easily enough, seal and shapes made for swimming. But the land-forms...I have no Kelpie blood in my veins" She trailed off, unable or

196

unwilling to articulate what he understood without words needing to be spoken.

She was not fully of Earth. Not bound entirely to its shapes and limitations. The forms tied to water came naturally to one whose heritage stretched to stars and oceans older than Scotland. But horse-form—purely terrestrial, evolved for running across ground rather than swimming through depths—that remained beyond her despite the Selkie blood she carried.

"Then you ride," Z'Landar said, understanding settling as simply as that. "Upon my back in horse-form. I'm strong enough to carry you. We'll move slower than if you had your own form, but we'll move fast enough."

"Z'Landar, I can't ask you to—after everything you've already—"

"You're not asking." He cupped her face gently, seeing past the exhaustion and doubt to the woman who had nearly killed herself channeling his power into magic that had saved them all. "You're accepting what I offer freely. What I need to offer because leaving you behind is unthinkable and you being here matters more than speed. And the Selkies among us must needs travel in human form, running their best, but still behind the pace of a horse."

Her eyes—those impossible eyes that had seen stars he could only imagine—filled with tears she didn't let fall. "Thank you," she whispered.

"Thank me by breaking the second egg's magic," Z'Landar replied. "Thank me by surviving what comes next. Thank me by being here when this ends and songs are written."

He kissed her then, brief and fierce, tasting smoke and exhaustion and love that had formed too quickly but felt ancient as the mountains they would soon run through. Then he stepped back, took the war-braid and secured it properly, and prepared himself for transformation.

"Ten minutes," he called to the others. "Then we run."

They departed Loch Ness as the sun climbed toward noon, Kelpies in horse-form thundering through shallows and up onto the southern shore where the dragon's fire had not reached, Selkies as human running their best. Beathan led, his dark coat gleaming wet, his movements showing the nervous energy of one who had already run these paths and knew the way. Behind him came Caelan, powerful and steady despite his wounds. Then Fionnuala, smaller but swift, her silver coat catching light like her mother's hair once had. Maelis ran with the ease of one who had taken this form so many thousands of times it felt as natural as her birth-shape.

And Z'Landar, carrying Andralia.

She sat astride him as humans rode horses, though nothing about this was typical riding. Her hands tangled in his mane—not pulling, just holding, maintaining connection that went beyond the merely physical. Her weight settled across his back in ways that should have been burden but felt instead like purpose. Like carrying something precious. Like being trusted with what mattered most.

They ran.

Not the desperate sprint of those fleeing death—that pace could not be maintained for six hours, would burn them out before they'd covered half the distance. But the ground-eating canter that Kelpies had perfected across centuries of ranging through Highlands that demanded both speed and endurance from those who would survive their vastness. When possible, Kelpies carried Selkies to maintain the canter, but when climbing it was the human form with the advantage.

They followed rivers where rivers would carry them toward their destination—splashing through shallows, swimming briefly through pools too deep for running, then emerging to run again when the water grew too narrow or the terrain demanded land-passage. They crossed glens where clans dwelt, where humans came to doorways and windows to watch the strange procession— horses and humans running with purpose that spoke of matters beyond mortal concern, one bearing a rider whose face showed neither fear nor excitement but only the particular focus of those who understand that everything depends on speed.

The land rose as they traveled south and west. The gentle hills near Loch Ness gave way to steeper slopes, to valleys carved deeper by ice and time, to country that grew wilder with each mile until civilization seemed a memory from another world entirely. They ran through purple heather that caught at their legs, forded streams that ran cold enough to numb, climbed paths that wound between peaks whose names were older than the language used to speak them.

And they ran in silence, saving breath for running rather than words, each lost in thoughts that ranged from desperate hope to quiet acceptance that they raced toward their ending as surely as they raced toward the egg.

Z'Landar felt Andralia's weight shift occasionally—adjusting for his gait, for the terrain, for the exhaustion he knew must be claiming her even though she made no complaint. He felt her hands in his mane, her thighs gripping his sides, her presence a constant reminder of why he pushed beyond what body and spirit both suggested was their limit.

For her. For Scotland. For parents who died believing their sacrifice mattered. For the army that holds ground because their king commanded it. For the hope—fragile as morning mist but real nonetheless—that maternal instinct might prove stronger than maternal rage.

The sun tracked across the sky, marking hours that felt both eternal and insufficient. Three hours. Four. The landscape grew more dramatic— peaks rising like ancient teeth, valleys plunging to depths where streams ran white with the force of their falling. This was the true Highlands— the place where Scotland showed its bones, where beauty and terror were names for the same thing, where humans built their small lives in the spaces between stone and sky and called it home because nowhere else would have them.

Five hours. The horses flagged despite Kelpie endurance, despite determination that pushed beyond merely physical limits. Sweat darkened their coats. Their breathing came harder. Caelan's limp—barely noticeable at the journey's start—had grown more pronounced. Even Beathan, who had already made this run once, showed signs of strain that spoke of limits approaching.

But ahead—rising above the surrounding peaks like a king among lesser nobles—Bidean Nam Bian thrust skyward in shades of gray and green, its summit lost in clouds that seemed to bow before its majesty. The mountain that held Glencoe in its shadow. The mountain beneath whose slopes a dragon had hidden her precious child.

The mountain they would climb to commit murder most necessary.

"There," Beathan gasped, his horse-form taking human shape as he stopped at the edge of a stream that tumbled down from heights above. He pointed upward, toward where the mountain's flanks held a basin barely visible from this angle. "The loch lies in that hollow—perhaps an hour's climb on foot, half that in horse-form if the path permits. But the way grows steep. Treacherous. And the water..." He paused. "The water will know we approach. Will know we come with ill intent. The magic that guards the egg—it's woven into the loch itself. We'll feel it the moment we enter those waters."

Z'Landar transformed, feeling his body protest the change, feeling muscles that had carried Andralia for five hours screaming their displeasure at being asked to perform yet another service. He helped Andralia dismount, his hands steadying her when her own legs proved uncertain after so long astride.

The others shifted to human form as well, all showing the journey's toll. Fionnuala's face was pale. Maelis moved with the careful deliberation of one whose age had finally caught up with determination. Caelan's wounds—reopened during the run—wept fresh blood that stained his clothing.

They were exhausted. Barely capable of what came next. And they had found the egg with perhaps an hour or two to spare before the dragon discovered her first loss and turned south again.

"We climb," Z'Landar said, because what else could be said? "We find the egg. Andralia breaks the magic. We destroy it. And we descend before the mother returns to find another child dead."

He looked up at the mountain—vast and ancient and uncaring of the small dramas played out by creatures who lived and died in spans that were to mountains less than heartbeats. Looked at the clouds that wreathed its summit. Looked at the path—barely visible, more goat-track than road—that wound upward toward where a loch waited with its terrible treasure.

"One hour," he said. "One hour to climb. One hour to save Scotland."

They began the ascent, leaving the gentle valley behind, climbing toward pure waters and purer purpose.

Behind them, at Loch Ness, an army waited and hoped and prayed to gods who had proven themselves distracted at best.

Ahead, beneath waters so clear they hurt to look at, an egg pulsed with life that dreamed of fire.

And somewhere in the northern Highlands, a dragon landed in an abandoned settlement and discovered that dreams—even draconic dreams—could end in shattered shells and golden ichor cooling on stone that remembered every grief ever suffered within its embrace.

The race was nearly run.

And soon—very soon—they would learn if maternal love meant fleeing to guard what remained, or returning to burn those who had dared to strike at a mother's heart.

Chapter Sixteen: The Breaking of Pure Waters

The climb tested them in ways the journey had not.

Not merely the steepness—though the path rose at angles that made each step a negotiation between forward motion and the pull of earth seeking to reclaim what dared ascend. Not merely the stone itself—though the rocks shifted treacherously beneath feet that sought purchase, and more than once a misstep sent cascades of scree tumbling down into valleys that seemed to mock their ambitions with echoes. Not merely the air— though it grew thin as they climbed, each breath requiring effort that left lungs burning and minds slightly disconnected from the bodies they commanded.

But all of it together. The accumulation of difficulty upon difficulty, of obstacle following obstacle, of a mountain that seemed to ask with each upward meter: *Are you certain? Are you determined enough? Do you truly wish to reach what waits above?*

They climbed regardless.

Beathan led, his young body showing the resilience of one who had made this ascent before, though even he moved with care that spoke of respect for stone that had broken stronger climbers than himself. Behind him came Caelan, his wounds protesting every movement, leaving small stains of blood on rocks where he paused to rest his hand. Fionnuala followed with the particular grace of youth not yet taught to fear falling, though Z'Landar saw how her hands trembled when she thought none watched.

Maelis climbed with the methodical patience of one who had learned across centuries that haste on mountains accomplished nothing save hastening one's descent—whether controlled or catastrophic. And Z'Landar brought the rear, his body remembering every mile of the journey south from the northern settlement, every hour carrying Andralia across country that had seemed designed to break will and body both, every moment since the dragon's fire had painted morning in shades of ash and grief.

202

But he climbed. Because the alternative was waiting below while others risked themselves. Because kingship meant leading from the front even when the front required ascending paths that goats would reject as unreasonable.

The sun tracked lower in the western sky as they climbed, painting the peaks in shades of amber and rose, casting shadows that lengthened like fingers reaching toward night. An hour had been Beathan's estimate. They were into their second hour when the path—if such generosity could be applied to what they traversed—finally began to level, when stone gave way to alpine grass, when the sound of water falling reached ears that had heard only wind and breathing and the occasional curse when rock betrayed grip.

"There," Beathan gasped, pointing ahead with hand that shook from more than exertion.

The loch spread before them like a jewel lost by some giant who had wandered these heights before the world learned to count its ages. Not large—perhaps two hundred yards across at its widest, less than half that in breadth. But *pure* in ways that defied mere description. The water held such clarity that the bottom—twenty, thirty fathoms down at the deepest point—showed as clearly as if only air separated eye from stone below.

And the light. By all the First Waters, the *light*.

The setting sun struck the loch's surface and shattered into brilliance that made eyes water and turn away, made the very air seem to catch fire with reflected glory. This was what Beathan had meant when he spoke of waters so pure they blinded. This was what the Puca had named when describing the second egg's hiding place.

Waters that had never known salt. That flowed from sources touched only by rain and snow and the particular blessing that high places sometimes bestow upon those patient enough to reach them.

And somewhere in those depths—invisible to eyes that should have been able to see everything through such clarity—an egg waited.

203

"I don't see it," Fionnuala whispered, her voice carrying the confusion they all felt. "If the water is this clear, if we can see the bottom stones—where is the egg? How can it hide?"

Maelis moved to the water's edge, her ancient eyes narrowing as she studied the loch with intensity born of lifetimes spent reading what others missed. "Invisibility," she said finally. "A spell woven around it, making it unseen to those who look with ordinary sight. Clever. In waters this pure, any object should be visible from surface to bottom. But make the object itself invisible—"

"And it becomes the one thing that *should* be seen but cannot be," Z'Landar finished. "Hidden by the very clarity that should reveal it. No wonder only the wee sprites could spot it."

"Can you break it?" Caelan asked, already moving toward Andralia with question implicit in his gaze. "Can you make it seen?"

But Andralia stood at the water's edge with an expression that Z'Landar had learned to read in the days since she'd appeared in his life bringing mystery and power in equal measure. Not confidence. Not the particular focus she'd shown before working the spell that compressed space itself around the first egg.

Doubt.

"I don't—" she began, then stopped, gathering words that seemed reluctant to form. "Invisibility isn't space or matter. It's perception. Making eyes slide away from what exists, convincing sight that nothing occupies space where something clearly does. I can't compress perception. Can't fold *not-seeing* into something too small to function."

"Then how do we find it?" Beathan's voice carried edges of desperation. "How do we destroy what we cannot see?"

Before anyone could answer, light flickered at the loch's edge—water sprites, dozens of them, emerging from the depths with the particular hesitance of creatures who had learned that approaching those who wielded power required care. They spun and darted, their luminescence painting patterns across water that held no other light save what sky granted.

204

And they congregated. Gathered above a point perhaps thirty yards from shore, perhaps fifteen fathoms down, where—

Nothing.

Even knowing where to look, Z'Landar saw nothing. Just clear water, visible stone, and sprites circling above what his eyes insisted did not exist.

"They can see it," Maelis breathed. "Creatures of pure light—they see what we cannot. They mark the spot for us."

"Then we know where it rests." Z'Landar began removing what little clothing his journey had required—the war-braid already secured, the shell-map safe in its pouch, nothing else that mattered save the pendant he never removed. "I'll swim down. Touch it. Feel its shape even if I cannot see it. And then—"

He dove before the sentence completed, taking seal-form mid-dive, the cold striking through fur and flesh with force that would have stolen breath if breath had been required in this shape. Down through waters so pure they seemed not water at all but some crystalline medium that happened to share water's properties. Down toward where sprites circled and something invisible waited.

Twenty fathoms. Twenty-five. The pressure built, the light dimmed despite the clarity, the sprites grew closer—

His nose struck something solid.

Not hard—he'd been moving slowly, carefully, hands extended before him seeking what eyes could not find. But solid nonetheless. Large. Smooth. Warm in ways that water this high and cold should never permit.

The egg.

He felt along its surface, mapping dimensions that were indeed larger than the first—perhaps twice his own length in seal-form, as wide as his horse-form stood tall at shoulder. Pulsing with that same terrible life, that same slow heartbeat of something growing toward wings and fire and devastation.

He surfaced, transformed, gasped air that felt precious after the cold below.

"It's there," he confirmed. "Thirty yards out, fifteen fathoms down. Large. Very large. And warm."

"The repulsion," Beathan said, and his voice carried warning that made Z'Landar's chest tighten. "I didn't mention—there was no time—but when we tried to touch it, when we attempted to strike it—" He gestured helplessly. "It threw us back. Not with violence, precisely. More like... rejection. Like the egg refuses to acknowledge physical contact, reflects it back upon whoever attempts approach."

Z'Landar looked at Andralia, saw her already understanding what this meant. Two spells protecting the second egg. Invisibility to hide it. Repulsion to prevent physical harm. The dragon had taken great measures—had protected her second child with magics layered and comprehensive.

"Can you break them?" he asked quietly. "Both spells together?"

Andralia moved to the water's edge, knelt, placed both hands beneath the surface. Her eyes—those impossible eyes—went distant, seeing past the merely physical into realms where magic existed as tangible as stone. After long moments that felt like ages, she withdrew her hands and met Z'Landar's gaze with expression that held sorrow and frustration in measures equal.

"No," she said simply. "The invisibility I might overcome—given time, given preparation, given strength I no longer possess after breaking the first egg's protection. But the repulsion..." She shook her head. "It's not a barrier. Not a shield. It's a fundamental redirection of force. Anything that touches the egg directly has its force returned to source. Strike it, and you strike yourself. Try to compress space around it—" her voice caught, "—and the compression reflects back into whoever attempts the working. I would destroy myself trying to harm it."

Silence held for three heartbeats that felt like hammers striking anvil.

"Then we've failed," Fionnuala whispered. "We've climbed all this way, raced the dragon, gambled Scotland's survival—and we cannot touch what we came to destroy."

"No," Z'Landar said, the word emerging with certainty he did not entirely feel but kingship demanded he project. "We've learned we cannot touch it *directly*. But who speaks of direct touch?"

He looked around—at the stone that formed the loch's basin, at the cliffs rising above them, at the mountain itself that had watched their ascent with the particular patience of things that measure time in ages rather than heartbeats.

"If force applied to the egg reflects back," he said slowly, working through the logic even as he spoke it, "then we don't apply force to the egg. We apply force to what surrounds it. We make the mountain itself do our work."

"You mean—" Maelis's eyes widened with understanding. "Collapse stone upon it. Bury it beneath weight too vast for any repulsion to reflect."

"Can you do that?" Caelan asked, skepticism and hope warring in his voice. "Can you move stone on that scale?"

Z'Landar looked at his hands—at flesh that had channeled power into Andralia's working, that had carried Andralia across six hours of country, that had swum and fought and endured across days that felt like years compressed. He thought of what Andralia had sensed during the first egg's destruction—his power surging through her, vast beyond her expectations, nearly consuming her with its magnitude.

He thought of what Maelis had said about the star-travelers, about heritage that stretched beyond Scotland to places where power was measured differently.

He thought of his parents, standing in the Heart of the Loch, choosing death so he might be born carrying possibilities they could only imagine.

"I can try," he said. "And trying will have to suffice."

He moved to where the loch's basin met the cliff face—where centuries of water flowing across stone had carved channels and weakened structures that appeared solid but held fractures invisible to casual observation. He placed both hands against stone that felt cold enough to burn, that radiated the particular permanence of mountains, and he reached *inward*—seeking the power that Andralia had glimpsed, that he himself barely understood.

It rose like tide responding to moon's pull. Like water remembering it had once been part of oceans that covered worlds now dust. Like something fundamental acknowledging that stone, for all its seeming permanence, was merely slow water—frozen in forms that patience and force could reshape.

The stone groaned.

Not loudly. Not with the violence of earthquake or avalanche. But with sound like the world adjusting its weight, like bones settling after long stillness, like something ancient agreeing—reluctantly, grudgingly—to move at the behest of one who asked with sufficient authority.

"Back," Z'Landar gritted through teeth clenched against the effort. "Away from the edge. This will not be gentle."

They retreated—all save Andralia, who remained close enough to touch, her presence somehow making the working easier, as if she amplified not the power itself but his *connection* to it, his ability to channel what lived within him into the world beyond skin and bone.

The cliff face shuddered. Cracks appeared—hairline fractures spreading like lightning frozen in stone, branching and diverging, seeking weaknesses that centuries of water and ice had carved. Small stones fell first, splashing into the loch with sounds like thunder's distant cousins. Then larger rocks, tumbling down with crashes that made the ground shake.

Then section the size of a cottage tore free, falling with majesty terrible and slow into waters so pure they seemed to protest being thus invaded. The splash rose higher than the cliff itself, a wall of water climbing skyward before gravity reclaimed it and pulled it back down in curtains of spray that caught dying light and scattered it in rainbows fleeting as hope.

The falling stone struck where sprites had circled.

Struck what eyes could not see but Z'Landar's power *knew* existed—egg hidden by invisibility, protected by repulsion that could turn aside force applied directly but proved helpless against the simple weight of mountain falling from above.

The water churned. Boiled. Something beneath the surface *screamed*—not with voice, not with sound that ears could process, but with a cry that registered in bones and blood and the places where life recognized its ending.

More stone fell. The cliff face—undermined by Z'Landar's power, by cracks expanded beyond their capacity to hold—began shedding pieces like a tree losing leaves to autumn's command. Tons of rock, accumulated across ages, tumbled into the loch with force that raised waves that broke against shores and sent spray high enough to wet those who had retreated to what they thought was safety.

The egg broke beneath that weight.

Not cleanly, as hammer had broken the first. But crushed—shell and membrane and the thing growing within all compressed together beneath stone that cared nothing for dragon magic, that answered only to gravity's ancient and implacable law.

Golden ichor bloomed in pure waters, spreading in clouds that seemed obscene against such clarity. The loch—which moments before had shown every pebble on its bottom with perfect definition—grew murky with the dying of what should never have been born.

Z'Landar fell to his knees, hands still pressed against stone that had moved at his command, feeling the power drain from him like water from a broken vessel. Not the hollow exhaustion of the first working—that had been Andralia channeling his strength through herself. This was different. This was spending his own power directly, shaping reality through will alone, learning in one terrible moment exactly how much

209

force he could command and how little he understood about controlling it properly.

Too much. He had used too much. The cliff face continued crumbling, more stone than necessary falling into waters that needed no further violence to accomplish what had already been done.

"Stop," Andralia said, her hands on his face, turning it away from the destruction he had wrought. "Stop, beloved. It's done. The egg is destroyed. You can stop now."

Her voice reached through the roaring in his ears—sound like a river in flood, like water remembering it wanted to be free, like power seeking any outlet rather than remaining contained. With effort that felt like lifting mountains from within his own chest, Z'Landar pulled back, closed doors he hadn't known were open, let the power settle back into whatever depths it normally occupied.

The cliff face groaned one final time, shed one final load of stone, then went still.

Silence descended—broken only by water finding new equilibrium around obstacles that had not existed moments before, by breathing harsh and fast from six people who had witnessed something beyond their capacity to fully comprehend.

"By the First Waters," Beathan whispered. "What *are* you?"

Z'Landar had no answer. Barely had consciousness to process the question. He slumped against Andralia, feeling her arms around him, feeling her strength supporting him when his own had been spent reshaping a mountain's face to serve purposes mountains were never meant to contemplate.

"It's done," Caelan said, his voice carrying relief and something that might have been awe. "The second egg. Destroyed. We've struck her twice in places she thought untouchable. Surely now—"

He stopped.

Because sound carried across the Highlands—traveling from north to south, from peaks to valleys, from wherever the dragon had flown after discovering her first child shattered. Not roar. Not the battle-cry she had loosed above Loch Ness. Not the fury that had painted morning in fire.

This was worse.

This was the sound of a mother realizing that death had claimed not one child but two. That protection—however carefully crafted, however layered with magics ancient and powerful—had proven insufficient. That enemies existed who could reach what she most valued despite her best efforts to shield them.

This was maternal grief given voice.

The shriek split the evening sky, made stones tremble and water shiver, sent birds fleeing from roosts and caused every creature within hearing to pause and acknowledge that something fundamental had broken in ways that could not be mended. It rose and fell and rose again, cycling through octaves that held notes no throat should produce, building until the very air seemed to crack beneath its weight.

Then it changed.

The grief remained, but something else joined it. Not rage—rage she had already demonstrated, rage they had survived. This was different. This was *fear*. The recognition that two eggs lost meant patterns emerging, meant enemies who could strike again, meant the third child—hidden in Ireland where she'd thought it safe—now stood as vulnerable as the first two had proven.

The shriek dopplered, growing fainter with each repetition.

She flew.

Not toward them. Not south to Loch Ness where an army waited bloodied but unbowed. Not toward vengeance or fury or the burning that grief and rage together might have demanded.

She flew west. Toward Ireland. Toward the third egg. Toward the single child that remained hidden and therefore still saveable.

211

She fled to guard what could be guarded.

The strategy had worked.

Z'Landar wanted to feel triumph. Wanted to rise and proclaim that Scotland had survived, that maternal love had indeed overridden maternal rage, that his gamble on dragon psychology had proven sound.

Instead, he simply knelt in alpine grass beside waters no longer pure, beside a cliff face carved into new shapes by power he barely controlled, and felt consciousness slipping away like water through fingers too exhausted to close into fist.

"Rest," Andralia whispered, easing him down to earth that felt impossibly solid after all that had moved at his command. "You've earned it. Scotland survives. The dragon flees. And we—" her voice caught, "—we live to see another dawn."

The others collapsed around them, exhaustion claiming what adrenaline and determination had held at bay. Six bodies sprawled in grass, beside a loch that would carry golden stains until time wore them away, beneath a sky that darkened toward the night that waited patient as mountains for small dramas to complete themselves.

Far to the west, a dragon flew with speed born of desperation, wings beating with rhythm that spoke of the terrible mathematics survivors understand—that living children matter more than dead ones, that protection sometimes means retreat, that maternal love calculates in ways maternal rage cannot comprehend.

Scotland had survived the morning's fire.

Scotland had gambled on dragon psychology and won.

But Z'Landar, lying in grass with Andralia's warmth beside him and his friends scattered around him like pieces of a war that had been fought and survived, understood something that would trouble his dreams in nights to come:

They had only won time.

The dragon would guard her third child with fury redoubled. Would let nothing—*nothing*—threaten what remained of her line. And when time came to face her again, she would remember the two who had been taken from her.

Would remember, and would make Scotland pay the price that grief demanded.

But that was tomorrow's problem.

Tonight, they rested.

Tonight, Scotland breathed.

And tonight, for the first time since fire descended, Z'Landar allowed himself to believe that perhaps—*perhaps*—they might survive what came next.

The dice had been cast.

Scotland still stood.

And the dragon, for now, flew away.

It would have to be enough.

Chapter Seventeen: The Standing Stones

They descended from Bidean Nam Bian as dawn painted the eastern sky in shades that seemed too gentle for a world that knew dragons. The journey down proved harder than the climb—legs that had carried them upward through desperate necessity now trembled with exhaustion that would not be denied, and more than once a misplaced step sent stone tumbling into valleys that waited patient as mountains for those foolish enough to test their mercy.

But they descended regardless. Because Scotland waited below, and armies required their king even when their king could barely manage one foot before the other.

Two days the return journey consumed—two days of swimming through rivers that ran cold with autumn's approach, of pausing to rest when rest became necessity rather than luxury, of watching the landscape shift from wild highlands to the more settled country surrounding Loch Ness. Two days during which Z'Landar felt his body slowly remember what it was to move without agony, felt strength return in measures grudging and insufficient.

The army they returned to was changed.

Not broken—they had been broken after the dragon's fire, after losing four hundred souls to flames that cared nothing for courage or determination. But *changed*. Those who remained moved with the particular care of people who had looked into their ending and survived only through fortune's caprice. They tended the wounded who would carry scars until death claimed them. They honored the dead who lay in rows awaiting rites that would send them to whatever waters received those who died far from home.

And they prepared. Because the dragon had fled west, and everyone who could think understood that fleeing dragons eventually stopped fleeing.

Z'Landar found Queen Mhairi on the loch's southern shore, where healers fussed over her with the determined futility of those who knew their efforts made little difference but refused to acknowledge that knowledge. The burns she had taken during the dragon's assault covered her left side—shoulder to hip, angry red against skin that had known three centuries without such marking. But worse than the burns were the shadows beneath her eyes, the way her breath came shallow and careful, the particular stillness of one who moved only when movement could not be avoided.

"Your Majesty," Z'Landar said quietly, approaching with Andralia at his side. "You should be resting."

Mhairi's smile held edges worn by pain and time both. "I have been resting, young king. Resting while you swam north and south and climbed mountains to murder dragon eggs. Resting while my people prepared for wars I am too old and too wounded to lead them through." She paused, gathering breath for words that clearly cost her. "Tell me you succeeded. Tell me the second egg lies as dead as the first."

"It does," Andralia confirmed, moving to kneel beside the queen with gentle grace. "Crushed beneath a mountain's weight. The dragon knows her children die in places she thought untouchable. She has fled to Ireland to guard what remains."

"Then Scotland breathes." Mhairi's eyes drifted closed for a moment. "For how long, I wonder? How long before maternal grief becomes maternal rage, before she returns with fury we barely survived the first time?"

"She will not return," Z'Landar said, speaking with certainty he did not entirely feel. "Not while a living child remains vulnerable in Ireland. She will guard it. Let nothing threaten it. We have bought time—not days, but weeks perhaps if fortune favors us."

"Time to do what?" The queen's eyes opened again, focusing with intensity that belied her weakened state. "To recover? To rebuild? To prepare defenses that proved worthless against her fire?" She shook her head slightly. "No. You plan to go after her. To Ireland, where she hides. To finish what you started when you broke her first child's shell."

215

It was not a question. Z'Landar did not insult her by pretending otherwise.

"We must," he said simply. "Two eggs remain. One she carries, one hidden somewhere in Ireland. We cannot leave her to guard them indefinitely. Cannot give her time to strengthen protections, to plan vengeance, to hatch what grows within her body. We must strike while she is wounded—not in flesh, but in spirit. While maternal fear overrides maternal rage."

"You will need an army." Mhairi's gaze traveled across the loch, taking in the survivors who moved with such careful determination. "But the clans are broken. Lost too many. Cannot field the forces that Ireland deserves from its neighbor." She paused. "The water-folk will go. My Selkies. The Kelpies. The Merrow who crossed from Ireland to stand with us. We will swim where ships cannot quickly reach, will fight where human warriors cannot breathe."

"You will lead them?" Andralia asked quietly.

Silence held for three heartbeats. Five. Then Mhairi's expression shifted into something that held grief and acceptance in measures that made Z'Landar's chest tighten.

"No," the queen said, her voice carrying weight of centuries acknowledging their ending. "I am old. Three hundred years I have ruled the Selkies—longer than any queen before me, watching generations be born and die while I endured. I have fought wars and won them. Have led my people through trials that should have broken us. Have survived because I was strong and wise and willing to do what survival demanded." She touched her burned side gently. "But dragon-fire cares nothing for strength or wisdom or willingness. It burns what it touches, and what it touched in me..." She trailed off, then continued with voice grown softer. "I am dying, Z'Landar. Not today, perhaps not tomorrow. But the healers know it. I know it. And I will not lead my people into Ireland's waters only to fail them when they need me most."

"Your Majesty—" Andralia began, but Mhairi raised one hand.

"Hush, child. I have lived longer than any Selkie has right to expect. Have seen wonders and terrors both. Have ruled well and poorly in turns, as all who rule must. But I will not—*will not*—carry my people into battle I cannot survive, leaving them leaderless in enemy waters facing a dragon whose fury I can barely imagine." She looked at Z'Landar with eyes that had seen empires rise and crumble. "You are King of All Waterfolk now. The Selkies will follow you to Ireland. Will fight under your command. Will trust that you value their lives as I have valued them."

The weight of those words settled onto shoulders already carrying more than seemed bearable. Z'Landar wanted to protest—wanted to tell her that she would heal, that healers worked miracles, that three centuries of rule could not end with burns from dragon-fire and a war still unwon.

But looking at her—truly looking, seeing past the queen to the person beneath who had given everything to her people and now gave the last thing remaining—he understood that protest would be cruelty masquerading as kindness.

"I will guard them as my own," he said quietly. "Will value each life as precious. Will lead them with the wisdom you have shown me. And when this war ends—when dragons are memory and eggs are dust—I will ensure that songs remember the queen who loved her people enough to let them go."

Mhairi's eyes glistened, though whether from pain or emotion or simple exhaustion, Z'Landar could not say. "Good," she whispered. "That is good." She gestured weakly toward the gathered forces. "Now leave me to my healers. You have planning to do. Forces to organize. And—" her gaze shifted to Andralia, "—parents to visit, I think. Yes. I see it in your eyes. Questions that need answering. Truths that cannot wait."

Andralia started, surprised. "How did you—"

"I am old, child. Old enough to recognize when young ones carry burdens they were not meant to carry alone. Old enough to know when cosmic matters press close and demand attention." She smiled faintly. "Go. Visit the high waters where your mother maps mysteries. Learn what you need to learn. Then return, and we will speak of Ireland and dragons and the wars that wait for those brave or foolish enough to seek them."

They departed Loch Ness at dawn two days later, swimming east and north toward waters that grew colder and higher with each mile. Maelis had provided directions—speaking of Loch Etchachan with the reverence one reserved for places that predated history, that held significance beyond the merely geographical. "The standing stones watch there," she had said, her ancient eyes distant. "Have watched since before the first Kelpie learned to take horse-form. Your mother chose that place for a reason, Andralia. To be close to what matters. To study what most would not recognize as worth studying."

The journey took two days—might have been done in one, but weary bones and even more weary souls required time to heal - swimming up rivers that grew narrow and cold, that flowed from sources touched only by rain and snow, that tasted of stone and sky and the particular purity that high places granted to water patient enough to wait for it. They traveled alone, leaving behind the army that prepared for Ireland, the councils that planned for war, the weight of kingship and responsibility and all the small necessities that consumed days when days should be spent otherwise.

They swam in silence mostly, saving words for when words mattered, but the silence felt comfortable rather than awkward. Z'Landar found himself watching Andralia as they traveled—the grace with which she moved through water, the way her impossible eyes caught light and scattered it in ways that seemed to defy natural law, the particular presence she carried that spoke of origins beyond Scotland, beyond Earth, beyond anything he could fully comprehend but was learning to accept as simply part of who she was.

"You're staring," she said without looking at him, amusement coloring her tone.

"I'm admiring," Z'Landar corrected. "There's a difference."

"Is there?" She glanced at him, smile playing at the corners of her mouth. "Admiring what, precisely? My seal-form's elegance? My swimming technique? The way my hair streams behind me in currents?"

"All of it," he said honestly. "Everything. The fact that you exist at all seems impossible—daughter of stars and sea both, carrying powers I cannot name but am learning to recognize. The fact that you chose to stay, to fight beside me, to love me—" He stopped, the word having emerged unbidden but feeling right nonetheless.

Andralia halted her swimming, treading water in a pool where the river widened enough to permit pause. Her eyes—those windows into distances he could barely imagine—fixed on him with intensity that made his breath catch.

"Love you," she repeated softly. "Yes. That's the word for it, isn't it? I have loved you since the moment I saw you in waters that should have killed me, saw you dive without hesitation to save a stranger. Have loved you through council meetings and dragon hunts and watching you reshape mountains with power you barely understand." She moved closer, her hand finding his beneath the water's surface. "I love you, Z'Landar. Beloved. My king. My heart."

He kissed her there, in cold waters that flowed from high places, with mountains watching their exchange with the particular indifference of things that measured time in ages. Kissed her with desperation and tenderness mixed, tasting the strangeness of her—salt and stars and something indefinable that spoke of origins his mind could not quite encompass.

When they parted, both slightly breathless despite water-breathing making such things irrelevant, Z'Landar pressed his forehead to hers.

"Whatever we learn at the stones," he said quietly, "whatever your mother reveals about spirals and patterns and cosmic significance—know that what I feel for you is choice, not destiny. That I love you because you are *you*, not because some universal pattern arranged our meeting."

"Can it not be both?" Andralia asked, her smile holding depths he was still learning to navigate. "Can we not be chosen by pattern and choosing each other both? Love that is meant and meant simultaneously?"

He had no answer. Perhaps there was no answer. They swam on, climbing toward waters that waited higher still.

219

Loch Etchachan lay cradled in the Cairngorms like a secret kept by mountains, surrounded by peaks that rose in shades of gray and purple against sky that seemed closer here, more immediate, as if the barrier between earth and heaven grew thin at this elevation. The loch itself was small—perhaps half a mile across at its widest point—but deep and cold and so clear that the bottom could be seen even in its center, where depth should have rendered such visibility impossible.

And on the shore, where stone met water in the eternal negotiation that defined shorelines everywhere, figures waited.

Andralia's mother had aged well—if aging was even the proper word for one whose nature included elements beyond time's normal jurisdiction. Kerinus stood at the water's edge with posture that spoke of someone comfortable in her own skin, her silver hair unbound and flowing in wind that carried scents of high places, her eyes—so like her daughter's, windows showing distances—fixed on the approaching swimmers with expression that held welcome and concern in measures equal.

Beside her stood Cormac—Selkie who had looked at a star-traveler and seen not strangeness but wonder, who had loved her despite the impossibility of their union, who had given Andralia a father's love even knowing she would always carry more of her mother's nature than his. He was older than Z'Landar had imagined him, silver touching his beard, lines carved around eyes that had watched his daughter grow into something magnificent and terrifying both.

"Andralia," Kerinus said as they emerged from the water, taking forms suitable for dry land, for conversation, for embraces. "Beloved daughter. You have been to war."

It was not a question. Andralia moved into her mother's arms with the particular relief of children who come home having borne more than children should bear. "We have fought dragons," she said, her voice muffled against Kerinus' shoulder. "Destroyed their eggs. Seen hundreds die in fire. And there is more fighting to come. More death. More—" Her voice broke. "Mother, I don't know if I'm strong enough for what comes next."

"You are," Kerinus said with certainty that brooked no argument. "You are strong enough because you must be. Because the pattern chose you—chose both of you—" her gaze shifted to include Z'Landar, "—for what comes. And the pattern, whatever its other qualities, does not choose poorly."

Cormac stepped forward, extending his hand to Z'Landar with the careful formality of fathers meeting those who love their daughters. "Z'Landar, son of Brannach and Isla. King of All Waterfolk. The man my daughter loves." His grip was firm, his eyes searching. "Welcome to our home. Such as it is."

"Thank you," Z'Landar managed, finding himself slightly off-balance in ways that combat and dragon-fire had never accomplished. "I—we came seeking answers. About the spiral pattern. About what it means. About—" He gestured helplessly. "About everything, I suppose."

"Then come," Kerinus said, releasing Andralia but keeping one hand on her daughter's shoulder. "The stones wait. They have been waiting since before Scotland learned its name. A few minutes more will not trouble them."

She led them along the shore, past rocks worn smooth by water and time, past alpine grass that grew in tufts where soil permitted, toward where—

Z'Landar stopped, breath catching despite himself.

The standing stones rose from earth like fingers reaching toward heaven, arranged in a circle perhaps thirty yards across. Not tall—none exceeded twice a man's height—but *old* in ways that made Maelis's three and a half centuries seem but a moment. They had stood here since before the ice retreated, since before the first humans crossed from continental lands to these islands, since before dragons woke from eggs and learned the taste of sky.

And every stone—*every single stone*—bore the cosmic spiral carved into its surface. The same pattern that marked dragons, that decorated Nerina's shell-map, that had appeared in the hidden chamber beneath the northern settlement, that seemed to follow them like a signature written by hands too vast to comprehend.

"By the First Waters," Z'Landar breathed. "What is this place?"

"This," Kerinus said quietly, "is one of the oldest places on your world. One of the places where the pattern first touched Earth, long before humans or water-folk or even dragons learned to call this planet home. The stones were raised by those who came before—star-travelers like my people, though from times so distant that even our records have forgotten their names."

She moved to the nearest stone, placing her hand against the spiral with gesture that spoke of long familiarity. "The spiral is universal. Appears on worlds separated by distances light requires millennia to cross. Appears in galaxies that will never touch, in dimensions that exist parallel to this one but forever separate. It is not a symbol. Not decoration. Not art." She turned to face them, her eyes holding depths that made Z'Landar's chest tighten. "It is a *signature*. A mark left by the force that shapes reality itself. The pattern that underlies existence—that determines which worlds will bear life, which species will rise, which individuals will matter when history turns on hinges invisible to those living through the turning."

Andralia moved closer to her mother, her hand finding the stone beside Kerinus'. "And it brought you here? To Earth? To Scotland specifically?"

"It called me," Kerinus confirmed. "As it calls all star-travelers eventually. We wander among worlds, seeking places where the pattern manifests strongly, where significant events will occur, where the future of species or civilizations or entire dimensions will be determined by choices made in moments." She looked at Z'Landar. "Your parents' sacrifice at the Heart of the Loch—do you think that was chance? Do you think they simply happened to choose that location, happened to perform a working that would create a child who could bridge species and carry powers beyond either parent's capacity?"

Z'Landar felt the words strike like physical blows. "You're saying the pattern—what? Arranged my birth? Determined what I would become?"

"I'm saying the pattern created the *possibility* of your birth. Created circumstances where your parents would be driven to the Heart of the Loch, where they would find the knowledge needed to perform a

222

working that should have been impossible, where they would love each other and their unborn child enough to die so that child might live." Kerinus' expression softened. "But the choices were theirs. The love was theirs. The sacrifice was theirs. The pattern provides opportunities. Individuals decide whether to seize them."

She gestured to encompass the standing stones, the loch, the mountains beyond. "This place is saturated with the pattern's presence. I have spent decades here, mapping how it manifests, tracking where it appears most strongly, trying to understand what it intends—if intention is even the right word for a force so vast it shapes galaxies." She looked at Andralia. "And I knew—*knew*—that eventually you would come here. That you would meet someone who mattered, who carried the pattern's touch as strongly as you do, who would need to understand what they are and why.

For, you see, these are not stones, not truly. They hold the appearance of stone, and that is by design, but they are technology, a concept you must become familiar with, a science of incredible abilities. They were placed here in the disguise of stones, so long ago that those people involved have faded from memory."

Cormac stepped forward, his mortal perspective offering balance to his wife's cosmic view. "She's making it sound more mysterious than it needs to be," he said with gentle humor. "Here's what matters: You're both special. Born of impossible unions, carrying powers that don't fit neatly into categories others understand. The universe has plans for you—big ones, apparently—but you're still people. Still making choices. Still responsible for what you do with what you've been given."

He moved to stand beside Z'Landar, placing one hand on the younger man's shoulder. "Your father was my friend. Good man. Brave man. Loved your mother more than life itself, and proved it by dying so you could be born. He knew—they both knew—that what they created would be unprecedented. Would carry possibilities neither fully understood." His grip tightened slightly. "But he also knew his son would be a person, not just a vessel for power. Would need to learn, to grow, to make mistakes and recover from them. Would need to be loved for who he is, not what he can do."

He glanced at Andralia, smile touching his weathered face. "And my daughter loves you. Not because the pattern arranged your meeting, though it did. Not because you can move mountains, though you can. But because you dove into killing waters to save a stranger. Because you lead from the front. Because you value lives over victory and people over power. Because you're *good*, in ways that matter more than magic or destiny."

Z'Landar felt his throat tighten, felt emotions he could not name threatening to overwhelm what little composure he maintained. "Then what do we do with this knowledge? How does understanding the pattern help us fight dragons or destroy eggs or survive what comes next?"

Kerinus' expression grew grave. "The dragon is drawn to pattern sites. Did you notice? Every egg hidden at a location where the spiral appears—the northern settlement had the marking in its hidden chamber. Bidean Nam Bian's pure loch lies beneath peaks where standing stones marked similar to these once stood before time toppled them. The fairy queen's cave in Ireland—Cruachan—bears spirals older than dragons themselves. And the final egg—" She paused. "The final egg will be at the strongest pattern site in Ireland. Where the veil between dimensions grows thin. Where Balor—"

She stopped, shook her head. "That is knowledge for another time. For now, understand this: You are fighting a war that matters beyond Scotland, beyond Ireland, beyond even Earth itself. The dragon serves forces older than her species. Not willingly—she thinks she acts from maternal instinct alone. But she is drawn to these places, compelled to nest where the pattern manifests most strongly, to create offspring who will..." She trailed off, searching for words. "Who will serve purposes she does not understand."

"And we're meant to stop her?" Andralia asked quietly. "We're the pattern's answer to its own machinations?"

"You're individuals making choices," Cormac interjected firmly. "The pattern may have arranged your meeting, may have given you abilities needed for this war. But you choose to use them. You choose to fight. You choose each other." He looked between them. "Don't let cosmic significance rob you of agency. You're not puppets dancing on universe's

224

strings. You're people who happen to have been positioned where they can make a difference—and who chose to do so."

Andralia moved to stand beside Z'Landar, her hand finding his, their fingers intertwining with the casual intimacy of those who had earned each other through fire and water both. "Then we return to Loch Ness," she said. "We gather the forces that can swim to Ireland. We assault the cave where the dragon hides. We destroy her and her children both. And we trust that the choices we make—the love we carry, the lives we value, the future we fight for—matter more than any pattern's design."

"Yes," Kerinus said softly. "That is precisely what you do. And know—" her voice strengthened, "—that I believe in you. That your father believes in you. That the pattern itself, if it can be said to believe in anything, believes you will succeed. Not because success is guaranteed—it is not. Not because you are invincible—you most certainly are not. But because you are exactly what this moment needs. What Scotland needs. What the worlds beyond Scotland need, and they already know your names and sing songs of your sacrifice."

Z'Landar looked around the circle of stones, at spirals carved in ages past by hands long turned to dust, at mountains that had watched empires rise and fall without comment, at a loch so pure it hurt to look at when sunlight struck its surface. He thought of his parents, dying in the Heart of the Loch so he might be born. Of Andralia, leaving safety to fight beside him. Of Queen Mhairi, three centuries old and dying from dragon-fire, entrusting her people to his care.

He thought of the army waiting at Loch Ness—broken but unshattered, prepared to swim to Ireland because their king commanded it. Of Highland chiefs who wanted to help but could not, who would watch them go with shame burning in hearts that valued honor above survival.

He thought of dragon eggs destroyed and those still waiting. Of battles fought and those still to come. Of death that had claimed hundreds and would claim hundreds more before this ended.

"We should go," he said finally. "The army will be preparing. Councils will be meeting. And Ireland waits with its mysteries and its dragon and its death."

"One thing before you leave," Kerinus said, moving to a small shelter constructed beside the loch—rough stone, barely more than a windbreak, but clearly home to two who needed little beyond each other and their studies. She emerged carrying something wrapped in oiled cloth, handling it with care that spoke of precious contents.

She unwrapped it slowly, revealing a object that made Z'Landar's breath catch.

A shell, similar to the map she had given Andralia, but larger, more intricate. The spiral pattern covered its entire surface, but this was not simple decoration. Each curve, each line, each subtle variation in depth showed something—locations, perhaps, or connections between places, or relationships too complex to grasp in single viewing.

"This," Kerinus said quietly, "is a map of pattern sites across Ireland. Every location where the spiral manifests strongly. Every place where dimensions press close. Every site where significant events have occurred or will occur." She handed it to Andralia. "The dragon hides at Cruachan—here." Her finger traced a point. "But the final egg will be elsewhere. Here." Another point, far to the southwest. "Where Balor once ruled. Where his influence lingers still. Where the veil grows thin enough that crossing between worlds becomes... possible."

"Thank you," Andralia whispered, taking the map with reverence it deserved. "Mother, I—"

"Hush, child. You need not speak it. I know." Kerinus pulled her daughter into an embrace that held centuries of love and moments of simple motherhood both. "Come back to me when this is done. Bring your king. Let me celebrate your survival rather than mourn your loss."

"I will try," Andralia said, her voice small in ways that made Z'Landar's chest ache.

"Trying is sufficient." Kerinus released her, turned to Z'Landar. "Guard my daughter. Love her. Let her love you in return. And when the pattern's design becomes clear—when you understand what you truly are and what you can become—remember that you remain a person. That choices matter. That love transcends destiny."

226

She kissed his forehead gently, a gesture that carried blessing and farewell both. "Now go. Fight your war. Destroy your dragons. Survive what comes. And know that we watch, we hope, and we believe in the choices you will make when choosing becomes the only thing that matters."

They swam back to Loch Ness through waters that seemed different somehow—as if understanding the pattern's presence changed perception of reality itself, as if every river and loch now carried significance beyond the merely geographical. They spoke little during the return journey, both processing what had been revealed, both trying to integrate cosmic significance with mortal urgency.

Z'Landar found himself studying Andralia as they traveled, seeing her differently now—not just the woman he loved, but a being whose nature spanned worlds, whose very existence represented possibilities that most minds could not encompass. And yet she remained Andralia. Still made small jokes during rests. Still moved with grace that took his breath away. Still looked at him with eyes that held love alongside their cosmic depths.

"I can feel you thinking," she said as they paused in a pool where two rivers met. "All those thoughts swirling behind your eyes. All those questions you're not asking."

"Just one question, really," Z'Landar admitted. "Does it change anything? Knowing that the pattern arranged our meeting, that cosmic forces want us to succeed—does it change what we feel? What we mean to each other?"

Andralia was quiet for a long moment, her gaze distant. Then she smiled—not the cosmic smile that spoke of star-traveler heritage, but the simple, human smile of a woman who loved a man and wanted him to understand what he meant to her.

"No," she said simply. "It changes nothing. The pattern may have positioned us. May have given us abilities we need. May have even ensured we would meet. But it could not make me love you. Could not make you see me as more than strange being from beyond Scotland.

227

Could not make us choose each other when choosing required sacrifice." She moved closer, her hand finding his face, cradling it gently. "I love you because you are worth loving. Because you are good and brave and foolish enough to move mountains trying to save people you barely know. Because when you look at me, you see Andralia—not star-traveler's daughter, not cosmic significance, not pattern's instrument. You see me. And that is choice, beloved. That is the only thing that matters.

Know this my love, I am with you because destiny demanded it. I fell in love with you because fate has allowed no escape from our bond. We are one because we choose."

He kissed her there, in waters where rivers met, with currents pulling at them from different directions, trying to separate what had chosen to remain together. Kissed her with understanding that deepened rather than clarity that resolved, with acceptance of mysteries that would remain mysterious, with love that transcended design because it was felt rather than calculated.

When they parted, both slightly breathless, both wearing expressions that held wonder and fear and hope tangled together, Z'Landar pressed his forehead to hers.

"To Ireland then," he said quietly. "To dragon caves and fairy queens and battles we may not survive. To whatever the pattern has planned and whatever choices we make despite those plans. Together."

"Together," Andralia agreed. "Always."

They swam on, toward Loch Ness where councils waited, where armies prepared, where Scotland held its breath before plunging into waters that might drown them all.

Behind them, at Loch Etchachan, standing stones marked with cosmic spirals watched their departure with the eternal patience of things that measured time in ages rather than heartbeats.

The pattern had positioned them. Had given them powers and purpose both.

But they swam forward by choice.

And that, perhaps, was all that mattered when the universe itself watched to see what mortals would make of opportunities immortals provided.

Scotland had survived the dragon's fire.

Now came the drowning.

And whether they would emerge gasping but alive, or sink beneath waters that cared nothing for courage or love or cosmic significance—

That remained to be seen.

The dice were cast.

The pattern watched.

And two who loved each other despite destiny swam toward the war that would define them, destroy them, or prove them worthy of the trust that mountains and mothers and ancient forces had placed upon shoulders barely adequate to their weight.

Ireland waited.

So did death.

So did the choices that would prove whether the pattern had chosen wisely, or whether even cosmic forces could be wrong about what mortals would become when pushed beyond what mortality should endure.

They would learn soon enough.

They all would.

Chapter Eighteen: The Return

Loch Ness rose before them as the sun climbed toward noon on the second day after their departure—familiar waters that had become home in ways that transcended mere geography, that had witnessed their transformation from separate peoples into something that might, with fortune's favor, be called unity. The shores still bore scars from dragon-fire, stone blackened where flames had touched, earth torn where the battle had raged. But life persisted despite those scars. Smoke no longer rose. The dead had been honored. And the living—the precious, stubborn living—continued their preparations with determination that spoke of those who had looked into ending and chosen to spit in its face.

Z'Landar felt eyes upon them the moment they broke the surface—hundreds of gazes turning to mark their return, to assess their condition, to read in their faces whether hope or despair should be the order of the day. He straightened despite exhaustion that went beyond the merely physical, despite carrying revelations that made the world seem simultaneously larger and more fragile than before. He straightened because kings did not return to their people bent and broken, did not allow weariness to show when others needed strength to draw upon.

This is what it means, he thought, swimming toward the southern shore where crowds had begun to gather. *Not the throne or the crown or the power to command. But this—being what they need even when you're not certain you possess what they require. Standing tall so they can stand tall. Believing so they can believe. Leading not because you know the way, but because someone must choose direction when all paths lead into darkness.*

Alasdair Fraser was first to reach the water's edge, his burns still visible but healing, his posture that of a warrior who had survived what should have killed him and took grim satisfaction in that survival. He extended his hand to help Z'Landar from the water—a gesture of respect between equals, between men who had faced fire together and would face worse before this ended.

"Your Majesty," Alasdair said, his voice carrying the particular roughness of one who had breathed too much smoke. "You return at a fortuitous moment. The councils gather even now—Kelpie Elders, what remains of Mhairi's court, the clan chiefs who survived the dragon's fury. All waiting to hear what comes next. Where we strike. How we finish what we started when we broke her children's shells."

"Then I will not keep them waiting," Z'Landar replied, his voice steady despite the fatigue that threatened to drag him down. "Gather them in the main assembly—humans and water-folk together, as it should be. What I have to say concerns all who would swim or sail to Ireland. All who would face the dragon in her lair and teach her that maternal grief, however terrible, cannot shield her from the consequences of bringing fire to Scotland's shores."

Something shifted in Alasdair's expression—a subtle straightening, a light kindling in eyes that had grown dim with grief and exhaustion. "Aye," he said, and his voice carried edges of something that might have been hope. "Aye, we'll gather them. And they'll listen, Your Majesty. They'll listen because you're the one who destroyed two eggs while the rest of us could barely survive her first assault. Because you're the one who gambled on dragon psychology and won. Because when you speak of facing her again—" he paused, choosing words carefully, "—we believe we might actually survive it."

He turned to where other clan chiefs had gathered—Dougal MacKinnon with his weathered face showing new lines carved by fire and loss, Iain MacLeod whose skepticism had been burned away by dragon-fire, Callum Graham who had questioned why Scottish blood should be risked for Ireland's problems and learned the answer written in flames. "Spread word," Alasdair commanded. "The King returns. The councils meet within the hour. All who would have voice in what comes next should present themselves."

They dispersed with the efficiency of men accustomed to following orders, but Z'Landar saw how they moved—not with the defeated shuffle of those who marched toward their doom, but with purpose rekindled, with determination that had found direction again. They had been adrift while he swam to distant lochs and climbed mountains seeking answers. Now their king had returned, and return meant leadership, and leadership meant someone had chosen a path forward even if that path led through fire and water both.

Andralia emerged from the loch beside him, and Z'Landar felt the subtle shift in the crowd's attention—the way eyes found her and softened, the way expressions that had been carved by grief gentled into something approaching affection. It had happened gradually over the days and weeks since she had appeared in his life carrying mystery and power in equal measure. At first they had watched her with wariness, with the suspicion that water-folk and humans alike reserved for those who could not be easily categorized, who fit no comfortable definitions.

But she had fought beside them at Loch Ness. Had channeled Z'Landar's power into magic that destroyed the first egg. Had ridden his back across six hours of country without complaint, had climbed mountains to break dragon protections, had stood beside their king when standing required courage most did not possess.

And more than that—more than her power or her courage or her willingness to bleed for a Scotland that was not technically her home— they had seen what she meant to Z'Landar. Had watched him become something more than the boy-king thrust into responsibility before he'd learned to carry it. Had seen him grow into leadership through her presence, through the love that steadied rather than distracted, through the partnership that made him stronger rather than weaker.

Fionnuala was there, pulling herself from the water with the particular grace of youth who had survived what should have killed her and was still processing that survival. She moved to embrace Andralia—not the formal greeting one gave to queens or cosmic beings, but the simple hug one woman offered another, friend to friend, sister to sister in all but blood.

"You're back," Fionnuala said, relief evident in her voice. "We were beginning to worry—four days gone, no word, just Maelis saying you'd gone to visit your parents and would return when ready." She pulled back, studying Andralia's face with eyes that missed little. "You learned something. Something that weighs on you. I can see it in how you hold yourself."

"We learned many things," Andralia replied quietly. "Some comforting. Others..." She trailed off, glancing at Z'Landar with expression that held concern. "Others less so. But all necessary. All part of understanding what we face and why."

232

Maelis appeared through the gathering crowd, her ancient face showing relief at their return mixed with the particular knowledge that came from living long enough to recognize patterns others missed. "The high loch treated you well, I trust? Kerinus and Cormac proved welcoming?"

"They did," Z'Landar confirmed. "And the standing stones—Maelis, you might have warned me about what waited there. About what the spiral means. About—" He stopped, shook his head. "No. You let us discover it as we needed to discover it. Thank you for that. For trusting us to seek answers rather than simply providing them."

"Answers provided carry less weight than answers earned," Maelis said, her amber eyes holding depths that three and a half centuries had carved. "You needed to see the stones, to hear Kerinus speak of the pattern, to understand that what you fight for extends beyond Scotland and Ireland both. Needed to know you carry significance that makes the burden heavier but also makes the bearing of it more crucial." She paused. "But you also needed to know you remain people. That choices matter. That love transcends destiny."

She turned to Andralia, reaching up to cup the younger woman's face with gesture that held grandmother's affection despite the absence of any blood relation. "You have become precious to us, child. Not just to your king—though the way he looks at you would melt stone harder than what forms mountains—but to all of us. You are the one who stands beside him when standing requires more strength than any single person should possess. The one who breaks dragon magic and rides into battle and loves our king with such fierce devotion that even the most cynical among us cannot help but believe that perhaps—*perhaps*—love matters more than power."

Andralia's eyes glistened, her composure cracking slightly under weight of words that clearly struck deeper than expected. "I only do what anyone who loved him would do. What anyone who saw his courage and his heart and his stubborn refusal to let Scotland burn would feel compelled to do."

"Precisely," Maelis said with a small smile. "Which is why we love you in return. Because you see in him what we see. Because you value what we value. Because when we watch you together—" her voice gentled, "—we see hope that the future might hold more than death and dragons.

233

That love persists despite fire. That partnerships can be forged in crucibles that should destroy all tender things. You remind us why we fight, child. What we fight to preserve. And that is gift beyond any magic you might wield or any eggs you might help destroy."

Others had gathered now—Kelpie warriors who had fought at Loch Ness and survived, Selkie courtiers who whispered among themselves with expressions that held approval, human warriors bearing scars from dragon-fire who watched the exchange with the particular softness of those who had learned to value what they once took for granted. And in their eyes, in the way they looked at Andralia and Z'Landar both, Z'Landar saw something that made his chest tighten with emotions he could not entirely name.

They believed. Not just in victory—that was too uncertain, too dependent on fortune and fury both. But they believed in *them*. Believed that their king would lead them well because he led from the front, because he valued lives over glory, because he made impossible decisions and bore the weight of those decisions without flinching. And they believed that his queen—though no formal coronation had occurred, though no ceremonies had blessed their union, still they thought of her as queen—would stand beside him through whatever came, would channel his power into magic that destroyed dragons' dreams, would love him with devotion that made even cosmic significance seem small by comparison.

It was a burden, that belief. A weight that settled onto shoulders already carrying more than seemed sustainable. But it was also a gift. Because belief, Z'Landar was learning, could be stronger than steel. Could hold armies together when all rational calculation suggested dissolution. Could make people stand when standing required more courage than most possessed in a lifetime.

"We should go to the council," he said finally, straightening to his full height, squaring shoulders that wanted to slump, finding the voice that command required even when exhaustion whispered seductive suggestions of rest and retreat. "The clans have waited long enough for answers. For direction. For whatever hope I can offer that Ireland will not be merely a longer, slower death than what we nearly suffered here."

He looked around at the faces gathering—human and water-folk, old and young, those who had fought beside him and those who had only heard tales of battles they had not witnessed. Looked and saw in their expressions the thing that made leadership possible when leadership should be impossible.

They wanted to follow him. Not because laws or traditions demanded it. Not because alternatives had proven less appealing. But because when he spoke of facing dragons in their lairs, when he stood tall despite exhaustion that should have broken him, when he looked at challenges that would daunt gods and saw only obstacles to overcome—they believed he might actually be mad enough to succeed. And if he could be that mad, that brave, that stubborn in his refusal to let Scotland burn, then perhaps they could be a fraction of those things themselves.

It was not enough. Would never be enough. But it would have to suffice.

Because Ireland waited with its mysteries and its dragons and its death.

And someone had to lead the way into that darkness.

Someone had to stand tall so others could measure themselves against that height and find courage they did not know they possessed.

Someone had to love and be loved in return, so that everyone who watched could remember what they fought to preserve and why preservation mattered more than survival.

Z'Landar took Andralia's hand in his—simple gesture that held volumes—and began walking toward where the councils gathered, toward where decisions would be made that determined whether Scotland's water-folk swam to glory or merely to a different shore on which to die.

And behind them, following with steps that held determination rather than desperation, came hundreds of souls who had decided that their king was worth following, that his queen was worth fighting for, that the love they shared and the courage they demonstrated and the stubborn hope they embodied was sufficient reason to swim toward Ireland's waters and whatever waited in their depths.

It would not be easy.

Would likely not even be survivable.

But they would swim regardless.

Because their king commanded it.

Because their queen stood beside him.

And because sometimes—*sometimes*—belief was stronger than dragons, and love was more powerful than fire, and the simple act of choosing to stand when every instinct screamed to flee was the only magic that mattered when the world itself held its breath to see what mortals would become when pushed beyond what mortality should endure.

The councils waited.

So did Ireland.

So did the dragon who had fled west with maternal fear driving wings faster than rage ever could.

So did the battles that would define them or destroy them or prove them worthy of the stories that would be sung when fire was memory and Scotland had learned whether courage was sufficient currency to purchase survival from a universe that cared nothing for courage or survival both.

They walked forward.

Together.

And that, perhaps, was all that mattered when the darkness gathered and the choices narrowed and the only path remaining led through fire and water toward whatever ending waited beyond.

Chapter Nineteen: The Councils of War

The gathering assembled on the southern shore of Loch Ness as afternoon sun painted the water in shades of copper and gold. They came in the sobered numbers of those who had survived the dragon's first assault—seven hundred souls, perhaps eight hundred if one counted generously. Warriors bearing scars from fire that had fallen from the sky. Clan chiefs whose tartans seemed heavier now, weighted with grief for those who would not stand beside them again. Water-folk who moved with the particular care of people who had looked into their ending and lived only through fortune's grace.

But not all could answer the call that waited.

Z'Landar stood at the council's heart, Andralia beside him where she belonged, and felt the weight of what was about to be asked pressing against his chest like stone. The dragon had fled to Ireland. Two eggs lay destroyed. Two remained—one carried within the dragon's own body, one hidden with protections they could only guess at. And between Scotland and those eggs lay water that must be crossed, allies who must be trusted, and a battle in a cave where the dragon would be strongest and they most vulnerable.

He looked across the assembly and saw the truth written in their faces: not everyone gathered here could make that journey.

Maelis called the council to order, her ancient voice carrying across the shore with authority earned through three and a half centuries of witnessing Scotland's turnings. "We gather to speak of Ireland. Of the dragon who fled our waters after we destroyed her second child. Of eggs that remain unbroken and threats that grow with each passing day." She turned to Z'Landar. "King of All Waterfolk—speak to us of what comes next."

Z'Landar took a breath, squared his shoulders, found the voice that leadership required. "Caoránach has fled to Ireland. She nests in Cruachan—the Cave of the Cats—a place where magic runs deeper than in most of Ireland. She carries the third egg within her own body now, protected by scale and fury and maternal fear that will make her more dangerous than she's ever been."

He paused, letting that truth settle across the assembly like morning frost.

"We destroyed two of her children. She knows we can reach what she tries to protect. She knows her magic can be broken, her defenses penetrated. And she has fled to the one place she believes we cannot easily follow—across water, into a cave that belongs to another power entirely, guarded by forces that care nothing for Scotland's survival."

"Then we must go to her," said Tormod of the Rapids, his weathered face grave. "Must swim to Ireland and finish what we started."

"Yes," Z'Landar agreed. "But not all of us can make that journey."

The silence that followed held weight heavier than the loch itself.

Alasdair Fraser stepped forward from where he stood among the Highland chiefs, his face showing the particular pain of one about to confess inadequacy. "The clans cannot march with you to Ireland."

Murmurs rippled through the assembly—shock and understanding in equal measure.

"We lost four hundred warriors when the dragon first struck," Alasdair continued, his voice thick with emotion barely contained. "Four hundred souls burned to ash or drowned in waters turned to boiling chaos. What remains—" He gestured to the humans gathered behind him. "What remains are survivors. Wounded men still healing. Young warriors not yet tested. Old chiefs who remember too many battles and carry too many scars."

238

Other chiefs nodded, their expressions showing the same grief Alasdair carried.

"And even if we had the numbers," Caelan MacLeod added, his young voice tight, "we lack the means. To move an army to Ireland requires ships—dozens of ships, properly provisioned and crewed. To gather such a fleet would take weeks, perhaps months. To sail across waters that grow treacherous as autumn deepens—" He shook his head. "We need time we don't have. The egg could quicken. The dragon could strike. Every day we delay is another day closer to hatching."

"So we cannot come," Alasdair said, and the words seemed to physically pain him. "Cannot sail fast enough. Cannot field sufficient force even if we could. Cannot be what you need when you need it most."

He turned toward where Muirgheal stood at the water's edge, her green hair dulled by hard swimming from Ireland, her eyes holding knowledge of what Scotland faced.

"Ireland sent warnings when the dragon first moved," Alasdair continued. "Sent Muirgheal to speak truth we would not hear, to offer aid we were too blind to accept. And now—now when Ireland bleeds from wounds the dragon has inflicted, when they need allies most—we cannot answer. Scotland's honor is wounded this day. Wounded in ways that shame cuts deeper than any dragon-fire could burn."

The old chief's voice broke on the last words, and Z'Landar saw tears tracking down weathered cheeks—tears other chiefs did not bother to hide.

Z'Landar felt his throat tighten. He had known this was coming, had understood during the journey from Loch Etchachan that human warriors with human limitations could not swim to Ireland in time that mattered. But seeing it spoken aloud, watching proud men confess their inability—

"There is no shame in impossibility," he said quietly. "Only in refusing to acknowledge it. You bled when the dragon struck. Lost sons and brothers and warriors you'd known since they were boys. You've paid whatever debts honor demands."

"Speak it as gently as you wish," another chief muttered. "We still watch water-folk swim toward death while we remain safely ashore."

"Then don't remain safely," Z'Landar replied. "Hold Scotland while we're gone. Guard the waters. Tend the wounded. Be ready for what comes after—whether that's victory to celebrate or graves to dig for those who don't return. That is service. That is honor."

"But it's not enough," Alasdair said hoarsely.

"It's what we have," Andralia said softly, speaking for the first time. "And what we have must suffice."

She moved to stand more fully beside Z'Landar, her presence a comfort he drew strength from. "The water-folk can reach Ireland in days, not weeks. We move through channels ships cannot navigate. We need no provisions except what the water provides. We are—" She paused, calculating. "Perhaps two hundred strong who can make that journey. Two hundred Kelpies and Selkies and water-sprites who can swim the distance and still have strength to fight when we arrive."

Two hundred.

The number hung in the air like a death sentence.

"Two hundred," Eilidh of the Deep Pools repeated, her voice holding disbelief. "Against a dragon?"

"Against a dragon and more," Z'Landar said, because hiding truth served no purpose. "The dragon nests in Cruachan—the Cave of the

Cats. That cave belongs to Fairy Queen Cliodhna, one of the Aos Sí. And Cliodhna is not our ally."

"She aids the dragon?" Tormod asked sharply.

"She hosts the dragon," Muirgheal confirmed, drawing all eyes to her. "Gives her sanctuary in a cave that should be sacred to fairy folk alone. We don't know why—whether for gold or power or reasons we cannot comprehend. But Cliodhna has allied herself with Caoránach. Has offered protection. Has turned her considerable magic toward keeping the dragon safe."

"So we must fight them both," Caelan said, understanding flooding his young face with something between horror and determination. "The dragon in her lair, where she's strongest. And a fairy queen whose powers we can barely imagine."

"Cliodhna is powerful," Andralia said carefully. "But not as powerful as some believe. She can be fought. Can be defeated if we're clever and quick and willing to pay the price that fighting her will demand."

"What price?" asked one of the Selkie nobles.

Andralia's expression grew distant, troubled. "I don't know yet. But fairy magic always demands payment. Always extracts cost from those who oppose it. We'll pay—in blood or power or something more precious still. But we'll pay it regardless, because the alternative is letting the dragon hatch her child and watching two dragons burn where one nearly destroyed us."

Z'Landar felt her hand find his beneath the water's edge, felt her fingers thread through his with the natural ease that had become second nature between them. Drew strength from that contact, from the certainty that whatever came, they would face it together.

"We won't be alone," Muirgheal said, her voice carrying across the assembly. "Ireland is not without forces willing to fight. The Merrow will stand with you—all who survived the dragon's wrath, all who remember friends burned in their own waters. We know Ireland's coasts, know the channels that lead to Cruachan, know where magic runs strong enough to offer protection."

"Beyond the Merrow?" Z'Landar prompted.

"The Púca have pledged aid," Muirgheal continued. "Shapeshifters— horse one moment, goat the next, human-seeming when it suits them. Tricksters by nature, but they hate the dragon for their own reasons. If you bind them with proper oaths, they'll fight beside you. Though expect chaos. Expect surprises. Expect help in forms you'd never choose if given option."

"The Aos Sí?" asked Eilidh warily.

"Some will fight with us," Muirgheal said carefully. "Not all fairy folk serve Cliodhna. Not all approve of her alliance with the dragon. Those who oppose her—those who remember older laws and older ways—they may join us. But they're unpredictable. Dangerous even as allies. You'll need to move carefully around them, speak carefully to them, remember that fairy folk play by rules we don't always understand."

"And Banshees," she added. "Death-seers who keen at dying. They've offered to guide us—to show which paths lead to death and which might yet hold survival. Their sight pierces veils we cannot. Whether we can bear to hear what they show us—" She shrugged. "That's our burden, not theirs."

Z'Landar looked around the assembly, seeing calculation on faces both human and not. Two hundred water-folk. Irish allies of uncertain loyalty and unpredictable power. Against a dragon in her chosen lair, protected by a fairy queen who had allied with forces that should be opposed.

The odds were impossible.

"We swim at dawn," he said, because what other choice existed? "Three days to reach Irish waters if we push hard. A day to coordinate with local forces. Then Cruachan. Then the dragon. Then whatever ending waits beyond."

"Strategy," said Tormod. "We should discuss how to fight her. How to coordinate forces that have never fought together. How to deal with Cliodhna while still having strength to face the dragon herself."

They spent the next hour bent over crude maps scratched in sand, voices rising and falling as those who had fought at Loch Ness and survived Bidean Nam Bian offered thoughts earned through blood. The cave was the dragon's advantage—confined space where her fire would reflect and multiply, where her size became weapon as much as her claws. But it was also potential weakness—she could not flee, could not maneuver as she had in open air.

Cliodhna was the unknown variable. Powerful but not invincible. Bound by fairy rules that might be exploited if they understood them well enough. Capable of turning steel to rust and making warriors forget their names—but vulnerable in ways they would need to discover through combat itself.

Z'Landar listened, contributed when his knowledge was needed, but felt his attention drifting despite the importance of every word. Felt his eyes pulling toward Andralia where she stood, her expression distant in ways that spoke of thoughts traveling beyond this shore, this moment, this mortal concern with tactics and survival.

The council continued around them—Maelis and Tormod working through approach vectors, Caelan discussing how to coordinate magic and steel, Muirgheal explaining the tides around Cruachan and when they ran strongest. Important discussions. Necessary discussions.

But Z'Landar found himself unable to focus fully.

Because beneath all the planning, beneath all the strategy and careful coordination—one truth remained inescapable:

They were swimming toward death with a force too small, against enemies too powerful, for stakes too high to contemplate failure.

Eventually, as the sun tracked toward western horizons and shadows lengthened, Maelis called the council to pause. "We'll resume at sunset. Work through final details. But for now—rest. Prepare yourselves. Departure is at dawn. Make peace with whatever gods you pray to."

The assembly dispersed—warriors moving toward food and rest, chiefs gathering to speak of matters councils did not address, water sprites resuming their movements though without their usual joy.

Z'Landar and Andralia drifted away from the crowds, moving along the shore toward where standing stones marked older boundaries. Neither spoke for long moments, both lost in thoughts that words seemed inadequate to contain.

Finally, Andralia broke the silence. "I'm afraid."

The confession hung between them, simple and devastating.

Z'Landar turned to face her fully, his hands coming up to cup her face with tenderness that felt almost profane given the violence they'd discussed mere yards away. "So am I. Terrified."

"Of dying?"

"Of losing you." His thumbs traced her cheekbones with touch that had become familiar over weeks that felt simultaneously like forever and no time at all. "Of watching you burn in Cruachan's darkness because I led you there. Of standing beside your body knowing I could have told you to stay safe in Loch Etchachan, could have faced this alone, could have—"

"Could have died alone," she interrupted gently. "Could have burned without anyone who loved you standing close enough to hold your hand while the fire came. Could have faced Cliodhna and the dragon and death itself without the one person who can channel your power into magic that breaks what cannot be broken."

"You make it sound almost reasonable."

"It's not reasonable." Her smile was sad, fierce. "It's insane. It's desperate. It's two hundred water-folk swimming toward a cave where a mother dragon guards her child and a fairy queen guards the dragon. It's impossible odds and certain death and every tactical consideration screaming that we should flee, should hide, should let Ireland burn rather than swim into fire ourselves."

She pulled his face closer, her forehead pressing against his. "But we're going anyway. Because two hundred is all we have. Because impossible doesn't mean we stop trying. Because—" Her voice broke. "Because I'd rather burn beside you in Cruachan than live a thousand years without you."

Z'Landar felt tears he hadn't known were forming track down his cheeks. "This isn't how it's supposed to be. We're supposed to have armies. Supposed to have advantages. Supposed to have some reasonable chance of survival beyond desperate hope and determination."

"When have we ever had reasonable chances?" Andralia asked, and despite the tears on her own face, she was smiling. "At the northern settlement, we had seven people against dragon magic. At Bidean Nam Bian, we climbed mountains and reshaped stone with power you barely understood. We've been impossible from the beginning, beloved. Why stop now?"

He kissed her then—desperately, fiercely, like she was oxygen and he was drowning. Kissed her like her lips held the only answer to questions he couldn't articulate. Kissed her like this moment might be their last peaceful embrace and he refused to let it pass without tasting what they'd become together.

When they finally parted, both breathless, the sun had nearly set.

"At Bidean Nam Bian," Z'Landar said quietly, "the dragon could flee. Could escape when pressed. But Cruachan—" He pulled back enough to meet her eyes. "In Cruachan she's trapped. Cornered. Protecting an egg she carries within her own body. She cannot flee. Will not flee. A mother's fury when defending young goes beyond any other force I know."

"I know," Andralia whispered.

"And Cliodhna—we don't even understand why she helps the dragon. Don't know what powers she'll bring to bear. Don't know how to fight fairy magic that can unmake warriors with words." His hands tightened on her shoulders. "We're swimming into the worst possible battlefield. Against enemies at the height of their strength. With a force too small to succeed. And I'm—" His voice broke. "I'm terrified that I'm leading you to your death. That I'm leading all of them to death. That courage and love and determination won't be enough when fire comes and fairy magic twists the world into shapes we cannot comprehend."

"Then we die," Andralia said simply. "We die together, trying. We die knowing we stood when standing required everything we had. We die having loved each other in ways that make even death seem small by comparison."

"That's not comforting."

"It's not meant to be." She pulled him close, her arms wrapping around him with strength that belied her frame. "Comfort is for times of peace. We're at war. War with dragons and fairy queens and forces that want us dead. Comfort is luxury we can't afford."

She pulled back enough to meet his eyes fully. "But love—love is necessity. Love is what makes swimming toward Cruachan seem somehow worthwhile. Love is what we fight for and what we carry with us and what we become together when we stand in places that ought to break us but don't because we refuse to break alone."

He held her as the sun set, as stars emerged over water that would carry them west toward death, as the weight of tomorrow pressed against them like the deep itself.

"Two hundred," he whispered. "Against a dragon and a fairy queen. In a cave where we have every disadvantage."

"Two hundred," she agreed. "Plus Irish allies we're not certain we can trust. Plus magic we barely understand. Plus whatever advantages love and desperation can create when combined."

"It's not enough."

"No," she said honestly. "It's probably not. But it's what we have. And what we have must suffice."

They returned to the council as full darkness fell, as warriors gathered for final planning, as the impossibility of what they attempted became more apparent with each tactical consideration discussed.

The Highland chiefs offered final advice, their voices thick with emotion at watching water-folk prepare to swim toward death while they remained behind. Muirgheal explained the currents around Cruachan one more time, the places where underwater channels might offer approach, the moments when tides might aid rather than hinder.

And through it all, Z'Landar felt Andralia's presence beside him like an anchor. Her hand in his. Her voice adding insights born of cosmic knowledge he still didn't fully understand. Her love surrounding him like armor that couldn't turn dragon-fire but could, perhaps, make him brave enough to face it.

When the council finally adjourned in the hour before midnight, when warriors dispersed to gather weapons and say goodbyes and make whatever peace they could with gods that might not listen— Z'Landar and Andralia stood alone on the shore.

"I love you," he said quietly.

"I know," she replied. "And I love you. Whatever comes. However it ends. I love you, Z'Landar. Beloved. My king. My heart."

"Promise me something," he said.

"Anything."

"If it comes to choosing between destroying the egg and saving yourself—choose the egg. Choose Scotland. Choose the mission. Don't let love make you hesitate when hesitation means dragons hatch and worlds burn."

Andralia was quiet for a long moment. Then: "I can't promise that. Won't promise that. Because if choosing the egg means losing you—" She shook her head. "Then I'd rather fail the mission and keep you alive than succeed and lose you. That's not heroic. Not noble. But it's true."

"Andralia—"

"No." She pressed fingers to his lips. "Don't ask me to promise I'll let you die. Don't ask me to choose Scotland over you. Because I won't. I can't. And if that makes me selfish, if that makes me unworthy of the cosmic heritage I carry—" She pulled his hand to her chest, pressing it against her heart. "Then I'll be selfish. I'll be unworthy. But I'll be those things with you alive beside me rather than heroic and noble with you dead."

He wanted to argue. Wanted to tell her that some things mattered more than love, that Scotland's survival was worth any price, that duty sometimes demanded sacrifice love could not accept.

But looking at her—at this woman who had chosen Earth over stars, who had stood beside him through fire and death and impossibility, who loved him with devotion that made cosmic forces seem small— he found he couldn't ask her to make that promise.

Couldn't ask it of himself, if their positions were reversed.

"Then we'll both be selfish," he said finally. "Both be unworthy. And we'll pray that love and selfishness and unworthiness combined are sufficient to destroy eggs and survive dragons both."

"Together," she whispered.

"Always," he agreed.

Dawn broke over Loch Ness in shades of crimson and gold. The water-folk gathered at the shore—two hundred strong, perhaps fewer if one counted honestly. Kelpies and Selkies, water sprites and those who had survived fire and were willing to face it again.

Such a small force.

Such impossible odds.

The Highland chiefs stood on shore watching, their faces showing grief and pride and shame in equal measure. Alasdair Fraser raised his hand in salute.

"May the stones guard you," he called. "May the lochs remember you. May you return victorious or not at all, because half-victories against dragons are just slow death by another name."

"Hold Scotland," Z'Landar replied. "Be ready to welcome us home."

"We will," Alasdair promised. "And if you don't return—we'll remember. Will speak your names until our grandchildren's grandchildren know who swam west when swimming meant death."

Z'Landar nodded once, then turned toward the west. Toward Ireland. Toward caves and dragons and fairy queens and death.

Andralia's hand found his beneath the water.

"Together," she whispered.

"Always," he agreed.

And they swam.

Two hundred souls following their king toward whatever ending awaited in Cruachan's darkness.

Behind them, Scotland held its breath.

Ahead, Ireland waited with its fire and mysteries.

Between them, in waters running cold with autumn's approach, love and courage and desperation combined into the only magic that mattered when odds were impossible and death was certain.

They swam west into dawning day.

And the world watched to see if two hundred could be enough.

If love could be sufficient.

If impossible could somehow become merely difficult.

The tale was far from finished.

The final battles had begun.

And in Cruachan's darkness, a dragon waited with her egg and her ally and her fury.

Waited to see if Scotland's courage would burn as bright as her fire.

Or if fire, in the end, would consume courage and leave only ash.

Chapter Twenty: The Western Waters

They swam west as dawn broke over Loch Ness, two hundred souls leaving Scotland behind for waters that held older magic and grimmer purpose. Z'Landar took the seal-form as naturally as breathing, feeling his body reshape with that familiar fluidity, feeling Andralia's presence beside him as constant as his own heartbeat. Behind them, the force followed—Kelpies powerful and steady, Selkies graceful and swift, water sprites flickering like thoughts through the deep.

The last glimpse of Scottish shore showed standing stones stark against morning sky, and Highland chiefs watching from the water's edge with expressions that held grief and pride in equal measure. Then the shore fell away behind them, and there was only the swim ahead, and the cold waters of the North Channel, and Ireland waiting beyond the horizon.

Two days the journey took.

They swam through waters that grew colder with each mile, through currents that had carved paths between Scotland and Ireland since before either land had names. The first day passed in steady rhythm—two hundred moving as one, finding pace that could be sustained, learning each other's swimming patterns, becoming something more than individuals scattered across the water.

Z'Landar watched them as they traveled, these warriors who followed him toward death with determination that should have been impossible. Watched the way the Kelpies moved with power born of river-strength, how the Selkies flowed through water like thought made fluid, how even the smallest water sprites kept pace despite their size. They were magnificent. They were doomed. They were his people, and he would lead them well or die trying.

Andralia swam beside him always, her presence a comfort that went beyond words. Sometimes their eyes met through the blue-green depths, and in those glances passed understanding that needed no speech—fear and love and grim determination all mixed together until they became indistinguishable from each other.

252

The second day brought rougher waters, autumn storms churning the surface far above their heads. They dove deeper to escape the turbulence, swimming through darkness broken only by the faint bioluminescence of deep-dwelling creatures who scattered at their approach. They rested that night in a sea-cave carved into underwater cliffs, too exhausted for words, huddled together for warmth that bodies accustomed to cold water still craved.

Z'Landar held Andralia in the darkness, feeling her breathe against his chest, feeling her heart beat steady and sure. "What if we fail?" he whispered.

"Then we fail together," she replied. "And at least we'll have had this. Had each other. Had us."

It wasn't comfort. But it was truth, and truth would have to suffice.

Their efforts finally brought them into Irish waters, and the difference was immediate. The taste changed—something older in it, something that spoke of magic that had saturated these seas long before Scotland knew Kelpies or Selkies. The water felt heavier somehow, weighted with histories that went deeper than the ocean floor. And beneath everything else, faint but undeniable, ran a current of wrongness—the taint of dragon-presence corrupting what should have been pure.

They surfaced at evening in a cove Muirgheal had described, where cliffs rose dramatic against darkening sky and standing stones marked thresholds between seen and unseen worlds. The Merrow was waiting, her green hair dulled by hard swimming, her eyes holding relief and something that might have been surprise.

"You came," she said as Z'Landar pulled himself onto the rocky shore, taking human form with Andralia beside him. "I wasn't certain you would."

"We said we would come," Z'Landar replied. "Scotland keeps its word. Eventually."

A ghost of a smile touched Muirgheal's lips. "Eventually," she agreed. "Rest tonight. Tomorrow you meet those who will fight beside you. And tomorrow—" Her expression grew grave. "Tomorrow you learn why Cruachan is only the beginning of what you face."

Z'Landar wanted to ask what she meant, but exhaustion crashed over him like a wave, and Andralia's hand found his, and Muirgheal was already moving away to help the arriving warriors find shelter in the caves that honeycombed the cliffs.

They slept that night in stone hollows carved by water and time, and Z'Landar dreamed of eyes that burned and caves that swallowed light and fire that cared nothing for courage or love or the stubborn refusal to surrender that had carried them this far.

When he woke, Ireland's dawn had broken gray and cold, and the Irish allies had arrived.

The Púca came first, appearing at the cave entrance with the particular unsettling quality of those who moved between shapes as easily as breathing. One moment empty air, the next a black horse standing where nothing had been, then a man with eyes that held too much knowledge and a smile that suggested secrets better left unspoken, then something between—neither fully horse nor human but carrying elements of both.

There were three of them, though the number seemed uncertain, as if they might be three or thirty depending on how one counted and from what angle one looked. The leader—if such beings acknowledged leadership—stepped forward wearing the shape of a tall man with wild hair the color of storm-clouds and a grin that belonged on a wolf.

"I am Ruadhan," he said, his voice carrying harmonics that suggested multiple throats speaking in unison. "We are the Púca of the western hills, and we have come because dragons bore us and fairy queens amuse us and watching mortals attempt impossible things entertains us more than anything else these dull centuries have offered."

Z'Landar met that unsettling gaze steadily. "We welcome any aid offered, however strange the reasons for offering it."

"Strange?" Ruadhan's grin widened. "Oh, young king, you haven't seen strange yet. But you will. You'll see strange and terrible and wonderful and horrific all mixed together until you can't tell which is which. That's what fighting fairy queens and dragons does to perception. Scrambles it. Makes everything uncertain." He cocked his head. "But you want certainty, don't you? Want to bind us with oaths so we can't betray you when betrayal would be most convenient."

"Can you be bound?" Andralia asked quietly.

"Oh yes." Something shifted in Ruadhan's expression—the trickster's grin remaining but edges growing harder. "We can be bound. Will be bound, if you speak the proper words. Púca keep oaths once sworn—that's our one reliable trait in a world of unreliable things. But understand this—" He leaned forward. "We help you our way. We fight beside you in forms you won't always recognize. We'll cause chaos because chaos is what we are. Sometimes that chaos will aid you. Sometimes it will complicate matters terribly. But we'll be bound by our word not to actively work against your purpose. That's the best you'll get from us. Take it or face the dragon without us."

Z'Landar glanced at Andralia, saw his own calculation reflected in her impossible eyes. Unreliable allies were still allies. Chaos that sometimes helped was better than no help at all.

"What words bind you?" he asked.

"Speak our names true three times while holding iron in running water," Ruadhan said. "Swear by stone and star and the deep places where old magic sleeps. Promise us entertainment—promise us that fighting beside you will be more interesting than any alternative. And we'll swear back—swear by our nature and our names and the forms we wear—that we'll fight your enemies and not betray your purpose, however much temptation whispers otherwise."

The ceremony took place in the cove where fresh water met salt, Z'Landar standing knee-deep with an iron knife borrowed from one of the warriors, speaking names that tasted strange on his tongue—Ruadhan and Síofra and Brígh—calling them three times each while water flowed cold around his legs and iron burned his palm. And the Púca swore back in voices that harmonized and split and reformed, promising aid in forms unpredictable and chaos that would serve rather than hinder.

When it was done, Ruadhan grinned his wolf's grin. "Now we're bound. Now you'll see what we can do. This will be fun." He glanced toward the others. "Terrifying and probably fatal. But fun nonetheless."

The Aos Sí arrived next, though "arrived" seemed inadequate for beings who had perhaps been there all along, simply choosing that moment to become visible. There were two of them, tall and impossibly graceful, wearing forms that looked almost human but wrong in ways that made eyes slide away from looking too long.

The first gave no name, speaking instead in a voice like wind through hollow hills: "We oppose what Cliodhna has done. We oppose the alliance she has made. We oppose the corruption of Cruachan with dragon-taint and maternal madness. So we will aid you—not from love of mortals, but from hatred of what our queen has become."

"Can you help us fight her?" Z'Landar asked.

"Fight her?" The being's laugh was bells heard underwater. "You cannot fight Cliodhna. Not truly. She is bound to Cruachan as root to earth, as stone to mountain. To fight her in her own cave is to fight the cave itself, and caves do not die when struck. But—" The Aos Sí tilted its head. "She can be... distracted. Confused. Her magic can be turned back upon itself if you know the words, know the ways, know the rules she herself must follow."

"Teach us these rules," Andralia said.

"We cannot teach what takes centuries to learn. But we can guide. Can whisper truths when truths matter most. Can show you paths through her magic that she will not expect you to see." The being paused. "But understand—every fairy gift carries cost. Every aid we provide will demand payment. Not from malice. Simply because that is what we are. Magic given must be balanced by magic taken. Help offered must be answered by debt owed. That is the law we cannot break even if we wished."

"What payment will you demand?" Z'Landar asked warily.

"We do not know yet. The cost reveals itself when needed, not before. You may pay in blood or memory or years of your life or things more precious still. Or you may pay nothing if fortune favors and our aid proves unnecessary. But know this—" The Aos Sí's eyes held depths that made even Andralia's cosmic gaze seem shallow. "Many will die in Cruachan's darkness. We see the futures branching. In some, you succeed but the cost empties you. In others, you fail and Scotland burns. In a few—very few—you win with something like victory. Which future arrives depends on choices not yet made."

The second Aos Sí spoke then, its voice carrying weight that made stone vibrate: "Know also that the dragon is not your only enemy. That Cliodhna is not your only obstacle. That Cruachan holds only one egg, and four were laid. The last rests elsewhere. Guarded by something older than dragons. More terrible than fairy queens."

Z'Landar felt cold settle into his bones. "What guards the fourth egg?"

"The eye that slays," the Aos Sí said cryptically. "The king who should have died. The one who watches from depths where even Fomorians fear to swim."

The Banshees came last, appearing without sound or warning, simply present where they had not been moments before. Three figures draped in gray that might have been cloth or mist, faces hidden but presence unmistakable. They keened softly—not the wail of death but something quieter, more sorrowful, like grief that had outlasted the mourning and settled into bones too deep to ever be dislodged.

They moved among the warriors, these death-seers, looking at each face with attention that made strong men flinch. Sometimes they paused, tilting heads, and the keening grew momentarily louder. Sometimes they simply moved on, leaving warriors to wonder if their survival was assured or simply not worth remarking upon.

When they reached Z'Landar, all three stopped. The keening built—not loud, but insistent, like wind that would not be denied. Then the central figure spoke in a voice that seemed to come from everywhere and nowhere: "Your fate is bound to the egg. Bound to the cave. Bound to the fire that waits in darkness. You will face death twice before your story ends. Once in Cruachan. Once beyond. Which death claims you—" The Banshee paused. "That depends on love and choice and things we cannot see because they have not yet crystallized into futures we can read."

She turned to Andralia. "Daughter of stars. You carry significance that makes our sight blur. We see you standing in Cruachan's heart. See you burning with light that is not fire. See you—" The Banshee's voice dropped to whisper. "See you falling. See him catching you. See endings that should not be but will be nonetheless. The price you pay is written in blood that has not yet been spilled."

Andralia's hand tightened in Z'Landar's, but she did not flinch. "Will we succeed? Will we destroy the egg?"

"You will face the dragon," the Banshee said. "That much is certain. What happens when you face her—how fire meets water, how love meets fury, how impossible odds become merely catastrophic—that shifts with every choice made, every word spoken, every moment that tips the balance toward one future or another."

She turned back to address the assembled warriors. "Many of you will not return. I see deaths in Cruachan's darkness—burned, drowned, broken by magic that unmakes flesh. I see cairns raised and songs sung and names carved in stone for those who will not see Scotland again. But I also see victory, if you are brave enough and desperate enough and loving enough to pay what victory costs."

"How many?" asked one of the warriors, voice tight. "How many of us die?"

The Banshee was silent for a long moment. Then: "Enough that survival will feel more like defeat. Few enough that Scotland might yet be saved. The precise number shifts. Changes. Depends on fortune and fury and a thousand small choices that seem insignificant until death follows from them."

She moved back to Z'Landar and Andralia. "But know this—your battle does not end in Cruachan. The fourth egg waits beyond. Guarded by one whose power makes dragons seem almost gentle. You will face Balor of the Evil Eye. And when you do—" The Banshee's keening grew so soft it was almost inaudible. "When you do, love will demand the price that love has always required. Sacrifice. Loss. The choice between survival and service. Between living and mattering."

They gathered in a larger cave as morning stretched toward noon, two hundred Scottish warriors and the strange allies Ireland had provided, and Muirgheal stood before them with expression that held knowledge earned through blood and grief.

"You've heard the warnings," she said. "Heard the Aos Sí speak of costs and fairy magic. Heard the Banshees keen over futures that hold more death than survival. Heard the Púca promise chaos. Now hear this—" She took a breath. "The dragon and Cliodhna are not your only enemies. There is a fourth egg. And it is guarded by something worse than either."

"Worse than a dragon?" asked Caelan, disbelief evident.

"Much worse." Muirgheal's green eyes held depths that spoke of having witnessed terrors that should not be survived. "Balor of the Evil Eye. Ancient king of the Fomorians. A giant so vast he makes dragons seem small, with a single eye that kills with looking. Not burns—kills. Instantly. Anyone who meets his gaze dies where they stand."

Silence fell like snow, cold and heavy and absolute.

"He hasn't been seen in centuries," Muirgheal continued. "Legends said he was dead, killed by his grandson in battles so ancient even our oldest songs barely remember them. But the Fomorians have been whispering. Speaking of their king returned. Speaking of something he guards in depths where no one dares swim. And now—" She gestured to the Aos Sí and the Banshee. "Now you have heard it confirmed. Balor lives. Balor guards the fourth egg. And when you finish in Cruachan—if you finish in Cruachan—you will need to face him."

259

Z'Landar felt something in his chest tighten until breathing became difficult. Two impossible battles. Two enemies that should not be survivable. And between them, a force of two hundred that was already insufficient for the first challenge.

"One battle at a time," Andralia said quietly, her hand finding his. "We face the dragon first. Destroy the third egg. Then we worry about the fourth."

"If we survive the third," Z'Landar replied, matching her quiet tone.

"If we survive," she agreed. "But beloved—if we spend all our time worrying about the battle after next, we'll die in the battle right in front of us. So let's worry about Cruachan. About the dragon. About getting that egg destroyed. Everything else can wait until after."

She turned to address the gathered warriors. "We came here knowing many of us would die. Knowing the odds were impossible. Knowing victory would cost more than we wanted to pay. Learning there's a second battle waiting doesn't change those facts. Doesn't make Cruachan any more deadly than it already was. So we do what we came to do—we swim into that cave, we face the dragon, we destroy her egg. And if we survive, if fortune favors and courage proves sufficient—then we'll face Balor. Together. The same way we've faced everything else."

Tormod of the Rapids stood. "The girl speaks sense. We can die worrying about two battles or die fighting one. I'd rather die fighting. So let's speak of Cruachan. Let's plan how to kill a dragon in her own lair. Let's decide who faces the fairy queen and who engages the mother dragon and who stands with our king when standing means burning."

They bent over the crude maps Muirgheal had scratched in sand, discussing approaches and tactics and the hundred small decisions that might mean the difference between death and slightly-less-immediate-death. The Aos Sí offered cryptic guidance about Cliodhna's magic— how it could be turned back on itself if they spoke true names, how it weakened at thresholds, how iron bothered fairy folk even if it didn't stop them. Ruadhan and the Púca promised chaos that would "probably help, definitely entertain, possibly doom them all." The Banshees stood silent, offering no guidance, simply present as reminders that death waited and would not be denied.

Z'Landar listened, contributed when his knowledge was needed, but felt his thoughts drifting toward the larger impossibility. Cruachan and Balor. Dragon and Fomorian giant. Three hundred years of peace shattered, and now two battles that should not be survivable stretching before them like roads that led only to graves.

"We'll divide our forces," Maelis was saying, her ancient voice cutting through the discussions. "Some to engage Cliodhna—keep her magic occupied, prevent her from turning all her power against our main force. The rest focus on the dragon. Z'Landar and Andralia at the center—they have the power to break dragon magic, to channel force sufficient to crack scale and reach the egg beneath."

"The Púca will move throughout," Ruadhan added, his grin suggesting things better left unspoken. "We'll shift and change and cause such beautiful chaos that neither dragon nor fairy queen will know which threats are real and which are merely us being ourselves."

"The Banshees will guide you through the cave," the central death-seer said. "We see the paths that lead to death and the paths that merely lead toward it. Follow where we indicate. Avoid where we warn. Some of you will die regardless. But fewer will die if you trust our sight."

"And the Aos Sí?" Z'Landar asked.

"We will do what we can," the first fairy-being replied. "Counter Cliodhna's magic where possible. Exploit the rules she must follow. Pay the prices that aid demands. But understand—we cannot guarantee victory. Cannot promise survival. Can only offer what small advantages our opposition to our queen provides."

The planning continued through afternoon and into evening, as every warrior learned their role, as every contingency was discussed, as hope and despair mixed together until they became indistinguishable. When darkness fell and the council finally adjourned, warriors dispersed to make their final preparations—sharpening weapons, speaking prayers, writing farewells for those who could write and asking others to carry words for those who could not.

Z'Landar and Andralia drifted away from the camps, moving along the shore until the sounds of preparation faded behind them. They found a hollow in the cliffs where stone curved to provide shelter and the sound of waves created privacy more complete than distance alone could offer.

"Tomorrow," Z'Landar said, the word tasting like ash.

"Tomorrow," Andralia agreed. She turned to face him fully, her hands coming up to cup his face with tenderness that made his chest ache. "If I die in that cave—"

"Don't—"

"Let me speak." Her thumb traced his cheekbone. "If I die tomorrow, know that loving you was the best choice I ever made. That standing beside you in Cruachan will matter more than a thousand years of safe living ever could. That whatever ending comes—I chose it freely. Chose you freely. And would choose the same again given a thousand chances."

"You're not going to die," Z'Landar said, though his voice carried no conviction.

"Perhaps not." Her smile was sad, certain. "But if I do—don't let it break you. Don't let grief stop you from facing Balor, from destroying the fourth egg, from finishing what we started. Promise me that."

"I can't promise that. If you die—" His voice cracked. "If you die, I don't know what I become. Don't know if I'll be strong enough or sane enough to continue."

"Then let me be strong enough for both of us," she whispered. "Let me love you enough that even dying won't stop me from giving you what you need to keep fighting."

She kissed him then, and in that kiss passed everything they had become together—fear and love and desperate hope and the particular intimacy of two people who had chosen each other despite destiny's demands and would choose each other again despite death's approach. They held each other as darkness deepened, as stars emerged over water that would carry them tomorrow toward fire, as the weight of what came next pressed against them like the deep itself.

What passed between them in that hollow is not for songs to tell or tales to recount. Some things remain private even when written in water and stone. Enough to say that they loved each other in ways that made even death seem small. That they held each other through the night. That when dawn broke gray and cold, they rose together with something like peace settled over them—not because fear had vanished, but because they had each other, and that would have to be enough.

The army gathered at dawn in water that ran cold with autumn's deepening. Two hundred Scottish warriors, their Irish allies scattered among them, all moving toward the channels that would lead to Cruachan. The Banshees floated at the front, their keening soft but insistent, showing the way through underwater passages that twisted and turned through stone carved by older forces than any present could name.

They swam in silence—too close to death now for words that might shatter fragile courage. Z'Landar led, Andralia beside him, and behind them came the force that would either save Scotland and Ireland both or die trying. Muirgheal swam to their left, her green hair streaming behind her. Ruadhan and the other Púca moved throughout the formation in forms that shifted—horse and seal and something between, causing ripples of confusion that might have been intentional or simply their nature expressing itself.

The Aos Sí were harder to track—sometimes visible, sometimes not, their presence felt more than seen as they moved through water like thoughts through dreams.

The channels grew narrower as they approached, the walls pressing closer, the magic growing stronger. Z'Landar could feel it now—Cliodhna's power saturating the stone, the dragon's heat radiating from somewhere ahead, the particular wrongness that came when two forces that should not coexist were pressed together in space too small to contain them both.

The water grew warmer. Impossible, at this depth, but warming nonetheless as dragon-presence bled into everything. Sulfur tainted the taste. Heat pressed against skin that knew cold as comfort.

Getting closer.

The Banshees stopped at a place where the channel opened into something larger, their keening building briefly before falling silent. The central figure turned to face the army: "Beyond lies Cruachan. Beyond lies the dragon. Beyond lies death for many and survival for few. The futures branch here. Which path you walk depends on courage and love and choices not yet made. Trust your king. Trust your queen. Trust each other. And trust that sometimes dying matters more than living, if dying preserves what living would destroy."

Then they moved forward into the opening, and the army followed, and the channel gave way to vastness.

Cruachan.

The cave stretched before them—a chamber so large that even two hundred warriors seemed small within it, so deep that the far end disappeared into darkness their eyes could not penetrate. The walls glowed faintly with phosphorescence, but beneath that gentle light ran something else—fairy magic like spiderwebs of power stretching from stone to stone, dragon-heat pulsing from the depths like a second heartbeat, and threading through everything, the particular wrongness that came when places meant to be sacred were corrupted by forces that cared nothing for sanctity.

Z'Landar felt Andralia's hand tighten in his as they swam into the chamber. Felt his own heart hammering against ribs that suddenly seemed too fragile to contain what beat within them. Felt fear clutch his throat until breathing became difficult.

But he swam forward regardless.

Because this was where they were meant to be. Where destiny and choice had carried them. Where love and duty and the stubborn refusal to let Scotland burn converged into this single moment, this impossible battle, this cave that held death and dragons and the slim chance that courage might prove sufficient after all.

The army spread out behind him, taking positions, readying weapons, preparing magic. The Banshees drifted to different points, marking paths and warning of danger. The Púca shifted forms, their chaos building. The Aos Sí positioned themselves at threshold points, preparing to counter Cliodhna's magic.

And from the depths of the cave came sound—not roar, not the battle-cry the dragon had loosed above Loch Ness, but something deeper, more primal. A mother sensing threats to her child. A creature cornered in her chosen lair. A force of nature preparing to defend what she valued more than her own life.

The water trembled.

Light bloomed in the darkness—not gentle phosphorescence but burning gold, dragon-eyes opening in the deep, fixing on the warriors who had dared enter her sanctuary.

And from the walls, from the ceiling, from the very stone itself—Cliodhna's laughter rang like bells heard underwater, like madness given voice, like fairy magic preparing to unmake those who had violated her domain.

"Welcome," the Fairy Queen's voice echoed through the chamber. "Welcome to Cruachan, foolish mortals. Welcome to my home. Welcome to your deaths."

Z'Landar felt Andralia's hand in his, felt his people readying themselves behind him, felt the weight of everything they had become pressing against his chest.

"Together?" he whispered.

"Always," she replied.

And together—two hundred souls and the king who would lead them well or die beside them—they swam forward into darkness.

Into fire.

Into whatever ending waited in Cruachan's depths.

Live or die, the time was now.

Chapter Twenty-One: The Fairy Queen's Fall

She manifested from the stone itself, stepping through the cave wall as if solid rock were merely mist that parted at her approach. Beautiful—impossibly, terribly beautiful—in ways that made mortal flesh seem crude by comparison. Cliodhna, Fairy Queen of Cruachan, wearing a form that was almost human but wrong in the way that starlight reflected in deep water was wrong, showing depths that should not exist in something two-dimensional.

Her hair fell like moonlight through moving water. Her eyes held colors that had no names in mortal tongues. Her skin seemed to shift between presence and absence, as if she existed partly in this world and partly in places where physics worked differently. She wore no crown, needed no symbols of authority—power radiated from her like heat from forge-fires, saturating the cave that was her domain, her kingdom, her flesh made into stone and water.

And she was laughing.

"Welcome," Cliodhna's voice rang through Cruachan like bells heard from the bottom of a well—beautiful and distant and wrong. "Welcome to my home, foolish mortals. Two hundred souls swimming toward their ending. Did you truly believe you could enter my domain and survive? That I would allow you to threaten what I protect?"

Her hand moved—casual gesture, almost dismissive—and fairy magic lashed out like whips made of light and malice.

Three Kelpie warriors in the front ranks screamed as their iron weapons turned to rust in their hands, the metal flaking away like skin from burned flesh. The rust spread—up their arms, across their chests, consuming them from the outside in. They died writhing, their bodies crumbling to powder that drifted through the water like snow made of death.

A Selkie noble forgot her name mid-stroke, forgot why she swam, forgot everything except confusion that left her floating motionless until the cave wall shifted and stone closed around her, crushing her before she remembered how to scream.

"First blood is mine," Cliodhna said, her smile sharp as broken glass. "Shall we continue? I have eternity to kill you all, one by one, until the water runs red with mortal arrogance."

"NOW!" Z'Landar's voice cut through the horror, and the battle began in earnest.

The army exploded into motion—practiced formations dissolving into controlled chaos as warriors engaged a threat that could not be fought with conventional tactics. Maelis led one wing, her ancient voice carrying commands that three and a half centuries had made instinctive. Tormod of the Rapids drove forward with twenty Kelpie warriors at his back, their river-strength pushing through water that Cliodhna tried to turn against them.

The Aos Sí positioned themselves at threshold points—places where cave walls met water, where stone touched emptiness, where one realm bled into another. They spoke words in languages that predated human tongues, unweaving the fairy magic that saturated Cruachan, creating gaps in Cliodhna's power like holes in fabric.

"By threshold and true name," one intoned, its voice resonating through dimensions mortals could not perceive. "By iron and oak and running water. By the laws you yourself must follow—we compel you!"

Cliodhna's laughter turned sharp. "You think knowing the rules means winning the game? How delightfully naive." Her power surged, and an Aos Sí shrieked—not in pain but in fury—as its form began to unravel, fairy magic turning on fairy flesh. It dissolved like salt in water, leaving only echoes that would haunt Cruachan for centuries.

But the opening had been created. Warriors poured through the gap, pressing forward, weapons raised despite seeing what Cliodhna could do to iron and flesh both.

The Púca struck from three directions simultaneously—Ruadhan as a massive black horse with eyes like coals, Síofra as something between seal and serpent, Brígh as a form that hurt to look at directly because it shifted too fast for eyes to follow. They moved through the battle like chaos given purpose, attacking Cliodhna and confusing her power and causing such beautiful havoc that even the Fairy Queen had to divide her attention.

"Tricksters!" Cliodhna's voice held something that might have been respect mixed with fury. "You bind yourselves to mortals? You, who should know better?"

"We bound ourselves to entertainment," Ruadhan replied, his voice carrying through horse-form like distant thunder. "And this—" He struck at her with hooves that might have been solid or might have been illusion, forcing her to respond either way, "—this is magnificent entertainment!"

Cliodhna's magic lashed out—trying to turn Púca flesh to stone, to bind them with true names, to unmake them as she'd unmade the Aos Sí. But Púca were harder to catch than wind, harder to hold than water, and her power kept striking where they had been rather than where they were.

Z'Landar swam through the chaos, Andralia at his side, watching his people die in ways that would haunt whatever dreams he had left. A young Kelpie warrior—barely twenty years old—caught Cliodhna's attention for a heartbeat. "What is your name, child?" she asked, and when he opened his mouth to answer, the word that emerged was his ending. His true name, spoken in her presence, gave her power over him. She twisted it like a knife, and he came apart at the seams, flesh separating from bone separating from the magic that had held him together.

"Stop her!" Maelis's voice carried desperation that three centuries had taught her to hide. "She's too strong in her own domain—we need more power!"

And Z'Landar understood. Cliodhna was winning. Despite the Aos Sí creating openings, despite the Púca causing chaos, despite two hundred warriors pressing forward with determination that should have been sufficient—she was winning. Because this was her cave, her kingdom, her flesh made into stone. Fighting her here was like fighting the mountain itself.

He needed more than physical strength. More than simple magic. He needed the power that made him different from every other Kelpie who had ever drawn breath.

But that power only worked in his water-forms.

"Andralia," he said, his voice tight. "I need to shift. Need seal-form to use my perception power. But if I do—"

"You can't speak to coordinate the warriors," she finished. "I know. Do it anyway. Shift. Use your power. I'll be your voice. I'll channel what you create into magic that breaks her hold. Together, beloved. Like we always do."

He looked at her—this woman who had chosen him, who had stood beside him through fire and death and impossibility, who loved him with devotion that made even fairy magic seem small—and found courage he didn't know he still possessed.

"Together," he agreed, and let the transformation flow over him.

The seal-form came as naturally as breathing, his body remembering shapes it had worn since birth. But this time felt different. This time, he felt the Heart of the Loch at his chest pulse with light so bright that warriors paused mid-stroke to stare. This time, he felt his power expand beyond his flesh, beyond his immediate presence, reaching out to touch the water itself, the stone, the space between things where perception lived.

And he saw.

Saw how Cliodhna perceived the battle—not as mortals did, tracking individuals and weapons, but as shifting patterns of threat and non-threat, power and weakness, danger and dismissal. Saw how her fairy-sight worked, how she read intentions before they became actions, how she knew what warriors would do because she could see the futures branching from each choice they made.

And he understood: to defeat her, he needed to make her see things that weren't there. To fill her perception with threats that would never materialize and hide real dangers behind illusions so convincing that her fairy-sight couldn't tell truth from fabrication.

Z'Landar reached for his power—the cosmic heritage that made him bridge between worlds, the star-traveler blood that let him shape perception as easily as Kelpies shaped water—and began to weave.

The cave filled with dragons.

Not one dragon, but dozens—false visions of Caoránach appearing throughout the chamber, each one perfect down to the smallest scale, each one radiating the same heat and menace and maternal fury as the real dragon who waited in the depths. The illusions moved with the serpentine grace of true dragons, opened jaws to show fire building in throats, beat wings that sent currents surging through water despite being nothing but shaped perception.

Cliodhna's laughter faltered. "Trickery? You think illusions will—" She stopped, her fairy-sight struggling to separate real from false. Because these weren't simple illusions—they were perceptions shaped by power that came from beyond Earth, woven by someone whose heritage included forces that could make reality uncertain at its foundations.

"Which ones are real?" she whispered, and for the first time, her voice held doubt.

Z'Landar pressed harder. Made her see her domain crumbling—stone walls developing cracks, water beginning to drain, the cave that was her flesh starting to die. Made her see the dragon calling for her help, roaring in fury at being abandoned by her ally. Made her see futures where she lost, where her power shattered, where Cruachan rejected her for corrupting what should have been sacred.

And through it all, Andralia channeled and amplified—taking his shaped perceptions and adding her own power, her cosmic heritage singing in harmony with his, making the false visions so convincing that even reality seemed to doubt itself.

The light from the Heart of the Loch grew blinding—not physical light, but illumination that came from somewhere else, showing truths and lies so intertwined that separation became impossible. Z'Landar felt his power surge beyond anything he'd achieved before, felt Andralia's presence wrapping around his like water around stone, felt their combined force pressing against Cliodhna's magic until something had to give.

"ENOUGH!" The Fairy Queen's shriek carried harmonics that made stone crack. Her hands moved in patterns too complex for mortal eyes to follow, gathering her power, preparing to unmake the illusions, to strike at Z'Landar directly, to end this game before it ended her.

But the Aos Sí saw their moment. While Cliodhna was distracted, while her attention was divided between false dragons and real threats, while her fairy-sight struggled to pierce Z'Landar's woven perceptions—they spoke the binding words.

"By your true name, Cliodhna of the Hollow Hills," they intoned in unison, their voices resonating across dimensions. "By threshold violated and sanctuary corrupted. By alliance made with forces that defile your sacred charge. By the laws you yourself cannot break—we compel you!"

Cliodhna screamed—rage and disbelief and something that might have been fear all mixed together. "You dare? You dare speak my true name against me?"

"We dare," the Aos Sí replied. "Because you broke faith first. You corrupted Cruachan with dragon-taint. You allied with forces of fire in a place meant for water and stone. You violated your own laws. And so those laws turn against you."

The cave itself rebelled. Stone that had been Cliodhna's flesh rejected her presence. Water that had carried her power turned hostile. The magic that saturated Cruachan began to unravel, pulling away from her control, seeking new equilibrium that didn't include a queen who had betrayed her sacred charge.

"NO!" Cliodhna's form flickered—presence becoming absence, solid becoming translucent. "This is my domain! Mine by right older than your pathetic mortality!"

272

"Was your domain," Ruadhan said, appearing in human form beside her, his grin sharp as knives. "But you broke the rules. And when fairy queens break their own rules—" He struck, his shapeshifting power combining with Z'Landar's perception magic and Andralia's amplification and the Aos Sí's binding words. "—they lose everything."

The combined assault hit like mountains colliding. Z'Landar felt his power surge through Andralia's channeling, felt it join with forces both mortal and not, felt it crash against Cliodhna's defenses with strength born of necessity and desperation and two hundred souls who refused to die without fighting.

And Cliodhna's magic shattered.

She screamed—a sound that would echo through Cruachan until stone itself forgot how to remember—as her power was torn from her like skin from flesh. The fairy magic that had made her queen, that had bound her to this place, that had given her dominion over stone and water and the space between—it unraveled thread by thread, pulled apart by forces she could not resist because she had broken the laws that protected her from such unmaking.

"I curse you!" she shrieked as her form began to dissolve. "Curse you all! You think defeating me means victory? The dragon will burn you to ash! And beyond her—beyond Cruachan—waits something worse! Balor will destroy what I merely wounded! You've won nothing but the right to die more slowly!"

Her power continued to unravel—not just her magic, but her very nature. The Aos Sí weren't just banishing her from Cruachan. They were stripping her of what made her fairy queen, reducing her to something less, something that could never threaten this place again.

"You cannot do this!" Cliodhna's voice grew fainter, more distant. "I am eternal! I am—"

"You were eternal," the Aos Sí corrected. "You were queen. You were many things. Now you are merely remnant, stripped of power, banished from domain, reduced to warning-tale that other fairy folk will tell when they wonder what happens to those who break sacred trust."

Cliodhna made one final sound—fury and grief and spite all compressed into wordless rage—and then she was gone. Not dead—fairies didn't die so easily—but banished to whatever realm accepted queens who had lost their kingdoms. Driven from Cruachan forever. Stripped of powers that would take centuries to reclaim, if they could be reclaimed at all.

The cave fell silent except for the sound of water finding new equilibrium, of stone settling, of magic that no longer had a queen to guide it seeking different patterns to follow.

Z'Landar shifted back to human form, exhaustion crashing over him like waves. His legs nearly buckled, and only Andralia's arms around him kept him upright. The Heart of the Loch still pulsed at his chest, but dimmer now, the light fading as his power retreated to levels that could be sustained.

"We won," he said, the words tasting strange. "We actually—"

"Count the dead," Maelis's voice cut through whatever celebration might have been building. "Count them and honor them and remember that victory is measured in blood."

The count, when it came, was devastating.

One hundred and three. One hundred and three warriors who would not return to Scotland. Who had died to fairy magic and Cliodhna's spite and the simple mathematics of fighting forces beyond mortal strength. Bodies drifted through the water or lay broken against stone where magic had thrown them. Some were recognizable. Others had been unmade so completely that only their weapons remained to mark where they had fallen.

Beathan. Z'Landar found him near the cave's western wall, his Kelpie strength insufficient against fairy magic that had turned his bones to sand inside his skin. He had died quickly—Z'Landar hoped he'd died quickly—his face frozen in expression of surprise rather than agony. Three hundred years he'd lived, fighting beside Brannach before Z'Landar was born, and he'd fallen in seconds to a power he couldn't comprehend let alone fight.

"He died well," Tormod said quietly, appearing at Z'Landar's shoulder. "Died fighting. That's all we can ask."

A Selkie noble named Eithne lay crumpled where Cliodhna's true-name magic had caught her. She'd been quick-witted and sharp-tongued, had made them all laugh during the journey from Scotland with stories of the ridiculous things mortals did for love. Now she was silent forever, her wit extinguished, her stories ended mid-telling.

And Cairbre—one of Muirgheal's Merrow, young and brave and convinced he'd survive anything because hadn't he already survived the dragon's initial wrath? Cliodhna had proven him wrong, had dissolved him like salt in freshwater until nothing remained but his red cap floating empty in the current.

The Banshees moved among the dead, keening softly—not in grief, exactly, but in acknowledgment that what they'd foreseen had come to pass. "We told you," they seemed to say without words. "We showed you the futures. We warned that many would not return. Now you understand what warning means."

Z'Landar wanted to weep. Wanted to rage. Wanted to undo the choices that had led one hundred and three souls to deaths they should not have died. But he had no time for grief, no space for doubt, because from the depths of the cave came sound that made every surviving warrior tense.

Movement. Massive displacement of water. Heat building rapidly toward levels that should boil flesh.

The dragon was coming.

Caoránach had waited while Cliodhna fought, had let her ally face the intruders first. Perhaps she'd believed the Fairy Queen would be sufficient. Perhaps she'd simply been preparing, gathering power, letting maternal fury build to levels that would make her unstoppable. Perhaps she'd known all along that she would have to face them herself and was merely conserving strength for the battle that truly mattered.

But now Cliodhna was gone. Now the fairy magic that had saturated Cruachan was broken. Now there was nothing between the dragon and

275

the warriors except water growing hot enough to hurt and darkness that pulsed with molten light.

The survivors gathered—barely one hundred now, exhausted and wounded and grieving for friends who would never see Scotland again. The Púca moved among them, still causing chaos but subdued somehow, as if even tricksters understood that what came next was not game but ending. The Aos Sí positioned themselves again, ready to do what they could though all of them understood that dragon-magic was different from fairy-magic, harder to bind, more primal in its fury. The Banshees floated at threshold points, keening constantly now, seeing deaths that were moments away rather than hours.

Z'Landar felt Andralia's hand find his, felt her fingers thread through his with familiar ease that spoke of how essential she'd become. He wanted to tell her to flee, to save herself, to let him face the dragon alone. But he knew she wouldn't go. Knew she'd choose to burn beside him rather than live without him. Knew that loving her meant accepting her choice even when that choice led toward fire.

"Together?" he whispered.

"Always," she replied.

The water exploded with light.

Caoránach emerged from the depths like nightmares given form—fifty meters of serpentine muscle and obsidian scales shot through with veins of gold that pulsed with inner fire. Her eyes opened—each one larger than a warrior's torso, burning with fury that went beyond rage into something pure and terrible and utterly maternal. Wings that should have been folded in confined space somehow had room to spread, membrane translucent and veined with gold catching the light from her own body and reflecting it in shades that hurt to see.

She was magnificent. She was terrible. She was everything the legends had promised and worse than any nightmare had prepared them for.

And she was only beginning to be angry.

"You killed my children," the dragon said, her voice resonating through water and stone and the chests of warriors who suddenly understood how small they were, how fragile, how utterly insufficient for the battle ahead. "You murdered my babies in places I thought safe. You destroyed my ally who offered sanctuary. You dare—DARE—enter my chosen nest to threaten what remains."

Her jaws opened, showing teeth like swords and a throat that glowed red-gold with fire building, building, ready to be unleashed.

"I will burn you all to ash," Caoránach declared, and her voice held certainty absolute as tides, inevitable as death. "Will scorch flesh from bone. Will boil water around you until you cook in your own bodies. Will make you scream for mercy that will not come because mothers protecting their young know nothing of mercy and care less of honor and value only the survival of what they would die a thousand times to preserve."

She inhaled—a sound like wind through caverns, like breath drawn before the end of the world—and the water around her began to boil.

"NOW!" Z'Landar's voice carried command earned through leading warriors into hell twice before. "SCATTER! Don't give her massed targets! Move, move, MOVE!"

The survivors exploded into motion—swimming in every direction, seeking shelter behind stone outcroppings, diving deeper or rising higher, anything to avoid being grouped where dragon-fire could claim them all at once.

Caoránach's fire came like the wrath of gods—a column of flame that shouldn't exist underwater but did anyway because dragon-magic cared nothing for physics or possibility. It struck where the warriors had been clustered, and the water there didn't just boil—it flashed to steam, creating a bubble of vacuum and heat and death that collapsed inward with force that pulverized stone.

Three warriors had been too slow. They died instantly, cooked inside their own flesh, their bodies floating lifeless in water that still bubbled with residual heat.

277

"Again," the dragon said, and inhaled once more.

Z'Landar looked at Andralia, saw his own understanding reflected in her impossible eyes. They had won against Cliodhna. Had broken fairy magic and stripped a queen of her power.

But the dragon was different. The dragon was worse. The dragon was a mother defending her last living child, and nothing—nothing—was more dangerous than that.

"This is it," he said quietly. "This is where we learn if love and courage and desperate determination are sufficient."

"Then let's find out," she replied, her hand tightening in his. "Together."

"Always."

The dragon's second blast of fire came like judgment, and the real battle—the impossible battle, the battle that would determine whether Scotland and Ireland survived or burned—began in earnest.

Behind them, one hundred and three bodies drifted in water that carried the taste of death and victory both.

Ahead, a dragon prepared to make that number two hundred and three.

And somewhere in the depths, an egg waited—protected by scale and fury and a mother's love that would burn worlds before allowing harm to reach it.

The tale was not yet finished.

But the ending—glorious or terrible or some mixture of both—was drawing closer with every heartbeat.

Every breath.

Every moment that warriors chose to stand rather than flee.

To fight rather than surrender.

To die if necessary, but to die trying.

Because that was what courage meant when courage was all that remained.

Chapter Twenty-Two: The Mother's Fall

The dragon's fire came again and again, each blast turning water to steam and stone to slag, each strike claiming lives that could not be reclaimed. Warriors scattered like schools of fish before predators, seeking shelter behind outcroppings that melted under sustained heat, diving deep only to find that depth offered no protection when dragon-fury heated water from above and below simultaneously.

Z'Landar swam through chaos that defied comprehension, Andralia at his side, watching his people die in ways that would haunt whatever dreams he had left. A young Selkie—Orna, barely eighteen, who had sung songs during the journey from Scotland with voice like morning itself—caught the edge of a fire-blast that wasn't even aimed at her. The heat cooked her instantly, and her body drifted past Z'Landar's vision still wearing the expression of someone who had been singing moments before death remembered she was mortal.

"We can't get close!" Tormod's voice carried over the sounds of battle, and Z'Landar saw the old Kelpie warrior bleeding from burns that covered half his torso. "Every approach is death! She protects her belly—the egg—won't let us near!"

He was right. Caoránach fought with the particular cunning of mothers who understood that their children's survival mattered more than their own. She positioned herself so that her vulnerable underbelly—where the egg rested within her body—was always shielded. Always protected. Attack from above and her wings became shields. Attack from the sides and her coils deflected strikes toward armored flanks. Attack from below and fire rained down until water itself became weapon.

The Púca darted in and out, causing chaos in forms that shifted too rapidly to track—horse and seal and something with too many teeth and not enough flesh to contain them. But even their trickster nature proved insufficient. Ruadhan took a glancing blow from the dragon's tail and went tumbling through the water, his form flickering between shapes like a candle guttering in wind.

280

The Aos Sí wove counter-magic, speaking words that should have bound dragon-power the way they'd bound Cliodhna's. But dragon-magic was older than fairy-magic, more primal, less concerned with rules that could be exploited. The spells slid off Caoránach's scales like water off oil, and one of the remaining Aos Sí shrieked as backlash caught it, unmaking its form until only echoes remained.

"We're losing," Andralia said quietly, her hand tight in Z'Landar's, her face tormented with the reality. "Beloved, we're losing."

He knew. Could see it in the way warriors moved—no longer with determination but with desperation, no longer attacking but simply trying to survive. Could see it in the bodies that drifted past, in the Banshees' keening that had become nearly constant, in the way even the bravest among them flinched when the dragon inhaled and fire built in her throat.

They were losing. And if they lost here, if they retreated or died or failed to destroy the egg—then Scotland and Ireland both would burn within a generation. Would become ash and memory and cautionary tales about what happened when courage proved insufficient against forces too terrible to comprehend.

He needed a plan. Needed strategy. Needed something beyond throwing warriors at a mother dragon who would die a thousand times before allowing harm to reach her child.

But all he had was exhaustion and grief and the growing certainty that victory would cost more than they could afford to pay.

Then Maelis swam past him, moving with purpose that three and a half centuries had taught her to recognize when others could not. She caught his eye for just a moment, and in that glance passed understanding that made Z'Landar's chest tighten with horror and comprehension both.

"No," he said. "Maelis, don't—"

But she was already gone, swimming not away from the dragon but directly toward her, moving with speed that belied her age, that spoke of final reserves being spent because there would be no after to save them for.

"FOR SCOTLAND!" Maelis's voice rang through Cruachan like bells tolling for the dead, like war-cries from battles fought before Scotland had a name. "FOR THE WATERS THAT BIRTHED US! FOR THE KING WHO LEADS US! FOR EVERYTHING WE FOUGHT TO PRESERVE!"

Caoránach's massive head swiveled toward her—distracted from the larger force by this single warrior swimming directly into her jaws, by courage so absolute it demanded attention, by defiance that made even dragon-fury pause in something that might have been respect.

"Foolish," the dragon said, and opened her mouth to unleash fire that would erase Maelis from existence.

"MAELIS!" Z'Landar's scream tore from his throat raw and desperate. "NO! RETREAT! THIS I COMMAND!"

But Maelis did not retreat. Did not slow. Did not falter even as dragon-light built in Caoránach's throat, even as death became not possibility but certainty, even as three and a half centuries of living approached their ending in fire and fury.

She looked back once—just once—and her ancient eyes found Z'Landar's across the chaos of battle. Her lips moved, forming words that somehow carried despite the distance and the noise and the roaring of blood in Z'Landar's ears:

"We will meet again in a land we do not yet know."

Then the fire came.

It struck Maelis directly, completely, without mercy or hesitation. There was no time for screaming, no moment of agony—just instant transition from living to ended, from presence to absence, from warrior to memory. Her body didn't drift away broken. It simply ceased to be, consumed so thoroughly that not even ash remained to mark where three and a half centuries of wisdom and strength and fierce devotion to Scotland had stood moments before.

Z'Landar felt something in his chest shatter—not physically but in ways that physical wounds could never match. Maelis was gone. The ancient

282

one who had taught him what it meant to lead, who had stood beside his father before Z'Landar was born, who had carried Scotland's memory through times when memory seemed insufficient to the task. Gone. Ended. Reduced to nothing by fire that cared less for centuries lived than for the simple mathematics of heat against flesh.

But her sacrifice had created what she intended—a moment of distraction, of vulnerability, where Caoránach's attention was divided and her defenses momentarily lowered.

Z'Landar wanted to weep. Wanted to rage. Wanted to stop the battle and honor what Maelis had given and scream at the universe for demanding such prices from those who could least afford to pay them.

But stopping meant her death was wasted. Meant Scotland burned anyway. Meant three and a half centuries ended for nothing.

So instead he swam forward, Andralia beside him, seeking the opening Maelis had purchased with her life.

Behind him, he heard the morale shatter like ice under spring sun. Heard warriors crying out in grief and horror. Heard some begin to retreat despite orders, despite determination, despite everything except the simple understanding that if Maelis could die—if the ancient one could be ended so completely—then none of them were safe, none of them sufficient, none of them equal to the task they'd undertaken.

"Hold!" Z'Landar's voice cracked with emotion he couldn't suppress. "HOLD THE LINE! She bought us this moment—don't waste it! Don't let her ending serve no purpose! HOLD!"

Some warriors steadied. Others continued to retreat. And Z'Landar understood with sick certainty that they were moments away from complete rout, from dissolution of the force into individuals fleeing for their lives, from failure that would make every death meaningless.

Then darkness came.

Not absence of light—the cave was already dim enough for that. This was different. This was presence, not absence. Darkness that moved like living things, that flowed into Cruachan from the entrance like smoke but with intention and malice and something that might have been hunger.

Warriors paused mid-retreat, confused and terrified. Caoránach herself stopped, her massive head turning toward the entrance, toward the darkness that came with sounds like wind through graveyards, like the breathing of things that should not breathe, like death given voice and form.

The Sluagh had arrived.

They came in forms that hurt to perceive directly—some bird-like with wings that seemed made of shadow and regret, some humanoid but wrong in ways that suggested humanity glimpsed through nightmare's lens, all of them dark and terrible and carrying the particular presence of things that had died but refused to properly end. The Host of the Unforgiven Dead, flowing into Cruachan like storm-front, like plague-wind, like all the deaths that Ireland had witnessed over centuries compressed into single force that cared nothing for dragon-fire because fire could not burn what had already burned and passed beyond burning's reach.

"The Sluagh!" Muirgheal's voice carried shock and relief in equal measure. "They actually came! I thought—I hoped—but I wasn't certain—"

The darkness coalesced into something almost like a leader—a figure that might once have been human but had forgotten what humanity meant, wearing tattered remnants that could have been clothing or skin or simply the idea of covering carried beyond death into whatever came after. When it spoke, its voice was wind through bones, was the last breath of dying men, was every keening cry that had ever marked someone's ending:

"We watched you from the western waters. Watched you fight impossible battles. Watched you die with courage that shames the living." The Sluagh-leader's form rippled like smoke. "We were uncertain. Uncertain if mortals still knew how to die well. Uncertain if flesh-bound creatures could demonstrate the devotion we remember from ages when death meant something more than simply ending."

Z'Landar found his voice despite horror that made speaking difficult. "You... you'll help us?"

"We help those who prove worthy of the dead's respect." The Sluagh-leader gestured toward where Maelis had fallen. "Your ancient one died well. Died as warriors should die—buying time for others, spending herself for purpose that transcended simple survival. That is worthy. You are worthy. And so—" The darkness surged forward. "We fight beside you. Dragon-fire cannot burn what is already burned. Death cannot claim what has already claimed itself. We are the Unforgiven. The Unredeemed. The ones who serve in death because life granted us no purpose. Let us serve now."

The Sluagh swarmed the dragon like a murder of crows made from nightmare, their forms flickering between solid and insubstantial, their shrieks filling Cruachan with sounds that made even hardened warriors flinch. Caoránach's fire came—blast after blast, turning the darkness luminous but failing to destroy it. Some Sluagh fell, their forms dissipating into true absence. But others pressed forward, clawing and biting and tearing with talons that were sometimes physical and sometimes merely the idea of harm made manifest.

The dragon thrashed, her massive body slamming against cave walls with force that cracked stone. Her wings beat, creating currents that would have scattered mortal warriors like leaves. But the Sluagh clung to her, dragged at her, distracted her with their sheer numbers and their refusal to be deterred by anything except complete dissolution.

"NOW!" Z'Landar's voice carried across the chaos. "While she's distracted! All forces, converge! This is our moment!"

The surviving warriors surged forward—fifty souls, perhaps fewer, all that remained of the two hundred who had entered Cruachan. The Púca joined the Sluagh in their assault, shapeshifting madly, adding chaos to chaos until even dragon-cunning couldn't track all the threats at once. The Aos Sí spoke their binding words, exploiting the moments when Caoránach's attention was divided. The Banshees keened directions— showing paths that led toward the dragon rather than away, guiding warriors through fire that would have killed them otherwise.

And Caoránach, distracted by the Sluagh, enraged by their persistence, driven to fury by these things that refused to die properly—exposed her belly.

Z'Landar saw it. The vulnerable point. The place where obsidian scales gave way to softer flesh, where the egg rested within her body, where a strike might penetrate if the striker possessed sufficient power and determination and desperation to attempt the impossible.

But weapons were insufficient. Swords had shattered against her scales. Spears had bounced off her hide. Magic had slid away like water off stone. Everything they'd tried had failed, and he had moments—perhaps seconds—before she realized her error and protected herself again.

"The water," Andralia said quietly, her hand finding his. "Beloved, you've been shaping perception. Making her see what isn't there. But you're also Kelpie. Son of water. You can shape more than just sight."

Z'Landar looked at her, understanding flooding through him like tide returning to shore. He'd been focused on perception—on making Cliodhna see illusions, on confusing enemies with false visions. But that was only part of his power. He was water-born. Son of Loch Ness. Child of sacrifice that had been paid in water and blood both.

He could shape the water itself.

"How?" The question emerged desperate.

"The same way you shape anything else." Her impossible eyes held certainty absolute. "Will it. Command it. Make it obey because you are what you are and water recognizes its own. And I'll—" She pressed closer. "I'll channel it. Amplify it. Make it real in ways that even dragon-scale cannot deny."

Z'Landar reached for his power—not the perception-shaping this time, but something deeper, older, more fundamental to what he was. Reached for the part of him that was water given form, that could swim as easily as breathing, that knew currents and tides and the way liquid moved through the world like blood through veins.

And the water responded.

286

It gathered before him—pulled from the cave, from the sea beyond, from every source within reach. Compressed under pressure that should have been impossible, solidifying in ways that defied every law of nature except the law that said power shaped reality when wielded by those whose heritage transcended simple mortality.

The Heart of the Loch at his chest blazed with light so intense that warriors had to look away, so bright that even dragon-fire seemed dim by comparison. Z'Landar felt Andralia's power joining his, felt her cosmic nature wrapping around his terrestrial strength, felt them become something neither could have achieved alone—synthesis of star-traveler wisdom and water-born fury, of love and desperation and the stubborn refusal to fail when failure meant Scotland burned.

The water took shape.

A sword longer than Z'Landar was tall, wider than his torso, forged from compressed water that had been made solid through will alone. Its edge gleamed like winter ice catching first light, sharp beyond anything mortal smiths could achieve because sharpness was simply another property to be commanded when water obeyed absolutely. Its blade pulsed with inner light—blue and silver and gold all mixed together, colors that came from the Heart of the Loch and from Andralia's amplification and from Z'Landar's own power finally unleashed without restraint or uncertainty.

It was beautiful. It was terrible. It was weapon that should not exist but did anyway because sometimes impossible was merely another obstacle to be overcome when necessity demanded and love provided the strength to demand.

Warriors stopped fighting to stare. The Sluagh paused in their assault, their darkness drawing back slightly as if even the dead recognized something profound in what Z'Landar held. The Púca's chaos quieted. The Banshees' keening faded to whispers.

Caoránach saw it too. Saw and understood that this was different from other threats, different from swords that shattered and magic that failed. This was something that could reach what she most needed to protect.

"NO!" The dragon's voice carried maternal fury beyond anything she'd demonstrated before. She tried to coil, tried to protect her belly, tried to shield the egg that was all she had left of her line.

But the Sluagh swarmed her again, holding her in place, and Ruadhan laughed his trickster's laugh and became three Ruadhans and then seven, each one pulling at different parts of her, each one real enough to demand her attention even if only some were truly physical.

Z'Landar raised the water sword. Felt its weight—or lack of weight, because it was water and water knew how to move at his command. Felt Andralia's presence wrapped around his consciousness, amplifying and focusing and guiding. Felt every warrior's hope pressing against his shoulders like physical force.

One chance. One strike. Everything they'd fought for, everyone who'd died, all the courage and love and desperate determination—it all compressed into this single moment, this impossible throw, this strike that had to be perfect because imperfect meant failure and failure meant Scotland burned.

He met Andralia's eyes. Saw love there, and trust, and certainty that he could do this because he was what he was and she would make him more.

"Together," she whispered.

"Always," he replied.

And threw.

The water sword flew like thought made manifest, like inevitability given form, like destiny compressed into single trajectory that could not be denied or deflected or stopped. It covered the distance between Z'Landar and the dragon in less than a heartbeat, moving faster than anything physical should move because it wasn't just physical—it was will shaped into weapon, power given purpose, love transmuted into force sufficient to pierce what could not be pierced.

It struck Caoránach's exposed belly precisely where Z'Landar had aimed—precisely where the egg rested within her body, protected by

288

flesh and scale and maternal devotion that would have been sufficient against any other threat.

But not against this.

The water sword punched through obsidian scales like they were paper. Drove deeper through flesh that tried to close around it. Kept going because Z'Landar willed it and Andralia amplified and together they were more than dragon-scale could withstand. Deeper. Into the chamber where the egg waited. Into the egg itself.

And the egg shattered.

Not with sound—it was too deep within dragon-flesh for that. But Z'Landar felt it through the connection his power maintained with the water sword. Felt the protective shell crack. Felt the magic that had kept the egg viable dissipate like smoke in wind. Felt the potential dragon-child die before it could breathe or see or spread wings that would never develop now.

Felt the third egg end.

Caoránach's scream was not roar or fury or even pain, though pain surely accompanied what Z'Landar had done. This was grief. Pure maternal grief that went beyond words or comprehension, that spoke of loss that unmade mothers more completely than any weapon could unmake flesh.

"MY CHILD!" The words tore from her throat like pieces of her soul being expelled. "MY LAST CHILD! WHAT HAVE YOU DONE? WHAT HAVE YOU—"

She thrashed, her massive body convulsing, the water sword still embedded in her belly like accusation made manifest. Blood—dragon blood that glowed faint gold and tasted of sulfur and fire—began to spread through the water, mixing with the carnage that already stained Cruachan.

"YOU KILLED THEM ALL!" Caoránach's voice grew weaker but no less anguished. "ALL MY CHILDREN! ALL MY LINE! EVERYTHING I—" She coughed, and fire came with the cough, but weak fire, dying fire. "Dragon-kind... will never... will NEVER be

289

defeated... Others remain... others will avenge... will burn your world to—"

Her voice failed. Her massive eyes—those burning gold orbs that had struck fear into every warrior who'd seen them—began to dim. Her wings folded against her sides one final time. Her coils loosened, and her body began to sink toward the cave floor with the particular finality of things that would not rise again.

"May the waters... remember... what mortals... forgot..." She managed one last whisper. "That mothers... would burn worlds... before allowing... harm to children..."

Then she was gone. Simply gone. Caoránach the dragon, ancient beyond most beings' reckoning, powerful enough to have destroyed Scotland if she'd wished, died not with fury but with grief, not cursing her killers but mourning her children, not threatening but remembering what it meant to be mother when being mother was all that mattered.

Her body settled onto the cave floor, and the impact sent tremors through stone that would take hours to fully quiet. The water around her glowed faint gold with her blood, and the heat that had made Cruachan nearly unbearable began to dissipate as dragon-fire extinguished forever.

Silence fell. Not peaceful silence—nothing about this could be called peaceful—but the particular quiet that follows battles when even survivors are too exhausted for celebration, too grief-stricken for triumph, too aware of costs paid to feel anything except hollow.

Z'Landar floated in the water, staring at what he'd done. The dragon was dead. The egg destroyed. Three of four eggs now gone. Scotland and Ireland were safer. The quest was nearly complete.

But Maelis was dead. And Beathan. And Eithne and Cairbre and Orna and ninety-five others whose names he knew, whose faces he remembered, whose deaths would haunt him until his own ending came.

Was it worth it? The question whispered through his mind like poison. All those deaths—for what? To kill a mother protecting her young? To destroy children before they could threaten? To do violence that felt less like heroism and more like necessary evil?

He didn't know. Perhaps he'd never know. Perhaps that was the weight of command—living with questions that had no comfortable answers, bearing guilt for choices that were simultaneously right and terrible.

"Beloved." Andralia's voice was gentle, her hand finding his. "Come. We need to tend the wounded. Honor the dead. Prepare for what comes next."

"What comes next is Balor," Z'Landar said hollowly. "What comes next is the fourth egg and a Fomorian giant whose eye kills with looking. What comes next is another impossible battle that will claim more lives I can't afford to lose."

"Yes," she agreed. "But not today. Today we honor those who fell. Today we remember Maelis and what she gave. Today we let ourselves feel the weight of what we've done and what it cost. Tomorrow—" She pulled him close. "Tomorrow we face whatever comes next. Together."

"Always," he whispered, though the word tasted like ash.

They gathered in the cave's center as what remained of the army swam among the dead, seeking friends and loved ones, confirming who had survived and who would need cairns raised and names carved and songs sung. The count, when it came, was worse than even the Banshees had predicted.

One hundred fifty-three.

One hundred fifty-three warriors who would not return to Scotland. Who had entered Cruachan with courage sufficient to shame gods and had paid the price that courage demanded when wielded against impossible odds.

Maelis, who had led them for three and a half centuries and died buying them moments they desperately needed.

Beathan the Kelpie elder, who had fought beside Z'Landar's father and survived three hundred years only to fall to fairy magic.

Eithne the Selkie noble, quick-witted and sharp-tongued, silenced forever.

Cairbre the Merrow, young and convinced of his own survival until Cliodhna proved him mortal.

Orna the singer, whose voice would not grace mornings again.

And a hundred forty-eight others whose names deserved to be remembered, whose deaths mattered, whose courage had been absolute even when survival proved impossible.

The Aos Sí had lost half their number—fairy folk who had opposed Cliodhna and paid for that opposition with endings that even immortals could not escape. The Púca were diminished—Síofra gone, dissolved by dragon-fire that had caught her mid-shift, leaving Ruadhan and Brígh to carry the chaos alone. And the Sluagh—impossible to count the Sluagh, but Z'Landar thought their darkness was less deep than before, their numbers reduced by dragon-fury that could harm even the dead if applied with sufficient heat and determination.

"We won," Tormod said, swimming up to where Z'Landar floated with Andralia. The old Kelpie's burns had been tended, but he moved with pain evident in every stroke. "Dragon dead. Egg destroyed. We actually won."

"Did we?" Z'Landar asked quietly. "Look around, Tormod. Look at the price we paid. Was this victory? Or just survival purchased at cost too high to justify?"

"It was both." The Sluagh-leader materialized beside them, its form rippling like smoke over water. "Victory and cost are not opposites, young king. They are companions. Always have been. You won because you were willing to pay what victory demanded. You lost because victory always demands more than anyone wants to give." The darkness shifted. "That is what it means to lead. To make choices where all options cost blood and courage requires spending lives you cannot afford to lose."

"Maelis—" Z'Landar's voice broke.

"Died as she chose to die," the Sluagh-leader said. "Died buying time for others. Died with purpose. That is more than most achieve, more than the Sluagh ourselves managed before death claimed us. Honor her choice, young king. Don't diminish it by wishing she'd chosen differently."

"Will you stay?" Andralia asked the Sluagh-leader. "The fourth egg remains. Balor guards it. We must face him next."

"We will stay." The darkness pulsed. "The dead fear nothing. We will fight beside you until the last egg is destroyed or you all join us in whatever realm waits beyond living. Balor's eye kills with looking, but we have already died. What is looking to those who see only endings anyway?"

Muirgheal swam over, her green hair matted with blood that wasn't hers. "We'll need time before facing Balor. Days at least. Maybe weeks. The survivors are broken. Not in spirit—" she added quickly, "—but in body. They need healing. Rest. Time to grieve properly."

"We don't have weeks," Z'Landar said. "The fourth egg—if it hatches before we reach it—"

"Will not hatch for months yet," one of the remaining Aos Sí said, its voice like bells through fog. "We can sense these things. The egg with Balor is younger than the others were. Still developing. You have time— not much, but some. Use it wisely. Because Balor is worse than dragon. Worse than fairy queen. Worse than anything you've faced yet."

"How much worse can it be?" Caelan asked, swimming closer. The young chief bore burns and cuts but had survived Cruachan where so many had not. "We faced a mother dragon in her lair. Fought a fairy queen in her own domain. How much worse can a Fomorian giant be?"

"Much worse," Muirgheal said quietly. "Balor is legend given flesh. Ancient beyond reckoning. His eye doesn't just kill—it unmakes. Doesn't just end life—it erases it as if it never was. The dragon could kill you. Balor can make it so you never existed. That's the difference."

Silence followed her words, heavy and cold as deep water.

Finally, Z'Landar straightened, squaring shoulders that wanted to slump, finding the voice that command required even when command felt impossible. "Then we rest. We heal. We honor our dead properly. We give the survivors time to remember why we fight and what we fight for. And when we're ready—when we've recovered as much as we're going to recover—we swim to face Balor. We find the fourth egg. We destroy it. We end this."

"And if we can't?" Fionnuala asked quietly. Z'Landar's half-sister had survived, though barely—her left arm hung useless, burned nearly beyond function. "If Balor proves too powerful? If his eye kills us all before we can strike?"

"These are thoughts we cannot give host. If we die, we die trying," Z'Landar said simply. "Die knowing we did everything mortality could do. Die having stood when standing required everything we had. That's all we can control—not victory, not survival, but the choice to stand regardless. And that—" He looked around at the forty-seven survivors, at the Sluagh's darkness, at the bodies that drifted or lay still. "That has to be enough. Because it's all we have."

They dispersed slowly—moving to tend wounds that needed tending, to sit with dead friends one final time, to find whatever comfort could be found in the aftermath of battles that should not have been survived. Z'Landar stayed in the center of the cave, staring at the dragon's body, at Caoránach who had died not cursing him but mourning her children, who had demonstrated a mother's love in ways that transcended species or morality or any simple division between good and evil.

"You did what was necessary," Andralia said quietly, appearing at his side.

"Necessary doesn't mean right."

"No. But it means we survive. Scotland survives. Ireland survives. Isn't that worth something?" Her hand found his. "Maelis thought so. She bought us this victory with her life. Don't dishonor that by drowning in guilt for choices you couldn't avoid making."

Z'Landar turned to her, this woman who had stood beside him through fire and death and impossibility, who loved him despite knowing what leadership cost and what command demanded. "How do you do it? How do you stay so certain when I can barely hold myself together?"

"I'm not certain," she admitted. "I'm terrified and grieving and questioning everything just like you. But I've learned—" She paused, choosing words carefully. "I've learned that doubt and action aren't opposites. That you can question every choice and still make them. That certainty isn't required for courage—sometimes courage is acting despite certainty's absence."

She touched the Heart of the Loch at his chest, her fingers tracing the pendant's edges. "And there's something else you need to know. Something I should have told you before, but the time never seemed right, and then we were fighting for our lives, and—" She took a breath. "The Heart of the Loch has no magic."

Z'Landar stared at her, even in his fatigue he was energized by her words. "What?"

"It's just stone and memory," she said gently. "A symbol of what your parents sacrificed. A reminder of the love that brought you into existence. But the magic—" She pressed her hand against his chest, against the pendant, against his heart beneath. "The magic has always been you. Your cosmic heritage, enhanced by the solar rays of this planet. Your Kelpie nature. The power born of sacrifice paid in water and blood and love so absolute it shaped reality. The pendant just gave you something to focus through, something to believe in when believing in yourself seemed too difficult."

"But the light—the power—I felt it—"

"You felt your own power," she said. "Shaped by your will. Focused through the pendant because you believed it helped. But fundamentally, always, it was you. The water sword you just created? That was your power. The perception-shaping that defeated Cliodhna? That was you. Everything you've achieved—" Her eyes held his. "Everything has been you, beloved. Not borrowed magic. Not artifact-granted strength. Just you, being what you are, doing what you were meant to do."

Z'Landar touched the pendant with shaking fingers. Felt it solid and real beneath his touch. Just stone. Just memory. Just symbol of parents he'd never known who had loved him enough to die so he could live.

But the power—that had been his all along.

"Why tell me now?" he asked.

"Because you need to know before facing Balor," she said. "Need to understand that your strength comes from within, not from external sources that could be lost or taken or destroyed. The pendant is meaningful—will always be meaningful—but not because it grants power. Because it reminds you who you are, what you carry, why you fight. That's more valuable than any magic it might have contained."

She pulled him close, her arms wrapping around him with strength that belied her frame. "You are enough, Z'Landar. You always have been. And when we face Balor—when his eye turns toward us and death becomes certain—remember that. Remember that your power comes from who you are, not what you carry. Remember that love and sacrifice and cosmic heritage combined make you more than any single force could unmake. Remember—" Her voice dropped to whisper. "Remember that I believe in you. I always have. I always will. However this ends."

He held her there in the cave where dragons had died and fairy queens had fallen, where one hundred fifty-three warriors would never breathe again, where victory and grief mixed together until they became indistinguishable. Held her and felt something in his chest settle—not peace exactly, but acceptance. Understanding that the burden he carried was his own, that the power he wielded came from within, that the choices he made were his to own regardless of their cost.

"One more battle," he said quietly.

"One more," she agreed.

"Then what?"

"Then we find out if courage was sufficient," she said. "If love was strong enough. If forty-seven warriors and the Host of the Unforgiven Dead can face a Fomorian giant and survive. If—" She paused. "If we get

296

to have an after at all, or if Cruachan was just prelude to endings we can't prevent."

"Cheerful thoughts."

"Honest thoughts." She pulled back enough to meet his eyes. "I won't lie to you, beloved. Won't pretend Balor is survivable when everything we know suggests otherwise. Won't offer false comfort when truth serves better. But I will promise this—" Her hand found his face, thumb tracing his cheekbone. "Whatever comes, whatever ending waits, whatever price Balor demands—I'll pay it beside you. Together."

"This I know, this I believe," he whispered.

And in that moment, in that cave where death saturated every stone, where grief and victory mixed like blood in water—Z'Landar understood that always might be very short indeed.

But it would be enough.

Because it was all they had.

And sometimes, when darkness gathered and impossible battles waited and the only path forward led through fire—all you had was enough, if you chose to make it so.

They swam toward where the survivors gathered, toward the wounded who needed tending and the dead who needed honoring and the living who needed reminding why they'd come this far and why they'd go farther still despite odds that should have broken them already.

Behind them, the dragon's body cooled.

Above them, the cave that had been Cliodhna's kingdom waited to see what new purposes survivors would make of it.

Ahead, somewhere in depths where even Fomorians feared to swim, Balor waited with his eye that killed with looking and his power that unmade existence itself.

The tale approached its ending.

But first, they would honor the dead.

And remember that dying well mattered more than living safely when living safely meant the world burned.

Chapter Twenty-Three: The Cairns of Sorrow

The Fiery Cross went out from the shores of Loch Ness three days after the survivors returned from Ireland, carried by teenaged runners whose legs knew every hill and glen, whose voices could wake sleeping settlements with news that demanded hearing. The cross itself was ancient—charred at both ends where flame had kissed wood in ceremonies that predated memory, wrapped with white cloth that spoke of death and honor in equal measure. Each runner who received it knew what it meant: victory purchased in blood, warriors fallen far from home, and a gathering called where Scotland met Ireland's waters to honor those who would not return.

Alasdair Fraser himself had sent the cross forth, his weathered hands trembling as he passed it to the first runner. "Spread word," he'd said, his voice carrying the weight of one who had watched water-folk swim toward death and could do nothing but wait. "Tell them Cruachan is won. Tell them the dragon is dead. Tell them the egg is destroyed. And tell them—" His voice broke. "Tell them one hundred fifty-three souls paid the price. Tell them we honor them as they deserve—water-folk and Irish allies both. Tell them to come to the shore between our lands, where sea meets stone, and bring whatever grief they carry. We will honor it all."

The cross traveled fast. Through glens where autumn had turned bracken gold and red. Past lochs that reflected morning sun like mirrors of copper and flame. To settlements that had cowered when dragon-fire first fell, that had sent warriors who would not return, that deserved to know their sacrifices had mattered. Each household that received the cross sent runners onward, spreading word like ripples from stones dropped in still water, until all of Highland Scotland knew: the battle was won, the dead were many, and honor demanded presence at their remembering.

Z'Landar watched the preparations from Loch Ness's southern shore, feeling exhaustion that went beyond flesh into something deeper, something that made even standing seem effort beyond his capacity. Three days they'd taken to swim back from Cruachan—three days through waters that tasted of autumn's approach and carried currents that seemed gentler than they should, as if the sea itself understood what had been paid in Irish caves and offered what small comfort water could provide.

Forty-seven survivors. That was what remained of the two hundred who had entered Cruachan with determination absolute and courage sufficient to shame gods. Forty-seven souls bearing wounds that would heal and memories that would not, carrying grief too heavy for words and pride too fierce to be diminished by death's accounting.

"The clans are gathering," Andralia said quietly, appearing at his side with the particular silence she'd mastered. "Alasdair sent word—they'll meet us at the shore between our lands. Where Scotland's stone reaches toward Ireland's waters. Where both peoples can honor what both peoples lost."

Z'Landar nodded, not trusting his voice. The last three days had been strange—swimming through water that should have felt like victory but tasted only of grief, watching his people move with the particular care of those who had looked into their ending and survived only through fortune's grace, feeling Maelis's absence like a wound that would not close because wounds required flesh to heal and she was simply gone, consumed so completely that not even memory seemed sufficient to hold her shape.

"You should rest," Andralia continued, her hand finding his. "The ceremony doesn't begin for days yet. Time for the clans to travel. Time for—"

"Time to pretend I'm not drowning in guilt for one hundred fifty-three deaths I ordered?" The words came harsh, bitter. "Time to forget that Maelis died buying moments I used to kill a mother protecting her child? Time to—" He stopped, breathing hard. "I'm sorry, I'm not in my right mind just now."

"Nothing about this is fair," she replied. "Not to me, not to you, not to anyone who survived or anyone who fell. Fair died when dragons chose to nest in Scotland. What remains is necessary. Is surviving. Is honoring those who paid what we asked them to pay." Her fingers tightened in his. "Come. Walk with me. The water helps. It always helps."

300

They walked along the shore as evening painted sky in shades of crimson and gold, as survivors tended wounds and prepared for the journey that would take them to the shore between lands, as the weight of what came next pressed against them both like stones carried underwater. The Púca had come with them from Ireland—Ruadhan and Brígh moving in forms that shifted between horse and human and things between, causing small chaos even in grief because chaos was what they were and denying nature seemed pointless when death had claimed so many already.

But the Aos Sí had not come. Had disappeared after Cruachan as if fairy folk found mortal grief too raw to witness or perhaps simply returned to whatever realms they inhabited when not fighting dragons in caves. And the Banshees—the Banshees had keened once as survivors left Irish waters, a sound like all the grief Ireland had ever known compressed into single note, then fallen silent and drifted away like smoke in wind.

And the Sluagh—the Host of the Unforgiven Dead who had turned the battle, who had swarmed Caoránach when defeat seemed certain—they had simply vanished. No farewell, no promise to return, no indication whether they would appear again when Balor was faced or if their service had been rendered and their interest exhausted. They were gone, and Z'Landar could only hope that when the final battle came, when the eye that killed with looking turned toward them, the dead would remember what they'd promised and fight beside the living one last time.

"Do you think they'll come back?" he asked quietly. "The Sluagh?"

Andralia was silent for a long moment. "I don't know. The dead follow their own paths, answer to obligations we don't understand. They judged us worthy once. Whether we remain worthy when facing Balor—" She shrugged. "We'll discover when we need them most. Either they'll be there or they won't. Planning around their presence seems foolish."

"So we plan to face a Fomorian giant whose eye unmakes existence with forty-seven exhausted warriors and two Púca whose chaos is as likely to doom us as save us." Z'Landar's laugh held no humor. "Excellent. That should be easy enough..."

"Perhaps it will," Andralia said. "Perhaps facing impossible odds is simply what we do now. What we've become. The people who look at battles that should not be survived and swim toward them anyway because someone must stand and we've forgotten how to run."

They walked in silence until full darkness fell, until stars emerged over water that reflected them like scattered diamonds, until the cold drove them back toward the camps where survivors huddled around fires and spoke in quiet voices of friends who would not share warmth again.

The journey to the shore between lands took two days—not because the distance was great, but because the Highland clans traveled with them, and clans moved at the pace of grief rather than urgency. Alasdair Fraser led his people with the particular dignity of one who had sent warriors to die and could do nothing but honor that sending. Other chiefs came too—MacLeod and MacKenzie, Cameron and MacDonald, bearing tartans that seemed heavier now, weighted with loss for those who had worn them and would not again.

They traveled through glens that had witnessed generations of battles, past cairns raised for warriors who had fallen in struggles that seemed almost quaint now—clan feuds and border raids, conflicts where death was personal and enemies at least had the courtesy to be human rather than dragon or fairy queen or ancient giants whose eyes killed with looking.

Z'Landar swam parallel to the land-bound clans, watching them move with the solemn purpose that Highlanders brought to grief. He saw children walking beside parents, learning what it meant to honor the dead. Saw old warriors whose campaigns were finished but who came anyway because memory demanded presence. Saw women carrying supplies for the two-day ceremony—food and drink and wood for fires that would burn without ceasing, marking time sufficient for sorrow and sufficient to brace courage for what lay ahead.

Andralia swam beside him, and he noticed how the survivors watched her. How they whispered when they thought she couldn't hear—telling stories already growing into legend about the woman from stars who had stood beside their king, who had channeled power sufficient to break fairy queens and forge weapons from water itself, who bore wounds that marked her as warrior rather than just wise woman or cosmic visitor. Her left shoulder carried burns from Cliodhna's magic that had splashed past Z'Landar's defenses. Her arms showed scratches from dragon-scale encountered too closely. Her face held exhaustion that went beyond simple tiredness into something that spoke of power spent beyond comfortable limits.

She was beautiful in her wounded presence. Terrible in her unyielding determination. And the army loved her for it—loved her for standing beside their king when standing meant burning, for amplifying his power when amplification cost pieces of herself, for choosing them over safety when safety would have been so much easier to claim.

"They're making you legendary," Z'Landar said quietly as they swam. "I hear them talking. 'Andralia who channels stars. Andralia who stood in Cruachan's heart. Andralia who loved the king enough to burn beside him.' You're becoming myth before you've finished being mortal."

"Good," she replied. "Let them make me myth. Myths give courage when courage seems insufficient. If they need to believe I'm more than I am to face what comes next—let them believe. Whatever gets us through Balor and to the other side."

"If there is an other side."

"There will be." Her certainty held weight he couldn't match. "We didn't survive Cruachan just to die before finishing what we started. We'll face Balor. We'll destroy the fourth egg. We'll end this. And then—" She paused. "Then we'll see what comes after. Together."

"Always," he whispered, though the word tasted like ash.

They reached the shore between lands on the third day after leaving Loch Ness—a place where Scottish stone met Irish waters, where tides had carved beaches from cliffs over centuries, where standing stones older than memory marked thresholds between seen and unseen worlds. It was perfect for what was needed: neutral ground where both peoples could gather, where water-folk could swim close enough to shore to join ceremonies but not so close that salt water became prison, where fires could be lit and stones could be raised and grief could be given the space it required to be felt fully.

303

The Highland clans arrived first, moving with efficiency born of long practice at raising camps and lighting fires and creating spaces where ceremony could unfold. Alasdair Fraser directed the placement of standing stones—three score of them, hauled from quarries and carried by strong backs, each one waiting to be carved with names that deserved remembering. The stones formed a circle large enough to hold thousands—water-folk and humans both, living and dead existing in the same space for once, united by loss that transcended the usual divisions between those who breathed air and those who breathed water.

The fires were lit as sunset painted sky in shades of blood and gold— great pyres arranged around the stone circle, fed with wood that had been blessed by druids who remembered older ways, tended by warriors too wounded to fight but not too wounded to serve. The flames caught and built and settled into steady burning that would continue for two days without pause, marking time sufficient for grief and courage both.

Z'Landar swam into the shallows as darkness fell, taking human form with Andralia beside him, feeling the weight of what was about to unfold pressing against his chest like the deep itself. Forty-seven survivors gathered behind them—Tormod and Caelan and Fionnuala, Muirgheal and the remaining Merrow, Selkies and Kelpies bearing wounds that would scar and memories that would haunt. The Púca drifted at the edges, their forms flickering between shapes as if even tricksters understood that some moments demanded respect beyond their nature's usual irreverence.

And all around them, gathering in numbers that made Z'Landar's throat tighten, came the clans. Thousands of them—every Highland family that could travel, every settlement that had sent warriors or simply heard the Fiery Cross's call and understood that presence mattered. They filled the spaces between standing stones, bearing torches and grief and the particular pride that Highlanders brought to honoring their dead.

Alasdair Fraser approached as full darkness fell, his weathered face showing the tracks of tears he'd stopped trying to hide. "The stones are ready for carving. The fires burn. The people have gathered." His voice was thick. "Speak to them, young king. Tell them what was won and what was lost. Tell them—" He stopped, unable to continue.

Z'Landar took a breath, squared his shoulders, found the voice that leadership required even when leadership felt impossible. He walked to the center of the stone circle, Andralia at his side, and felt thousands of eyes fix on him—water-folk and human both, living witnesses to what had been paid in Cruachan's darkness.

"I have known battle, and I have known loss. I have stood steady when my legs craved collapse, my heart pounding. I have done these things, but I don't know if I have the strength to speak words here in the presence of our bravest fallen. We gather to honor the dead," he said, his voice carrying across the assembly with clarity born of necessity rather than volume. "To speak their names. To remember their courage. To acknowledge what they gave so that Scotland and Ireland both might survive what threatened them."

He paused, letting that truth settle.

"One hundred fifty-three warriors entered Cruachan and did not return. Water-folk and Irish allies both, united in purpose, divided only by death's accounting. They faced a fairy queen in her own domain and broke her power. They faced a mother dragon protecting her last child and destroyed the egg despite knowing the cost. They paid with their lives for victory that keeps our homes from burning and our children from knowing dragon-fire's touch."

His voice grew stronger, though tears tracked down his face and he made no effort to hide them.

"But I will not speak long. This ceremony is not about me. Not about what I witnessed or what I ordered or what I carry in guilt that will haunt me until my own ending comes. This is about them. About the one hundred fifty-three who deserve better than a king's words when family's remembering serves more truly."

He gestured to the standing stones, to the tools laid beside them for carving. "In the Celtic tradition—in the way our ancestors honored their fallen—one from each family will stand. Will speak of loss and pride. Will carve names into stone that will outlast our memories and stand as testament to courage that transcended mortality. That is how we honor them. That is how we remember."

He stepped back, and Andralia moved with him, her hand finding his. She said nothing—did not speak, did not offer wisdom, simply stood beside him bearing wounds that marked her as warrior and exhaustion that spoke of power spent beyond comfortable limits. But her presence was enough. The survivors saw her there, saw the legend already forming around her, saw the woman from the stars who had chosen to burn beside their king rather than watch safely from distance.

And one by one, the families began to speak.

A Kelpie elder stepped forward first—ancient beyond most present, bent with centuries but still strong enough to stand. "I speak for Beathan," his voice cracked. "My brother in all but blood. Three hundred years we swam together. Three hundred years we fought beside each other and laughed at death because death seemed distant and we were young even in our age." He moved to a standing stone, began to carve with tools that knew his hands. "He died to fairy magic in Cruachan's darkness. Died quickly—I pray quickly—turned to dust by power he couldn't comprehend. But he died fighting. Died standing. Died knowing that his ending mattered." The carving took shape: BEATHAN. KELPIE ELDER. DIED IN CRUACHAN FOR SCOTLAND'S LOVE. "I will miss him until water forgets how to flow. And I will remember him as he deserves—warrior who never faltered, friend who never failed, brother who chose courage when courage was all we had."

A Selkie woman came next, her face showing grief too deep for easy tears. "I speak for Eithne. Quick-witted. Sharp-tongued. Who made us laugh when laughter seemed impossible and sang songs that reminded us why living mattered." She carved while speaking, her hands steady despite emotion that should have made them shake. "She died when Cliodhna spoke her true name. Died confused about why she fought, who she was, what anything meant. That is what kills me—that she died uncertain, died with her sharp mind unmade before her body followed." The name took shape in stone. "But she chose to come. Chose to swim to Cruachan despite knowing the risks. That choice—that courage—is what I'll remember. Not her ending but her decision to stand regardless."

One after another they came—water-folk and Highland families both, speaking of warriors who had fallen and pride that transcended grief. A father speaking of his son who had been nineteen and convinced of his immortality. A sister speaking of a brother who had promised to return and broken that promise in Cruachan's fire. A Merrow speaking of Cairbre, young and brave and wrong about his survival but right about his courage. Each one carved names into stone—ORNA. CAIRBRE. Names that would outlast their speakers, that would stand as testament when memory itself failed.

And when a space opened—when the carving paused and grief needed moment to catch breath before continuing—Alasdair Fraser stepped forward. His weathered hands trembled as he approached the largest standing stone, the one at the circle's center, the one that would bear the name deserving greatest honor.

"I speak for Maelis," he said, and his voice broke immediately. He stopped, gathered himself, tried again. "I speak for the ancient one. Ten years ago I knew neither her nor her wisdom, but through battle and sacrifice I came to learn of her courage, her strength and her loyalty. A true warrior. Three hundred forty-seven years she lived. Three hundred forty-seven years she guided us and taught us and carried Scotland's memory when memory seemed insufficient. She—" His voice failed entirely.

Z'Landar found himself moving before conscious decision, stepping forward to stand beside Alasdair, placing his hand on the old chief's shoulder. "Let me," he said quietly.

Alasdair nodded, unable to speak, and stepped aside.

Z'Landar took up the carving tools with hands that shook, began to inscribe letters into stone that would outlast kingdoms. "Maelis taught me what it meant to lead," he said, his voice carrying across the assembly. "Taught me that courage wasn't absence of fear but action despite fear's presence. Taught me that sometimes dying well mattered more than living safely, that sacrifice given freely was gift beyond measure, that love expressed through ending was still love and still mattered and still counted even when counting seemed impossible."

The letters took shape beneath his hands: MAELIS. SELKIE. THREE HUNDRED FORTY-SEVEN YEARS. ANCIENT ONE WHO DIED SO OTHERS MIGHT LIVE.

"Her last words to me were: 'We will meet again in a land we do not know.'" Z'Landar's vision blurred with tears that made carving difficult but not impossible. "I don't know what land she meant. Don't know if such places exist or if hope was all she offered. But I know this—" He finished the carving, stepped back to see it whole. "She died as she chose to die. Died with purpose. Died making victory possible when victory seemed impossible. And that—" His voice broke. "That is more than most achieve. More than I'll likely achieve. More than anyone has right to ask but what warriors sometimes give because giving is what makes them worthy of remembering."

He turned to face the assembly, tears streaming down his face, making no effort to hide them because hiding seemed dishonest and dishonesty served nothing. "She was my mentor. My guide. My link to parents I never knew. And she died in fire buying moments I used to forge a weapon that killed a mother protecting her child. That is what leadership costs. That is what victory demands. And I will carry that weight—carry her sacrifice—until my own ending comes. And I will try—" His voice dropped to whisper that somehow carried across the stone circle. "I will try to be worthy of what she gave. Try to lead as she taught me to lead. Try to make her death matter for more than just another name carved in stone and another grief carried by those who survived."

Silence followed his words—heavy and profound and broken only by the crackling of fires that would burn for two days without ceasing.

Then, slowly, one by one, the assembly began to sing, the great highland bagpipes rising behind them. Not organized hymns or practiced songs, but the natural melodies that Celts brought to grief—laments that had been sung for fallen warriors since before Scotland had a name, songs that wove between languages and traditions, human voices mixing with water-folk harmonies in ways that created something neither could achieve alone.

The singing continued as more families came forward—as more names were carved into standing stones, as more stories were told of courage and love and sacrifice that transcended simple accounting. The fires burned. The stars wheeled overhead. And somewhere in the darkness between stone and sea, between memory and grief, the dead were honored as they deserved.

The first night of the ceremony passed in waves of remembering and silence both. Z'Landar found himself drifting between conversations—listening to warriors speak of friends who had fallen, hearing Highland chiefs discuss what Cruachan's victory meant for Scotland's future, watching Andralia move through the crowds with the particular grace that made people stop and stare and whisper her name like prayer or legend both.

Near midnight, he found himself at a fire with Muirgheal and several other survivors, the Irish Merrow poking at embers with some crooked stick that had been carved with symbols he didn't recognize. Tormod sat across from them, his burns bandaged but healing slowly. Caelan was there too, the young leader looking older than his years after witnessing Cruachan's horrors.

"Something's been bothering me," Muirgheal said quietly, her green eyes reflecting firelight in ways that made them seem deeper than eyes should be. "Something the dragon said as she died."

Z'Landar felt his chest tighten. "What about it?"

"She said her children were dead. All of them. That you'd killed them all." Muirgheal's voice was careful, measured. "But there's still one egg. The fourth egg hidden away with Balor. So why would she say all her children were gone?"

Silence fell around the fire as warriors processed the question.

"Perhaps she was dying and confused," Caelan offered. "Perhaps grief made her forget—"

"Dragons don't forget their eggs," Tormod interrupted. "Not ever. Not even dying. A mother might forget her own name before forgetting her children. So if Caoránach said all her children were dead—" He looked at Z'Landar. "What does that mean?"

Z'Landar felt understanding dawn like cold water over skin. "She didn't count the fourth egg as hers."

"Exactly." Muirgheal poked the fire again, sending sparks spiraling upward. "She counted three eggs. Three children. The ones we destroyed were hers—laid by her, protected by her, loved by her with devotion that made her fight impossible battles. But the fourth egg—" She paused. "The fourth egg wasn't given to Balor. It was taken by him."

"For what purpose?" Fionnuala asked from where she sat nursing her wounded arm.

"We don't know," Muirgheal admitted. "Perhaps he wants a dragon as servant. Perhaps he sees power in controlling something that could burn worlds. Perhaps—" She shrugged. "Perhaps Fomorian purposes are beyond our comprehending and speculation serves nothing. But what matters is this: the egg with Balor isn't Caoránach's child in the way the others were. It's something else. Something he took for his own reasons. And that makes it different. Dangerous in ways we might not anticipate."

"It's still an egg that will hatch," Z'Landar said quietly. "Still a dragon that will burn Scotland if we don't destroy it. Whether Caoránach counted it as hers doesn't change what we have to do."

"No," Muirgheal agreed. "But it might change how Balor fights to protect it. A mother defending her children fights with desperation that makes strategy irrelevant. But someone protecting stolen property— someone with purposes beyond simple maternal devotion—that's different. That's calculated. That might be worse in ways maternal fury could never be."

The fire crackled, and Z'Landar watched sparks rise toward stars that seemed suddenly very distant and cold.

"So we face a Fomorian giant," Tormod said slowly, "who has taken a dragon egg for purposes we don't understand, who guards it with power that can unmake existence, and who might be even more dangerous than a mother dragon because his reasons confound and deny simple love." He laughed without humor."

"It will end," Z'Landar said, though conviction felt hollow. "One way or another. We'll face him. We'll destroy the egg. We'll finish this."

"If we can find him," Caelan muttered. "If we can fight him. If we can survive his eye long enough to strike. If—"

"Enough ifs," Andralia said, appearing from the darkness with the particular silence she'd mastered. She settled beside Z'Landar, her presence immediately comforting despite the gravity of what they discussed. "We know where ancient tales place him. Deepest waters between Scotland and Ireland. Waters where even Fomorians fear to swim because what dwells there predates their kind. We'll search those depths. We'll find him. And we'll do what we came to do."

"How can you be so certain?" Fionnuala asked.

"Because uncertainty is luxury we can't afford," Andralia replied simply. "Because doubt paralyzes and paralysis kills. Because sometimes faith that we'll succeed is the only thing separating survival from despair, and despair serves nothing when battles wait and eggs need destroying, truly despair is the enemy." She took Z'Landar's hand. "So I choose faith. Choose certainty. Choose to believe we'll find him and face him and finish this. Not because evidence supports that belief, but because believing anything else makes swimming toward Balor impossible."

Muirgheal nodded slowly. "The cosmic one speaks wisdom. Faith when faith seems foolish. Certainty despite odds that should crush certainty absolutely. That's what we need for Balor. That and—" She looked at Z'Landar. "That and whatever power the king can bring to bear. Whatever magic lives in him that forged water into weapons and shaped perception until fairy queens couldn't tell truth from illusion. We'll need all of that and more."

"If it's enough," Z'Landar said quietly.

"It will be," Andralia said with passionate conviction that made him almost believe. "Because it has to be. Because we've come too far to fail now. Because—" Her voice dropped. "Because I have faith in you, beloved. Faith absolute. And sometimes one person's faith can carry many when many have forgotten how to carry themselves."

The conversation drifted to other topics—practical discussions of where to search, how to coordinate with survivors too wounded to fight effectively, whether the Sluagh would return or if facing Balor meant

311

forty-seven warriors and chaos-loving Púca against forces that unmade existence itself. But Z'Landar found his attention wandering, found himself watching Andralia in firelight, memorizing the way flames painted her face in shades of gold and shadow, trying to hold this moment despite knowing that moments couldn't be held any more than water could be grasped.

Eventually the fire burned low, and warriors dispersed to find rest or continue their grieving in privacy. Z'Landar and Andralia walked away from the crowds, moving along the shore until the sounds of ceremony faded and only waves against stone marked their passage.

And they divided. Andralia went camp-to-camp, tending to the wounded, holding hands burned from unearthly fire, speaking words of comfort to those who might never again know comfort. Her presence among them was almost as a spirit, or a goddess, so loved was she.

And Z'Landar, walking through the midnight shadows between campfires, hearing story after story of his magical victories against creatures most in the glen could never understand. His legend already beyond the greatest of highland myths. But, once coming into the soft glow of campfire, the stories stopped, and the eyes glowed knowing their king was with them.

"Come," Andralia said quietly, rejoining him hours later, leading him toward a tent that had been raised for them—simple canvas structure, but private, sheltered from wind and eyes both. Inside, blankets had been laid and a small fire burned in a small portable brazier, creating space that felt almost safe despite everything that waited beyond canvas walls.

They settled onto blankets, and Z'Landar felt exhaustion crash over him like waves—not physical tiredness alone, but soul-deep weariness that came from carrying grief and guilt and knowledge that one more impossible battle waited and this time there might not be survivors to carve names or sing songs or remember what had been paid.

"Talk to me," Andralia said softly, her fingers threading through his. "Don't carry this alone. Whatever you're thinking—whatever doubt or fear or guilt is gnawing at your soul, you—speak it. Let me help carry it."

312

"I'm terrified," he admitted. "Terrified of facing Balor. Terrified of losing you to his eye that kills with looking. Terrified that everything we've done—everyone who's died—will be for nothing because we can't survive what comes next."

"I know," she whispered. "I'm terrified too."

"You don't seem it. You seem certain. Seem strong enough for both of us."

"That's performance," she said gently. "That's what I show others because they need someone to seem certain when certainty has abandoned everyone else. But inside—" She pulled his hand to her chest, pressing it against her heart. "Inside I'm as frightened as you. As uncertain. As aware that we're swimming toward an ending that might claim us both."

"Then why keep going?"

"Because stopping means Scotland burns anyway. Means Maelis died for nothing. Means one hundred fifty-three warriors paid with their lives so we could give up before finishing." She shifted closer, her warmth against him a comfort that meant more than words. "And because loving you means I'll face Balor at your side rather than watch you face him alone. That's not courage. That's just love expressed in ways that look like courage to those who don't understand the difference."

Z'Landar held her, feeling her breathe, feeling her heart beat steady against his chest. "There's something else I need to tell you," she said after long silence. "Something about why I was so exhausted after our first battle together. After the northern settlement."

He pulled back enough to see her face. "You nearly collapsed. I thought—I thought using so much of your power had nearly killed you."

"It nearly did," she admitted. "But not for the reason you think. Not because of my power, but yours, not because channeling your energy is inherently dangerous or because your power is toxic to touch. It nearly killed me because—" She paused, choosing words. "Because I tried to channel all of it. Every drop of power you possess. I didn't know how

313

much you carried, didn't understand the depths of what lives in you. I just opened myself completely and tried to hold everything you are."

Understanding dawned. "And it was too much."

"It was infinite," she whispered. "Or close enough that infinite seems the appropriate word. Your cosmic heritage isn't just bloodline or interesting ancestry. It's real. It's vast. It's power that comes from sources I barely comprehend despite being star-born myself. The mutations brought by Earth's sun are unique. And when I tried to channel all of it—" She shuddered. "It nearly unmade me. Not from malice. Just from magnitude. Like trying to hold the ocean in a teacup. The container simply isn't sufficient."

"So now—"

"Now I've learned," she said. "Learned to channel carefully. To take what's needed rather than everything available. To work with your power rather than trying to contain it all. That's why I wasn't as exhausted after Cruachan. Not because the battles were easier—they were worse—but because I'd learned how to manage the flow. How to amplify without trying to encompass."

Z'Landar felt something shift in his understanding. "So at the northern settlement, when you collapsed—that was you nearly dying because my power is greater than you expected."

"Much greater," she confirmed. "Greater than you know even now. The water sword you forged? That was but a fraction of what you carry. The perception-shaping that defeated Cliodhna? Another fraction. You're like—" She struggled for comparison. "Like ocean pretending to be pond. And I'm learning to channel streams from that ocean rather than trying to drain it entirely."

"Does that mean—" He stopped, fear clutching his chest. "Does that mean when we face Balor, if I need to use everything—"

"Then I'll do what I did at the northern settlement," she said simply. "I'll try to channel all of it. And it might kill me. Might unmake me the way your power nearly unmade me before. But if that's what survival requires—if that's what destroying the fourth egg demands—then that's

314

what I'll do. Because loving you means I'll pay whatever price keeps you alive, even if that price is myself."

"No." The word came fierce, desperate. "I won't let you—"

"You don't get to decide," she interrupted gently. "This is my choice. My power to wield as I see fit. My life to spend how I choose. And I choose—" Her hand found his face, thumb tracing his cheekbone. "I choose to stand beside you. To focus and multiply your power. To make you more than you could be alone. And if that kills me—" She smiled sadly. "Then at least I'll die having loved you absolutely. Having given everything I had to someone who deserved it. That's more than most achieve, beloved. More than I dreamed possible when I chose Earth over stars."

Z'Landar wanted to argue. Wanted to forbid her from risking herself. Wanted to face Balor alone rather than watch her burn in cosmic fire that came from trying to channel power too vast to contain.

But looking at her—at this woman who had chosen him, who loved him with devotion that transcended survival, who would die beside him rather than live without him—he found he couldn't demand she choose differently.

Because he would make the same choice if their positions were reversed.

Would burn himself to nothing if it meant keeping her alive.

Would pay any price to ensure her survival even if that price was himself.

"Together," he whispered, pulling her close.

"Always," she replied.

And in that tent, on the first night of ceremony honoring the dead, they held each other and tried not to think about the fact that always might end very soon.

That Balor waited with his eye that killed and his power that unmade.

That forty-seven exhausted warriors might not be sufficient for the battle ahead.

That love, for all its strength, couldn't turn dragon-fire or stop giant-kings or guarantee survival when survival required miracles.

But it could make the waiting bearable.

Could make the fear manageable.

Could transform impossible into merely catastrophic.

And sometimes—when darkness gathered and endings loomed and hope seemed foolish—that was enough.

And so they slept, one night of peace in a reality of harsh conflict. And so they slept.

The second day of ceremony dawned gray and cold, autumn asserting itself with wind that carried hints of winter approaching. The fires had burned through the night, tended by warriors who understood that tending flame was service when service was all they could offer. More names were carved into standing stones as families continued their remembering—speaking of warriors who had fallen and pride that transcended grief.

Z'Landar moved through the crowds with Andralia beside him, accepting condolences from Highland chiefs who gripped his hand too tightly and spoke words that tried to comfort but mostly just reminded him of costs that couldn't be undone. He watched as Ruadhan and Brígh drifted at the edges, their Púca nature making them uncomfortable at formal grief but their presence itself a statement that even tricksters could join forces when the enemy threatened all.

By evening, all one hundred fifty-three names had been carved, wet hands rubbing ashes deep into the carving to stain the words into prominence. All the families had spoken. All the grief that could be expressed in two days had been given voice and stone and flame to mark its passage.

316

As the sun set on the second day, Alasdair Fraser stood at the circle's center and spoke words that had been spoken for Highland dead since before memory: "We have honored them as they deserve. Carved their names in stone that will outlast our bones. Spoken their deeds so stories might survive when we do not. And now—" His voice grew stronger. "Now we must be worthy of what they gave. Must finish what they started. Must face whatever battles wait with courage they demonstrated and determination they embodied. That is how we honor the dead—not just by remembering, but by continuing. By standing when standing is all that remains."

The assembly responded with voices raised in ancient words—half song, half prayer, entirely Celtic in its understanding that grief and glory mixed together until they became indistinguishable.

As darkness fell and the ceremony concluded, as families began their journeys home and warriors prepared for whatever came next, Z'Landar stood before the stone that bore Maelis's name. Andralia stood beside him, silent support, her hand in his.

"We will meet again in a land we do not know," he whispered to stone that would carry her name long after he was gone. "I don't know when. Don't know where. Don't know if such lands exist or if you offered only hope when hope was all you had to give. But I promise—" His voice broke. "I promise to be worthy of what you taught. To lead as you showed me to lead. To face Balor with the courage you demonstrated. And if I fall—if I fall—I'll do it having tried. Having stood. Having refused to surrender when surrender would have been so much easier."

Andralia's fingers tightened in his. "She would be proud," she said quietly. "Is proud, wherever she is now. You honor her through continuing. Through refusing to let grief paralyze. Through swimming toward Balor despite knowing the cost."

"The cost," Z'Landar repeated hollowly. "Always the cost. Always blood and death and grief that never quite heals."

"Yes," she agreed. "That is what leadership demands. What protecting Scotland requires. What love costs when love is expressed through sacrifice." She turned him to face her, her impossible eyes holding his. "But we knew that when we started. Knew that this path led through fire

317

and death and endings that would hurt more than we could bear. We chose it anyway. Choose it still. Because the alternative—letting dragons hatch and worlds burn—is worse than any price we might pay.

My king, you did not choose to be king, the crown chose you. You, your life, was always meant to lead, and there was never any way for you to deter away from your destined path."

He pulled her close, breathing her in, trying to memorize this moment because moments were all they had and moments couldn't be held any longer than water could be grasped.

"Where do we find him?" he asked finally. "Where does Balor hide with his stolen egg and his eye that kills?"

"The deepest waters between Scotland and Ireland," Andralia said. "That's what ancient tales claim. Waters so deep that light never reaches bottom. Waters where even Fomorians fear to swim because what dwells there predates their kind. That's where we'll search. That's where we'll find him."

"And if we're wrong? If he's somewhere else?"

"Then we'll search until we find him," she said simply. "However long it takes. However far we must swim. We have strong and queer allies, beings with natures we cannot understand, and they wander in places we cannot. We'll find him and face him and finish this." Her voice dropped to whisper. "Together."

"Again, though it tears at my being to bring you into harm" he replied, though the thought tasted like grief and determination both.

They stood there as the last fires burned low, as the ceremony concluded and warriors prepared for whatever came next. Stood before stones that would outlast them, bearing names that deserved remembering, marking costs that had been paid and costs yet to come.

Behind them, Scotland waited.

Ahead, somewhere in depths that predated memory, Balor waited with his eye and his egg and his power that unmade existence itself.

318

Between them—forty-seven exhausted warriors, two chaos-loving Púca, and hope that somehow courage would prove sufficient when courage was all that remained.

And in the deepest waters, where light died and ancient things dwelled, a giant-king stirred.

Sensing prey approaching, preparing to demonstrate why Fomorians were feared.

Why his eye had become legend.

Why some battles couldn't be won but only survived... or not survived...

Chapter Twenty-Four: The Ravens' Message

The sorrowful ceremony concluded as evening painted sky in shades of ash and blood, the fires burning low but still sustained by those who understood the significance of gestures and traditions. The last names had been carved into standing stones that would outlast kingdoms, the last families had spoken their grief and pride, and now the clans began their departures—moving away from the shore between lands with the particular solemnity that Highlanders brought to endings that could not be undone.

Z'Landar stood at the stone circle's edge with Andralia beside him, watching thousands disperse like water finding separate channels after confluence. The memorial would remain—three score standing stones bearing one hundred fifty-three names, marking costs that had been paid and courage that deserved remembering. But the living had to continue, had to return to glens and settlements and lives that would never quite be the same after Cruachan's accounting. Centuries hence, people would wonder what caused such a stand of monuments.

"We need to know where to search," Andralia said quietly, her hand finding his. "The waters between Scotland and Ireland are vast. We could spend weeks searching and never find him. Never find the egg."

"I know." Z'Landar's voice carried exhaustion that went beyond flesh. "We know he's somewhere between our lands, somewhere deep. But that describes half the Irish Sea. We need—" He stopped, uncertain what they needed beyond miracles and fortune they'd already exhausted.

Then the ravens came.

They arrived as movement, almost a shimmer against an ugly and gray sky—dark shapes that might have been clouds except clouds didn't move with such purpose, didn't descend with such intent. Not one raven, not a dozen, but hundreds of them, flowing down from autumn's cold heights like smoke given form, like darkness that had learned to fly.

A murder of ravens, converging on the stone circle.

Warriors looked up, tension spreading through the remaining crowds like ripples from stones dropped in still water. Highland chiefs reached for weapons they weren't carrying, water-folk moved closer together, and even the Púca—chaos-bringers who feared nothing—went still with attention that suggested they recognized significance in what descended.

The ravens landed on the standing stones.

Perched on freshly carved names, on memorial markers still showing chisel marks, on stone that bore weight of one hundred fifty-three deaths and would carry that weight until erosion claimed what grief could not. Black feathers caught fading light, sharp beaks opened and closed, and eyes—too intelligent, too knowing, too aware—fixed on the gathered warriors with attention that made even brave souls flinch.

The largest raven settled on Maelis's stone—the one at the circle's center, bearing her name and her three hundred forty-seven years. It was bigger than any natural raven, ancient-looking in ways that suggested it had witnessed endings before Scotland had a name, carrying presence that made the space around it seem heavier, more significant, weighted with doom that had not yet arrived but would.

The sounds began.

Harsh cawing, sharp croaking, calls that held no beauty or melody but carried meaning nonetheless. Not random bird-noise but purposeful communication—pattern in the harshness, intent in the croaking, message in sounds that hurt to hear because they spoke of things no one wanted acknowledged.

Death. Endings. Battles that would be lost. Warriors who would not return. Doom approaching like tide that could not be turned.

"Ravens on death markers," someone whispered, voice tight with superstitious fear. "That's ill omen. They gather when death comes. When battlefields wait for bodies."

"Should we drive them away?" asked another.

But no one moved. Because driving them away seemed wrong somehow, seemed like denying truth that would arrive regardless, seemed like the kind of futile gesture that changed nothing except the comfort of ignorance.

Z'Landar watched the largest raven—perched on Maelis's stone, cawing with sounds like wind through bones—and felt certainty settle over him cold as deep water. These ravens hadn't come randomly. Hadn't simply been drawn to fresh death markers out of scavenger instinct. They had come with purpose. With message. With knowledge of what waited and where waiting would end.

But who could understand them?

Maelis had been able to speak with water sprites—had possessed some gift for communication that bridged usual divisions between species. But she was gone, consumed by dragon-fire, reduced to name on stone that ravens now desecrated with their presence.

Who among them spoke bird-tongue?

Then Ruadhan moved.

The Púca had been standing at the circle's edge in human form—tall man with storm-cloud hair and wolf's grin that suggested secrets better left unspoken. But now the grin faded, replaced by expression Z'Landar had never seen on trickster's face before: seriousness. Gravity. The particular attention that came when even chaos-bringers recognized that some truths claimed triumph over their usual irreverence.

Ruadhan walked toward the ravens with steps that seemed reluctant despite their steadiness. Stopped near Maelis's stone, tilted his head, and listened to harsh cawing with an intensity that made warriors hold their breath.

"They speak," the Púca said finally, his voice carrying none of its usual playful quality. "The ravens speak of what they've seen. Of where death waits. Of doom gathering in waters between your lands and ours."

"You can understand them?" Z'Landar asked, moving closer.

"Púca understand all tongues," Ruadhan replied, not looking away from the ravens. "Human, water-folk, beast, bird—we shift between forms, we carry languages with us. That's what we are. Bridges between things that should not communicate but do anyway." He paused as the largest raven cawed again, long harsh sound that made several warriors step back. "And ravens—ravens speak truths no one wants to hear. That's what they are. Harbingers. Doom-bringers. Witnesses to endings."

"What are they saying?" Andralia asked quietly.

Ruadhan was silent for long moment, listening to cawing that built and fell and built again like waves against stone. His face grew graver with each harsh call, even trickster's nature unable to find amusement in what ravens revealed.

"They've flown over the waters between Scotland and Ireland," he said finally. "Over the Irish Sea. Over and over, many times, drawn by currents and winds and things that draw ravens to places where death will come. They know those waters better than any creature that swims."

The ravens cawed louder, more insistent, and Ruadhan's hands clenched at his sides.

"They've flown over the island in the middle. The island between your lands and ours. The one named for Manannán mac Lir—the sea-god who guards boundaries between mortal world and Otherworld, who rules mist and magic and the spaces where things that should not meet can touch."

"Isle of Man," Muirgheal breathed, appearing at Z'Landar's shoulder. "They speak of Isle of Man."

"Yes." Ruadhan nodded slowly. "And they've seen—" He stopped, listening as ravens grew almost frantic in their calling. "They've seen wrongness in the deep waters around it. Darkness that predates darkness. Ancient power stirring in trenches and caves beneath the island, where light dies, where pressure should crush bone, where even Fomorians dwelt in old times when the world was younger and more terrible."

Z'Landar felt cold settle into his chest despite knowing, despite having suspected. "Balor. They've seen Balor."

"They've seen where he waits." Ruadhan's voice was flat, careful. "The one-eyed king in his chosen domain. In waters so deep that reaching them requires swimming beyond comfortable limits, beyond safe depths, beyond places where retreat remains possible. He guards something there. Something precious. Something that pulses with heat and malice both."

"The egg," Andralia said.

"The egg," Ruadhan confirmed. He looked at Z'Landar finally, and in the Púca's eyes—usually dancing with mischief and chaos—Z'Landar saw only certainty grim as grave-stones. "Balor waits at Isle of Man. In the deepest waters on the western side, where trenches drop away into darkness that has never known sun. That's where you'll find him. That's where the fourth egg is kept. That's where—" He glanced at the ravens. "That's where the ravens expect to feast soon."

Silence fell like snow—cold and heavy and absolute.

"Why do they tell us?" Z'Landar asked finally. "Why reveal his location if they're just here to watch us die?"

Ruadhan listened to more harsh cawing, then shook his head slowly. "They don't tell you out of kindness. Don't offer knowledge from desire to help. They tell you because—" He paused, seeming to search for words. "Because they always gather where death will be greatest. Where battles are fought that make the earth remember. Where enough blood is spilled that even stones learn to weep. They're not helping you. They're simply ensuring they're present for the feast. By telling you where to go, they guarantee they'll be there when you arrive. When you fall. When you join the one hundred fifty-three already honored in stone."

The largest raven—still perched on Maelis's stone—cawed once more. Long, harsh call that sounded like laughter heard from the bottom of a grave, like amusement at mortals who thought courage could substitute for strength, like doom announcing itself with certainty beyond question.

Then it took flight.

Wings beat against cold air, lifting the ancient creature skyward. The other ravens followed—hundreds of them rising at once, swirling around the stone circle like some curious storm made of feathers and death-knowledge, circling overhead once, twice, three times with harsh calls that filled the air with sounds of endings approaching.

Then they flew west.

Toward Ireland. Toward Isle of Man. Toward the waters where Balor waited with his eye and his egg and his power that unmade existence itself.

"They go ahead of us," Ruadhan said, watching them disappear into distance. "To wait. To watch. To feed on what remains when courage proves insufficient and determination becomes just another word for dying." He turned to face Z'Landar. "That's what ravens do. That's what ravens are. And they're never wrong about where death will come."

They gathered around the largest fire as darkness fell—forty-seven survivors, Púca, remaining Merrow, Highland chiefs who had stayed to see the sacred ceremony concluded. The question hung over everything now, given shape and location by ravens whose honesty was cruel as winter but at least offered certainty where uncertainty had paralyzed.

Isle of Man. Balor waited at Isle of Man. In the deepest waters between their lands, in trenches that dropped away into darkness, in caves where only Fomorians had dwelt when the world was younger and more terrible.

"I know that island," Muirgheal said, her green eyes reflecting firelight in ways that made them seem deeper than eyes should be. "Every Irish water-dweller knows it. Central in the Irish Sea, between our lands and Scotland's. Sacred to Manannán mac Lir—the sea-god, the guardian of boundaries, the one who walks between mortal world and Otherworld with equal ease."

"What can you tell us of its waters?" Z'Landar asked.

"That they're treacherous," Muirgheal replied. "That currents run strange around it, mixing cold and warm in patterns that make no sense. That the island itself has mountains—Snaefell highest among them, rising over two thousand feet from sea level. That standing stones mark it as sacred ground, that ancient powers have always saturated its shores." She paused. "And that the waters on the western side drop away suddenly. Sharply. From shallows to trenches that reach depths where light never penetrates and pressure becomes weapon as deadly as any blade."

"How deep?" Tormod asked.

"Deep enough that swimming there requires determination beyond normal. Deep enough that many water-folk have tried and failed to reach bottom. Deep enough that—" Muirgheal's voice dropped. "Deep enough that Fomorians chose it. In old times, before they were driven to the margins of the world, they dwelt there. Built there. Carved chambers in stone that should not be carved, created spaces where even sea-gods feared to swim. That's where Balor has returned. To the ancient dwelling-places of his kind."

"Why there?" Caelan asked. "Why not somewhere even more remote? Even deeper?"

"Because Isle of Man is liminal space," one of the remaining Highland chiefs said—old warrior whose name Z'Landar didn't know but whose weathered face spoke of decades witnessing things that should not be witnessed. "It's between. Between Scotland and Ireland, between mortal lands and Otherworld, between sea and stone. Places like that hold power. Hold magic. Now, when we are well into the time of man. If Balor wants to raise a dragon as servant, wants to corrupt what should not be corrupted—" He shrugged. "He'd choose ground that's already between things. Already liminal. Already touched by forces that make reality uncertain."

Z'Landar stared into the fire, watching flames dance and trying to imagine what waited in trenches so deep that light died before reaching them. Trying to picture Balor—Fomorian giant-king, ancient beyond reckoning, bearing eye that killed with looking—dwelling in darkness absolute, guarding egg that pulsed with heat and potential for destruction that would make Caoránach's maternal fury seem gentle by comparison.

"We need strategy," he said finally. "We can't simply swim to Isle of Man and throw ourselves at him. Can't just hope our courage proves sufficient when every indicator suggests otherwise."

"Strategy for fighting what we cannot gaze upon," Tormod muttered.

But they tried anyway. Spent hours discussing approaches that might work, tactics that might give them some advantage, ways to fight a giant whose eye unmade existence and whose power made frivolous anything they'd faced before.

Attack from multiple directions—surround him, strike from all sides simultaneously so he couldn't focus his gaze on all threats at once. But coordination in deep water was difficult, and Balor would sense them coming, would know every approach through territory that was his in ways that went beyond simple ownership.

Use Z'Landar's perception-shaping—make Balor see false threats, confuse where real attacks originated, overwhelm his senses until truth and illusion became indistinguishable. But would that work on a Fomorian king? On something ancient enough to predate most forms of magic? Uncertain, and more…unlikely.

Andralia would channel and amplify Z'Landar's power—make his perception-shaping strong enough that even Balor couldn't penetrate the illusions. But that meant she'd be channeling vast amounts of uncontrolled force, trying to hold that dammed ocean in a teacup, risking the unmaking that had nearly claimed her at the northern settlement. Z'Landar watched her across the fire and felt his chest tighten with fear that went beyond concern for his own survival into terror at losing what made survival worthwhile.

"If the Sluagh return—" someone offered tentatively.

"They won't," another interrupted. "They disappeared without word or whisper. Without promise. We can't plan around forces we don't have."

Many, perhaps all, of the highland chiefs struggled to follow, their minds in conflict with the understanding of so many mythical creatures living among them.

But Z'Landar found himself hoping anyway. Hoping that the Host of the Unforgiven Dead would remember what they'd promised, would judge the final battle worthy of their presence, would appear when needed most because the dead feared nothing and Balor's eye could not kill what had already died.

The planning continued until exhaustion made thought difficult and strategy became just another word for desperate hope. Eventually the gathering dispersed—warriors seeking rest or continuing their grieving in privacy, chiefs preparing for journeys home, water-folk floating in shallows and trying to imagine how twenty-five or thirty souls could face what two hundred had been insufficient to defeat in Cruachan. In tent after tent, loved ones wrapped tender arms in fear and hope, trusting everything on their new king and queen.

Because that was what it came to, in the end. They couldn't take everyone. Couldn't ask warriors too wounded to swim properly to face a Fomorian giant in his deepest stronghold. Couldn't waste lives that would be spent just reaching the battlefield, leaving no strength for battle itself.

The triage was brutal but necessary.

Fionnuala—Z'Landar's half-sister, bearing left arm so damaged by Cruachan's fire that she could barely move it—would have to stay. She protested, tears streaming down her face, insisting she could fight one-handed if needed. But Z'Landar held firm, hating himself for it, hating the necessity that made him deny her the right to finish what she'd helped start.

"Someone has to stay," he told her gently. "Someone has to tend these stones, to remember us if we don't return, to tell Scotland what was paid. Let that be you. Let that be your service."

She finally nodded, unable to speak, and Z'Landar moved to the next wounded warrior and repeated the cruelty until fifteen souls who desperately wanted to continue were told they must stay behind.

Twenty-eight would swim to Isle of Man. Twenty-eight out of the two hundred who had entered Cruachan with determination devoid of hope. Twenty-eight to face the final egg, the final battle, the final accounting of whether courage had ever been sufficient or if they'd simply been

328

delaying inevitable defeat through stubborn refusal to acknowledge reality.

Dawn broke gray and cold on what might be their last morning on Scottish soil, or indeed life itself. Z'Landar stood at the stone circle's center as first light painted standing stones in shades of ash and old blood, as survivors prepared for departure, as Highland clans gathered to witness what might be a final farewell to warriors who had given everything and might yet give more.

Alasdair Fraser approached with steps that seemed heavier than his years alone could account for—old chief who had sent countless warriors to their deaths over decades of leadership but had never grown comfortable with that sending. He stopped before Z'Landar and Andralia, his weathered face showing tracks of tears he'd stopped trying to hide days ago.

"I've watched you become king," he said, his voice thick with emotion that made each word effort. "Watched you grow from boy uncertain of his heritage—unsure if you were Kelpie or something else, unsure if you belonged anywhere—to leader who carries Scotland's fate on shoulders that should not have to bear such weight." He gripped Z'Landar's shoulders with muscled hands that trembled. "And I've watched you—" He turned to Andralia. "I've watched you stand beside him. They call you woman from stars who chose earth and water over cosmic distances, who chose him over safety, who became queen not through ceremony or crown but through devotion that shames every love song ever sung."

His voice broke. He stopped, gathered himself, tried again.

"Whatever happens at Isle of Man—whatever ending waits in trenches where light dies and ancient powers dwell—you need to know this." He looked between them, old eyes holding certainty and sorrow. "You've already honored your parents' sacrifice, Z'Landar. Already proven worthy of the crown you never asked for and the burden you've carried since the moment you understood what being king meant. And you—" He focused on Andralia. "You've proven that love can be fierce as any weapon, that devotion can stand against dragons and fairy queens and

329

Fomorian giants if devotion is given absolutely enough. Even without him you are worthy to be queen of Scotland."

Alasdair released Z'Landar's shoulders, stepped back, and with deliberate ceremony raised his right hand in salute that Clan Fraser gave only to those deemed worthy of ultimate respect and loyalty.

"I pledge the eternal good right arm of Clan Fraser," he said, his voice carrying across the assembly with strength that belied his tears. "To the King of Waters who leads when leading means dying. To the Queen from Stars who stands when standing costs everything. To both of you, together, for as long as either draws breath or until Scotland herself forgets how to remember courage. The Clan Fraser stands with you. Has always stood with you. Will continue standing even should you fall, because that is what loyalty means when loyalty is tested against impossible odds."

The salute held—right arm raised, hand open, pledge given in words older than most present could trace.

Z'Landar felt something in his chest break that wasn't quite grief but wasn't far from it either. He stepped forward, embraced the old chief with strength that should have hurt but Alasdair seemed to welcome anyway, and tried to speak past tightness in his throat that made words nearly impossible.

"Thank you Honored Chief," he managed finally. "For everything. For teaching me what it means to lead. For standing with water-folk when humans had every reason to fear. For—" His voice failed entirely.

"No thanks needed, lad." Alasdair's arms tightened around him. "Just—" He pulled back enough to meet Z'Landar's eyes. "Just swim well. Fight well. And, gods save us, you fall—" His voice dropped to a husky whisper. "Fall knowing you mattered. Fall knowing Scotland will remember. Fall knowing you were loved by those who should have feared you and followed by those who should have been wise enough to run."

He released Z'Landar, turned to Andralia, and offered the same embrace—old human chief holding a curious woman from distant stars with reverence that acknowledged what she'd become, what she'd chosen, what she'd given to stand beside a king who led toward endings rather than victories.

"And you, lass—" Alasdair's voice was barely audible. "You chose well when you chose him. That matters too. That will be remembered. Our queen."

Then he stepped back, saluted once more, and moved away before emotion overwhelmed the dignity that Highland chiefs brought to farewells that might be final.

Other chiefs came forward—MacLeod and the very proud MacKenzie, Cameron and MacDonald—offering their own pledges and farewells, speaking words that tried to express what words couldn't hold. But none matched Alasdair's weight, none carried the particular gravity of a man who had watched Z'Landar grow from uncertain boy to king who would lead Scotland's last defense against forces that should not exist.

The survivors gathered at water's edge as the sun climbed higher— twenty-eight souls preparing to swim west, toward Ireland, toward Isle of Man, toward trenches where Balor waited with eye that killed and egg that threatened. They took human forms for this moment because words required mouths and farewells deserved the dignity of faces rather than seal-shapes or horse-forms or the fluid bodies that served for swimming but failed for proper goodbyes.

Tormod was there despite burns that made movement painful—old Kelpie warrior who had fought beside Beathan for three centuries and would not be denied the right to finish what his friend had died starting. Caelan, young chief who had aged decades in weeks, who carried wounds from Cruachan but not wounds sufficient to stop him from continuing. Muirgheal and several Merrow, Irish allies who had stood with Scotland through dragon-fire and fairy magic and would stand through whatever Fomorian fury brought. Others whose names Z'Landar knew, whose courage he'd witnessed, whose deaths he would carry if this ending claimed them.

Ruadhan and Brígh drifted at the edges in forms that flickered between shapes—Púca nature unable to settle even for farewells, chaos persisting because chaos was what they were and denying nature seemed pointless when death waited regardless.

331

And Andralia stood beside him—always beside him, constant as his own heartbeat—bearing wounds from Cruachan that marked her as warrior rather than just cosmic visitor. Her left shoulder showed burns where Cliodhna's magic had splashed past his defenses. Her arms carried scratches from dragon-scale encountered too closely. Her face held exhaustion that went beyond tiredness into something that spoke of power spent beyond comfortable limits and determination to spend more regardless of cost.

She was beautiful in her war scars. Terrible in her devotion. And looking at her—knowing what she'd risk, what she'd spend, what she'd give if facing Balor required channeling his full power—Z'Landar felt fear clutch his chest until breathing became difficult.

"Together again, once more into futile battle?" he asked quietly, the word carrying weight beyond its simple syllables.

"Always, you know that, always together" she replied, her hand finding his.

They took seal-forms and entered the water.

The swim toward Isle of Man took two days through waters that grew colder with each mile, through currents that seemed to carry warnings in their flow, through the Irish Sea that had witnessed countless journeys but few toward destinations as grim as the one they sought.

And the ravens came with them.

Not just the hundreds that had descended on the stone circle, but more— so many more that they darkened the sky like storm-clouds made of feathers and doom-knowledge. They flew overhead in numbers that defied counting, circling and cawing with harsh calls that filled the air with sounds of death approaching, of endings inevitable, of battles already lost in futures the ravens could see but mortals could not.

A cloud of ravens. That's what it became. A moving darkness above swimmers who represented Scotland and Ireland's last defense against forces that should not exist. The birds didn't attack, didn't threaten—

simply followed, watching with eyes too intelligent and waiting with patience that suggested they knew exactly when patience would be rewarded with feast they'd traveled so far to witness.

"They're like carrion birds following dying cattle," Muirgheal said during a rest on the first night, her voice tight. "Waiting for the fall. Certain it will come. Just patient about when."

"Let them watch," Z'Landar replied, though his voice held less conviction than his words suggested. "Let them gather and wait and expect our deaths. We'll prove them wrong or die trying. Either way—" He looked up at the dark cloud overhead. "Either way, they'll witness what we are. What we chose. What we paid. And, we owe debt. Their services might be selfish, but they did provide us with the location we could not know. "

But the ravens' presence weighed on everyone. Made the journey feel less like swimming toward battle and more like swimming toward execution, with witnesses already gathered and graves already dug and only the final moment of falling still uncertain in its timing if not its arrival.

The first day passed in cold water and silence broken only by harsh cawing from above. Warriors swam with grim determination, each processing approaching death in their own ways—some praying to gods who might listen, some simply swimming because stopping meant acknowledging terror that paralysis would make unbearable, some trying to remember why they'd chosen this path when choosing differently would have been so much easier.

Z'Landar swam beside Andralia, matching her pace, feeling her presence as comfort without need for words. They'd spoken little since departure—what was there to say that hadn't been said already? That they loved each other absolutely? That they were terrified? That swimming toward Balor felt less like courage and more like fated suicide? They knew these truths already, had acknowledged them in darkness while holding each other, had accepted that some paths led only toward endings but had to be walked regardless.

Night fell, and they rested in shallower waters with Isle of Man visible in the distance—dark shape against darker sky, mountains rising from sea with presence that seemed heavier than geography alone could account for. The island looked peaceful, beautiful even, bathed in starlight that made it seem innocent rather than harboring ancient evil in trenches beneath its shores.

But the wrongness was palpable now. Growing stronger with each mile. Ancient power saturating the water like poison too diffuse to see but present nonetheless, making each stroke slightly harder, each breath slightly more labored, each moment of continuation requiring determination beyond what should be necessary for simple swimming.

"Can you feel it?" Andralia asked quietly, floating beside him in the dark.

"Yes." Z'Landar stared at the island. "Like something vast is watching. Waiting. Aware that we're coming."

"Balor knows." Her voice held certainty grim as the ravens overhead. "Has known since we left Scotland. Probably knew before that. Knew when the dragon died. Knew when the egg was destroyed. Knew that we'd come for the fourth eventually because we had no choice." She paused. "He's had time to prepare. Time to ready whatever defenses he's crafted. Time to ensure that when we arrive, we arrive on ground of his choosing against odds of his making."

"Frightening, thoughts, but true for all that."

"Honest thoughts." She turned to face him, her impossible eyes catching starlight in ways that made them seem to hold galaxies. "I won't lie to you, beloved. Won't pretend this is survivable when everything suggests otherwise. Won't offer false comfort when truth serves better. But I will say this—" Her hand found his face. "Whatever ending waits, I'm grateful I'm facing it beside you. Grateful I chose earth and water over stars and distance. Grateful that loving you gave meaning to everything I am, even if everything I am proves insufficient for what comes next."

He pulled her close, feeling her breathe, feeling her heart beat against his chest. Around them, other warriors rested or prayed or simply stared at Isle of Man with expressions that acknowledged they were looking at their probable grave. Above them, the ravens settled in nearby trees and rocks, dark shapes against darker sky, waiting with patience that

334

suggested they'd waited for countless deaths before and would wait for countless more after.

"Tomorrow," Z'Landar said. "Tomorrow we reach it."

"Tomorrow we find where he dwells," Andralia agreed.

"Tomorrow everything changes."

"Does it. I feel this has been brewing since the stars were new. We are but players, aren't we?"

"If so, those that play us choose well to put you in my life."

They held each other through the night while stars wheeled overhead and ravens watched and Isle of Man waited with secrets buried in depths where light never reached and pressure crushed hope as efficiently as it crushed bone.

The second day brought them to the island itself as the sun climbed toward noon—pale autumn light doing little to warm waters that grew colder with wrongness rather than temperature. Isle of Man rose before them—mountains dramatic against sky, Snowfall highest among them reaching over two thousand feet, slopes showing bracken gold and green even this late in season. The coastline was rugged, beautiful—cliffs carved by millennia of waves, beaches where stone met sea with the particular grace that only time could craft, coves and caves that spoke of sanctuary rather than danger.

It seemed innocent. Peaceful. A place where humans might someday dwell in harmony with sea, where standing stones marked sacred ground without threatening, where the only conflicts were between wind and water and stone in their eternal dance of erosion and resistance.

But beneath the beauty ran wrongness that made Z'Landar's chest tighten with each stroke closer. The water tasted wrong—not poisoned exactly, but carrying flavors that should not exist, that spoke of ancient magic saturating everything, that warned of powers that predated the island itself dwelling in depths beneath its shores.

335

"The trenches are on the western side," Muirgheal said, appearing beside him. "That's where we'll find him. Where the sea floor drops away suddenly from shallows to depths that reach—" She paused. "No one knows how deep, exactly. Deep enough that many who've tried to reach bottom have failed. Deep enough that water-folk tell stories about what might dwell there, what Fomorians built in old times when the world was younger and more terrible."

They swam around the island, following its coastline toward the western shore. The water grew progressively darker as they moved—not from clouds overhead, which remained constant gray, but from depth increasing beneath them. Z'Landar could feel it—the sense of void below, of vast emptiness opening beneath his fins, of swimming over abyss that waited patient as the ravens for the moment when mistake or exhaustion made falling inevitable.

Then they reached the trench.

It was like swimming to the edge of the world and finding the world simply ended—no gentle slope, no gradual descent, just sudden termination where relatively shallow waters gave way to darkness absolute. One moment they were swimming over sea floor visible perhaps fifty feet below. The next, there was no bottom at all. Just void. Just black. Just depths that made even seasoned water-folk pause because some places spoke to primal fears that transcended courage and touched something more fundamental about what it meant to be small and mortal and swimming over darkness that could swallow entire kingdoms without notice.

The wrongness here was not subtle. It pressed against them like physical force, making breathing difficult, making continuation require active will rather than passive motion. The water was warmer—not from sun, but from something below. From heat that pulsed like heartbeat, rhythmic and regular, speaking of dragon egg developing in depths, growing stronger, moving closer to hatching with each day that passed.

And beneath the heat, beneath the wrongness, beneath everything—presence. Vast and ancient and aware. Knowing they'd come. Waiting for them. Patient as the deep itself because patience cost nothing when you'd lived longer than memory and would live longer than any who swam above.

Balor. In the trenches below. In darkness where light died. In pressure that should kill. Waiting.

"There," Muirgheal whispered, pointing toward where trench wall showed opening—vast cave mouth carved into stone, or perhaps not carved but deliberately crafted, shaped by forces that made stone obey in ways stone should not. "That's Fomorian work. That's old. That's where he dwells."

Z'Landar stared at the opening. It was huge—large enough to admit beings whose size made dragons seem small, wide enough that the twenty-eight of them could swim through it side by side without crowding. The edges showed marks—not erosion, but deliberate shaping, patterns that suggested purpose beyond simple excavation, symbols that might have been language or warning or both.

"This was a breeding ground," one of the older Merrow said, voice hushed with horror or awe or both. "In old times, before Fomorians were driven to the world's margins, they bred here. Raised their young in these depths. Built chambers and halls and places where even gods feared to swim. That's what this is. That's why Balor chose it. He's returned to ancestral dwelling, to place of power, to ground that remembers his kind and welcomes their darkness."

The twenty-eight gathered at the trench's edge, staring down into darkness that seemed to have weight, substance, malice. Above them, the ravens circled—hundreds of them, maybe thousands, dark cloud against gray sky, waiting for the moment when swimmers below would become feast.

Z'Landar felt Andralia's presence beside him, her hand finding his even in seal-form, their connection transcending the limitations of bodies that didn't have proper hands to hold.

This was it. The final threshold. The last moment before swimming into darkness that would claim most of them, into presence of power that unmade existence, into ending that might take all of them or might—if fortune favored and courage proved sufficient—leave just enough alive to destroy the fourth egg and finish what they'd started.

337

"We should wait," Tormod said quietly. "Rest. Prepare. We're exhausted from two days' swimming. Going in now—"

"Gives us no advantage," Z'Landar interrupted gently. "Waiting just gives fear more time to work on us. Gives doubt space to grow. Gives Balor more time to prepare whatever welcome he's crafted." He looked at the twenty-eight warriors who had swum this far, who had survived Cruachan and Cliodhna and dragon-fire and now faced something worse. "We go now. We go together. We do what we came to do. And if we fall—" His voice steadied. "If we fall, we fall having tried. Having stood. Having refused to surrender when surrender would have been easier and safer and completely insufficient for what Scotland requires."

He took human form—needed a mouth for what came next, needed face rather than seal-shape for words that deserved the dignity of human speech.

The others followed—twenty-eight taking forms that could speak, that could meet each other's eyes, that could acknowledge what they were about to do with the particular gravity that only humans managed when facing endings.

"I don't know what waits in those depths," Z'Landar said, his voice carrying across the small group. "Don't know if we can survive Balor's eye or fight in darkness that absolute or endure pressure that should crush us. Don't know if twenty-eight souls are sufficient when two hundred barely managed Cruachan. Don't know—" He stopped, took breath. "Don't know anything except this: someone has to stand. Someone has to swim into that darkness. Someone has to face the final egg and finish what we started. And it's us. Twenty-eight souls who've come too far to stop now, who've lost too much to let those losses be meaningless, who love Scotland and Ireland enough to die protecting them if dying is what protection requires."

He looked at each face—Tormod and Caelan, Muirgheal and the Merrow, Ruadhan and Brígh, the others whose names he knew and whose courage he'd witnessed. Saw fear in every expression. Saw determination too. Saw understanding that this was ending—probably their ending, likely final and absolute—but that ending didn't change necessity.

"Thank you," he said simply. "For swimming this far. For standing when standing meant burning. For following a king who's led you only toward death and danger and costs that should never be asked. Thank you for—" His voice broke. "Thank you for being more courageous than I have right to expect. More loyal than I've earned. More willing to die for Scotland than Scotland has right to demand."

"We don't do it for Scotland alone," Tormod said gruffly. "We do it for each other. For the ones who fell in Cruachan. For Maelis and Beathan and all the others whose names are carved in stone. We do it because we've become something together—not just warriors or water-folk or defenders of Scotland, but family forged in fire and grief and determination that pushes us beyond simple survival. So we'll swim into that darkness together. Fight together. Fall together if falling is what comes. But together. Always together."

"Together," the others echoed, and the word held weight beyond its syllables.

They prepared to take seal-forms again, to descend into the trench, to swim toward the cave where Balor waited. Z'Landar reached for Andralia, pulled her close one final time, held her with desperate strength that tried to convey everything words couldn't hold.

"I love you," he whispered against her hair.

"I know." Her arms tightened around him. "I love you too. Have loved you since before I understood what loving you would cost. Still love you despite knowing that cost now. Will love you until either I cease to be or you do or we both fall into darkness that erases even love's memory."

They released each other, took seal-forms, and dove.

The descent was like swimming into oblivion—light fading rapidly as they went deeper, pressure building with each meter, cold intensifying not from temperature alone but from some wrongness that saturated everything. The twenty-eight swam close together, drawing comfort from proximity when comfort was all that remained, following Z'Landar and Andralia toward darkness that seemed to have weight, substance, hunger.

Z'Landar's power pulsed at his chest—the Heart of the Loch glowing with light that had nothing to do with the pendant itself and everything to do with his unique heritage finally unleashed, with power drawn from sources that made even deep trenches seem shallow by comparison. The light pushed back darkness somewhat, revealing stone walls that dropped away on either side, showing the trench's immense depth, illustrating just how far they'd have to descend before reaching caves where Balor dwelt.

Andralia swam beside him, her own form glowing faintly with starlight that came from within rather than without—her otherworldly nature expressing itself in ways that defied simple physics, making her visible even when all other light failed. Together they illuminated enough space that warriors behind could see, could follow, could continue descending despite fear that made each stroke require active will.

The heat grew stronger as they descended—dragon egg pulse becoming palpable, rhythmic, speaking of life developing in depths, of potential for destruction growing with each heartbeat-like throb. It was warmer now than it should be at this depth, warmer than any natural process could account for, warmer in ways that suggested fire sleeping but not extinguished, waiting for the moment when shell broke and fury emerged to burn everything it could reach.

The stone walls began to show marks—deliberate shaping, patterns that were definitely language or warning or both. Fomorian work. Ancient beyond most present comprehension. Symbols that hurt to look at directly because they carried meanings that mortal minds weren't shaped to contain, that spoke of powers and purposes that predated humanity and would persist long after humanity forgot how to remember its own name.

Then they reached the cave.

The opening was exactly as they'd glimpsed from above—vast entrance carved or crafted into the trench wall, large enough to admit creatures whose size made dragons seem small, shaped with purpose that defied simple excavation. But from within—from close, with Z'Landar's light revealing details—it looked less like a cave entrance and more like some threshold between worlds, like a doorway into a realm where different rules applied and returning might prove impossible even for those who entered willingly.

The edges bore more symbols—clear now, detailed, speaking in language Z'Landar couldn't read but could feel. Warning? Welcome? Statement of purpose? All of those and more, compressed into shapes that carried meaning beyond simple translation.

And beyond the entrance—darkness absolute. Not just absence of light but presence of darkness, weight of it, malice of it, hunger of it. A darkness with appetite. Darkness that had swallowed countless things and would swallow countless more, that cared nothing for courage or determination or love expressed through dying together.

They gathered at the cave entrance—twenty-eight souls hovering in water that pressed against them like physical force, staring into darkness that waited patient as death itself. Z'Landar felt each heartbeat like drum in his chest, felt Andralia's presence beside him like anchor in storm, felt the weight of what came next pressing against his shoulders until standing upright seemed effort beyond his capacity.

This was the threshold. The final moment before swimming into ending. The last chance to turn back, to flee, to choose survival over Scotland's protection and accept that some battles couldn't be won but only witnessed.

No one turned back.

Z'Landar met Andralia's eyes—impossible cosmic depths that had seen distances he couldn't imagine and had chosen to focus on him, on earth, on water and stone and the stubborn refusal to let dragons win—and he found courage he didn't know he still possessed.

"Together," he said, though no one could hear in seal-form.

But she understood anyway. Nodded. Moved closer. Her presence wrapping around his like water around stone.

They swam forward.

Into darkness.

Into the cave that Fomorians had crafted as their breeding ground, that Balor had claimed as dwelling, that held the fourth egg and a power that unmade existence itself.

Behind them, the twenty-eight followed—swimming into ending because someone had to, because standing mattered more than surviving, because love and duty and stubborn courage were all they had and all they needed and all they'd ever been.

The darkness swallowed them.

The cave entrance faded behind.

And from somewhere ahead—somewhere deeper in the Fomorian-crafted depths, somewhere in chambers where pressure should kill and darkness should blind—something stirred.

Vast. Ancient. Aware.

Knowing they'd come.

Ready for them.

Balor of the Evil Eye.

The one-eyed king.

The Fomorian giant whose gaze unmade existence.

Opening.

Eye opening.

And then, as hope seemed its most fragile, as darkness pressed closest, as the twenty-eight swam deeper into caves that should not exist—light came from behind.

Not physical light. Not illumination in any sense that eyes could process. But presence. Force. The particular awareness that came when the dead decided to honor their promises and fight beside the living one final time.

The Sluagh.

They materialized from darkness like darkness given purpose—the Host of the Unforgiven Dead flowing into the Fomorian caves with sounds like wind through graveyards, like grief that had outlasted mourning, like endings that refused to properly end. Forms flickered between solid and insubstantial—some bird-like with wings made of shadow and regret, some humanoid but wrong in ways that suggested humanity glimpsed through death's distorting lens, all of them dark and terrible and carrying presence of things that had died but refused to accept death's finality.

Hundreds of them. Maybe thousands. Flowing past the twenty-eight living warriors like a flood of spectral force, like an army that answered to no mortal command but had decided—for reasons known only to the dead—that this battle warranted their attention.

The Sluagh-leader—if such beings acknowledged leadership—manifested beside Z'Landar. Its form rippled like smoke over water, wearing shape that might once have been human but had forgotten what humanity meant.

"We told you we would come," it said, voice like wind through bones. "Told you the dead fear nothing. Told you we would fight beside you until the last egg was destroyed or you all joined us in whatever realm waits beyond living." The darkness that was its face turned toward the caves ahead. "Balor waits. His eye kills with looking. His power unmakes what should not be unmade. But we have already died. Already been unmade. What is his eye to those who see only endings anyway?"

Then the Sluagh surged forward—flooding deeper into the caves, flowing past the twenty-eight with determination that was more than simple courage into something that looked like vengeance or justice or simply the particular purpose that the dead brought to battles the living could not win alone.

Z'Landar felt hope flare in his chest—not certainty of survival, not confidence in victory, but simply the understanding that they were not alone. That the impossible had become merely catastrophic. That whatever ending waited in the depths, they would face it with forces that defied easy death and refused to surrender even when surrender was the only logical response.

Andralia's presence wrapped tighter around his. He felt her relief, her renewed determination, her understanding that the Sluagh's arrival changed calculations enough that survival shifted from impossible to merely unlikely.

Together—living and dead both—they swam deeper into the Fomorian breeding ground.

Knowing that doom approached.

But uncertain—perhaps for the first time in millennia—whether doom approached for warriors who swam toward him or for himself.

Chapter Twenty-Five: Into the Deep

They swam deeper into darkness that had weight.

The Fomorian breeding ground was vast beyond comprehension—chambers carved from stone by forces that made stone obey in ways stone should not, connected by halls sized for beings whose scale made dragons seem small. Symbols covered every surface, writing that hurt to look at directly, patterns that carried meanings mortal minds weren't shaped to contain. Z'Landar's light from the Heart of the Loch pushed back the darkness somewhat, and Andralia's cosmic glow provided additional illumination, but even together their radiance barely penetrated the black that pressed against them like malice given substance.

The Sluagh flowed ahead through the chambers—hundreds of spectral forms scouting the path, moving with purpose that suggested they knew exactly where Balor waited. The Host of the Unforgiven Dead made sounds like wind through graveyards as they went, like grief that had outlasted mourning, like endings that refused to properly end.

Behind them, twenty-eight living warriors followed. Water-folk in seal-forms, swimming through halls where pressure should crush bone but somehow didn't, where heat from the dragon egg pulsed stronger with each meter descended, where wrongness saturated everything until even breathing became labor requiring active will.

A Selkie named Rónan swam too close to a wall, curiosity or carelessness drawing his attention to a symbol that pulsed with faint light. His flipper brushed the carved stone.

The symbol flared.

Rónan's scream lasted less than a heartbeat before he simply dissolved—not torn apart, not burned, just unmade as if he'd never been. One moment a living warrior swimming beside his companions. The next: nothing. Not even memory seemed sufficient to hold his shape.

Z'Landar felt the death like ice in his chest but didn't stop swimming. Couldn't stop. Stopping meant thinking about how they'd lost another warrior before even reaching the battle, meant acknowledging that the breeding ground itself was hostile in ways that killed without warning or mercy.

Twenty-seven now. Twenty-seven out of the two hundred who had entered Cruachan with determination absolute.

The Sluagh-leader materialized beside Z'Landar, its form rippling like smoke over water.

"Two chambers ahead," it said, voice like wind through bones. "He waits in the deepest part. The egg is with him—we feel its heat, its malice. He knows we come. Is ready." The darkness that served as its face turned forward. "This is his ground. His chosen battlefield. We enter at every disadvantage."

"We enter anyway," Z'Landar replied.

"Yes," the Sluagh-leader agreed. "We enter anyway."

They swam through another chamber—this one showing evidence of what the breeding ground had been. Bones lay scattered across the floor, some enormous beyond easy comprehension, others merely large. Fomorian young who hadn't survived the culling? Enemies thrown here to die? Sacrifices to whatever power dwelt deepest? The bones spoke of darkness that raised children through cruelty, that made survivors strong by killing the weak, that cared nothing for mercy or kindness or any quality except power earned through suffering.

This was what they faced: a king who was product of such breeding, who had survived when others failed, who carried strength forged in darkness that should have killed him but made him mighty instead.

Then they saw it.

The final chamber's entrance loomed ahead—vast opening carved into stone, doorway sized for giants, threshold to Balor's domain. Darkness within was absolute, swallowing even Z'Landar and Andralia's combined light as if illumination itself was unwelcome. Heat pulsed from inside in

346

rhythmic waves—dragon egg calling, drawing them forward, marking the location of what they'd come to destroy.

And beneath the heat, beneath the darkness, beneath everything—presence. Vast and ancient and aware. Knowing they'd come. Waiting for them. Patient as stone because patience cost nothing when you'd lived longer than memory and would live longer than any who swam toward you.

Balor.

The twenty-seven gathered at the threshold. Sluagh flowing forward, living warriors positioning themselves, everyone knowing their role without need for lengthy discussion. They'd fought together through Cruachan and Cliodhna's fury. This was just... bigger. More terrible. More likely to kill them all.

But the strategy was simple enough: Sluagh first to create chaos and distraction. Warriors split into groups—some to draw Balor's attention and his eye's deadly gaze, others to strike at the egg if opportunity arose. Z'Landar would shape perception, create illusions that made truth indistinguishable from false. Andralia would channel and amplify his power until even a Fomorian king couldn't penetrate the deceptions.

And then they'd either win or die.

Probably die.

But at least they'd die trying.

Tormod swam close, his burns from Cruachan still visible but his eyes fierce with determination rather than pain. "For Beathan," he said quietly. "For Maelis. For all of them. Let's finish this."

Others echoed agreement—short fierce words that spoke of warriors ready to fight, not philosophize. They'd come too far to hesitate now. Come through too much death to falter at the final threshold.

This was what they came for.

Z'Landar reached for Andralia's presence, felt her attention shift to him, pulled her gently away from the others toward a small alcove in the hall. Just a few meters of privacy. Just enough space for words that needed saying before everything changed.

She came without question, taking human form as he did, and when they faced each other in the darkness her impossible eyes held understanding that made his chest tighten until breathing hurt.

"You're going to channel all of it," he said. Not question—statement. He knew. Had known since they'd entered the breeding ground, since they'd approached this threshold, since he'd felt the magnitude of what waited in that chamber ahead.

"Yes," she replied simply.

"It will kill you."

"Yes."

"Then don't." The words came desperate, fierce. "We'll find another way. There's always—"

"There isn't." Her voice was gentle but absolute. "You know there isn't. To destroy that egg, guarded by a Fomorian king in his own domain, protected by power that unmakes existence—we need everything. Every drop of what lives in you. The ocean. The infinity you carry from your cosmic roots. And I'm the only one who can channel it."

"Even if it unmakes you?" His hands found her shoulders, gripping tight enough to hurt but she didn't flinch. "Even if trying to hold all of it tears you apart from the inside? You said it yourself—at the northern settlement you nearly died channeling a fraction of my power. Actually channeling everything—"

"Will definitely kill me," she finished. "Let's be honest about that. Not 'probably' or 'might.' Will. Channeling your full power means trying to hold the ocean in a teacup, means containing infinity in a vessel shaped for mortality. And that—" Her voice caught. "That will unmake me more completely than Balor's eye ever could."

348

"Then I'm ordering you not to." Desperation made him cruel, made him reach for authority he'd never used on her. "As your king—"

"You're not my king in this." She pulled his hands from her shoulders, held them in hers instead. "You're the man I love. And I'm choosing how I spend myself. You don't get to stop me."

"Andralia—"

"Listen to me." Her fingers tightened in his, urgent and fierce. "I came from stars. From distances and cold and nothing that mattered. Cosmic spaces between me and anything real. Then I found you. Found THIS." She pressed one of his hands against her chest, against her heart. "Found love so absolute it gave meaning to everything I'd been, everything I am. These months with you—worth more than centuries before them. Worth more than anything I left behind. Worth dying for."

"Don't say that." His voice broke. "Don't make this sound like it's beautiful when it's just—it's just you dying. You ceasing to be. You leaving me alone to face everything that comes after and I can't—" He pulled her close, desperate. "I can't do this without you."

"You can." Her arms wrapped around him, holding tight. "You will. Because you have to. Because Scotland needs its king and survivors need their leader and someone has to carry this forward after I'm gone. And because—" She pulled back enough to meet his eyes. "Because I'll be waiting. Somewhere beyond this. Energy doesn't just end—it transforms. What we are together, what we've become—that's too powerful to simply cease. So I'll wait. In stars, in whatever realm comes after water and stone. And when your time comes, when your duty is done and Scotland no longer needs you—you'll find me again."

"Promise me." The words came hoarse, pleading. "Promise you'll be there. That this isn't just ending. That always means something beyond this moment."

"I promise." She touched his face, thumb tracing his cheekbone with tenderness that hurt worse than any wound. "We will meet again in a land we do not know. Just like Maelis said. Not here, not in these waters, but somewhere. In cosmos, in stars, in whatever waits when flesh fails

349

and only what matters most remains. I'll be there. I'll wait forever if I have to. However long it takes you to come for me."

He kissed her then—desperate and tender both, trying to memorize everything about this moment because moments were all they had and this one was ending too fast. Her taste, her warmth, the way she fit against him like water against stone. Everything that would be gone soon. Everything that mattered more than breath or life or duty or any other consideration except this: that he loved her and she was dying and there was nothing he could do to stop it.

When they finally separated both were crying, tears mixing with the wrongness and pressure and heat that saturated the breeding ground.

"I love you," he whispered. "Gods, I love you so much it hurts."

"I know." Her smile held sorrow and certainty both. "I love you too. Have loved you since before I understood what loving would cost. Still love you knowing the cost now. Will love you until—" She couldn't finish.

"Until always."

"Until always." She pulled him close one final time, held him with strength that suggested she never wanted to let go. "However long always takes. However many realms we have to cross. However far apart we are—always together in ways that matter. In memory. In what we became when we chose each other. In love that nothing can unmake, not even Balor's eye, not even death itself."

They stood there in the darkness, holding each other, trying to make the moment last while knowing it couldn't. Knowing that duty called and battle waited and the egg pulsed ahead like heartbeat counting down to ending.

Finally—too soon, always too soon—they separated. Took seal-forms again. Returned to where the others waited.

Z'Landar saw them watching, saw understanding in their eyes. Tormod nodded once, grim acknowledgment of sacrifice that was coming. Caelan

350

looked away, unable to meet their gaze. Muirgheal's face showed grief for loss that hadn't happened yet but would.

The warriors were ready. Not contemplative now but fierce, determined, energized for battle. They'd done their mourning, their preparing, their accepting of approaching death. Now they were simply ready to fight.

Tormod's voice carried across the small group: "Let's finish this. For everyone we lost."

Caelan added: "For Scotland. For Ireland. For all of us."

Muirgheal, grim smile showing teeth: "Time to show this Fomorian bastard what happens when he threatens our lands."

Even Ruadhan was grinning now, chaos returning to his expression after the uncharacteristic seriousness of the descent. "Let's make this memorable."

Others voiced fierce agreement, weapons ready though everyone knew weapons might prove useless against what waited. But having something to hold, something to strike with, made the impossible seem merely catastrophic.

The Sluagh gathered at the threshold—hundreds of spectral forms flowing together, darkness given purpose, death incarnate preparing to face something that killed with looking. They would enter first. Would create initial chaos. Would draw Balor's attention and his eye's deadly gaze. Give the living warriors chance to position, to strike, to do what the dead could not do alone.

Behind them, warriors split into groups without need for lengthy orders. Tormod leading ten toward the left—distraction group who would attack openly, draw Balor's eye, knowing they were probably sacrificing themselves but creating openings for others. Caelan and Muirgheal leading eight toward the right—strike group who would try to reach the egg while Balor was occupied. The Púca flickering between forms, chaos incarnate, ready to add confusion to whatever madness unfolded.

And Z'Landar with Andralia, guarded by three warriors whose job was keeping them safe enough to maintain focus. Because Z'Landar's

351

perception-shaping required concentration, required Andralia's amplification, required them both surviving long enough to do what needed doing.

Z'Landar wanted to speak. Wanted to give some final rallying cry, some words that made this seem noble rather than desperate. But looking at the twenty-seven warriors gathered at darkness's edge, he found he had nothing left except truth.

"We swim now toward ending," he said, voice carrying despite being hoarse with emotion. "Some of us won't return. But we swim anyway. For Scotland. For Ireland. For everyone who died getting us here. For each other."

He paused, meeting as many eyes as he could in the darkness.

"Together."

"ALWAYS!" The response came back fierce, defiant, absolute. Living and dead both. United in determination that made no sense except that sense had abandoned them chambers ago and all that remained was stubborn refusal to surrender when surrender meant failure.

The Sluagh surged forward first—flooding into the chamber like a spectral tide, flowing into darkness that swallowed their forms, making sounds like wind through graveyards as they went. The sound built and echoed and filled the halls behind with noise that spoke of death claiming its own, of endings approaching, of battles that would be written in stone and blood and memory.

Then the warriors followed.

No hesitation. No final pause. Just movement—swimming into the chamber, into heat that struck like physical force, into pressure that should crush them, into darkness so absolute that even Z'Landar and Andralia's combined light barely penetrated a few meters ahead.

The chamber was vast. Impossibly vast. The ceiling—if there was a ceiling—lay beyond their lights' reach. The walls disappeared into black on all sides. They swam through space that felt less like room and more like void, like swimming through the heart of some massive beast that might close around them at any moment.

Heat pulsed from ahead. Stronger now. Overwhelming. Dragon egg no longer distant promise but immediate presence, somewhere in this darkness, somewhere close, throbbing like heartbeat that made water itself vibrate with each pulse.

And then—movement.

Something vast stirring in the darkness ahead. Something so large that the water itself shifted with its motion, currents pushing against the swimmers, making them fight to maintain position.

A voice came. Not voice—force. Like stones grinding against each other deep underground, like earthquakes given speech, like malice that predated language learning how to make sounds that mortal ears could process.

"SO YOU'VE COME AT LAST."

The voice filled the chamber, came from everywhere and nowhere, resonated in bones and water and stone.

"GOOD. I'VE WAITED. GROWN BORED IN MY WAITING. NOW—"

More movement. Something enormous shifting position. Water displacing.

"—NOW I WILL SHOW YOU WHAT IT MEANS TO FACE A FOMORIAN KING IN HIS OWN DOMAIN. WHAT IT MEANS WHEN THE EYE OPENS. WHAT IT MEANS TO BE UNMADE."

Light appeared in the darkness ahead.

Not light—wrongness made visible. Anti-light. The opposite of illumination, somehow glowing while making everything darker, making shadows deeper, making the darkness itself seem to have substance and hunger.

The eye.

Balor's Evil Eye.

Opening.

Slowly, deliberately, lid pulling back to reveal something that should not exist, that mortal minds weren't shaped to perceive without breaking.

A Merrow named Sean looked up. Couldn't help it—instinct to see what spoke, to face what threatened. His eyes met the gaze of the opening eye.

He screamed.

Brief, terrible scream that cut off mid-sound because there was suddenly no one there to make it. Sean didn't die. Didn't fall wounded. Didn't have time for final words or thoughts or even understanding of what was happening.

He simply ceased.

Not dead—UNMADE. Erased from existence as if he'd never been. The water where he'd been swimming showed no trace of his passage, no memory of warrior who had fought through Cruachan and survived dragon-fire and made it all the way to this chamber only to be ended with a glance.

Twenty-six now. Twenty-six out of two hundred.

"Don't look at him!" Z'Landar's voice cut through the horror. "Don't meet the eye! Attack but don't look directly—"

The Sluagh swarmed forward, spectral forms flooding toward where Balor's presence loomed in darkness, and warriors moved with them— groups splitting, attacking from different angles, weapons raised though everyone knew weapons might prove useless, courage absolute though fear should have paralyzed them.

Z'Landar felt Andralia's presence wrap around his consciousness, felt her beginning to channel his power, felt the first stirrings of perception-

354

shaping magic building between them. He reached for his ability to make minds see what wasn't there, to confuse reality until truth and illusion became indistinguishable.

And pushed.

False warriors appeared in the darkness—dozens of them, swimming from every direction, attacking from impossible angles, each one as solid-seeming as the real fighters. Sounds multiplied—screams and battle-cries and the particular noise of weapons striking stone, all of it false but real enough that even Z'Landar momentarily doubted which was which.

Andralia amplified. He felt her power wrapping around his, taking the perception-shaping and making it stronger, deeper, more real. Her cosmic nature channeling his water-born magic until the illusions stopped being tricks and started being forces that could deceive even ancient kings.

The eye turned. Searching. Trying to find real threats among the false ones. Its anti-light swept across the chamber, and wherever it looked warriors screamed and scattered because meeting that gaze meant ending absolute.

But the Sluagh swarmed it. Already dead, they feared the eye less than living warriors feared it, and though even they could be harmed by that terrible gaze they pressed forward anyway, clawing and shrieking and pulling at something vast in the darkness—Balor himself, hidden in the black, protected by his eye's deadly power.

Andralia's voice came to Z'Landar through their connection—not words spoken aloud but thought shared between minds linked by love and magic both:

Whatever happens—remember. Always.

Always, he replied, pouring everything he felt into that single word. *However this ends—always.*

Then the battle truly erupted.

Warriors attacking from darkness, real and false mixed together until even Z'Landar couldn't track which was which. Sluagh swarming something massive ahead, their spectral forms flickering and dissolving when the eye caught them but always more flooding forward to replace those lost. The Púca shapeshifting madly—Ruadhan becoming three Ruadhans and then seven, each one pulling at different parts of the vast presence, each one real enough to demand Balor's attention even if only some were truly physical.

Heat pulsing stronger. Dragon egg calling. Close now. So close.

Z'Landar shaped perception until reality bent. Shaped it until he couldn't tell anymore what was real and what was illusion. Shaped it until his head pounded and his vision blurred and only Andralia's channeling kept the power flowing, kept the magic building, kept the impossible assault continuing against a king who should have ended them all with a glance.

And somewhere in the darkness, in the chaos, in the fury of desperate courage meeting ancient malice—

Balor laughed.

Deep, terrible sound like mountains cracking, like the earth itself finding amusement in mortal presumption.

"YOU THINK ILLUSIONS WILL SAVE YOU? YOU THINK NUMBERS MATTER WHEN THE EYE CAN UNMAKE EXISTENCE ITSELF? FOOLISH CHILDREN. BRAVE, BUT FOOLISH. LET ME SHOW YOU WHAT POWER TRULY MEANS."

The eye opened wider.

Much wider.

And the true battle—the final battle, the ending that would determine everything—

Began in earnest.

Chapter Twenty-Six: The Eye and the Ending

The eye opened wider and warriors died screaming.

Tormod led his distraction group forward with a roar that held three centuries of fury—charging toward where Balor's massive form loomed in darkness, drawing the eye's terrible gaze. The anti-light swept across them and three warriors simply ceased mid-stroke, unmade so completely that water filled the spaces where they'd been without ripple or disturbance.

But Tormod kept coming, kept swimming, kept attacking with weapon raised and courage absolute, until the eye caught him directly and the old Kelpie—who had survived three hundred years of battles, who had fought beside Beathan and Maelis and every other fallen friend—was erased from existence with less ceremony than morning erasing stars.

Z'Landar felt each death like a blade to his chest but didn't stop shaping perception, didn't stop creating illusions that swarmed from every angle. Couldn't stop because stopping meant their deaths were wasted, meant Tormod's sacrifice bought nothing, meant—

Caelan's group struck from the right, swimming fast and low, trying to reach the pulsing heat that marked the egg's location. The young chief moved with desperate courage, leading seven warriors toward their goal, and for a moment Z'Landar thought they might actually reach it—

Then Balor's massive arm swept through the water.

Not seen, just felt—displacement so enormous it created currents that scattered warriors like leaves in storm-wind. Caelan and two others were caught directly, crushed against stone walls with force that shattered bone and ended thought simultaneously. The remaining five kept swimming, kept trying, and Z'Landar created false images of them— dozens of phantom warriors all swimming toward the egg, making Balor divide his attention, making the eye search for real threats among illusions—

357

The eye found them anyway.

It swept across the group and warriors unmade, dissolved, ceased. Five became three became one became none, and the path to the egg remained blocked by a king whose size and power made their assault seem less like battle and more like insects attacking mountain.

More, Andralia's presence whispered through their connection. *Give me more. I can channel more. We need MORE.*

Z'Landar poured more power into the perception-shaping, felt it amplified beyond anything he'd achieved before, felt illusions becoming so real that even he couldn't distinguish them from warriors actually attacking. The chamber filled with false threats—hundreds of them, thousands, swarming from every direction, making the darkness itself seem alive with assaulting forces.

Balor roared frustration. The sound was physical force, was pressure that crushed, was fury given voice. Warriors closest to the source screamed and clutched their heads, blood streaming from ears and noses, and when the roar finally ended half of them floated motionless, killed by sound alone.

Muirgheal swam through the chaos with determination that honored every Irish warrior who'd ever lived, leading her Merrow toward the egg with single-minded focus. She'd survived Cliodhna and Caoránach both—surely she could survive this, surely courage meant something against even impossible odds—

The eye caught her.

For just an instant Z'Landar saw her face—saw recognition of what was happening, saw understanding that this was ending, saw fierce pride that she'd made it this far—and then she was gone. Unmade. Erased. The Merrow with her dissolved moments later, and the Irish alliance that had seemed so important, so necessary, ended with warriors who died far from home defending a land not their own because some causes demanded sacrifice beyond reason.

MORE, Andralia demanded, and Z'Landar felt the strain in her voice, felt power flowing through her beyond what any being should channel, felt

358

her burning from within as cosmic forces meant to exist in stars were compressed through mortal flesh. *Give me EVERYTHING. We're close. So close. Just—MORE.*

He gave her more.

Gave her everything he had, everything he was, everything his cosmic heritage provided. Perception-shaping became reality-shaping, illusions became forces that could actually harm, and when phantom warriors struck at Balor now the Fomorian king bled—not much, but bled, proof that what Z'Landar created was more than mere tricks of light and confusion.

The Sluagh swarmed endlessly, spectral forms clawing and biting and pulling at flesh that was stone-hard, at power that should have been untouchable. The eye destroyed them by hundreds—dissolving the already-dead into true non-existence, unmaking even those who had already been unmade—but more flowed forward, Host of Unforgiven Dead living up to their name by refusing to stop, refusing to surrender, refusing to acknowledge that some battles couldn't be won through determination alone.

Ruadhan shapeshifted madly, becoming dozen versions of himself, becoming things with too many teeth and not enough form to be easily targeted, adding chaos to chaos until Balor roared again and swept his arm through where the Púca danced. Half the forms dissolved—false images destroyed by force alone. But one was real, one was actually Ruadhan, and the impact sent the trickster spinning through water trailing blood from wounds that even shapeshifter healing couldn't immediately fix.

Brígh dove to help her companion, took forms that pulled Ruadhan away from immediate danger, and for a moment Z'Landar thought the Púca might survive—

Then the eye found them both.

They dissolved together, chaos-bringers who had added confusion and trickery to every battle, who had translated ravens and caused small madness wherever they went, ended in silence and stillness that made their absence somehow worse than their deaths.

The warriors were dying. All of them. Dying with courage that shamed gods, dying with determination that should have meant something, dying because Balor was simply too vast, too powerful, too ancient to be defeated by courage alone no matter how absolutely that courage was given.

Z'Landar felt his power draining, felt exhaustion building beyond anything he'd experienced, felt perception-shaping becoming labor rather than gift. His vision blurred. His body—even in seal-form—ached with strain that suggested bones might crack under pressure of forces he channeled.

But Andralia kept taking it, kept amplifying it, kept pushing power through herself that burned brighter and hotter with each passing moment. He felt her through their connection—felt her determination, her love, her absolute refusal to fail even as channeling forces meant for cosmos through frame meant for mortality began to tear her apart from within.

The egg, she whispered. *I can see it. Through the power, through the channeling—I can SEE it. Hidden behind him. Protected. But I can reach it if you give me EVERYTHING. If you hold nothing back. If you trust me to—*

NO, he screamed through their connection. *Not if it kills you. Not if—*

It's already killing me, she replied, and her voice held strange peace, terrible acceptance. *I've been dying since I started channeling this much. Since I tried to hold ocean in teacup and found the ocean was bigger than I imagined. But I can still DO something with it. Can still use what's burning through me. Can still—*

She didn't finish with words.

She finished with action.

Z'Landar felt her pull everything—every drop of his power, every bit of cosmic heritage, every force that lived in him drawn forth and channeled through her and shaped into weapon or will or reality-bending force too complex to name. Felt her burning, felt her screaming silently, felt her dying—

And through it all, felt her love. Absolute and unwavering and worth dying for.

The egg shattered.

Not seen directly, not witnessed, but FELT—dragon egg that had pulsed like heartbeat through chambers suddenly going silent, potential dragon destroyed before hatching, fourth egg ended and quest completed and Scotland saved at cost that made saving seem inadequate word for what was paid.

Balor roared.

Not frustration now but PAIN, but fury absolute, but understanding that what he'd guarded had been destroyed despite his power, despite his eye, despite being Fomorian king in his own domain. The sound filled the chamber, made water itself vibrate with rage, made stone walls crack under pressure of voice that should not exist.

And through their connection—through the link that bound Z'Landar to Andralia through magic and love both—Z'Landar felt her die.

Not unmade by Balor's eye. Not killed by external force. But consumed from within by power too vast to contain, burned away by trying to channel infinity through mortality, dissolved not into non-existence but into energy that returned to cosmos from which she'd come.

She was simply... gone.

The connection that had been constant presence since they'd met—that had wrapped around his consciousness like warmth, like home, like everything that mattered—

Went silent.

And something in Z'Landar broke.

Not his body. Not his mind exactly. But something deeper, more fundamental—the part of him that had learned to love, that had become more than king or warrior or water-born being with cosmic heritage. The part that had been completed by her presence and couldn't exist whole in her absence.

He screamed.

Sound that came from seal-form but carried human grief, carried loss that made Balor's fury seem quiet by comparison, carried rage not at enemy but at a universe that demanded such prices, at fate that made love cost everything, at gods who allowed beings to love absolutely and then took that love away.

And with the scream came power.

Not controlled. Not shaped. Not perception-tricks or illusions or anything resembling strategy. Just raw force—cosmic heritage unleashed without restraint, without concern for consequences, without anything except need to HURT something, to make something PAY for what he'd lost, to destroy until destroying was no longer possible and only then could grief be allowed to consume him.

His body changed.

Even in seal-form he grew—larger, more massive, as if the strength that should have been horse-body in his Kelpie form was forcing itself into his current shape. Muscles bulged. Bones thickened. He became something between seal and something else, something that carried power meant for forms not yet achieved, for potential not yet realized, for cosmic heritage finally expressing itself without his conscious direction.

And he threw that power at Balor.

Mindlessly. Endlessly. Without thought or strategy or anything except fury that gave form to forces that should not have form. Water became weapons—not elegant swords like he'd forged against Caoránach but crude massive things that existed only to batter, to crush, to hurt. Reality itself bent around him as perception-shaping became reality-shaping became simple overwhelming of what was with what he WILLED to be.

The Sluagh swarmed with him, adding their spectral fury to his cosmic rage. Balor's eye swept across them, destroying hundreds, thousands, but

362

the Host of Unforgiven Dead was nearly infinite and the few hundred destroyed were nothing against tide of wrathful spirits who recognized kindred fury in the grieving king.

Balor fought back. His massive arms swept through water, his eye unmade everything it caught, his voice roared challenges and curses and threats. But Z'Landar didn't care about dying anymore, didn't care about surviving, didn't care about anything except making Balor PAY, making SOMETHING pay, destroying until destruction was exhausted and grief could finally claim him.

The last living warrior—a Selkie whose name Z'Landar would never remember because grief had consumed memory—was caught by Balor's arm and shattered against stone. Twenty-six became none. Every warrior who had entered the chamber was dead or ended or ceased, leaving only Z'Landar and the Sluagh and fury absolute.

Z'Landar kept attacking.

Kept throwing power that came from sources he'd never fully accessed, never fully understood, never wanted to understand because understanding meant control and control meant restraint and restraint was impossible when Andralia was GONE and nothing mattered except—

Balor fell.

Not dramatic. Not with final curse or threat or acknowledgment of defeat. Just... fell. The massive presence that had filled the chamber, that had loomed in darkness like mountain given malice, simply collapsed. Wounded beyond healing, weakened by egg's destruction, overwhelmed by forces he'd thought beneath his notice, the Fomorian king who had survived millennia died to grief-maddened water-born wielding power that made no sense except that love given absolute expression could break even ancient evil.

The eye closed. The presence ceased. And in the darkness, in the silence that followed roaring, Balor of the Evil Eye was ended.

Z'Landar floated in water that tasted of blood and death and victory that felt like failure. His body—still enlarged, still carrying strength that shouldn't fit seal-form—shook with exhaustion that went beyond physical into something that suggested his very essence had been spent beyond recovery.

Around him, the Sluagh began to fade.

Not destroyed. Not unmade. Just... leaving. Their service complete, their promise fulfilled, their interest in mortal affairs exhausted now that the battle was won and the feast consumed. They dissolved into darkness like smoke dispersing, like shadows when light arrives, like anything insubstantial returning to the formless state from which it came.

The Sluagh-leader was last to go. It manifested beside Z'Landar one final time, its form already translucent, already more absence than presence.

It said nothing. What was there to say? The dead understood grief better than the living ever could. Understood that some losses couldn't be comforted with words, couldn't be diminished by sympathy, could only be endured until endurance itself became unbearable.

The Sluagh-leader simply nodded once—acknowledgment of warrior who had fought well, of king who had paid costs that should never be asked, of being who had loved absolutely and lost everything that made loving worthwhile.

Then it faded. And Z'Landar was alone.

Alone in a chamber where twenty-six warriors had died. Alone with Balor's massive corpse. Alone with egg fragments that spoke of quest completed and price paid and victory that tasted like ash and blood and ending.

Alone.

He took human form without conscious decision, finding he needed hands for what came next, needed face that could express grief rather than seal-features that couldn't show the depths of what he felt. His body was changed—larger than before, muscles more prominent, strength that belonged to horse-form somehow compressed into human shape. His face was gaunt, sallow, as if channeling forces meant for cosmos had burned him from within and left only hollowed version of what he'd been.

His eyes—when he caught reflection in dark water—were haunted. Held shadows that hadn't been there before. Held grief that would never fully fade. Held understanding that he'd saved Scotland but lost everything that made Scotland worth saving.

He swam through the chamber, searching. Needing to find her. Needing to see what remained. Needing—

He found her near where the egg had been.

Not unmade like warriors caught by Balor's eye. Not dissolved into nothing like Sluagh destroyed beyond even death's persistence. But ended nonetheless—body that remained after cosmic force had burned through it, after channeling infinity had consumed what made her her, after love absolute had been spent for cause she deemed worthy of spending.

She looked like barely more than a rag doll dropped by child grown tired of playing. Limp, emptied, used completely. Her cosmic glow was gone—no starlight emanating from within, no sense of vast distances contained in mortal frame. Just body that had held those things but held them no longer.

Z'Landar gathered her to him with hands that shook, pulled her against chest that heaved with sobs that came from places deeper than lungs, held her like holding could somehow bring her back even though he knew—KNEW—that what had been Andralia was gone, returned to cosmos, existing now in forms and spaces his mortal comprehension couldn't touch.

"I'm sorry," he whispered to body that couldn't hear. "I'm sorry I let you do it. I'm sorry I wasn't strong enough alone. I'm sorry—" His voice broke. "I'm sorry I love you this much. I'm sorry it hurts this badly. I'm sorry—"

But sorry was meaningless now. As meaningless as victory, as salvation, as Scotland saved and eggs destroyed and duty fulfilled. All of it ashes compared to her absence, all of it insufficient payment for what he'd lost.

He held her in darkness, in chamber that smelled of death and endings, held her until even grief became exhausting and numbness began to creep in around the edges. Eventually—time meaningless here, could have been minutes or hours—he realized he couldn't stay. Couldn't remain in breeding ground that had claimed everyone he'd led here, that had taken twenty-six warriors and the woman he loved and left him only victory that felt like punishment.

He had to leave. Had to return. Had to bring her body back because leaving her here was unbearable, was abandoning her in darkness when she'd spent herself for light.

He took seal-form—body still enlarged, still wrong, still carrying strength that didn't fit—and carried her gently in his mouth, the way seals carried their young, the way Kelpies carried precious things through water when human hands weren't available.

The swim back through the breeding ground was nightmare given form. Through chambers where warriors had died, past walls carved with symbols that spoke of purposes he'd never understand, through halls that echoed with silence that should have been filled with voices, with laughter, with sounds of survivors processing victory.

But there were no survivors.

Only him. Only Z'Landar who had led them here, who had promised they'd finish this together, who had failed to mention that together might mean him alone at the end carrying grief too heavy to bear.

He swam through the trench that led to surface, through darkness that gradually gave way to deep twilight blue, through pressure that slowly decreased until breathing no longer required active will. Up and up, carrying her, refusing to let go even when exhaustion made his muscles scream and his lungs burn and his enlarged body demand rest he couldn't allow.

Up toward light he couldn't face, toward world he couldn't inhabit without her, toward Scotland saved at cost that made saving seem like cruelest joke ever told.

Eventually he reached shallower waters. Saw surface above, pale and distant but achievable. Saw Isle of Man's shore—rocky beach where water met land, where he could rest, where he could process what remained of his shattered existence.

He surfaced in late afternoon light that seemed too bright after chamber's darkness, too cheerful for what he carried, too indifferent to the price that had been paid in depths below. The water around the island was calm, gentle, beautiful—as if the Irish Sea had no understanding of what had occurred beneath its surface, as if Balor's death and warriors' sacrifice meant nothing to tides that would continue their eternal rhythm regardless of how many died beneath them.

Z'Landar swam toward shore, toward rocky beach where he could take human form, where he could sit with her, where he could try to understand how he was supposed to continue when continuing meant existing without her.

He reached the shallows and transformed, his enlarged body making the shift strange, awkward, more difficult than it should have been. His human form was bigger now—taller, more muscular, as if cosmic heritage had decided that grief required physical expression, that loss this profound needed body capable of carrying it. His face remained gaunt, haunted, marked by exhaustion that went deeper than flesh into whatever served as soul for beings born of sacrifice and cosmic convergence.

He carried her to the beach—body that had been woman from stars, that had chosen earth and water over cosmic distances, that had loved him absolutely—and laid her gently on stone worn smooth by millennia of tides.

Then he sat beside her.

Just sat.

Looking at nothing, feeling nothing except hollow where love had been, understanding that he'd won but winning meant nothing, that Scotland was saved but Scotland would have to survive without its king because being king required caring about continuation and caring required pieces of himself that had died with her.

Overhead, movement.

The ravens came.

Not hundreds now but thousands—every raven that had followed them from Scotland, that had circled overhead during journey, that had known death would come and had waited patient for feast they'd been promised.

They landed on rocks around the beach, perched on outcroppings and stones, filled the shore with dark shapes that watched with eyes too intelligent and too knowing.

But they were silent.

No harsh cawing. No croaking calls of doom. No sounds at all—just presence, just witness, just acknowledgment that feast had been consumed and death had claimed its due and now there was nothing left except watching, waiting, bearing quiet witness to grief that made even ravens hesitate to disturb.

They'd gotten what they came for. Twenty-six warriors dead in depths below. The greatest battle they'd witnessed in generations, perhaps centuries. Blood and courage and sacrifice that would be sung about if anyone remained to sing.

But now—sitting on shore with the spent body of a woman who had saved Scotland, with king who had lost everything winning—they were simply quiet. Simply present. Simply bearing witness to aftermath of doom they'd known was coming.

Z'Landar sat with Andralia's body beside him, with ravens silent overhead, with late afternoon sun painting sky in colors that seemed obscene in their beauty, and tried to understand how he was supposed to continue.

How he was supposed to return to Scotland and tell survivors that everyone who'd entered the breeding ground had died except him. How he was supposed to face those left behind—Fionnuala and the others too wounded to fight—and explain that courage hadn't been enough, that determination hadn't mattered, that twenty-six warriors had paid everything and the only one who survived was the one who had led them to their deaths.

How he was supposed to rule Scotland when Scotland's salvation had cost him the only thing that made ruling bearable.

How he was supposed to exist in waters that held her memory in every current, her absence in every moment, her love in every reason he'd ever had for caring about continuation.

He had no answers.

Just sat there as sun moved toward horizon, as shadows lengthened across beach, as ravens watched in silence, as waves lapped against stone with rhythm that suggested nothing had changed, nothing mattered, nothing would ever again approach the magnitude of what had been lost.

The quest was complete.

The eggs destroyed.

Balor dead.

Scotland saved.

And Z'Landar—King of Waters, victor of impossible battles, wielder of cosmic power—

Sat on rocky shore holding grief that would never fade, carrying victory that felt like punishment, trying to understand how he was supposed to care about tomorrow when yesterday had taken everything that made tomorrow worth seeing.

The ravens remained silent.

And the waves, indifferent, continued their eternal rhythm.

Chapter Twenty-Seven: The Return and the Reckoning

The swim from Isle of Man to Scotland should have been impossible.

Two days of constant swimming through the Irish Sea, carrying a body that couldn't be left behind, exhaustion absolute and grief heavier than any physical burden. Z'Landar's transformed body—larger now, muscles that belonged to horse-form somehow compressed into seal-shape—moved through water mechanically, without thought or awareness beyond the necessity of continuation.

He carried her gently in his mouth, the way seals carried their young, the way precious things were borne when human hands weren't available. Her body was light, empty, all the cosmic force that had made her brilliant now gone, returned to stars from which she'd come. What remained was just flesh, just memory made physical, just everything that mattered reduced to weight he could carry but never set down.

The water tasted of salt and grief. Each stroke pulled at muscles that screamed for rest, each breath drew in exhaustion that made the next stroke harder. His mind stayed trapped in the chamber where she'd died—replaying the moment her presence ceased, the instant their connection went silent, the understanding that love absolute had been spent and nothing remained except hollow where warmth had been.

He swam anyway. Because stopping meant acknowledging reality too terrible to face. Because Scotland waited. Because duty persisted even when nothing else did.

The first seal appeared near dawn of the first day.

Old bull seal, scarred from long life, swimming alongside in silence. Then another. And another. Dolphins came next—pod of them, moving with grace that seemed reverent somehow, keeping pace but not crowding, bearing witness without intruding.

By midday, dozens swam with him. By evening, hundreds.

They knew. Somehow they knew what had happened beneath Isle of Man. Word spread through waters in ways humans never understood—through currents and songs whales sang, through connections water-folk shared that went deeper than language, through the particular awareness that ocean creatures possessed when something significant occurred in their realm.

They knew about the battle. About sacrifice paid and victory won. About king who had saved them all but lost everything that made saving worthwhile.

An ancient seal—female this time, gray-muzzled and wise—swam directly into Z'Landar's path. He stopped, too exhausted to navigate around her, too hollowed to care about delays.

She communicated not with words but with the particular language water-folk used when words were insufficient: *Let us carry her.*

Z'Landar wanted to refuse. Carrying her was duty, was honor, was the least he could do when he'd failed to save her. But his body was failing, muscles trembling with exhaustion, and the ancient seal's eyes held understanding that made refusal seem like pride rather than devotion.

You have carried enough, she insisted. *Let us bear this burden. Let us honor her.*

He released Andralia's body with gentleness that hurt worse than any wound, watched as dozens of seals gathered around her with reverence that suggested they understood what she'd been, what she'd given. They worked together—weaving kelp into platform, creating bier that floated stable and secure, lifting her onto it with care that would have made human pallbearers seem clumsy.

Dozens of seals positioned themselves around the platform, swimming in perfect formation, bearing her like queens were borne in old times when ceremony mattered and honor demanded visible expression.

Z'Landar swam beside them, no longer carrying her physically but burden remaining in his chest where it would stay forever. At least now he could simply swim, could focus on grief instead of exhaustion, could process loss without fighting his body's demands for rest.

371

He wasn't sure that was an improvement.

The procession grew.

Word spread faster than they swam, carried by dolphins who ranged
ahead and returned with more escorts, by fish who schooled in thousands
around the formation, by currents themselves which seemed to carry
news to everything capable of understanding. By the second day, the
procession stretched for miles—sea creatures of every kind swimming
together in unity that should have been impossible, predator and prey
both recognizing that this moment demanded something beyond usual
patterns, beyond normal behavior.

The whales came at midday.

First a pod of humpbacks, massive and ancient and wise, surfacing near
the procession with breaths that sounded like sighs, like grief too deep
for smaller throats to express. They didn't speak—whales rarely
communicated directly with smaller creatures—but their songs filled the
water with sounds that were mournful and magnificent both, telling tale
of battle fought in depths, of cosmic woman who died saving lands not
her own, of king who wielded power beyond comprehension and paid
price beyond bearing.

More whales arrived. Orcas came, their black and white patterns stark
against blue water, killers showing respect for fallen warrior in ways
their nature rarely allowed. Blue whales—largest creatures Earth had
ever known—surfaced at the procession's edge, their presence making
everything else seem small, their songs so deep they resonated in bone
and stone and the water itself.

The ocean mourned. All of it. Every creature capable of understanding
loss, capable of recognizing sacrifice, capable of acknowledging that
what had been paid in Balor's chamber mattered not just to Scotland but
to all waters, all life that depended on waters remaining free of dragon-
fire and ancient evil.

Irish Merrow joined the procession—survivors who had stayed behind,
too wounded to fight, swimming now to add their presence to the honor

guard. They bore news that Muirgheal had died well, that Irish alliance had held to the end, that the price paid was shared between peoples and grief would be borne together.

By the time they approached the waters between Ireland and Scotland—where fishing boats often ventured, where humans might witness what passed—the procession numbered in thousands. Impossible to count. Impossible to comprehend. The ocean itself seemed to escort Z'Landar home, bearing witness to this ending and beginning both, to victory that felt like defeat and survival that tasted like failure.

The fishing boat appeared in late afternoon, badly weathered Scottish vessel out for catch that would feed families through coming winter. Old fisherman at the helm saw the procession approaching and called to his crew with voice that held awe and confusion both.

"What in God's name—"

They watched as thousands of creatures swam past—seals and dolphins, whales surfacing and diving, fish schooling in numbers that darkened water, all of them moving with purpose that suggested this was no natural migration but something orchestrated, something meaningful, something that demanded witnessing.

The fisherman recognized water-folk shapes among seals. Recognized the kelp bier borne by dozens. Saw body of woman laid on platform with reverence that spoke of honor beyond usual understanding.

"That's them," he breathed. "That's the king's warriors. But why so many? What happened?"

The procession swam close, not avoiding the boat but passing near enough that humans could see clearly. Could see the still body on crafted platform—beautiful even in death, peaceful in ways that suggested peace had been hard-won. Could see Z'Landar's transformed form swimming beside—larger than seals should be, wrong in ways that suggested something had changed him beyond recognition, face gaunt and hollow when he surfaced briefly before diving again.

Understanding settled over the fishermen like cold.

"The battle," the old fisherman said quietly. "They won. They must have won. But the cost—" He looked at the thousands escorting single body home. "The cost was everything."

He turned the boat toward shore immediately, abandoning nets and catch and everything except need to spread word. Scotland had to know. Had to prepare. Had to understand that king was returning but returning broken, that victory had been achieved but everyone who'd entered battle was dead save one, that salvation had come but at immeasurable price that made salvation seem cruel joke.

"Send word to the clans!" he shouted to crew. "The king returns! The battle is won! But prepare—" His voice caught. "Prepare for grief that will shake Scotland to its foundations."

By the time Z'Landar approached Scotland's coast, everyone knew.

Not just that he was coming, but what had happened. The Sluagh— before fading completely after the battle—had appeared to those with minds capable of receiving their gifts. To warriors and chiefs, to water-folk and some humans, to anyone strong enough to bear what the Host of Unforgiven Dead chose to share: visions.

Visual memories of battle in Balor's chamber. Of courage without limit and sacrifice beyond comprehension. Of Tormod's charge and his ending, of Caelan's death against stone, of Muirgheal dissolved by the eye that killed with looking. Of twenty-six warriors dying with determination that should have meant something but proved insufficient against ancient power.

Of Andralia channeling forces meant for cosmos through frame meant for mortality, burning from within, dying not to Balor's eye but to love expressed through ultimate sacrifice.

Of Z'Landar's transformation when she died—his body changing, his power unleashing, his grief-fueled rage throwing mysterious forces at the

374

dread Fomorian king until ancient evil fell and egg was destroyed and quest was completed at cost no one should have to pay.

The Sluagh had shown it all. Every moment of battle witnessed, every death acknowledged, every act of courage recorded in visions that burned themselves into minds strong enough to receive them. And those who received shared with others, and word spread until all of Scotland knew what had happened beneath Isle of Man before Z'Landar even reached shore.

Legend before he arrived. Tale complete before he could speak it himself.

Water sprites—small ethereal beings that Maelis had been able to communicate with, that others could reach with effort and focus—had carried message beyond Earth. Somehow, through means not fully understood, they'd touched cosmic spaces and delivered word to beings who dwelt among stars:

Your daughter fell in battle.

She died saving this world.

Come for her ceremony.

And the stars had listened.

Thousands gathered on Scotland's shores. Highland clans assembling in numbers not seen since—since ever, perhaps. All the chiefs, all the warriors who could travel, all the families who had sent loved ones to Cruachan and Isle of Man and wanted to witness what their sacrifice had purchased. Water-folk filled the shallows—Kelpies and Selkies, Merrow who had traveled from Ireland, others whose names Z'Landar didn't know but who came anyway because what had been done mattered beyond Scotland, beyond Ireland, beyond any single realm or people.

They waited in silence as the somber procession approached. Thousands of sea creatures in water, thousands of humans on land, all watching as kelp bier came closer, as Z'Landar's transformed form became visible, as understanding settled that this was ending and beginning both, that what returned was victory for all and grief that would never heal.

Z'Landar reached shallows and took human form for the first time since entering Balor's chamber.

The transformation was wrong. He knew it as soon as he stood—taller than he'd been, perhaps six and a half feet now, muscles more prominent than before as if strength meant for horse-body had forced itself into human frame. His face was gaunt, hollow, cheekbones sharp and eyes holding shadows that would never leave. He looked like himself but also like a stranger, like someone who had gone into depths and returned as something else, something not quite mortal anymore, something that carried distances in its gaze and power in its bones that didn't fit earthly constraints.

The gathered crowds gasped. Not at his transformation exactly, but at seeing it confirmed—at understanding that their king had become something beyond what he'd been, that power wielded in Balor's chamber had changed him in ways that might never be undone, or understood.

Sea creatures brought the kelp bier to shallows gently, laying it where water met sand, where Highland warriors could come forward and lift her with reverence. They did—six chiefs, Alasdair Fraser among them, bearing her from water to prepared place on shore with ceremony that suggested they understood what she'd been, what she'd given, what her death had purchased.

Z'Landar followed like ghost, walking from water toward where they carried her because what else could he do? Stop and collapse? Allow grief to consume him completely? Duty demanded presence even when presence required everything he had left.

Fionnuala came toward him—his half-sister, arm still damaged from Cruachan's fire, face showing tears that wouldn't stop. She wanted to embrace him, wanted to offer comfort, wanted to say something that might help.

"Brother—" she started.

He shook his head slowly. Not ready for words. Not ready for comfort. Just... not ready. She understood, stepped back, let him pass without further attempt at connection he couldn't provide.

Alasdair Fraser approached with careful steps, old chief seeing transformation in his king that went beyond physical into something that made approaching seem almost dangerous, like nearing force that might lash out not from malice but from simple inability to control what it had become.

"Lad—" Alasdair's voice was thick with emotion he couldn't hide.

Z'Landar met his eyes briefly. Alasdair saw grief there—saw depths of loss that made the old chief step back despite himself, saw shadows that suggested this king was broken in ways that might never heal, saw understanding that Z'Landar existed now only because duty demanded existence and nothing else mattered enough to keep breathing.

Alasdair said nothing more. What could be said? Sometimes grief was too deep for comfort, too profound for words, too absolute for anything except witness and acknowledgment and letting the grieving grieve without demanding they perform recovery they couldn't achieve.

The preparations had been made with remarkable speed. Scotland knew how to honor its dead—had centuries of practice raising stones and lighting fires and creating spaces where grief could be expressed and courage acknowledged. But this was different. This was not just funeral but victory celebration, not just mourning but triumph, not just sorrow but pride in what had been accomplished.

Both needed recognition. Both deserved ceremony. So both would happen simultaneously, contradictory as that seemed, necessary as breathing even if breathing hurt.

Standing stones were being raised—twenty-six of them plus one larger than others at the circle's center. Names were being carved even now, chisels striking stone with sounds that rang across the shore like bells, like heartbeats, like promises that fallen would not be forgotten. Fires were lit—great pyres that would burn for days, marking time sufficient for grief and celebration both. Food was prepared, songs were being written, space was being created for thousands to gather and process what had been won and what had been lost.

Andralia's stone was largest, most central. They carved it now while Z'Landar watched with eyes that saw but didn't process, that registered motion without comprehending meaning:

ANDRALIA OUR QUEEN DIED SAVING EARTH

Simple words for sacrifice beyond words. Insufficient but necessary. What else could be carved that would capture what she'd been? What she'd given? What her loss meant to king who stood hollow and haunted, watching strangers carve her name while her body lay nearby and her absence consumed everything that mattered? Scotland had no king, no queen, but the humans had adopted Z'Landar and Andralia as the closest thing, and in respect for their true royalty among the waterfolk.

The mood was solemn but not defeated. Proud but not jubilant. Everyone understood: great thing had been done, terrible price had been paid, and both deserved acknowledgment. You didn't diminish victory by grieving fallen, didn't dishonor dead by celebrating survival. You did both, held contradictions, accepted that life was complicated and significant moments were never simple.

Z'Landar moved through preparations like some ghost haunting his own existence. Speaking when absolutely necessary, otherwise silent, hollow, barely present. People gave him space, understood he wasn't really there—body functional but soul elsewhere, perhaps still in the darkest chamber where she'd died, perhaps already following her toward unknown stars, perhaps simply scattered across distances too vast for mortal frame to contain.

Then the sky changed.

It wasn't clouds. Wasn't weather. Wasn't anything natural or explicable in terms Earth's inhabitants understood. The light bent somehow, twisted, as if reality itself was being pulled aside like a shimmering curtain to allow passage of something that didn't quite fit mortal realm, that existed in spaces between what was and what could be.

Stars became visible in daylight—impossible but happening, constellations appearing against blue sky as if darkness had been invited to manifest without waiting for night. The gathered thousands felt it before seeing it: presence approaching, power beyond comprehension descending, something unknown and vast and otherworldly coming to collect what was theirs.

Warriors reached for weapons instinctively. Chiefs called orders. Water-folk tensed, ready to dive, to flee, to do whatever was necessary when faced with forces beyond understanding.

But Z'Landar simply looked up. And understood.

They came.

Two beings descending from obscured sky that wasn't quite sky anymore, from spaces that might have been between stars or between moments or between realities. Not quite physical, not quite spirit, but existing in states that mortal comprehension could only approximate, could only see as vaguely humanoid shapes containing distances, depths, infinities that hurt to perceive directly.

Cormac and Kerinus. Andralia's parents. Cosmic entities who had bore their daughter on Earth, who had watched from distance as she'd loved absolutely and died for it, who came now to collect what remained and say goodbye to a world that had taken their child.

They were beautiful beyond description. Terrible in their otherworldliness. Bodies that shimmered between solid and light, between here and elsewhere, between physical and something that made physical seem like crude approximation of what form could be. Eyes that held galaxies, that saw distances mortal eyes couldn't approach, that carried ages and wisdom and grief that made even ancient Highland chiefs seem like children.

Cormac's presence was like solar winds—constant, powerful, carrying heat that wasn't quite temperature but felt like warmth nonetheless. Kerinus moved with grace like nebulae forming, like star-birth captured in motion, like creation itself given purpose and direction.

The gathered thousands fell silent. Not commanded to silence but choosing it because what else could you do when faced with beings who dwelt among stars and came to visit Earth only when loss demanded their

379

presence? People had been calling Andralia the child of the stars, not because they believed it, but because they had heard others speak thus. But now, now…

They descended toward where Andralia's body lay on the hastily prepared platform, stones being raised around her, fires burning nearby, ceremony in progress but paused now because otherworldly parents commanded attention simply by existing.

They approached her. Knelt—if kneeling was appropriate word for beings who didn't quite follow physical laws—and touched her with hands that were light and substance both, with grief visible even in beings so alien that understanding their emotions should have been impossible.

But grief was universal. Loss transcended species, realms, the usual boundaries between what could be comprehended and what couldn't. Parents mourning child—that was truth that held across every form of existence, that needed no translation, that spoke directly to every heart capable of understanding what love meant when love ended.

Kerinus spoke first, voice carrying across shore without needing volume, simply existing in awareness of everyone present simultaneously:

"We knew when we came to Earth that she might not return to us." The words held sorrow ancient as stars themselves. "She was always drawn to mortal realms. To connections we couldn't provide. To love expressed in ways that required mortality to understand."

Cormac continued, his voice like wind across solar systems: "We let her go to Z'Landar knowing this might be the beginning of the ending. Because keeping her from her destiny would have been cruelty worse than loss. She needed to burn. Needed to love. Needed to spend herself absolutely rather than persist eternally without meaning."

"She chose well," Kerinus said, touching Andralia's face with tenderness that made thousands watching have to look away because witnessing such grief seemed like intrusion. "Chose love over distance. Chose meaning over eternity. Chose to spend herself for others rather than hoard existence for herself alone. That is more than most achieve. Cosmic or mortal both."

They stood—or rose, or simply became vertical again—and turned toward where Z'Landar stood apart from crowds, hollow and haunted and barely holding together.

They approached him. And every instinct Z'Landar possessed screamed that he should kneel, should bow, should show proper respect to beings who made even Fomorian kings seem small. But his legs wouldn't obey, wouldn't bend, wouldn't do anything except keep him upright because if he fell now he'd never rise again.

Cormac and Kerinus didn't seem to mind. Just came closer, studied him with eyes that saw everything—transformation, grief, power barely contained, cosmic heritage finally realized but not understood, potential that extended beyond Earth's capacity to hold.

"We meet again because you are the one she loved," Kerinus said. Not question—statement carrying weight of cosmic certainty. "We are not here in physical bodies, these are merely projections, although they have the power to influence matter around us."

"We see her in you," Cormac added. "See what you became together. See what her love made possible."

They circled him slowly, studying, assessing, understanding. Z'Landar felt their attention like physical force, like being examined by entities who saw not just surface but depths, not just present but potential, not just what he was but what he could become.

"You have evolved," Cormac said finally. "Become more than you were. More than even you understand. In truth, even more than we understand."

"Your cosmic heritage has fully expressed," Kerinus continued. "Grief and power and love combined to unlock what was always there but dormant, waiting. She helped you become what you were meant to be. Even in dying, she completed you."

Z'Landar found his voice, hoarse and broken: "I couldn't save her."

"No," Cormac agreed gently. "Because she didn't want saving. She wanted spending where spending had meaning. There's difference."

"You wielded forces that shouldn't exist in the mortal realm of Earth," Kerinus said. "Shaped reality itself. Threw cosmic power with grief as fuel. That is not water-born magic alone. That is star-stuff, cosmic force. Your father's heritage finally realized."

"But you don't yet comprehend what you are," Cormac added. "What you've become. That will take time, exploration, understanding beyond Earth's scope."

Kerinus moved closer, her presence wrapping around him like warmth, like comfort he couldn't accept but couldn't reject either. "We suspected her fate would be short." The admission was sorrowful but not regretful. "She burned so bright, loved so absolutely. That kind of intensity rarely sustains. Burns out quickly, leaves brilliance behind. We hoped we were wrong. But suspected we weren't."

"Then why let her come?" Z'Landar's voice broke completely. "Why allow her to Earth, to me if you knew—if you thought—"

"Because we could have forbidden her coming," Cormac replied. "Could have kept her in stellar distances where she'd be safe. But that would have death of a different kind. Slow fading rather than brilliant burning. She needed this. Needed Earth. Needed you."

"She needed to love absolutely even if briefly," Kerinus said. "We gave her that chance. Even knowing the cost. Because keeping her from her destiny would have destroyed her more completely than dying for it ever could."

She touched Z'Landar's face, her hand warm and cool simultaneously, real and not-real both. "We don't blame you. She chose. You didn't take her from us. She gave herself. That's different. She spent herself as she wished, for cause she deemed worthy, for love she considered sufficient reason. That was her choice. Her right. Her glory."

"I tried to stop her," Z'Landar whispered. "Tried to order her not to channel so much. She refused. And I needed—I wasn't strong enough alone, needed her amplification to reach the egg. So I let her die for me."

"No," Cormac said firmly. "She died for herself. For cause she chose. Using power she possessed. Making decision that was hers alone. You didn't fail her. You honored her choice. That's what love means—allowing beloved their agency even when their agency leads to ending."

Silence held for long moments. Thousands watching, witnessing, understanding something profound was happening even if they couldn't fully comprehend what.

Then Cormac spoke again, voice carrying new weight: "You cannot stay here."

The words fell like stones into still water. Z'Landar looked up sharply, met wise eyes that held certainty.

"Your evolution is complete," Kerinus continued. "But Earth cannot contain what you've become. These waters are too small now. This realm too limited for what you carry."

"I saved Scotland—" Z'Landar started.

"And Scotland is grateful," Cormac interrupted gently. "But gratitude doesn't change reality. You're not just water-born anymore. Not just Kelpie with cosmic heritage. You've become something between. Between water and stars. Between mortal and cosmic. Something new, something undefined, something that doesn't fit mortal realms anymore."

Kerinus moved closer. "You saved it. Protected it. That duty is fulfilled. But continuing here would be half-life. Would be denying what you've become. Would be trying to fit ocean back into teacup. Impossible. Destructive. Fatal, eventually."

"Scotland's waterfolk needs its king," Z'Landar said, but the words held no conviction, no belief, just desperate attempt to hold onto something familiar when familiar was crumbling.

"They need a king who can be present," Cormac replied. "Who can love these waters. Who can care about continuation. You love only her now. Everything else is duty without heart. That's not kingship. That's martyrdom."

"Your heart left these waters when hers stopped beating," Kerinus said, and her voice held compassion that hurt worse than any cruelty. "Your soul followed her to spaces beyond. Only your body remains, going through motions. That's not living. That's haunting. And haunting helps no one—not you, not Scotland, not Kelpie nor Selkie, not anyone."

Cormac extended hand—appendage—something that suggested offering: "Come with us. Take your place among the stars. Where distances match your power. Where scope fits your nature. Where—" He paused significantly. "Where your fate waits."

"We don't demand answer now," Cormac added. "There are ceremonies to complete. Fallen to honor, victories to celebrate. But know that path exists. When you're ready. When Earth has said goodbye. We will wait for you in the depths of Loch Etchachan. And offer passage to the stars."

They began to fade—not leaving exactly, but becoming less present, blending into sky that had returned to normal, into starlight that remained visible despite daylight, into cosmic distances that were their true home.

"When you're ready," Kerinus's voice came from everywhere and nowhere. "We'll be waiting. Both of us."

Then they were gone. And Z'Landar stood on shore with thousands watching, understanding settling over him like weight: he would leave. Not if, but when. When ceremonies concluded. When Scotland had been properly honored. When grief had been adequately expressed.

Then he would go. Would swim through dark blue waters toward stars. Would follow her to spaces beyond. Would take his place among cosmic beings and finally understand what he'd become, what he had been born to become, what she'd helped him become, what loving absolutely had cost and what it had purchased.

The ceremonies began at sunset.

Andralia's funeral came first—her stone complete now, bearing simple words that couldn't capture what she'd been but tried anyway. Songs were sung by water-folk and humans both. Highland chiefs spoke of courage beyond understanding, of sacrifice that shamed even their proudest warriors, of a woman from the stars who chose Earth and died saving it.

Whales sang offshore—deep mournful sounds that resonated through stone and water and bone, that spoke grief in language older than humanity, that acknowledged loss that mattered beyond single species or realm.

Z'Landar was supposed to speak. Everyone expected it. But when he approached the stone, when he stood before gathered thousands with her body lying nearby and her absence consuming everything, he found words insufficient.

"She came from distances I can't imagine," he managed finally, voice hoarse and barely audible. "Chose Earth, chose love over eternity. Chose to spend herself so others could live. She—"

His voice broke. He couldn't continue. Just stood there, hollow and haunted, until Alasdair came forward and gently guided him away, let others take over the speaking because some grief was too deep for words, too profound for ceremony, too absolute for anything except witness.

They honored all the fallen next. Twenty-six stones raised, twenty-six names carved, each one spoken aloud so Scotland would remember. Tormod who had charged knowing he'd die. Caelan who had led despite fear. Muirgheal who had honored Irish alliance to her ending. All of them. Every name. Every story. Every act of courage that had purchased Scotland's survival.

The victory celebration happened simultaneously—fires burning bright, food shared among thousands, songs of triumph mixed with laments. People danced and mourned both, laughed and cried, celebrated salvation while grieving those who'd paid for it. Life asserting itself even in death's presence, joy persisting even through sorrow, because that was what living meant—holding contradictions, accepting complexity, understanding that significant moments were never simple.

Z'Landar moved through it like a reluctant ghost. Present physically but absent in every way that mattered. Speaking when duty demanded, otherwise silent, hollow, barely holding together. People understood, gave space, didn't demand he perform a recovery he couldn't achieve.

The ceremonies continued for three days. Three days of honoring fallen and celebrating victory, of grief expressed and pride acknowledged, of Scotland processing what had been won and what had been lost. Three days of gathering that would be remembered as long as Scotland remembered anything—as moment when realm was saved, when heroes fell, when king became something more than king and less than whole.

Z'Landar looked back at Scotland's shore, at standing stones bearing names of fallen, at water-folk and humans who had fought beside him, at realm he'd saved and couldn't inhabit anymore. At everything he was leaving behind because staying meant haunting rather than living, meant existence without meaning, meant half-life that dishonored her sacrifice by refusing to move beyond it.

Fionnuala stood at shore's edge, crying but understanding. Alasdair raised hand in final salute—eternal good right arm of Clan Fraser pledged even in farewell. Others gathered, watching, bearing witness to departure that felt like ending but might be beginning, that looked like abandonment but was actually transformation.

Camp was breaking, people returning to their lives, seafolk too long from their proper waters were going home. But Z'Landar spoke, and his voice carried, "I must leave, travel to lands unknown by means I cannot fathom. But before I go I will visit you all in your homelands, to say goodbye properly, to share your companionship one last time."

And behind him, Scotland watched its king depart. Watched transformation to horse. Watched his lonesome travels begin. Watched grief become journey. Watched ending become beginning.

The waves continued their eternal rhythm.

The stones stood bearing names that would outlast kingdoms.

Chapter Twenty-Eight: To the Stars

Z'Landar swam through Scotland's waters in seal-form, moving south toward where the Selkies gathered in numbers sufficient to witness what came next. The funeral ceremonies had concluded three days past—three days of honoring fallen and celebrating victory, of grief expressed and pride acknowledged, of Scotland processing salvation purchased at cost that would haunt generations. Now came the leaving. Six weeks to say goodbye to everything he'd known, to everyone who'd stood with him, to the realm he'd saved but could no longer inhabit.

His transformed body moved through water with power that felt wrong for these depths, too strong for Scottish seas, too vast for lochs and channels that had seemed infinite when he was young but now felt constraining, limiting, insufficient for what he'd become. The future called him stronger with each passing day—pulling him toward stars, toward distances his cosmic heritage demanded, toward her family waiting in spaces beyond mortal comprehension.

But first: duty. However hollow duty felt, however much his heart had departed these waters when hers stopped beating, he owed proper farewells to those who'd followed him, fought beside him, trusted him to lead when leading meant probable death. Six weeks estimated. Then the stars. Then whatever came after.

The Selkie gathering place was ancient—protected cove where his mother's people had met for ceremonies since before Scotland had a name, where Maelis had been young once, where tradition held weight heavier than any modern consideration. They were assembled when he arrived, perhaps three hundred of them, floating in waters that caught afternoon light and made their seal-forms seem gilded, touched by sun that knew what was ending and offered beauty as benediction.

Fionnuala waited at the gathering's center. His aunt become sister, youngest daughter of his Selkie grandmother, bearing damaged arm from Cruachan's fire but standing—floating—with dignity due a princess. She'd known this was coming. They all had. The moment Z'Landar announced he was leaving, the succession became clear: she was rightful heir, proper ruler, the one who could love these waters in ways he no longer could.

The elders floated around her in formal pattern—seven of them, ancient beyond most present reckoning, carrying Scotland's memory in their bones. They acknowledged Z'Landar with nods that held respect and sorrow both, understanding that what departed was their king who'd saved them but also warrior who'd been legend, to Maelis who'd guided for three and a half centuries, to ways that were ending because everything eventually ended and holding tight only made letting go hurt worse.

Z'Landar took human form—standing in shallows where transformation was easier, where his enlarged frame could be seen properly. Taller now, perhaps six and a half feet, muscles that belonged to horse-form somehow compressed into human shape, face gaunt and haunted but determined. Eyes holding depths that hadn't been there before, carrying distances that spoke of what he'd become, what he'd witnessed, what he could no longer ignore.

"I'm leaving," he said without preamble, voice carrying across still water. "You know this already. The Sluagh showed you visions of what happened beneath Isle of Man. You understand what I've become. What I can no longer be."

Silence held. No one contradicted, no one protested. They'd seen through Sluagh's gifts—seen him transform in grief, seen cosmic power unleashed, seen king become something that no longer fit mortal constraints.

"Fionnuala will rule the Selkies." He gestured toward his half-sister. "She's rightful heir, proper successor. She'll serve you better than I could now. She can love these waters. Can care about continuation. Can be present in ways I can't anymore, won't ever be able to again."

He moved toward her through shallows, feeling every eye watching, feeling weight of moment pressing against shoulders that had carried too much already. When he reached her he took both her hands in his, met eyes that held tears she wouldn't let fall.

"I'm not ready," she whispered, voice meant just for him though everyone present could hear. "Not as ready as you were."

"I wasn't ready either," he replied gently. "No one is. But you're strong, Fionnuala. You proved that by surviving Cruachan—not the battle, but the staying behind. That took different courage. Harder courage, perhaps. You'll be better than I was. More whole. More present. More able to love what you lead."

"You're really leaving? Really going to the stars?"

"I have to." His hands tightened in hers. "There's nothing for me here anymore. Not without her. And something in me pulls toward those stars now—like destiny I've always felt but never understood. Now I understand. Now I must follow."

"Will I ever see you again?"

The question hung between them like plea and acknowledgment both. Z'Landar wanted to lie, wanted to offer comfort that might make parting easier. But lies served nothing, and she deserved truth even when truth hurt.

"I don't know. Honestly, I don't know. But—" He pulled her into embrace, holding tight. "You don't need me. You never did. You just thought you did. The Selkies will thrive under your rule. You'll be what they need—their leader who can be present, who can care, who isn't hollowed by grief that makes caring impossible."

"I'll miss you." Her voice broke completely.

"I'll miss you too. But missing is better than staying when staying means haunting rather than living. You deserve a living leader, not ghost of brother who can't move past loss." He released her, stepped back, looked at gathered Selkies. "She is your queen now. Follow her as you followed me. Love her as you—" He stopped, unable to continue.

The elders moved forward in ancient pattern, speaking words that had been spoken for successions since before memory—releasing old ruler, accepting new one, binding oaths that made transitions official and irrevocable. Fionnuala accepted their blessings with grace that suggested

389

she'd been preparing for this moment longer than anyone realized, that she was more ready than she'd claimed, that leadership might fit her better than it had ever fit him.

Z'Landar stayed for two days. Not longer—couldn't stay longer, his future pulled too strongly, made comfort impossible. He answered questions from those who asked, shared meals with families who wanted to see him one final time, blessed young ones who would grow up in the Scotland he'd saved but would never know him except through stories.

On the morning of the third day, he took seal-form and swam away. Didn't look back. Couldn't look back. Looking back meant acknowledging that this goodbye was final, that Fionnuala would rule for decades or centuries without him, that the Selkies would continue and he would be memory, legend, king who saved them and departed, leaving only stories and standing stones to mark where he'd been.

The Kelpies gathered in different waters—deeper, colder, more suited to beings who were horses in water as easily as seals. His father's people, though his father had died before Z'Landar drew first breath, raised him after his mother died in birthing, taught him what being Kelpie meant, prepared him for kingship he'd never wanted but accepted because duty demanded and refusing meant Scotland burned.

The council of elders waited—five of them this time, old stallions who'd survived centuries through wisdom and strength both. They acknowledged him with respect that held finality, understanding that what came next was ending rather than continuation, was release rather than succession.

"You're leaving," the eldest said. Not question—statement carrying certainty.

"Yes," Z'Landar replied simply.

"The Kelpies will return to council governance," another elder continued. "As we ruled before your father, before you. No single king. Just elders guiding, deciding together, sharing burdens that shouldn't rest on single shoulders."

"That's wise," Z'Landar agreed. "I was never meant to rule. Was meant to save. To fight. To destroy eggs and defeat Balor. That's done. Now you return to ways that serve you better than kingship ever did."

"You fulfilled duty your father couldn't," the eldest said, voice heavy with emotion elder Kelpies rarely expressed. "He died creating you— paying a price forces demanded for being who carried power sufficient to face what threatened. You lived that purpose. Saved Scotland. Destroyed eggs. That was what you were born to do."

"And now it's complete," Z'Landar said quietly. "Now I'm released."

"Yes." Simple word carrying weight of ages. "You're released. Go. Find what waits in these stars of yours. Become what you were always meant to become. We'll remember. We'll tell stories. We'll make sure Kelpies know what you were, what you did, what you paid. But we don't need you anymore. And you—" The elder's eyes held understanding profound. "You don't need us. Haven't needed us since grief remade you into something beyond what we can comprehend."

The ceremony was brief. Kelpies didn't waste words when actions served better. They acknowledged his departure, blessed his journey, released him from oaths that had bound him since becoming king. Then it was finished. No lengthy farewells, no attempts to convince him to stay. Just understanding: he'd done what was needed, now he must go, and holding him here would be cruelty rather than love.

He stayed another day. Mostly in silence, swimming through waters where Tormod had taught him to fight, where Beathan had shown him what honor meant, where countless centuries of Kelpie wisdom had prepared him for battles that would claim nearly everyone he led. The memories hurt. Everything hurt. But pain meant he'd lived, meant connections had mattered, meant loss was real because what was lost had been valuable.

On the third morning he left. The elders watched from depths, making no gesture of farewell because farewell had already been spoken and repetition would diminish rather than honor. Z'Landar swam north, toward where Highland clans waited, toward human connections that needed acknowledgment before stars could claim him.

He took horse-form for the Highland journey—great black stallion with strength that seemed supernatural because it was, moving through glens and over mountains with endurance that defied natural limitations. The transformation felt more comfortable now than it had before Balor—as if his body had finally accepted what it was, had stopped fighting the contradictions of being seal and horse and human and cosmic force all compressed into a single frame that struggled to contain them.

Six weeks total he'd allocated for farewells. Two days with Selkies, two with Kelpies plus travel left four weeks for everything else. For the clans who'd stood with him, for the humans who'd followed water-folk king despite every reason to fear, for the families who'd lost sons and daughters and husbands and wives in chambers deep where twenty-six had died so Scotland could live.

Most of that time was travel. Through autumn-touched Highlands where bracken turned gold and red, where mountains wore first snow on their peaks, where every valley held memories that hurt to touch but couldn't be avoided. He stopped at every settlement, every village, every gathering of humans who'd heard what he'd done and wanted to see him before he departed.

The pattern became familiar: arrive in horse-form, transform to human, accept hospitality from simple folk who offered what they had—bread and cheese and ale, stories and gratitude and tears. They'd all felt dragon-fear during the months when eggs threatened, when fire from the north spoke of monsters that might spread south, when nightmares held images of children burning and homes destroyed and everything familiar consumed by forces beyond human resistance.

He'd ended that fear. Had saved them in ways they couldn't fully comprehend but understood enough to be grateful for. They welcomed him like their true hero, like legend, like king who'd proven that different didn't mean dangerous, that water-folk could be allied with, that sometimes salvation came from unexpected sources wearing unfamiliar faces.

Z'Landar accepted their welcome with grace that felt hollow but necessary. Shared meals, blessed their homes, told them they were safe now—eggs destroyed, Balor dead, threats ended. Answered questions about battle when asked, though he kept details sparse because some horrors didn't need full description and imagination was often kinder than reality.

They saw his transformation—couldn't help seeing it. He was taller than any man they'd known, stronger in ways that suggested more than simple muscle, marked by something that made them uncomfortable even while grateful. His eyes held distances that made meeting them difficult, his presence carried weight that felt like standing near cliff's edge, like proximity to forces barely contained.

But he was kind. Patient with their questions, gentle with their children, respectful of their grief when they spoke of family lost. That mattered more than strangeness. That made him theirs even if he was leaving, even if he'd become something they couldn't fully understand.

The clans required more formal visits. MacLeod welcomed him with ceremony that acknowledged what he'd been to Scotland, what his departure would mean. MacKenzie warriors spoke of honor he'd brought to alliance between species that had eyed each other warily for centuries. Cameron chiefs offered blessings for his journey to the stars, accepting his leaving as necessary rather than abandonment. MacDonald—youngest of the major chiefs, barely thirty—stood in awe, unable to speak properly, just gripping Z'Landar's hand and nodding repeatedly as if words were insufficient and physical contact could convey what voice couldn't.

Each visit lasted two days maximum. Couldn't stay longer—unknown future pulled too strongly, made comfort impossible, made lingering feel like resistance rather than respect. He moved constantly, driven by something he couldn't name but couldn't ignore, pulled forward by destiny that had always called but now screamed, demanded, would not be denied much longer.

But he saved Fraser for last. Saved the most important for when journey neared conclusion, when only Loch Etchachan remained before departure became real rather than theoretical, before portal opened and Earth became past rather than present.

He arrived at Clan Fraser lands in early evening, sun painting sky in shades of blood and gold that seemed appropriate for endings. Alasdair waited in stone arched doorway of his hall—old chief who'd pledged eternal good right arm, who'd stood with water-folk when standing seemed madness, who'd become grandfather figure to this being who'd never known human family, who'd taught Z'Landar what human love meant when love seemed like concept rather than reality.

The old man had aged in the weeks since the funeral. Grief did that—wore people down, carved years into faces that had held strong against time until sorrow proved stronger than resilience. He moved slowly as he approached where Z'Landar stood in human form, stepped carefully as if bones protested continuation, but his eyes held clarity and love that made Z'Landar's chest tighten until breathing hurt.

"Lad," Alasdair said simply, and the word held everything—welcome and sorrow, pride and loss, understanding that this goodbye would be final.

"Honored Chief," Z'Landar replied, using proper title that had always been slightly wrong because Alasdair had never been just chief to him, had been something more, something that Scottish language didn't have proper word for.

They embraced in the doorway—old human and transformed water-born, grandfather and grandson in ways that transcended blood, connection that defied easy categorization but mattered more than definitions ever could. When they separated both were crying, neither bothering to hide it because some emotions were too large for dignity, too profound for pretense.

"Inside," Alasdair said gruffly. "We'll talk properly. Just us. Don't need witnesses for this."

The hall was warm, fire burning bright, familiar space where Z'Landar had eaten meals and told stories and learned what human hospitality meant. Alasdair poured ale with shaking hands, passed cup to Z'Landar, settled into chair that creaked under his weight.

For a very long moment they just sat. Drinking, watching fire, existing in silence that held more meaning than words could approach. Finally

Alasdair spoke, voice careful, as if testing words before committing to them:

"Is it true, then? You're actually going to the stars? Or is that just myth folk tell themselves to make your leaving easier?"

Z'Landar met the old man's eyes, saw desperate hope there, saw need to believe that departure wasn't abandonment but transformation, that losing grandson-figure wasn't loss but necessary continuation.

"It's true," he said quietly. "Andralia's parents came. Cormac and Kerinus—cosmic beings from distances I can barely comprehend. They showed me—" He paused, choosing words. "They showed me possibilities of places. In realms I don't understand yet but will. They're offering passage. Instant travel across distances that should be impossible."

Alasdair took long drink, processing. "And you believe them? Believe you'll find your fate there?"

"I don't know if I believe. But I know I can't stay here. Can't exist in these waters without her. Every current holds her memory. Every wave reminds me she's gone. Staying would be slow death—drowning in grief until grief was all that remained. Going—" He stared into fire. "Going might be living again. Eventually. When grief fades enough to allow it."

"I've lived seventy-three years," Alasdair said slowly. "Seen more death than any man should. Lost wife, lost sons, lost warriors I loved like brothers." He leaned forward, firelight painting his weathered face in shades of amber. "And I can tell you—grief doesn't fade. It just becomes part of you. Becomes weight you carry. Some weights make you stronger. Some crush you. Depends on the weight, depends on the man."

"Which kind is this?"

"The kind that crushes if you don't move. The kind that needs journey, not staying." Alasdair reached across, gripped Z'Landar's shoulder with strength that belied his age. "So you're right to go. Right to follow her family to those stars. Right to choose living over haunting. I don't want to lose you, lad. But losing you to a new future in the stars is better than watching you fade here, becoming a ghost of what you were, existing without living."

He stood suddenly, formal now, and Z'Landar stood with him because something in Alasdair's bearing demanded response, suggested ceremony rather than simple conversation.

"You came to us as half-breed nobody knew what to do with," Alasdair said, voice carrying weight of pronouncement rather than casual speech. "Water-folk and cosmic both, fitting nowhere, belonging to nothing. We didn't know if we could trust you. Didn't know if water-folk could be allied with, could be understood, could be anything except feared and avoided."

He moved closer, gripped both Z'Landar's shoulders now. "You taught us different. Taught us that courage exists beyond humanity. That love transcends species. That honor isn't bound by blood or form or origin. That sometimes salvation comes from sources we'd never expect, wearing faces we couldn't imagine."

His voice grew stronger, more formal, carrying echoes of oaths spoken for centuries, of traditions that predated Scotland's current form:

"You're Fraser, lad. Might not carry our blood, but you carry our honor. Fought for us, led us, saved us. That makes you clan. That makes you family. That makes you FRASER in ways that matter more than blood ever could."

He released Z'Landar's shoulders, stepped back, raised right arm in strong salute that Z'Landar had seen before, at funeral, when eternal good right arm was pledged. But this was different—this was not pledge to serve but charter to carry, commission to spread rather than stay.

"So I charter you—Z'Landar of Loch Ness, King of Waters, Son of Sacrifice and Stars—I charter you to carry Fraser name to whatever worlds you find. To spread our clan across cosmos if cosmos is where you're bound. To remember that you came from Scotland, from these highlands, from people who loved you despite not understanding you, who stood with you despite fear, who followed you despite knowing following might mean death."

Alasdair's voice broke but he continued: "To BE Fraser wherever you go. However far you go. However long forever takes. You're ours, lad. Always will be. Distance doesn't change that. Stars don't change that. Nothing changes that you're FRASER and Fraser stands with family, stands with clan, stands with honor even when standing costs everything."

Z'Landar couldn't speak. Couldn't find words adequate to what Alasdair offered—not just acceptance but belonging, not just tolerance but claim, not just understanding but love that would persist across distances that made physical proximity impossible. He pulled the old chief into embrace instead, holding this man who'd become grandfather, who'd taught him what human connection meant, who'd shown that family could be chosen rather than born.

"I'll remember," Z'Landar managed finally, voice thick with tears that wouldn't stop. "I'll carry Fraser honor to my stars. I'll make you proud."

"You already have, lad." Alasdair's arms tightened. "You already have. From the moment you chose to protect us despite owing us nothing. From the moment you led warriors knowing leadership meant probable death. From the moment you loved her absolutely despite knowing love would hurt when it ended. You've been Fraser in everything that matters. Now you'll be Fraser among the stars. And we—" His voice broke completely. "We'll be proud. Always. However far away you are."

They stood there holding each other while fire crackled and evening deepened into night, while everything that needed saying passed between them in silence more eloquent than any speech could be. Eventually they separated, both understanding that prolonging this moment wouldn't make parting easier, would just delay the inevitable and make delay itself become pain.

"When you find her—and you will find her, I know you will—tell her something for me," Alasdair said.

"Anything."

"Tell her this old Highland chief said thank you. Thank you for loving you. Thank you for giving herself. Thank you for showing us that some things matter more than survival, that some causes are worth any price, that love expressed through sacrifice is still love and still beautiful even when it hurts." His eyes held tears that streamed freely now. "Tell her the Fraser remembers. And always will."

Z'Landar left Fraser lands at dawn. Looked back once from a heathered hilltop, saw Alasdair standing in that grand stone doorway of his hall, raising hand in final salute. Eternal good right arm of Clan Fraser, pledged to king who served among stars now, to grandson-figure who'd go farther than either had imagined but would carry clan honor across whatever distances cosmos demanded.

Both were crying. Both understood. Both knew this was goodbye—final, absolute, forever in terms that mortality understood.

But love persisted anyway. Connection mattered despite ending. And that—perhaps—was what made parting bearable rather than impossible.

The remaining days passed in a numbing blur of faces and names and brief encounters with families who'd lost loved ones in chambers deep beneath Isle of Man. Parents who wanted to know if sons died well. Siblings seeking confirmation that sisters' courage had mattered. Spouses needing understanding that husbands' deaths purchased something real rather than just ending.

Z'Landar gave them what he could—truth when truth served, comfort when comfort was possible, acknowledgment that every death had mattered, that Scotland was saved because twenty-six had been brave enough to swim into darkness knowing light wouldn't follow them out.

Each encounter was brief but meaningful. Each family received his attention, his respect, his promise that fallen would be remembered not just in stone but in continuation, in children growing without dragon-fear, in Scotland that persisted because warriors had been willing to pay everything ensuring it could.

The weight of it accumulated. Twenty-six families, each carrying grief that mirrored his own, each surviving what shouldn't be survived, each trying to understand how to continue when continuation seemed impossible. He bore witness to their sorrow, acknowledged their loss, and moved on because staying too long anywhere made future's call unbearable, made destiny's pull feel like physical force demanding obedience.

Six weeks concluded. All farewells made. All duties fulfilled. Only one destination remained—Loch Etchachan where it had all begun, where he'd first understood cosmic heritage during those moments of connection with Andralia who showed him what he was before either fully understood what showing that would cost.

He traveled there in seal-form, swimming through Scotland's waters one final time, passing Loch Ness where he'd been born, where parents had paid everything to create him, where Maelis had taught him what leadership meant before dying to demonstrate it. The memories pressed against him like weight, like stones carried underwater, like everything he was leaving compressing into a single burden that made swimming labor rather than instinct.

But he continued. Because stopping meant acknowledging finality too terrible to face. Because motion meant not-yet rather than goodbye. Because arriving at Loch Etchachan meant portal and departure and transformation from might-leave to have-left.

The loch was remote, high in mountains where few ventured, where water was cold even in summer and autumn painted surrounding peaks in shades that suggested the world was ending beautifully rather than simply changing season. He surfaced in the center of the loch, took human form, floated there feeling weight of moment pressing against chest until breathing became conscious effort.

Then he dove.

Deep. Deeper than normal beings could reach, deeper than pressure should allow, into secret waters below where Cormac and Kerinus waited, where technology that seemed like magic created spaces that shouldn't exist, where a mysterious glowing portal stood ready to swallow him and deposit him distances away that made distances meaningless as measurement.

The chamber beneath Loch Etchachan was exactly as he remembered—vast space carved or created or simply existing through means he couldn't comprehend, filled with equipment that glowed and pulsed and spoke of sciences so advanced they made his Scottish understanding seem like child playing with stones while adults built cities.

Cormac and Kerinus stood near the portal, their cosmic forms shimmering between solid and light, between present and elsewhere, watching as Z'Landar entered their domain for what might be the final time or might be first of many, depending on futures neither could predict with certainty.

"You came," Kerinus said, and her voice held relief mixed with sorrow. "We weren't certain you would. Weren't sure if six weeks among those you're leaving might make leaving impossible."

"I gave my word," Z'Landar replied, taking human form and standing in shallows of the impossible chamber. "And staying would be dying slowly rather than living. You were right about that. Scotland needs a living ruler, not ghost who can't move past grief. I released them. They released me. Now—" He looked at portal that stood dormant but humming with potential. "Now I go forward."

"First," Cormac said, gesturing to equipment that filled chamber, "you should understand what waits. Should see what you're agreeing to, what journey entails."

He moved to panels that glowed with symbols Z'Landar couldn't read, touched surfaces that responded to his presence, activated displays that showed images and words and patterns that hurt to look at directly because mortal minds weren't shaped to process information presented this way.

"This is science," Cormac explained as Z'Landar approached hesitantly, drawn by curiosity that was first emotion besides grief he'd felt in weeks. "Technology. Understanding of universe's laws and how to manipulate them. You can't comprehend it yet—not after a short single lifetime in mortal realm where magic and science blur together until distinction becomes meaningless. But you'll learn."

The panels showed—something. Images? Projections? Representations of concepts that required visual form? Z'Landar saw what might have been stars, what might have been worlds, what might have been distances compressed into manageable displays. Words scrolled across surfaces but he couldn't read them, couldn't make sense of symbols that weren't Fomorian but equally alien, weren't any language Earth possessed but something cosmic, universal, fundamentally OTHER.

"You'll spend years learning this," Kerinus said gently, seeing his confusion. "Decades perhaps, understanding what these devices do, how technology works, what's possible when you grasp forces that govern the universe rather than just forces that govern water and earth. Don't be overwhelmed. Everyone feels this way their first time. Even cosmic beings born to this technology feel overwhelmed when first encountering sciences beyond their understanding."

Z'Landar touched a panel carefully, saw it respond to his presence—colors shifting, displays changing, something happening that he didn't understand but recognized as reaction rather than random occurrence. His reflection showed in darkened portions—tall figure, gaunt face, eyes holding shadows and distances, body that was wrong for Earth but might be right for somewhere else.

"Her aunt and uncle wait on the other side," Cormac said, gesturing toward the portal that stood at chamber's center. "They're eager to meet you. Eager to help you understand what you've become, what you're capable of, what your heritage means when fully realized rather than partially expressed."

"Will they—" Z'Landar stopped, unsure how to ask.

"They know about Andralia," Kerinus said, understanding question before it finished. "Know what she did. Know what it cost. They grieve too. But they're also proud—so proud of what she became, what she chose, what she gave to save a world that wasn't hers but became hers when she chose you."

She moved closer, her presence warm and cold simultaneously, comfort and awe both. "They'll teach you. Guide you. Help you navigate your new worlds that will seem strange at first but will become familiar with time. And in time you might learn your destiny, for if any living being has a destiny it is truly you."

"How long?" His voice was hoarse, desperate. "How long until I find understanding?"

"We don't know," Cormac admitted. "Time works differently in cosmos. What seems like moments might be years. What seems like years might be moments. But you'll find it. That much we know with certainty."

He approached the portal, touched controls that hummed under his fingers. "This will take you there. One step, and you'll be on a world so distant that Scotland would need technologies not yet invented to even see its star. But travel will be instant. No time passing between here and there. Just... transition. Earth to elsewhere. Mortal realm to cosmic one."

"Will I—" Z'Landar stopped again, multiple questions crowding throat.

"Will you be able to return?" Kerinus finished. "Yes. Eventually. When you've learned enough. When you understand technology that makes portals possible. Then you could come back, could visit. But—" Her expression held compassion that hurt worse than any cruelty. "But why would you? What's here except memories that hurt? What's in Scotland that calls you forward rather than backward?"

Z'Landar had no answer. Because she was right. Scotland held only past—beautiful past, meaningful past, past worth remembering but not worth inhabiting. The future waited elsewhere. In stars. In cosmos. In wherever she had existed in life before entering his life.

"We won't see you again," Cormac said, and his voice held finality that suggested this goodbye was absolute. "Not for long time. Distances between us will be vast once you're on that world, learning from her aunt and uncle. But know this—" He placed hand/appendage/light on Z'Landar's shoulder. "You carry our love. Our pride. Our understanding that you were indeed perfect match for our daughter. That together, you were magnificent. That apart—" He paused significantly. "You're still magnificent. Just incomplete. For now. Not forever."

Z'Landar embraced them both—awkward contact between transformed mortal and cosmic beings, but meaningful nonetheless. Thanked them for

402

letting Andralia come to Earth, for giving him a path forward, for understanding that staying would be slow death while leaving might be eventual life.

Then he stood before the portal. Cormac activated it with touches to panels Z'Landar couldn't read, with manipulations of technology that seemed like magic but was science beyond his current comprehension. The circular gateway hummed louder, light appearing within it—not quite light, something else, something that showed distance and depth and ELSEWHERE made visible.

Through the portal Z'Landar saw shapes that weren't familiar, colors that Earth's sky never held, space that didn't follow rules he understood. Not threatening—just utterly different. Foreign. OTHER in ways that should have terrified but instead called, beckoned, promised that different didn't mean wrong, just meant NEW.

And beneath the strangeness, through the unfamiliarity, he felt it: her presence. Not seeing her, not yet. But sensing her. Waiting. Just beyond threshold. In forms he couldn't perceive with mortal senses but cosmic heritage recognized anyway.

She waited. And that was enough.

Z'Landar took his final breath of Earth's air, final moment in the realm he'd saved but could no longer inhabit, final instant of being king and warrior and water-born creature who'd done impossible things and paid impossible prices and survived only because dying seemed like betraying everyone who'd already fallen.

Then he thought what needed thinking, what made stepping through the portal necessary rather than optional, what crystallized everything into words he'd carry forward:

I don't know that I will ever understand how she came to me, or why. It seems we two were created to be together, yet now there is only one where there should be two. I will take this journey because there is no life for me here as only one.

Scotland is safe. That matters. Duty is fulfilled. That matters. But what matters most is that she was once with me. And I can't stay here when

403

there means possibility of growing even in her absence. Can't remain in waters that hold only memory when stars might hold reality.

So I go. Not running from grief. Following fate. Not abandoning duty. Completing transformation that began when cosmic father and water-born mother paid everything to create me. They gave me life. She gave me meaning. Now cosmos gives me continuation.

Together. Always. However far always reaches.

He squared his shoulders. Raised his head. Walked forward with determination that defied fear, with certainty that transcended doubt, with boldness that suggested he knew exactly where he was going even though he didn't, couldn't, would only understand once arrival made understanding possible.

One step toward portal.

Light—not-quite-light—surrounded him.

Earth disappeared.

Scotland vanished like distant dream upon waking.

Everything familiar ceased.

Everything unknown began.

And Z'Landar—King of Waters, Son of Sacrifice and Stars, Fraser chartered to carry clan to cosmos, being who'd saved realm but lost everything making salvation possible—

Stepped through.

Gone.

To distant world where aunt and uncle waited.

To technology he'd spend years understanding.

To life without her, if that could be possible.

To continuation beyond grief.

To transformation complete.

To unknown future that called stronger than past could hold.

The portal closed behind him. The chamber beneath Loch Etchachan fell silent. Cormac and Kerinus faded back to whatever cosmic distances they called home, their daughter's beloved delivered to his next stage of journey that would eventually—inevitably—lead to family and future they'd promised.

In the loch above, water returned to stillness. No evidence anyone had been there. No sign that portal had opened and king had departed and Scotland's salvation had walked away from what he'd saved because saving didn't mean staying, because duty fulfilled meant release rather than eternal binding.

The water-folk would continue without him. Would tell stories of what he'd done, what he'd paid, what he'd become. Would raise stones bearing his name alongside Maelis and Tormod and all the others who'd died so Scotland could live. Would remember that different didn't mean dangerous, that cosmic and water-born could combine into something magnificent, that sometimes heroes left not because they stopped caring but because caring required them elsewhere.

The Highlanders would sing songs of King of Waters who saved them and departed to distant stars, who carried Fraser honor to distances unimaginable, who loved absolutely and lost everything but found a path forward through loss into continuation beyond grief.

And somewhere—distances away that made distance meaningless, on a world whose name Earth didn't know, in spaces where technology and magic blurred into science that seemed like wonder—

Z'Landar arrived.

Stepped through portal into elsewhere.

Found himself surrounded by strangeness and beauty both.

Found aunt and uncle waiting, cosmic beings ready to teach.

Found future that called him forward.

And somewhere—not close but not unreachable, not visible but not gone, not present but not absent—

She lived in his heart and his memories.

Love that persisted beyond death.

Promise that "always" meant exactly what it suggested.

Together.

However far always reached.

In land he did not know.

But would.

In Scotland, the waves continued their eternal rhythm.

The stones stood bearing names that would outlast kingdoms.

And the stars shone brighter that night, as if welcoming home one of their own.

As if celebrating a destined transformation complete.

As if understanding that some stories didn't end.

They just continued elsewhere.

Beyond sight.

Beyond comprehension.

But real nonetheless.

Always.

Epilogue

The sun rose different here.

Not wrong—Z'Landar had learned that different didn't mean wrong, had spent two years understanding that lesson in ways that went deeper than words—just different. Three suns actually, painting sky in colors Earth had never known, creating shadows that fell in patterns Scottish eyes would find confusing but eyes adjusted to cosmic realities recognized as simply another way light could behave when rules changed.

He stood alone on the vast patio that overlooked forests stretching hundreds of miles in every direction—trees that weren't quite trees, bearing leaves that weren't quite leaves, growing in patterns that suggested intelligence or intentionality or simply other rules for how living things could organize themselves. Beautiful beyond anything Scotland had offered, though that beauty was alien, strange, required adjustment before recognition could become appreciation.

But he'd adjusted. That was what two years had purchased—adjustment, understanding, transformation from water-born king who could barely comprehend cosmic technology into being who could navigate between worlds, who could read the symbols that scrolled across panels, who could understand sciences that made magic seem crude by comparison.

He was larger now. Not just the transformation that grief and battle had wrought, but further development—mountain of a man, easily seven feet tall, muscles that belonged to something beyond human or Kelpie or any single form, body that had finally accepted what it was: synthesis of water-born strength and cosmic potential, container for forces that required physical expression even when physical seemed inadequate to what was contained.

His eyes held distances that two years of star-living had deepened rather than diminished. Memories lived there—of Scotland left behind, of waters that had birthed him, of funeral where thousands gathered to honor woman who'd died saving a world not her own. Of walking away from everything familiar toward portal that promised nothing except continuation and possibility of a new life.

Two years since that step through light-that-wasn't-light into elsewhere that had become here. Two years of learning from aunt and uncle whose names he could finally pronounce properly, whose kindness had been absolute even when teaching was difficult, whose grief for Andralia mixed with pride in what she'd done and gratitude that her beloved had come to them broken but willing to heal.

Two years of technology lessons that rewired how he understood reality. Of cosmic sciences that explained forces he'd wielded instinctively during battle but hadn't comprehended consciously. Of navigation between stars and manipulation of energies and understanding that universe was vaster than Scotland had prepared him to imagine but not so vast that love couldn't cross its distances.

Two years of preparation for the moment that was approaching like tide that couldn't be turned, wouldn't be delayed much longer, demanded recognition that readiness had been achieved.

He heard movement behind him—gentle sounds of beings who could move in silence but chose not to, who respected his need for solitude but also understood that some solitudes needed interruption before they became prisons.

Her aunt and uncle emerged onto the patio, beings who'd become family in ways that blood couldn't predict but choice could create. They'd lost Andralia too—beloved niece who'd ventured to a primitive world and fallen in love and spent herself absolutely for cause she'd deemed worthy. But they'd gained him—the one she'd loved, the one she'd chosen, the one who carried her memory like sacred trust and honored it by continuing rather than collapsing.

They stood on either side of him—not touching but present, not speaking but communicating through the particular awareness that beings who shared space long enough developed, that transcended words and approached something like knowing without needing to ask.

The aunt—whose name translated roughly as "She Who Guides Through Distances"—finally spoke: "You feel it?"

"Yes," Z'Landar replied simply. No need to elaborate. They understood what he felt because they'd felt it too, had recognized the moment approaching when student became ready, when preparation transformed into action, when two years of learning reached conclusion that enabled beginning.

"It's been waiting," the uncle said—his name meaning something like "He Who Maintains Connections Through Darkness." "Patient. Because what have doesn't require urgency. Exists outside time in ways that make waiting meaningless as measurement."

"But it will be glad you're ready now, your destiny awaits you, indeed hungers" the aunt added, and her voice held warmth that suggested devotion that made Z'Landar's arrival not intrusion but gift, not burden but blessing.

Z'Landar turned slowly from forest view that had become familiar over two years, faced beings who'd taught him everything—how to navigate cosmos, how to read technologies that seemed like magic, how to understand his own power now that understanding was possible, how to exist as something between mortal and cosmic without belonging fully to either category but creating his own.

They'd been patient. Hadn't rushed him. Hadn't demanded he find his path before he was ready because finding it required comprehension of forms, of energy states, of cosmic existence that couldn't be perceived with water-born senses alone no matter how enhanced by heritage those senses were.

But now—after two years learning, adjusting, growing into what he'd become rather than resisting it—he was ready. Could perceive what he couldn't before. Could navigate spaces that had seemed impossible. Could recognize the possibilities of whatever form energy took when mortality released its constraints.

"I'm ready," he said, and the words held certainty absolute, carried weight of transformation complete, spoke of journey that had reached its transition point. "Ready to go out and meet my destiny."

The aunt smiled. "She would be so pleased. She knew you would come someday. Knew you'd learn what needed learning. Knew love that absolute couldn't be stopped by something as trivial as death or distance or different forms of existence."

Z'Landar looked out at the alien forest one final time—at beauty that had been strange but became familiar, at this world that had been foreign but had become temporary home, at space that had held him while he learned what needed learning. Gratitude filled him for aunt and uncle who'd taught without demanding, who'd guided without controlling, who'd given him tools and time and trust that he'd use them when ready.

Now he was ready.

Ready to leave this temporary home for permanent destiny.

Ready to discover what always meant when always extended beyond death, beyond distance, beyond every limitation mortality had suggested was absolute.

He turned back to them, this family that had become his when blood family was light-years away and connections had been redefined by necessity and choice both.

"Thank you," he said simply. "For everything. For teaching me. For being patient. For believing I could become what I needed to become. For loving her enough to love the one she loved."

"Thank you," the aunt replied, "for coming to us. For honoring what she gave by continuing. For becoming what she knew you could become. For proving that her choice—choosing you, choosing Earth, choosing to spend herself for love—was right."

The uncle placed hand-light-appendage on Z'Landar's shoulder one final time. "Go. Be what you were always meant to be. And know—" His voice held emotion cosmic beings rarely expressed. "Know that we're proud. Of her for choosing so well. Of you for honoring that choice."

Z'Landar nodded once. Squared his shoulders. Raised his head. Checked coordinates that glowed on panels he could finally read, that showed pathways he could finally navigate, that marked destination he'd been preparing two years to reach.

Then he activated the transition.

Not portal this time—he'd learned other methods, other technologies, other ways that cosmic beings moved between spaces when spaces obeyed rules different from mortal understanding.

Light surrounded him. Not quite light—something else, something cosmic, something that carried him from here to there in ways that transcended distance by acknowledging that distance was relative, that what seemed far became close when you understood properly, that separation was illusion when beings who belonged together finally learned how to navigate the cosmic between.

And Z'Landar—mountain of a man, student who'd become adept, king who'd become citizen of stars, beloved who'd crossed death itself to reach his destiny—

Went.

To meet that destiny that had always waited.

To discover what always meant when always had no limits.

In Scotland, the waves continued their eternal rhythm.

The stones stood bearing names that would outlast kingdoms.

The Highlanders sang songs of a water-born king who saved them.

And somewhere in far galaxies—distances away that made distance meaningless, in spaces where energy danced in forms that mortal eyes couldn't perceive but cosmic understanding recognized immediately—

Hie life began anew.

THE END

Author's Notes… Whew, this one beat me up. It just wouldn't work. I wrote it twice, and I tossed it in the bin twice. Voices didn't sound right, wouldn't tell me the story, characters were off, frankly it was junk – twice. But then one day Andralia spoke to me and said, "Silly boy, you've been writing 'The Adventures of Z'Landar', but that isn't what this book is about – it's a love story."

And she was right! It is a love story, and once I understood that, the thing just launched, all the voices were telling me the same story, everything clicked. So there you go – it's a love story. Who knew?

And, right around chapter fifteen, I had another bolt of lightning hit me when I realized what the future (book three) holds for Z'Landar. He is destined to meet another one of my main characters, bringing two very different universes together. So stay tuned for that in 2026.

And finally, a special thanks to *Tailgaters Il Primo* and *The Roadhouse*, both Cave Creek, because that's where I do most of my writing. All you dolls that keep my glass full while I furiously write – thanks!

Yours aye, Kevin

www.ingramcontent.com/pod-product-compliance
Lightning Source LLC
Chambersburg PA
CBHW031449260626
47154CB00016B/66